ᴛᴀʟᴇѕ ᴏꜰ ʟᴀʀᴋɪɴ

THE GREAT GATHERING

TALES OF LARKIN

THE GREAT GATHERING

WRITTEN AND ILLUSTRATED

BY

ALAN W. HARRIS

--❦-❦--

Fruitful Tree Publishing

Lexington, South Carolina 29072

This book is published by:

Fruitful Tree Publishing

Lexington, South Carolina

www.TalesOfLarkin.com

Copyright © 2014 by Alan W. Harris

Printed in the United States of America.

All rights reserved.

ISBN-13: 978-0-9773633-8-4

Ebook ISBN: 978-0-9773633-9-1

Library of Congress Catalog Card Number: 2014912642

Cover illustration by Alan W. Harris

1. Harris, Alan W. 2. Christian 3. Fantasy 4. Adventure 5. Family
6. Teen 7. Young Adult 8. Character Development 9. Faith
Building
10. Nature Tales I. Harris, Alan W. II Title

This novel is a work of fiction. Names, characters, places and incidents are either the work of the author's imagination or are used fictitiously. Any resemblance to actual events, locales, organizations, or persons living or dead is entirely coincidental.
For information about special discounts for bulk purchases for sales promotions, corporate use, conferences or resale contact Alan at: larkinwriter@yahoo.com.

I wish to dedicate this book to

Mark Gable and **Ken Neller**,

two of my dearest friends who kept the faith and finished their course. While they were on this Earth they not only loved me but encouraged me to love God. By their godly examples they challenged all who knew them to use the gifts God has given each of us for His glory.

I miss you guys!

CONTENTS

List of Illustrations

PREFACE

I can hardly believe that I have finished my third novel in the *Tales of Larkin* series. To be honest with you, I really didn't have time to do this. I'm a full-time veterinarian, a business owner, a husband, father, and grandfather, plus I'm over sixty years old. This is crazy! I should be taking naps. If it were up to me, I probably would be, but my children are a tough crowd. They continued to ask, *"What happens next, Dad"?* So I blew the dust off my keyboard, cranked up the ol' creative juices, and started again.

I did feel an obligation to several friends who read my first book. These particular friends said that they couldn't wait for me to write the second book so they could find out what happens to their favorite characters in the first book. Those of you who have faithfully read my second book, *Larkin's Journal*, know that didn't happen. My second book was not a sequel to the first book, but rather a prequel.

I actually did start to write *The Great Gathering* as my second book, out of deference to my friends. I wrote maybe two and a half pages and then realized that I didn't know where to take the story. I usually spend a lot of time thinking about a story before I try to write it, and I just hadn't thought about this story. On the other hand, I had thought a lot about *Larkin's Journal*. So with encouragement from my wife Valerie, I put *The Great Gathering* aside and wrote the story that was begging to get out of my brain, *Larkin's Journal*.

With that story out of the way and with apologies to my friends, the creative corner of my mind was now free to wrestle with the sequel to the first book. I was becoming curious myself to know what happened to my old friends from Book One. It really turned out to be very enjoyable to renew the old relationships with Hawthorn, Rush, Jay, Tobin and, of course, Eldan. This third story takes place two years after the events of the first book, *Hawthorn's Discovery*, and includes many of the prominent and one or two not-so-prominent characters from Book One. There are also quite a few fun new personalities who thrust themselves into the narrative. In fact, some of the new characters are so much fun that I may have to write a story just about them.

One of the more satisfying parts of writing the third book was the opportunity it gave me to explain more of some of the interesting details of the Larkin and the Makerian ways of life. As I wrote *The Great Gathering*, I was surprised to discover that the Makerians are more technologically advanced and organized than I had realized. Now, I know what you're thinking. You're thinking, *Hey, aren't you the guy who makes all of this stuff up? Why are you surprised?* I was surprised because, as I write these stories, it's not all simply writing down a story. In my mind it has to make sense (at least as far as stories about one-inch-tall people can make sense). So some of the story-writing process is discovering how these small people would accomplish difficult tasks with what they know and what's available to them. Some of you have informed me how much you enjoy the inventions by the Makerian people, so I try to put a lot of thought into how they might do things. I know that all of this stuff comes out of my head, but I was honestly amazed when I found out how they communicate long distances.

Admittedly, *The Great Gathering* does not contain as much raw adventure as the first book, *Hawthorn's Discovery*. Neither does it possess the mystery and intrigue of Book Two, *Larkin's Journal*. But I believe you will find all of the fun and excitement that you expect from a *Tales of Larkin* book as you go undercover on a covert Makerian mission. The followers of Jehesus risk their lives to infiltrate the Larkin's Great Gathering for the purpose of bringing their most precious possession to the Larkin people. It's a story that allowed me to help visualize to my family what following the Maker sometimes looks like and what it costs.

As always, this third offering in the *Tales of Larkin* series has passed the Harris family Larkin Night reading test. As I would finish some chapters, we would gather together either in person or online and continue our family tradition of my reading the new chapters to the family, complete with voice characterizations by yours truly. I must admit that the family test is getting tougher to pass since, with marriages, the family is getting bigger. I did have to tweak the story a bit here and there to satisfy all of the family members' questions and concerns, but I am proud to tell you that the final product has received the Harris Family seal of approval, i.e., the coveted *Thumbs Up*!

I want to offer my deepest appreciation and gratitude to my wonderful wife Valerie for her many hours of work in editing this book. With this being my third book you would expect that I had learned a few things and made the editing job easier. Unfortunately, I think my aging brain synapses are acquiring more rust. It seems that Valerie has to work harder and harder to make me look like a competent writer. I'm not so sure that doing that is even possible, but I am very grateful that she tries so hard. "Thank you so much, Sweetheart!"

It is my sincere hope that each of you enjoys *The Great Gathering*. May it encourage you to draw closer to the Maker and His Son, and may it give you a vision of what God can do with your life as a true follower of His.

Alan W. Harris

Lexington, South Carolina

May 21, 2014

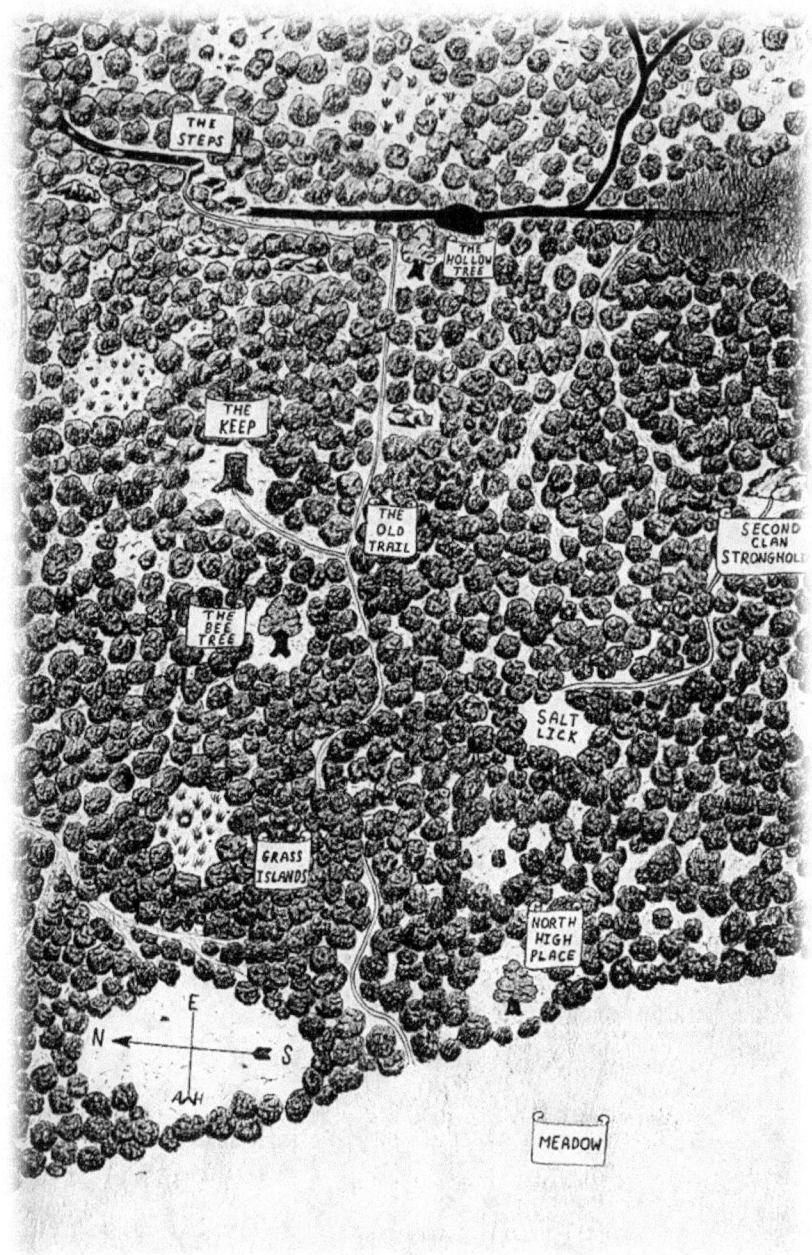

CHAPTER ONE

All In a Day's Work

Though the sun's hot rays beat intently upon the leafy roof of the ancient forest, only a few of the beams were able to penetrate the thick canopy of foliage to illuminate the forest floor far below. A light breeze wafted among the trunks and limbs, dispelling the summer heat and freshening the humid air near the ground. Like an army of giants, the stately trees filled the scene in every direction as far as the eye could see, which wasn't far, owing to the denseness of the forest. There were the tall and straight yellow poplars, the smooth barked hickories, and the huge blackjack oaks with their spreading branches. The tree nearest at hand was a stately shag bark hickory, which was anchored firmly in the ground at the base of a low moss and lichen-covered hill. Snaking its way up into this tree, looking very much like a large rope, was an old wild grape vine of proven quality. As it had for so many previous seasons, this faithful old vine once again produced a vast quantity of large, deliciously sweet, bronze-colored wild grapes known as scuppernongs. Many of the forest creatures traveled to this spot in the late summer to feast on the tasty fruit. There was, in fact, a rather unique woodland creature gorging himself on them at that moment.

1

ALL IN A DAY'S WORK

One particularly large and very ripe-looking grape was lying by itself on top of a dry leaf. A rounded hole had been cut through its skin, and through this hole were a pair of tiny legs covered in tan leather leggings and ending in a pair of dark brown leather boots.

"Hawthorn, are you gonna eat that whole thing?" a voice called out from nearby.

The legs began to kick and squirm as they backed out the hole in the scuppernong. Slowly the full body of a tiny person emerged from the grape, revealing a small woodsman in a belted leather tunic who was less than an inch tall.

"I might!" the one named Hawthorn returned with an annoyed look on his face.

Hawthorn and his companions were members of a race of insect-sized people who were unknown to man. Their small size and the fact that they lived deep in the woods where few men ever walked kept their existence a secret. They were also a people who were masters of woodlore—so much so that man's dulled senses had little hope of detecting the presence of these miniature folk when they chose not to be detected. These tiny people called themselves *Larkin* in the same way that man would refer to himself as *man*.

Their name came from a great ancestor from whom they all descended. He, Larkin, was literally the father of these people. Larkin had seven sons, and their descendants made up the clans of Larkin. There had originally been seven clans, but now almost three centuries later, only five clans remained. The individual clans lived separately in their own strongholds scattered throughout the forest. Though each clan existed independently of the other clans, they were ruled by authoritarian religious leaders from the First Clan, who were known as Shaman. The Shaman had been in charge longer than anyone could remember, and no one questioned their authority for one primary reason: the Larkin people believed that only the Shaman could speak to

God the Maker, because only the Shaman knew the Maker's secret prayer language. In this way the Shaman controlled access to the Maker, and because of this, they had been able to maintain their power over the clans for many generations. The Shaman not only ruled the clans, but they also served as judges. Anyone who refused to obey or submit to their authority was declared a Renegade and banished from the clans.

As a matter of survival, the banished criminals known as Renegades had joined together to form their own tribe, but their culture was based on cruelty, hatred, and the strong dominating the weak. These savages roamed the woods, looking for food and opportunities to seek revenge on their Larkin enemies.

Hawthorn was from the Third Clan of Larkin. Today he was serving as a member of a work party sent out to gather wild grapes for the clan's food supply. Though only seventeen seasons old, in some ways he seemed much older. He and five others from the Third Clan had experienced some amazing adventures two summers ago, and Hawthorn had returned with a maturity and wisdom that surprised all those who knew him. He had also returned with something else—a fantastic secret that he valued more than his own life. He and his friends had discovered another culture of tiny people living in the woods that most Larkin didn't know existed.

These mysterious people called themselves the Maker's Children, or simply Makerians. They originally had been Larkin from the First Clan but had been banished by the Shaman. This came about when one of the Larkin religious leaders whose name was Micah read some of the Maker's Words which he had found in an ancient journal. He then shared his discovery with several others. These holy writings revealed that anyone could pray to the Creator without the need for any kind of prayer language. This meant that not only were the Shaman unnecessary, but they were actually a hindrance to the people getting to know the Maker. From the holy words Micah also learned that the Creator was not a terrifying God eager to punish people as the Shaman portrayed Him. Instead, He loved the whole world so much that He sent His Son to die for all people so any who believed in the Maker's Son could become His children. Micah tried to share his discoveries with the Shaman leaders, but because of this threat to their authority, they rejected the truth and decided to banish Micah and all those with whom he had discussed his discovery. These banished people formed a new community, basing their whole culture on obedience to the words of the Maker. Over the years the Makerians continued to seek the Maker's will in all they did, prayed about all their needs, and actively loved their enemies.

Two summers ago after Hawthorn and five of his friends were rescued from their Renegade enemies by the Makerians, they had lived with their rescuers for a short time until the Larkin could return to their clan. When they did return home, Hawthorn, his father Savin, and two others in their party, Jay and Rush, carried with them a new faith in the Maker's Son, whom they called Jehesus. Knowing that the Shaman would banish them or worse if they found out about their faith in Jehesus, the four believers decided to keep their faith a secret for as long as possible in order to try to share the truth with others in their clan.

As Hawthorn stood beside the scuppernong, he pulled out his leather water pouch and began washing the sticky juice from his hands and face. His companion, who looked to be about the same age as Hawthorn, was standing next to another of the large, ripe, bronze-colored grapes. He was holding a straight stick that was as tall as two Larkin and was sharpened on one end.

"You're clean enough," the young Larkin holding the long stick called to Hawthorn. "Hurry up; the haulers are coming back down the hill."

4

"Keep your tunic on, Garnet," Hawthorn returned. "I'm coming."

Putting the wooden stopper back in his water pouch and laying it on the ground next to his backpack, Hawthorn quickly moved over to where Garnet was standing. With Garnet using his stick as a lever and with Hawthorn pushing hard with his shoulder, they were able to roll the large grape over onto its side. Then Garnet took the sharpened end of the tall stick and started shoving it into the place on the grape where the stem had been attached to it.

"All right, Thorn. It's in. Grab the hammer and drive it through."

The hammer consisted of a smooth, oblong rock that was flat on one end. This stone was attached to a hickory handle with leather lashing. Picking up the heavy tool, Hawthorn began pounding at the end of the long stick, driving it deeper and deeper into the wild grape. He continued at this until Garnet indicated that he had driven the stick through the entire body of the large fruit. Just as Hawthorn dropped the hammer, six other Larkin approached carrying a coil of rope.

"Now that's a pretty one!" one of the Larkin said as he patted the firm skin of the large grape. "Find us three more as big as this one, and we can call it a day."

"I don't know, Jay," Garnet spoke up. "The way Hawthorn's been eating them, I'd say we only have half enough."

Jay, who was twenty-two seasons old and was the leader of the work detail, cut his eyes over at Hawthorn. Hawthorn's only response was a big smile.

"So what do you think, Thorn?" Jay asked with a faint smile. "Do we have enough grapes?"

"Oh, I think so," Hawthorn said thoughtfully. "But I'm not sure what the rest of the clan's gonna' eat."

5

"Great snakes!" exclaimed another Larkin named Cedar, who was close to Jay's age. "That boy's gonna' have us haulin' grapes till midwinter!"

"Well then, I'd guess we'd better get at it." Jay announced, as he took the rope and slipped a small loop tied in one end of the rope over one of the ends of the stick driven through the grape. Another of the Larkin named Fennel grabbed the small loop on the other end of the rope and placed it over the opposite end of the grape stick. As they did so, two of the Larkin began wrapping long leather strips tightly around the ends of the stick to keep the loops from sliding off. When the rope was secure, the six haulers stepped inside the rope as it lay on the ground. Picking it up, they began to pull the large grape up the hill. Hawthorn and Garnet helped get the grape rolling by pushing from behind.

Once he could see that the haulers had the large scuppernong rolling steadily up the hill, Hawthorn called after them, "Be careful, fellas! I don't want you bruising my private stock."

Hawthorn then turned to Garnet. "Well, since you found that last beauty, I guess it's up to me to find the next one."

"Great!" answered Garnet as he lay down on a patch of moss. "Wake me up when you locate it."

Hawthorn knew that it wouldn't take him long. There were hundreds of the plump grapes all over the ground. He walked past several smaller ones and two nice-sized ones with soft spots in their sides before he spotted the one he wanted. It was the biggest one he had seen, and there was not a single bruise on it. As he trotted up to it, the large grape gave a sudden shudder, and a big red scorpion charged out from behind it. The scorpion, which was half again as long as Hawthorn was tall, was ready to fight. She had staked a claim to this grape and was not about to give it up. With a snarling hiss she came straight at the young Larkin. Hawthorn ran to his left and circled the large grape with the deadly killer right behind him. Being much longer than Hawthorn, the scorpion could not run around the large grape as quickly as the young Larkin. Rounding the grape on a dead run, Hawthorn raced back toward his friends, yelling as he ran, "WHIPTAIL! WHIPTAIL!"

When Garnet looked up, he spotted Hawthorn running furiously with a huge red scorpion right behind him. Realizing that they were both headed straight for him, he jumped to his feet and raced up the hill as fast as he could run.

Jay had also heard Hawthorn's cry, and stopping the haulers, he looked back down the hill in time to see Hawthorn emerge from the fallen grapes with the maddened scorpion gaining on him.

Hawthorn had run almost to the place where Garnet had been resting when he decided to look back. The scorpion was almost on him, so he dodged behind another grape lying nearby. The killer insect slid to a stop in front of the grape behind which Hawthorn now hid.

Jay could see Hawthorn clearly as he crouched behind the grape just at the bottom of the hill on which Jay and the other workers stood. "Fennel, grab the left side of our grape! Cedar, you grab the right! Quickly!" Jay was barking orders rapidly. "As soon as they've got it, the rest of you get out of the rope!"

Cedar and Fennel ran to the sides of the grape and grabbed the ends of the stick protruding from it. When they had the large round fruit securely held, the others dropped the rope and ran out of the way—all but Jay. He ran to the right side of the grape.

"Fennel, hold your end tight. Cedar, help me line this thing up!" Jay grabbed the stick, and he and Cedar began pulling their end uphill. "Now hold it and let me look!" Jay barked.

When he knew Cedar had a firm grip on the stick, Jay ran back up the hill a few paces so he could look over the top of the grape. "We pulled it too far, Cedar! Drop it back down just a little!"

"Would you guys hurry? I can't hold this thing much longer!" Fennel cried out from the other end.

"That looks good!" Jay shouted as he sighted over the top of the grape. "Okay, both of you turn loose NOW!"

Jay ran forward as he said this. As the two Larkin released the grape, Jay threw himself into the back of it, giving it a powerful shove.

Hawthorn heard Jay's shout and looked uphill in time to see the huge round grape rolling down towards them, gaining speed every second. At first he thought that the careening fruit would crush him, but then he realized that Jay had aimed it at the scorpion. The noise of its approach warned the scorpion, and she jumped backwards at the last moment. She lashed out with her venomous tail at the grape as it flew past, tearing open a gash in its side.

"No!! We missed!!" yelled Jay. "Come on! We've got to help Hawthorn!"

When Hawthorn saw that the huge insect was momentarily distracted, he turned and ran. His quick movement caught the attention of the scorpion, and she again took up the chase. Hawthorn knew the killer insect would have him in less than five seconds if he didn't do something. Just in front of him was the large grape out of which he had been eating earlier. At a full sprint, Hawthorn launched himself headfirst through the opening in the side of the grape. The enraged creature wasn't about to let her enemy get away. She grabbed the sides of the grape into which Hawthorn had dove and began to shake it violently. Finally, out of frustration, she drove her long, poisonous, stinging tail viciously into the grape. Her attack was so powerful that the tip of her tail went clean through the fruit and out the other side.

Just at this moment Jay and the others arrived. Jay quickly whipped out his sting, which was a long rapier-like sword made from the thorn of the prickly pear, and drove it through the joint of the tail next to the scorpion's stinger which was sticking through the backside of the grape. This kept the creature from withdrawing her stinger and also kept her on the opposite side of the grape from the rescuers.

"Quick! Get him out of there!" Jay ordered.

Sharp flint knives instantly appeared, and the thick grape skin was slashed open. A strong-looking Larkin named Ash threw himself into the oozing pulp and in a moment had Hawthorn by the arms and was dragging him out.

By now the scorpion was insane with rage and was trying to tear the grape to pieces.

"We've got him! Let's move!" Jay yelled above the roar of the monster. "Back up the hill—quickly!"

Hawthorn's feet hardly touched the ground as he was rushed away from the danger.

"Are you all right, Thorn?" Garnet asked when he joined the party on top of the hill a short time later.

"Yeah, I'm fine," he responded as he tried to wipe the juice off his hands and face with the skirt of his tunic. When he looked up and saw who asked the question, he added, "No thanks to you."

"What was I supposed to do—fight a whole whiptail by myself?" Garnet returned defensively.

"Don't get your hackles up, Garnet! I was just teasing," Hawthorn answered. "There wasn't anything you could have done. Besides, you didn't see me standing my ground, did you?"

"Hee, hee," Garnet snickered, "I've never seen ANYBODY run that fast."

"I don't know about that," another Larkin named Dock spoke up. "From where I was standing, it looked to me like you two would have had a close race."

"Yeah, you were movin' pretty swift yourself, Garnet," added Fennel.

"I was . . . uh . . . just trying to get out of Hawthorn's way," Garnet replied sheepishly.

"Well, friends," Jay announced as he watched the scorpion in the distance continue to try to free her tail, "it looks to me like our grape gathering is over for today. We'll help the other crews finish hauling home the ones that we got and come back in a few days to get more when the whiptail's gone.

"I'm sorry we lost one for your private stock, Hawthorn," Jay added with a smile.

"That's all right," Hawthorn answered. "I've had about all the grapes I need for a long time. I'm soaked to the bone in juice. Everything I've got is sticky!"

"I hate to hear what your mother's going to say when she sees you," Jay chuckled. "You're going to look like a walking leaf ball when we get you back to the Keep.

"Oh—and by the way," Jay continued, "you owe me a new sting."

"I'll start working on it this afternoon." Hawthorn nodded in agreement. "Thanks for saving my life. Thanks to all of you . . ." a sly smile began to creep across Hawthorn's face as he added, ". . . except Garnet."

Later, as they were walking back to the Keep, which was what Larkin in the Third Clan called their stronghold, Jay moved over closer to Hawthorn.

"The Maker was sure looking out for you today," he said in a low voice that only Hawthorn could hear. "When I saw that whiptail after you, I figured you were a dead Larkin if you didn't get some help. I guess I must have said the fastest prayer in the world."

"And I must have said the most earnest prayer in the world—on the run," Hawthorn whispered back. "I'm just glad the Maker hears us."

"That is a good thing," Jay returned, "'cause you sure keep Him busy."

"You do remember about the gathering tonight, right?" Hawthorn whispered.

"What gathering?"

"You know; we planned it last week. Mother's cooking a big pot of stew for all of us, and after we eat, we're going to talk about Jehesus."

"Is that tonight? Are you sure?" Jay asked with a surprised look on his face.

Hawthorn nodded.

"Then I'll be there. I'll just have to get someone to swap guard duty with me. Clover will do it; he owes me a favor. Does Rush know about the meeting?"

"He's supposed to," Hawthorn whispered back, "but if he forgot, I'm sure my father will remind him. They're both gathering honey today."

CHAPTER TWO

LOST AND MOSTLY LOST LEGGINGS

The Larkin gathered their honey from an old giant beech tree. This timeworn tree had survived several lightning strikes over the many decades it had existed and was a habitat for a number of different forest creatures. A large hive of honey bees had made their home perpetually in a deep hollow in the trunk of the massive beech.

In order to reach the honeycomb without having to confront the bees, the Larkin had carved a sloping pathway in the bark of the tree up to a place on the same level as the opening to the beehive but on the opposite side. From this place on the tree, the industrious Larkin had years ago carved a tunnel which allowed them to arrive at the back side of the bee's honeycomb. By carefully carving through the wax forming the back wall of the comb, the Larkin were able to safely reach the honey that the bees had sealed in the cells.

Through the carved tunnel a line of Larkin workers was steadily moving buckets of the precious, sweet liquid from where it was being dipped from the opened cells. When the full buckets were handed out of the tunnel opening, workers standing there would hook the buckets onto a rope which was attached to the trunk of the tree just above the tunnel entrance and was stretched at a steep angle down to the ground some distance from the base of the huge tree. The buckets then slid down the rope and were collected by workers on the ground.

"So how're we doin', Birch?" This question was asked by the deep-chested, burly Larkin who was in charge of the operation.

"I think we're doing pretty well, Rush," Birch answered. "Other than that slow start we had getting to the part of the comb where the good honey is, everything has been going smoothly. The buckets of honey have been moving steadily up the tunnel for the last few hours."

"Well, let's keep it up," Rush returned with some concern in his voice. "We've just about collected our quota. It'd do me a world a' good to finish this job up today and not have to come back here tomorrow. I get powerful nervous around bees!"

"Oh, I don't mind them so much," Birch said with a smile, "as long as they stay on the other side of the honeycomb. Besides, Savin's in charge of the honey dipping, and I think he's got it under control."

"Wel-l-l," Rush drawled, "maybe I'll stroll on up the line an' see if we can con-clude this project."

Rush made his way further into the carved tunnel, passing by those who were hauling the full buckets out. The closer Rush got to the honeycomb, the louder the buzzing sound became. The sound was almost deafening as Rush arrived at the back of the comb. Sweat began to pop out on Rush's forehead as he considered what was on the other side of that thin wall of wax. He was still contemplating that thought as he heard his name being anxiously called. Looking up, he saw a Larkin just a little younger than himself approaching him.

"What's up, Savin?" Rush asked.

"I know you said that you wanted the younger Larkin to get experience in all of the jobs," Savin began in a hushed voice that only Rush could hear. "Well, Poke's been hauling buckets all day, and I wanted to let him have a chance to dip out the honey before we finished. So I called him up a little while ago, but he's going to get himself killed, and I can't stop him!"

"What's he doin'?" Rush growled as he and Savin began walking toward the part of the comb where the honey dipping was taking place.

"He's almost fallen through the comb twice. He's being very careless, and he's got this attitude. He refuses to listen to anything I tell him."

"Why didn't you send him back to the bucket line?" Rush snapped.

"I tried to, Rush, but he wouldn't leave, and I didn't think standing beside the honeycomb was a very good place to pick a fight."

"I know he's just worried about his dad's health," Rush said, shaking his head, "but thunderation, Savin, I don't know how much more of his sullenness and disrespect I can take!"

"Well, you won't have to worry about that if he falls through the honeycomb," Savin shot back.

"All right! All right! I'll deal with him!" Rush growled as he stalked down the narrow path along the back of the honeycomb till he came to the collecting spot. Three Larkin stood there, organizing the wooden buckets that had been filled with honey.

"Where is he?" Rush asked, looking around.

"You mean Poke?" one of the workers responded. "Oh, he climbed over the edge and is dipping honey from below."

"You mean he's climbing on the COMB?" Rush said incredulously. "Great snakes! He's gonna' get us all kilt!" Rush moved quickly over to the edge of the wooden walkway and leaned over. What he saw made his knees weak. A short distance below him, the young Larkin stood with one foot on the wood of the tree and one foot in an empty open cell of the wax honeycomb. He was leaning against the comb as he dipped one of the buckets into on open cell to fill it with the sweet thick liquid.

"Poke!" Rush called out.

Hearing his name, the young Larkin glanced upward. On recognizing his leader, Poke turned back to his work. "What do you want?" he called back over his shoulder.

"I want you to stop what yer doin' an' climb back up here right now!"

Poke made no reply but continued to fill his bucket. When Rush saw that his order was being ignored, a low growl sounded from his broad chest. He waited until Poke had filled his bucket and was lifting it up to Rush.

With anger in his eyes, Rush reached down, but instead of grabbing the handle of the bucket, Rush grabbed Poke's wrist. Poke shouted an angry protest as he was being lifted forcefully back up onto the wooden walkway. As Rush released his grip on the young rebel's wrist, Poke, who was still holding the honey bucket, angrily swung it toward Rush's head. The older warrior saw the bucket coming and was able to duck and allow the heavy pail to fly over his head, but as the full container swung around, its weight pulled Poke off balance, causing him to tumble off the side of the walkway and smash into the waxy honeycomb. There was a sickening crack as the weight of Poke's body slammed into the thin wax plates forming the wall of the comb. The broken wall began to fold inward. Crushed and broken honey cells began to pour out their thick, sticky contents. Honey and broken wax chips began to ooze over the young Larkin. In a panic, Poke began to thrash wildly, trying to free himself, but he only succeeded in breaking more cells and becoming even more stuck.

By now the buzzing noise on the other side of the slowly collapsing wall was deafening and reaching a fever pitch. Rush quickly turned to his three companions. "Those bees will be through that wall and on us any moment! Ash, run back up the tunnel and get everyone out of here now!"

Looking up from his sticky tomb, Poke saw the Larkin named Ash drop his buckets and run back down the passageway. "Don't leave me!" he screamed in terror.

Rush and the other two workers looked back at their trapped companion. "I'm gonna' need some help getting' him out," Rush said.

"We're with you, Rush. Let's get to it!"

"Come on then," Rush cried as he led the way over the wooden ledge to the place where Poke had been standing before he fell. "Calamus, you hang on to me," Rush ordered, "and Moss, you hang on to him. I'll try to grab Poke; then you two pull us back."

They quickly locked arms with each other to form a chain, moving toward Poke. They had to stretch as far as they could to reach him. Poke frantically grabbed Rush's outstretched arm, but Moss, who was the only one who had adequate footing, couldn't pull hard enough to budge Poke.

"We can't do it, Rush!" Moss finally called out.

"Here come the bees!" Calamus yelled.

They looked up in time to see a large piece of the comb wall that had broken begin to slide down. It didn't slide far before the jagged pieces of broken wax caught on the sticky broken wax below it, but it was enough to leave a gap in the wall. Through this gap, antenna, legs, and wings began to appear.

"The honey dripping down from above the break is slowin' 'em down," Rush observed.

"But that honey will stop real soon," Calamus added, "and when it does, those bees will be all over us!"

"Don't leave me!" Poke cried again. "Please don't leave me!"

Rush's mind was racing to come up with a plan. He began looking all around them for something to use.

"You looking for this?" called a voice from above them. Looking up, they saw Savin holding a coil of rope.

"Quick, toss me the end o' that thang," Rush yelled.

16

Grabbing the end of the rope that Savin tossed him, Rush drove his hand into the sticky mess holding Poke and worked the line around the young Larkin's body.

"Pull me up—quick!" Rush called as he handed the rope to Poke and allowed the young Larkin to finish tying the line around himself.

As the four Larkin strained against the rope, they began to feel Poke moving toward them. "It's working!" Poke cried. "Don't stop!"

The top half of Poke's body was free of the honey, but the sticky ooze still gripped his legs. At that moment a louder buzzing was heard above them. Looking up, they saw that they had been spotted by a bee whose head was sticking through the gaping hole in the broken wax wall. The angry insect was fighting furiously to get through the last of the dripping honey in order to reach those who had caused the damage.

"We're outta time!" Rush yelled. "PULL!"

The four Larkin leaned hard against their load and, with bellowing cries, heaved on the rope with all of their might. Poke screamed with them as the tense rope dug into his armpits. Then suddenly Poke broke free and flew across the space, landing on his friends.

"My pants, my pants!" Poke yelled. "They're still stuck in the honey with my boots!"

"Yer gonna lose mor'n yer clothes if'n ya don't start runnin'!" Rush barked at the barelegged youth.

By now all of the Larkin were on their feet and sprinting back up the tunnel. All at once the buzzing noise echoing up the tunnel intensified dramatically.

"Whoo-oo! Run fellers!" Rush's frantic voice called up from behind. "They're after us an' comin' fast!"

Savin was the first one out of the tunnel. He could hear the wings of the furious insects beating against the sides of the tunnel as they were charging up the passageway behind the Larkin. He realized that they would never make it if they tried to descend the path that was carved into the side of the tree. Quickly he unlatched his belt and threw it over the silken rope down which the filled honey buckets had traveled to the ground.

"Follow me, lads!" he called as he grabbed both ends of his belt and jumped off the edge. "It's our only hope!"

One by one the frantic Larkin jerked off their belts, tossed them over the rope, and jumped after Savin. When Rush reached the opening, he saw Poke standing hesitantly on the wooden ledge, watching their friends slide down the tight cord.

"Quick, use yer belt!" Rush screamed as he glance back over his shoulder at the rapidly approaching bees.

"I don't have a belt!" Poke screamed back.

Rush already had his own belt off and, running up, he threw it over the rope. "Then grab ME!"

Poke leaped behind Rush and wrapped his arms tightly around the stout Larkin's chest just as Rush flung them out into space. Rush was a heavy Larkin anyway, but with Poke's added weight, the two of them began gaining speed as they slid down the steeply sloping rope.

"The bees aren't following us!" Poke called out as he glanced back over his shoulder and saw a thick cloud of the killer insects swarming around the opening to the tunnel.

"That's the least of our worries!" Rush shot back.

Turning back around, Poke saw that they were rapidly approaching the slider in front of them.

"Look out, Moss!" Rush yelled. "I cain't slow us down!"

When he heard Rush call, Moss glanced back and saw his speedily approaching friends. He had just enough time to tighten his grip on both ends of his belt when Rush and Poke slammed into him. But instead of slowing them down, Moss was carried along in their swift descent.

RUSh AND POKE

They were still gaining speed when they caught up with Calamus. They tried to yell a warning, but Calamus never looked back. They were still many leagues above the ground when Moss hit him. The blow was too much for the unsuspecting Calamus. The belt slipped from one of his hands and down he plunged. The quick-thinking Moss stuck his feet out and caught his falling comrade under both armpits.

The blow had also been more than Poke's tired arms were prepared for, and he lost his grip around Rush's chest, but he managed to regain it around Rush's waist. He discovered his perilous position too late as Rush's beltless pants began to slide down.

"WHAT ARE YOU DOIN'?" Rush screamed as he saw he was losing both Poke and his leggings. Throwing his legs as wide as he could, Rush tried to stop the descent of his friend and his clothing. "Grab me, not my pants!"

Poke seized each of Rush's legs and held on for dear life.

"Oh, no!" they heard Moss gasp. "We're on fire!" Looking up, they saw thick smoke streaming off both of their belts. The added weight on Rush and Moss was not only making them go faster, but it was also producing much more friction on the leather belts.

By now all four of the Larkin were yelling as they rocketed down the rope. Savin heard the racket and looked back over his shoulder. He saw his terrified friends careening towards him like a screaming meteor. He had just enough time to say, "Lord Jehesus, help us!" when they bowled into him. By the grace of the Lord, as Savin later declared, he was able to retain his grip on his belt, but now all five of them were zipping toward the ground at an alarming rate. Fortunately the weight of all of them together stretched the silken rope so that, as they approached the end, they began sliding across the ground a short distance before they reached the trunk of the small tree to which the rope was tied. That slide, although it caused the loss of a significant amount of skin, especially for those without pants, also slowed them down enough to save their lives when they came to a sudden stop at the base of the tree.

"Is everyone alive?" Savin asked as they began to painfully pick themselves up. Poke, Calamus, and Moss all nodded their heads in response.

"Praise the Maker," Rush called out loudly as he stood there, pulling his torn britches back up, "but I don't EVER want to do that again!"

CHAPTER THREE

FELLOWSHIP

"Enough of your foolishness, Rush!" Rose snapped as she spun around to face the burley Larkin. "You tell me right now! How badly were you hurt this afternoon?" Rose had her left hand on her hip, and her right hand was pointing a wooden cooking spoon straight at Rush's nose.

Rose was the wife of Savin and the mother of Hawthorn. She was preparing stew and seed meal cakes for their special friends whom they had invited to their living quarters for the evening. She had brown eyes and shoulder-length dark brown hair with just a few wisps of grey at her temples. She was petite and was known for her kind, soft-spoken manner, but that was not the side of her that was showing now.

"It ain't that bad, Rose," Rush said defensively. "Honest. I lost some hide when we was a scootin' along the ground, and I probably won't be doin' much sittin' fer a while, but I'll heal."

Rose was still giving Rush her same hard look.

"I promise, Rose. It ain't no worse than after my father got done with me that time I set my brother's pants on fire."

"And what about young Poke?" Rose demanded as she looked around at all of them.

This time the answer to her question came from Savin, who was sitting on a bench holding a bowl of stew with bandaged hands.

"Other than lots of scrapes on his legs and backside, the only serious injury he received was a long deep gash on the outside of one of his thighs. We got him cleaned up and bandaged before we took him back home."

"Is he going to be all right?" Rose asked with concern.

"Oh, he'll heal," Rush returned, "but that boy's got bigger problems than his wounds. He's mad at the world."

"It's not the world he's mad at," Jay said, rising up from where he sat hunched over his bowl of stew, "it's us. He didn't start acting like this until his father got hurt while we were trying to escape from the Renegades a couple of seasons ago. I think he blames us for Sycamore's head injury."

"He does," Hawthorn spoke up. "I've heard him say that."

"He's just scared and worried about his father," said Savin, "and his mother dying last season didn't help either."

"Is Sycamore getting any better?" Rose asked, turning to Rush.

"Between Jay and me, we try to get by and see him every few days. His memory is better. He is starting to recall some of the details of his capture and escape from the Renegades."

"He's even starting to remember the Makerians," Jay added, "so Rush and I have begun trying to tell him about Jehesus. We just have to do it when Poke's not around, 'cause he gets real mad when he hears us talking about that stuff."

"Recently," Rush began again, "Sycamore has been having these really bad spells where he passes out and

23

starts thrashing around wildly. They don't last very long, but they are terrible when he has them."

"The poor dear," Rose sighed. "When we finish our meeting tonight, Hawthorn, you and I are going to take them some stew and bread."

Hawthorn looked up from his bowl with a mouth full of stew and nodded his agreement.

Suddenly a loud feminine voice was heard coming from just outside the front door. "Well, hey there, Shaman Agnus!"

At that moment everyone in the room froze, and nervous eyes cut back and forth at each other. "That sounds like Juniper," Rose whispered to her husband Savin.

"She must be trying to warn us," Savin whispered back.

Juniper was a small young lady who, like Hawthorn, was seventeen seasons old. She and her widowed mother Verbena had become followers of Jehesus ten months ago after Rose had spent several afternoons talking with them about the Maker's Son. The petite Juniper had jet black hair that grew in such tight curls that it resembled a black cloud surrounding her head. She also had large expressive brown eyes which at this moment were locked onto the tall, bearded figure of Shaman Agnus as he stood close to the doorway of Savin and Rose's living quarters.

"We don't usually get to see any of the Shaman up here in this part of the Keep," the young lady continued with a big smile, "but I'm really glad I ran into you."

Shaman Agnus shifted his eyes between the girl and the nearby door. Finally he adjusted his long brown robe nervously, and with a stiff smile, he turned to face the approaching Larkin girl. "And how are you today, Juniper?"

"Oh, I'm just as fine as I can be!" Juniper returned with her usual enthusiasm.

"And your mother?" the Shaman added politely.

"She's fine, thank you," Juniper answered quickly. "Well, she's not really fine. In fact, she's not good either. Actually, she's sick. She's been sick for these last four days."

"I'm sorry to hear that," the Shaman said, looking around him.

"That's very kind of you, Shaman Agnus," Juniper shot back, still smiling broadly. "It will just make Mama's day when she finds out that I bumped into you and you asked about her. I'm hoping she'll be better soon. Did I tell you she's been sick these last four days?"

"Uh, yes . . . as a matter of fact . . ."

"Three days isn't too bad," Juniper began again, cutting him off. "Nose sickness, throat sickness, even ear sickness all last about three days. But when they go to FOUR days . . . well, that's when I start getting nervous. Although I was sick for six days once, but that's because Aunt Lobelia was giving me yellow dock root instead of skullcap tea. Great Snakes, but that was a cleansing experience! I spent the next two days in the 'little girls' room,' if you know what I mean. Hee, hee, hee!"

"Well, that's all very interesting," the Shaman began, "but I'm sure that you have . . ."

"Oh, Shaman Agnus!" Juniper exclaimed. "I have a wonderful idea! Since you are up here visiting in the living areas, you can come by and visit with my Mama."

"No, uh, I mean," Agnus stammered, "that may not be such a . . ."

"It will be great!" inserted Juniper. "Once I pick up the soup Lady Rose fixed for us, then you can walk with me back to our home. It would just raise Mama's spirits to spend the afternoon talking with you. And I'll be there, too!"

"Now, Juniper," the Shaman began again, "your mother has been sick for four days. I'm sure she needs all the rest she can get. I think you should take that fine soup Lady Rose has prepared back to your mother and then

25

encourage her to get some sleep. That will help her as much as anything. I regret that I will not be able to come by to see her today since I am needed elsewhere, but rest assured that I will be speaking to the Maker on her behalf."

"But Shaman Agnus . . ." Juniper countered.

"I'm sorry, Juniper, but I must be going now." Quickly the Shaman turned and strode purposefully toward the hallway that led to the lower levels of the Keep.

"Juni," whispered a voice from nearby. Juniper turned and saw Savin standing in the doorway of his home. "Where was he standing?"

Juniper stepped over next to the wall and pointed to the spot where Shaman Agnus had been.

Savin positioned himself in that exact location, and with a nod, he beckoned the girl to enter his home.

"What was the Shaman doin' out there, young one?" Rush asked after Juniper was inside and Rose had replaced the heavy curtain covering the door to their living quarters.

"When I first saw him, he was standing right beside the outside wall of this home, and he was slowly moving toward the front door," Juniper answered. "Now I don't really know what he was doing there, but it sure looked to me like he was trying to listen to what was being said in here."

"How long do you think he had been there?" Jay wanted to know.

Juniper thought about this for a moment and then responded, "I don't think he had been there very long, or he would have already been right next to the doorway."

"Wel-l-l," Rush drawled, "it appears that the Shaman are still suspicious of us."

"Do you think he heard anything?" Jay asked.

"Let's find out," Rush returned. "SAVIN!"

Immediately Hawthorn's father stepped back in the room.

"What do ya think?" Rush asked. "Could ya hear what we was sayin' from out there?"

"I don't think he heard anything," Savin answered confidently. "I stood right where Juni said Agnus was standing, and even leaning as close to the door as I could, I wasn't able to make out what you were saying just now. But it's a good thing Juni came along when she did, or he would have been next to the door listening through the curtain."

"That was real quick thinking, Juni," Jay said encouragingly. "By speaking to the Shaman like that, you not only warned us, but you also completely took him off guard."

"Oh, Juni girl," Rose spoke up as she gave Juniper a big hug, "you saved us! Your mother's going to be so proud!"

"Wow! This is great!" Juniper exclaimed. "I've never saved anybody before. How about you, Hawthorn? Are you proud of me?"

Hawthorn was taken aback by the question. He stared up at the wide grin and the big expectant eyes of Juniper as she leaned towards him, eager for his answer. He took a moment to swallow the large spoonful of soup that was already in his mouth. "Uh, sure, Juni. We're all proud of you. You did a really good job."

Leaning closer to Hawthorn, Juniper looked deeply into his eyes and said, "I'm especially glad that you're proud of me, Thorn."

Hawthorn tried to smile in response but nervously cut his eyes over to his mother.

"Well, now, Juni girl," Rose said quickly as she put her hands on the young lady's shoulders and guided her to a chair across from Hawthorn, "why don't you sit right here at the table, and I'll get you some soup?"

Hawthorn picked up his bowl and quickly shoved the last few bites in his mouth. Then hopping up from his chair, he announced, "Since I'm finished eating, I think I'll go out and sit beside the door. That way I can watch for more spies, and I can listen through the curtain to what all of you are saying."

"I think that's a real good idea, Son," Savin returned. "It looks like we will have to start doing that for all of our meetings from now on."

"At least we know that the Shaman are suspicious of us," said Jay.

"Yeah, but they know we know," Rush returned, "so we're gonna have to be a lot more careful about gittin' together."

"Have any of you heard from our Makerian friends?" Rose asked expectantly.

"Rush said that he thought he heard Eldan's caller in the woods nearby when we were gathering honey," Savin answered.

"Oh, I definitely heard him," Rush added, "but we was so busy that I couldn't slip away to answer him. I think I've figured out a way to do it though."

"What you got in mind?" Jay wanted to know.

"Wel-l-l, when the bees got after us, we wound up havin' to leave a lot of the buckets and rope near the bottom of the tree. Since I was in charge of the honey gatherin', then it's up to me to make sure it all gets brought back to the Keep. So I'm recruitin' you two guys and Hawthorn out there to go back to the Bee Tree tomorrow and help me get all of our stuff collected so we can haul it back home. Since there won't be anyone else there 'cept us believers, I'll just give ol' Floppy a squawk on my trusty caller and get him to come meet with us."

"You really think Eldan will still be there tomorrow?" Rose asked.

"Well shor' he will. Floppy ain't got nuthin' better to do than wait for us to call him back."

"Well then, in that case," Rose announced, "I shall write a letter to Burdock's mother and sister. Since they became Makerians, they love hearing what is happening back here, especially from a lady's perspective."

"Could I say something to them, too, Lady Rose?"

"Of course you can, Juni. In fact, after our meeting and Hawthorn and I take some soup to Sycamore and Poke, I shall come by your home, and you and your mother can help me write it."

"That will be so fun, Lady Rose!" Juniper returned excitedly, "and will Hawthorn come, too?"

"No!" came a voice from the other side of the curtain.

Rather than spending time reading some of the Maker's Holy Words which the Makerians had given Hawthorn, they decided to pray together and end their meeting early.

Shortly after sunrise the next day, the thick wooden gates protecting the entrance to the Larkin fortress known as the Keep were pushed open by the gate guards, and out marched four guards followed by Rush, Savin, Hawthorn, and Jay.

There was only one entrance to the Keep. The gate was located on the southern side of the great cedar stump and was constructed of two large carved oak doors which could be quickly drawn closed and bolted securely at the first sign of danger. There had been many times in the past that the only things that stood between the inhabitants of the Keep and certain death were these stout oak doors and the defenders on the walls. As an added defense, there were two sealed casks made of wood located just beside the gates. These casks were filled with a thick black foul-smelling fluid which was an extract of a number of different plants and berries and, when spread on the ground in front of the gate, was a deadly poison to many of the insects that might attack the Larkin fortress.

FELLOWSHIP

The morning air was warming quickly under the rising summer sun. The birds and the insects were already busy welcoming the day and beginning their hunt for food. The small parade of troopers walked purposefully along the gate path which ran between two extended roots that formed the Keep entrance. When the four guards reached the end of the path, the two carrying lances stopped and took their positions on either side of the end of the path. The two guards with bows kept marching to take their posts about a stone's throw further out. The four friends stopped at the end of the path to let Rush report their destination and purpose to the guards. After the brief exchange, Rush gave a nod to his friends and led them in a long distance trot to the south in the direction of the Bee Tree.

The four traveled single file, following the old path that would lead them back to the huge oak. They each wore a helmet carved from an acorn cap with leather strapes which could be tied under the chin. A long-sleeved, tan leather tunic hung to the middle of their thighs. Their legs were covered with leather pants which were tucked inside dark brown boots. A wide dark leather belt circled the waist from which hung a cloth pouch on the right hip and a long sheath on the left. The sheath held their sting.

The sting was the primary weapon of a Larkin warrior. It was long and rapier-like, made from the straight thorns of the prickly pear plant. Each warrior carefully selected a thorn that had the desired weight and balance. Then the base of the thorn was carved into a handle which was wrapped with leather. Larkin warriors regularly practiced using bow and arrows, a staff, a sling, and a lance, but they spent the most time practicing with their sting.

The four friends carried backpacks behind which were slung their wooden shields. In addition to all this, every warrior had a flint knife stuck inside one of their boots and a bow with a small quiver of arrows over a shoulder. All of these weapons were needed, because outside the protective walls of the Keep, enemies were everywhere.

It took nearly two hours for the friends to reach the Bee Tree. When they finally arrived at the base of the great oak, they spent several minutes scouting to make sure that the bees had settled down.

"Things look peaceful today," Savin observed as he scanned the opening to the hive high up on the trunk.

"I reckon they're all busy cleanin' up the mess that Poke made yesterday," Rush returned. "That should give us time to collect all the buckets and rope that we had to leave behind.

"Savin, you take Jay and Hawthorn over to where the rope slide ends and start coiling ropes and getting' all the buckets together. I'm gonna' see if'n I can make contact with Floppy."

With a nod Savin led the way over to the long rope slide tied to the base of a nearby tree to begin the cleanup work. As the three walked away, Rush slid off his pack and pulled out an odd-looking device. It was a carved wooden cup a little smaller than his head. There was a tiny hole drilled through the bottom of the cup through which ran a cord that was almost as long as Rush was tall. The cord was knotted inside the cup so that it would not slip out. Rush kneeled down, placing his knee on one end of the cord. Holding the cup with his left hand, he lifted it up until he had stretched the cord tight. His right hand held a small block of hard pine sap. This he began drawing along the tight cord. An enormous croaking roar began to come from the open end of the cup. By the way Rush stroked the cord with the sap, he made the cup sound like it was speaking a strange language. There were long calls, then short calls, then combinations of long and short. After several minutes of this, he stopped and listened for some time. When nothing was heard, he pulled up his caller and repeated the bellowing calls. When again he received nothing but some distant bird cries for all of his efforts, he tried it a third time.

"Give it a rest," Jay called out. "If Eldan was in the area, he would have answered by now."

"I KNOW I heard him callin' yesterday," Rush said with emphasis. "I was shor' he'd still be here. It ain't like him to run off when he tries to contact us."

"Something probably just came up," Hawthorn suggested. "You know how those Makerian Rangers are. They're always coming and going and doing stuff."

"Wel-l-l, it cain't be helped," Rush growled. "If he ain't here, he ain't here. I might as well be productive and help you birds get all our stuff together."

Rush packed up his caller and set to work with his friends, trying to gather up all of the scattered ropes and buckets. Most of the wooden pails were spread around the base of the tree where the sliding rope was anchored. They spent some time collecting these and lining them up. They would run a long pole through all of the handles so that, with two Larkin on each end of the pole, they could carry them all back to the Keep.

After organizing all of the buckets close at hand, the four friends began ranging further out, looking for abandoned equipment. "What did you fellas do yesterday?" Jay called out a short distance away. "There are buckets way over here!"

"When word spread that the bees were after us," Savin answered defensively, "everyone bailed out of that tree pretty fast. When you're running for your life and something's in your way, it gets thrown aside."

"All I can say is that, if you had panicked a little less, there wouldn't be such a big mess to clean up," Jay shot back, holding up a very sticky bucket with dirt and bits of leaves stuck to it. "A lot of these buckets still had honey in them when they got tossed."

"Watch out, Jay!" Hawthorn yelled from nearby.

Jay turned just in time to see a fierce-looking black ant come charging from a grass patch behind him. Its antenna brushed Jay's leg as he leaped out of the way. The ant, now alert to Jay's presence, suddenly became agitated. With a hissing blast, a scented mist shot from its enlarged abdomen, and the enraged ant began racing around in all directions, tearing up everything it could get its powerful mandibles on. It grabbed the bucket Jay had dropped, and immediately the carved wooden pail exploded into splinters in the jaws of the terrible creature.

Black ants only came up to a Larkin's knee, but they were over a hundred times as strong and, even when calm, were not a creature to be messed with. A loud thrashing racket began in the grass clump from which the ant had come. Suddenly three more enraged black ants burst out of the grass and began charging around, destroying everything in their path.

"Hawthorn!" cried Savin. "There are two more behind you!"

Pulling his eyes from the rampaging ants in front of him, Hawthorn spun around to find two more ants carefully searching the ground behind him. "Where did they come from?" he shouted, as he began backing cautiously away from the danger in front and behind him.

"It's the honey!" Rush called out. "Honey was spilt all over the place when we knocked the buckets over tryin' to get away from the bees. Now the ants have found it."

"And they obviously don't like competition!" Jay yelled back as he began running from more of the aggressive insects.

"To me, Larkin! To me!" Rush ordered. Immediately Savin, Hawthorn, and Jay ran as quickly as they could to join their leader.

More ants began to appear, and as soon as one of the agitated insects got anywhere close to the others, then the calm ants were pulled into the wild frenzy.

"Thunder and sky fire!" Rush barked. "Them thangs is all around us, and they's goin' plum wild."

"This doesn't look good, Rush," Jay said with a look of concern.

"What do we do?" Hawthorn yelled. "They'll be on us any minute!"

"Well, we cain't fight 'em," Rush answered, thinking out loud. "All we can do is try to stay outta their way."

Looking around, Rush saw that the only thing close to them that offered any hope of escape was a small hickory sapling. "Hurry!" Rush exclaimed, running over to grab an empty bucket. "Somebody bring me some rope!"

Savin snatched up a coil he had been working on and ran to join Rush under the sapling.

"Tie it on quick!" Rush snapped as he held the bucket's handle up for Savin, who with nimble fingers rapidly knotted the rope securely in place.

"Now back off!" growled the burly Rush as he began whirling the bucket around rapidly. With a mighty heave and a yell, Rush sent the bucket and the rope flying over his head. As the bucket with the rope attached reached the top of its arch, it passed over one of the branches of the sapling and fell back to the ground. Grabbing the rope, Rush turned and shoved it into Hawthorn's hands. "Hold on to both ends of the rope as you climb, an' shoot up that thang like yer life depended on it, cause it does!"

Without hesitation Hawthorn began dragging himself up the rope as fast as his arms and legs would work.

"You next, Jay," Rush ordered. There was no argument. Every Larkin knew that the leader's orders were to be obeyed instantly. Jay grabbed the rope and sped up it after Hawthorn.

"The ants are heading this way fast!" Savin called out.

"I see 'em," Rush returned. "Get up the rope! I'll be right behind you."

Savin took the rope and climbed rapidly. Rush took a glance at the oncoming ants and quickly followed his friends in their climb for safety.

By now Hawthorn was trying to pull himself up onto the limb, and Jay was helping to push him on up. Savin, with Rush just behind, had almost caught up to Jay, who was now a little more than five-Larkin high above the ground. Suddenly there was a powerful jerk on the rope that even caused the limb on which Hawthorn lay to dip toward the ground. Looking down, they discovered that one of the berserk ants had found their rope and was savagely attacking it. Again the rope was jerked, this time even more powerfully, almost causing Hawthorn to lose his grip.

"We've had it!" Jay cried out.

"Not yet we ain't!" Rush shot back. The powerful Larkin released one hand from the rope to reach behind him and unhook his shield where it hung on his backpack. Holding it by its edge, he watched the fierce creature beneath him, looking for the right moment. Suddenly Rush released his grip on the rope, and giving his war cry, he dropped toward the dangerous insect below. As Rush crashed down upon the creature's back, he drove his shield with both hands into the joint where the ant's head attached to its thorax. With a loud crunching snap, the ant's severed head rolled a short distance away, the fierce mandibles still clamping at unseen enemies.

Rush painfully pulled himself off the thrashing body of the dying ant, and dropping his shield, he began to climb back up the rope. When the four friends were all safely up on the branch of the sapling, they quickly hauled the rope up after them.

They sat there on the bouncing limb for almost a quarter of an hour, watching the ants searching the ground near them for more honey, when suddenly a voice from below startled them, "Well, lookee there. I thought it was too early in the season for hickory trees to be bearing nuts, but there sits a cluster of them right there on that limb."

Below them stood a thin young warrior with a heap of flaming red hair piled on his head, freckles on his face, and a pathetic-looking sprig of red fuzz sprouting from his chin. "Eldan!" Hawthorn shouted down to his friend. "We didn't think you were going to show up."

"We'll drop the rope for you, Floppy," Rush added. "You better shinny on up here before them ants find you."

"Calm yourself, Wretch ol' buddy," Eldan called back with an amazingly wide grin. "You forget . . . it's ME!"

The redheaded warrior quickly whipped out his knife and began cutting open the abdomen of Rush's dead ant. Keeping a wary eye on the ants roving nearby, Eldan moved some of the ant's organs aside until he found two fleshy sacks lying very near to each other. Taking a moment to make sure he knew which way the headless ant was lying, Eldan selected the sack he wanted and removed it from the carcass.

"Better watch out, Eldan!" Hawthorn called. "One's headed right for you!"

"No worries, Chummy," Eldan returned with a smile. He reached inside his pack and removed a long pouch. From this he drew two smooth sticks, each as long as the distance from his elbow to his fingertips. As he watched the rapidly approaching worker ant, Eldan poured some of the smelly liquid from the sack he had removed from the ant onto both of his sticks.

Just then the fierce-looking black ant discovered the body of the dead ant. As the insect began her examination, Eldan reached down and began tapping her antennae with his two wet sticks. After tapping and rubbing his sticks in a repeated pattern along the ant's sensitive feelers, the insect suddenly turned and scurried away.

"I'm tellin' ya," Rush said with enthusiasm, "it just bakes my cake every time I see him do that!"

"I can teach you how to do it, Wretch," Eldan called up.

"There ain't no way, Floppy! I'm as close to them varmints as I ever intend to git!"

"You're gonna have to make an exception this time," Eldan answered. "You chums get down here pronto."

"What's going on, Eldan?" Hawthorn asked as Rush began lowering their rope.

"I need your help to save some of your Larkin buddies," Eldan returned, "and we don't have much time!"

CHAPTER FOUR

THE READY-MADE RESCUE PARTY

"I'll try to explain while you fellas get down here," Eldan called up to his friends, "but you need to hurry.

"Being the good Ranger that I am, this morning I was scouting a ways south of here near the salt lick when I heard what sounded like a battle going on. When I went to investigate, I found that a Larkin mining detail had gotten themselves surrounded by a large war party of Renegade warriors. As many Renegades as there were, it didn't look like the Larkin were going to have much a chance unless they got some help real soon. That's about the time I heard your caller, and I thought to myself, *Ah-ha! A ready made rescue party!* So I came to get you. And here I am, and there you are, and we've got to go. So come on!"

Grabbing their packs and weapons, the four Larkin quickly lined up behind Eldan as he led them across the ant-covered clearing. Eldan had to confront three more of the fierce black insects with his sticks to get his friends to the trail that led to the salt lick.

"Why didn't you contact your Ranger troop, Eldan?" Hawthorn asked as they ran down the trail.

"They were already busy, Chums," Eldan called back. "We got word that an army of Renegades was moving through the woods further south. They went to go check it out."

"Why didn't you go with 'em?" Rush asked.

"Ah, you know me, Wretch. I don't do groups very well. Besides, Ranger Troop Six is being led by Sir Comfrey, and he doesn't do me very well either—if you know what I mean. It's better for all concerned if I'm my own troop.

"Now I know what you're gonna say, Wretch," Eldan continued. "You're gonna say that I need to stay with my troop, and I'll admit you got a point. It's a little tougher surrounding Renegade war parties when you're by yourself. But, you know, me being by myself isn't totally my fault. I wouldn't have to leave the troop if they just went where I wanted to go."

The five friends ran quietly through the woods for almost an hour. They stopped once when a large grey lizard moved across the trail in front of them. "That dragon looks like he's hunting," Jay whispered as they peeked around the edge of the large blackjack oak leaf under which they were hiding.

"Yeah," Rush agreed. "We shor' don't wanna mess with him. While we give him a chance to move on outta our way, let's take a little food and water. We're probably gonna need it."

After their short rest and quick meal, the five would-be-rescuers were on their way again. As they approached the salt lick, Eldan pulled up and began to move forward with caution. Suddenly he stopped and addressed the others in a low whisper, "You fellas stay put while I go see what we're up against."

Eldan then disappeared quietly into the surrounding brush. He was only gone for a few minutes before he returned and drew his friends close around him. "The battle's over," he whispered. "Looks like the bad guys won. What's left of the Larkin miners are all tied up and sitting in a group surrounded by six Renegades. There were a lot more enemy fighters than that, but they appear to have left."

"We've all got bows," Rush observed. "Let's just slip up there; then each pick a target. That'll just leave one."

"No killing, fellas," Eldan said with resolve, "not unless we have to."

"So how do we do it?" Hawthorn asked.

"I've got just the thing," Eldan answered as he pulled his quiver of arrows from his shoulder.

Searching through the missiles, he found three with solid black feathers. Pulling these out, Eldan held them up so that his friends could see the tips.

"Why, they've all got round balls of rock on the tips of 'em!"

"Now aren't you just the observant one, Wretch," Eldan smiled. "That's exactly what they've got. You just aim for the head and let 'em fly."

"Hoo-wee," Rush exclaimed softly, "if you get hit with one a' them thangs, you'll definitely be catchin' up on yer beauty sleep."

"But Eldan, the Renegades will all be wearing those heavy wooden masks," Hawthorn observed. "Your special arrows may hurt them a little, but they may not knock them out."

"That's why the shooters will have to slip around behind them and shoot the Renegades in the back of the head where their masks won't protect them."

"That'll work," said Savin. "So how many of those arrows do you have?"

"I've only got three," Eldan answered.

"That means that we'll have to thin their numbers down a bit before we can use 'em," Rush spoke his thoughts out loud.

"I'm way ahead of you, Wretch," Eldan said with his characteristic grin. "Let me tell you fellas my plan."

A stone's throw through the woods was a small clearing in which sat a group of nine Larkin prisoners tied hand and foot. Six Renegade warriors lounged in a wide circle around them. The enemy fighters wore leather hunting shirts that were covered with each warrior's signs and symbols of rank. They also carried a shield and wore a frightening wooden mask. These masks were carved and painted in a wide variety of shapes and colors and were meant to strike fear in the hearts of their victims.

Suddenly a voice called out across the small clearing, "What's going on here?"

The Renegades turned and saw a lone young Larkin standing nearby, close to the edge of the brush.

"Hey! You're Renegades!" the young Larkin blurted out.

"Well, at lease yer eyes work," the Renegade closest to him sneered. "It's too bad that yer brain doesn't. You should'a kept yer mouth shut and stayed hid, you dumb kid. Now yer gonna be one of our slaves." As he said this, the Renegade strode purposefully toward his victim.

Immediately Hawthorn drew back and threw a rock he was holding straight at his enemy and ran back into the brush.

The Renegade warrior tried to dodge, but the rock hit hard against the upper part of his mask. With a cry of pain, the injured warrior jerked off his mask and began to rub his sore face. "You've had it now, kid!" the angry Renegade roared.

"Scar, you come with me. Da rest a yous stay here and guard our prisoners. We're gonna get dat kid."

Yelling their war cries, the two warriors charged into the grassy weeds and low-growing brush where they last saw Hawthorn. The remaining four Renegades stood there and spent the next several minutes entertaining themselves by guessing what their chief would do when he got hold of the young whelp. After several long minutes went by with no sign of their companions, the guards began to look nervously toward the brush where they had last seen them.

Just then a familiar voice called from their right. "If you're wondering when your friends will be coming back, it's going to be a while."

Quickly turning to find the source of the voice, the Renegades saw Hawthorn standing on the edge of the clearing. "Maybe you suckered the cap'n an' Scar into one of your traps," the guard closest to Hawthorn shot back, "but there's four of us an' only one of you." From behind the guard came the sound of three quick thuds.

At that point Rush stepped out of the brush and stood next to Hawthorn with his sting in his hand. "You might just want to check those numbers again, big boy," Rush said with a smile.

As the Renegade looked behind him, he discovered that his three companions were laying unconscious, face-down on the ground. A short distance behind them stood three determined-looking Larkin with bows in hand. Immediately the remaining warrior tossed his war club aside and extended his hands and arms away from his body as a sign of surrender.

"Jay, get these Larkin untied," Rush called across the clearing to his friends. "We can use their ropes to tie up our Renegade captives."

As Jay drew near to the group of bound Larkin, he suddenly stopped and gave a call of surprise. "Whoa! Hey, Rush, look at this!"

While the others guarded the Renagade prisoners, Rush quickly hurried over to join Jay by the seated cluster of Larkin captives. "Thunderation!" Rush exclaimed. "What happened to yer clothes?"

True enough, the shirts, pants, caps, and boots were all missing from the nine captives. "Well, I can tell you what happened, but I don't really know why." This was spoken by a middle-aged Larkin near the edge of the group.

Savin had removed the bindings from his wrists and legs, and the freed miner was just standing up. "I'm Bracken from the Second Clan."

"I'm Rush. We're from the Third Clan."

"We sure are grateful you fellas came along when you did," Bracken returned. Several of the others echoed his sentiments. "I'm the leader of this salt-gathering detail," Bracken continued. "There were twelve of us. We had been working for several hours when suddenly a war party of eighteen Renegades stepped out of the brush. They killed three of my people before we could get to our weapons. They had all of us take off our clothes. Then they tied us up and made us sit down. After that most of them took off their clothes and put on ours. Three of them even put on the clothes of our dead friends. They piled all of their Renegade clothes over there by that bush. They left their weapons and took ours. Six of them didn't have Larkin clothes, so they got left here to guard us. Then they took the salt we had mined and marched off to the south. That was about a half an hour ago."

"Now that don't make a lick of sense," Rush spoke his thoughts out loud.

"You know how Renegades are, Rush," Jay spoke up. "Maybe their clothes were getting worn out, and they just needed some new ones."

"If that's all there is to it, then why did they take the salt and leave their captives here under guard?" Savin countered.

"That's right," Hawthorn added. "I know from experience that Renegades always make their slaves do their carrying for them."

"Yeah, sumthin' ain't right. This whole thing just don't add up," Rush agreed.

"I'll bet I can find out what's going on," Bracken said as he snatched up one of the dropped war clubs and strode purposefully over to where the only conscious Renegade captive stood. The Larkin warrior rammed the pommel of the war club hard into the stomach of the Renegade, doubling him over. Then with a downward swing of the weapon, Bracken cut the legs out from under the enemy warrior, causing him to crash hard on his back. The angry Larkin stood over the injured Renegade with his war club raised.

"All right, you slimy piece of filth, you got three seconds to tell us what all this is about, or I'm gonna break every bone you got, starting with your ribs!"

"Swing away, muck face!" the Renegade spat back. "I'm tellin' you nothin'!"

"Take this, you scum!" the red-faced Larkin yelled and drew back the war club, intending to drive it with all of his might into his victim's side.

At that moment Eldan quickly stepped up and put his hands on Bracken's shoulders. "Now hold on a second, friend," Eldan said with a smile. "Let's not start acting like Renegades. Come on over here just a minute. I think I've got a better idea."

Eldan led Bracken over to where Rush stood. "Hey, Wretch, why don't we have our friends here get some clothes on? They'll have to make do with what the Renegades left till we get theirs back."

As the newly freed Larkin began to search through the pile of discarded clothing, Eldan moved next to Rush. "Try to keep these guys occupied while I spend a few minutes alone with this Renegade, Wretch," Eldan whispered. "I might be able get him to talk to me."

"Okay," Rush agreed. "Give it a try, but don't take too long. If we're gonna catch those rascals, we need to get movin'."

Eldan turned to Hawthorn, "Hey, Chummy, how about helping me with our guest?"

Following Eldan's direction, Hawthorn helped Eldan lift the injured Renegade to his feet and lead him off into the brush out of sight of the others. They came to a dead limb lying on the ground that was out of earshot of the rest of their party. Here they eased their captive down so he was sitting on the moss-covered branch.

"If you two puny squirts think yer gettin' anything outta me," the guard gasped, trying to get his breath, "then yer dumber than you look."

"I see you have some blood coming from your mouth," Eldan observed. "You must have bit your tongue when you got knocked down. How about a drink of water to wash your mouth out?" Eldan pulled out his leather water pouch to offer it to the Renegade.

"I ain't drinkin that!" the Renegade snarled. "It's probably poison."

Eldan smiled, pulled out the wooden stopper, and poured some of the water into his own mouth. Then he handed the pouch to Hawthorn, who at Eldan's encouragement took a drink as well.

"Well, how about it?" Eldan asked, once again offering the Renegade a drink. This time the warrior nodded in agreement.

Since the Renegade had his hands tied behind his back, Hawthorn stepped over and poured some water into the captive's open mouth. Hawthorn gave the injured warrior several good drinks before replacing the plug.

"Well," growled the Renegade, "I figure since you gave me water that you're probably not gonna torture me, so you're gonna make me your slave. Is that it?"

Eldan had been pacing back and forth, obviously deep in thought, when he finally turned to answer his captive's question. "Actually, uh . . . uh," Eldan suddenly paused with a questioning look on his face, "By the way, what's your name?"

"Pike," came the gruff answer.

"Well, actually, Pike, I'm going to let you go," was Eldan's response.

Both the Renegade and Hawthorn looked at Eldan with surprise. "Eldan, why would you let him go?" Hawthorn asked.

"I'm going to let all of them go," Eldan returned.

"Red Top," Pike chuckled, "you're nuttier than a loon. You know we'd kill you if we get the chance."

"Oh, I know you could," Eldan replied calmly, "but it's occurred to me that you've got bigger problems to worry about than us."

"Like what?" sneered the Renegade.

"Pack ol' buddy, you and your cohorts back there are going to be in deep muck when the leaders of the Renegade army that are secretly surrounding the Larkin's stronghold find out you let your captives escape and mess up their plans."

Suddenly the Renegade jerked his head up. "You're...you're bluffin'. You don't know nuthin'."

"What are you talking about, Eldan?" Hawthorn asked with a confused look on his face.

"It took me a while to figure it out, Chums, but it all makes sense now. You remember how I told you that the Ranger troop that I started out with was south of here watching an army of Renegades that was reported moving through the woods? Well, you and I both know that Renegade armies don't just move through the woods for no reason. They are always going someplace and are always up to no good. And what's about a two-hour march just south of here?"

"The stronghold for the Second Clan of Larkin!" Hawthorn exclaimed as he began to understand Eldan's reasoning.

"Right you are, Chummy! And if you were a Renegade army hiding in the woods around that stronghold, what could you do with twelve Renegades dressed up to look like a Larkin salt-gathering detail returning home?"

"Oh, no!" Hawthorn gasped as realization struck him. "Eldan, those twelve Renegades are gonna march right up to the gate of the stronghold and kill the guards before they even know they're in danger."

"Right again, Chums. Then the twelve Renegades in disguise will signal their friends and hold the gate open as the whole Renegade army charges inside."

"The Second Clan won't have a chance!" Hawthorn added.

"Ah, but they will now, Chums," Eldan returned, his broad smile spreading across his face. "You hurry back and tell Wretch what's going on. Have him take everyone and run after that group of twelve Renegades. The disguised enemy warriors haven't been gone very long, and they will be traveling slowly since they are carrying the salt. Our friends should be able to catch them easily before they get to the Larkin stronghold."

"I'll go tell him right now!" Hawthorn said excitedly.

"After you get them moving," Eldan yelled after his retreating friend, "come back here and help me. Tell Wretch to come back here when they've finished doing what they can to save the Second Clan, and let us know when it's safe to turn these Renegades loose."

When Eldan turned around to face his captive, he saw that Pike's head was down, and he was slowly shaking it back and forth.

"Yessiree," Eldan said, addressing the Renegade, "you and your buddies are going to have a lot of explaining to do when all your disappointed Renegade chums get a hold of you."

"Just stop talkin', will ya?" Pike snapped. "I gotta think."

After a couple of more minutes of silence, Hawthorn came trotting back up. "Our troops are on their way," the young Larkin reported. "What's with him?" he added when he saw the worried look on the Renegade's face.

"Oh, he's just trying to figure out a way not to get killed, but he's coming up empty. You see, Chums, ol' buddy Pork here is figuring that when we turn him loose, if he goes back to the Renegades, they'll be so mad at him for ruining their well-planned ambush that they'll kill him, which they probably will. So then he figures that instead of going back to the Renegades, he should try to survive on his own in the woods. But all three of us know that he wouldn't survive half a week without help. Those are the only two options he sees, and they both end in him getting killed."

"No wonder he's upset," Hawthorn said with concern.

"But you know, Chums, it's really not as bad as he thinks. Peck doesn't realize that there is another option."

At this point Pike looked up. "What other option?" he asked anxiously.

"You realize I'm not a Larkin, don't you?" Eldan asked with a smile.

Pike studied Eldan's clothing and equipment for a moment and said, "You're a Gooder, ain't you?"

"Right you are, Speck ol' buddy! Right you are! And while we Makerians don't take slaves or torture our prisoners, we do offer people like you a chance to start a new life. That is—if you're ready to stop being a Renegade."

"I can't stop being a Renegade!" Pike barked. "It's who I am!"

"My father did," Eldan said proudly.

"Your father's a Renegade?"

"He was until he became a Makerian . . . a Gooder."

"What's his name?" Pike asked suspiciously.

"His Renegade name was Ripfang," Eldan answered.

A gasp escaped the warrior's lips. "Ripfang the Vicious? I remember him from when I was just a kid. He was fierce! But they said he died fightin' you Gooders."

"He was severely injured in the battle," responded Eldan, "but he didn't die. The Makerians cared for him for weeks until he was well, and then they offered to help him get back to his people."

"Well, if that's true, then why didn't he ever come back?" Pike asked accusingly.

"I can tell you the answer to that question in his own words. He said, 'The Makerians should have hated me for what I did to them. But instead, when I was completely at their mercy, they showed me more love, compassion, and tender care than I had ever received in my life. After experiencing so much goodness and kindness, the thought of going back to the Renegade Lair to live like a savage among savages was disgusting to me. I begged them to let me stay. I even offered to be a slave to all of them. They said that they didn't keep slaves but that I was free to return to the Renegades or to stay with them, so I stayed. I figured that people that good needed someone to fight for them.'

"So he did. And later, when he found out where their goodness came from, he became one of them."

"I can't believe it!" Pike exclaimed. "Ripfang the Vicious became a Gooder?"

"He sure did, Peek," Eldan returned. "He changed his name to Ripgood, and he even got married. Then he had ME . . . uh, and my brother. So if my father could change, then you can change."

"I still think yer nuts," growled the Renegade.

"That may be," Eldan answered with a large grin, "but if you ask me, your other options don't look very appealing. The choice will be up to you, Spike. Once Chummy and I have kept you and your buds under wraps long enough to give our people plenty of time to stop the Renegade attack, then we're going to cut all of you loose. After that, it will be your decision whether you go back and try to square things with your Renegade chums or go with us to start a new life."

"I hear what yer sayin', Red," Pike snapped, "but how can I do that? The only thing I know how to do is be a Renegade."

"I'm not saying that it would be easy, Perk ol' buddy. But there are several Makerians who used to be Renegades, and so you would make lots of help. Plus, I know this guy who can give you all the power and motivation you need to make the changes."

"Who's that?" Pike asked curiously.

"His name is Jehesus," answered Eldan, "and He's a personal friend of ours.

"Hey, Chummy," Eldan said, turning to Hawthorn, "Why don't you start telling our friend Punk about Jehesus while I go check on the rest of our guests?"

Rush led his party of Larkin warriors on a long distance run, following the trail left by the disguised Renegades. They had been running for almost an hour when he pulled up to give everyone a brief rest. "Hey, Jay," Rush called out.

The young Larkin walked over and sat down next to Rush. "What's up?" Jay asked.

"Are you feelin' up to a little extra runnin'?"

"I got my special running boots on," Jay answered. "What do you want me to do?"

"We got to be gettin' close to them ya-hoos, and I don't want to mess up our surprise by runnin' up on 'em unawares. So how about you sprintin' on ahead an' see if you can spot 'em?"

"Right," Jay eagerly returned as he jumped to his feet and sprinted off.

"Mercy!" Rush exclaimed as he watched Jay quickly disappear up the trail. "Don't that boy ever get tired?"

After their short break, Rush got his party back on the trail. They had only been running a few minutes before Jay came sprinting back. Rush quickly called a halt.

"They're only about the length of two bow shots ahead of us," Jay reported breathlessly. "That salt they're carrying must be pretty heavy because they've just stopped to give everyone a breather."

"That's good; that's good," Rush said more to himself than to Jay.

"Hey, Bracken," Rush called to the leader from Clan Two. Bracken, who was standing nearby, stepped over to Rush and Jay. "Bracken, Jay here tells me that the Renegades we're looking for are only two bow shots ahead of us. He said that whole muckeree of 'em are pooped from totin' all yer salt, so they're takin' a rest. We're gettin' close to yer stronghold, so you should know these woods purdy well. Is there some way we can get past those birds without 'em spottin' or hearin' us?"

A grin began to spread across Bracken's coarse features. "Oh yeah," he nodded. "Follow me." Bracken then took off running to the right away from the trail as the rest of the group hurried after him.

"Awright, you lazy bunch a' slugs!" the Renegade leader screamed at his troop. "Get off yer buckets an' pick up dat salt. Da whole army's waitin' on us, so let's get movin'."

With much growling and complaining, the Renegades who were dressed as Larkin got up and re-formed their marching line. Six of the Renegades picked up the salt. Each of the three piles of salt had been loaded onto a large rectangular mat. The two corners of one end of each mat were pulled up and tied together, and the same was done to the two corners on the other end. A long pole had been placed through the tied ends of the mats, and each of these poles was again lifted by two Renegades, one on each end.

This procession had only been moving again for a few minutes when suddenly two Renegades with hideous-looking masks stepped onto the trail in front of them. "Hold it right there, Larkin," one of the Renegades called out. At that moment ten more warriors stepped from the brush on either side of the marchers.

"Cork da barrel, brother!" the leader of the salt detail called excitedly. "Don't be so hasty! We ain't really Larkin. We're just dressed up like 'em."

"You ain't getting' out of dis dat easy," the masked Renegade growled back as all of the warriors moved closer to the members of the salt detail, their weapons at the ready.

"I'm tellin' you, you bone head, yer makin' a big mistake! We're a Renegade war party from Troop Five of the Wolf Tribe."

"Well, I'm convinced," declared the Renegade with the mask. "Hey fellas, dis guy here says dat dey ain't Larkin, but dat de're really Renegades. So I says, let's treat 'em like Renegades." As soon as he said this, all of the warriors surrounding the salt detail screamed their war cries and waded into them with clubs swinging. The fight, if you could call it that, only lasted a few moments.

"Good work, fellers," Rush called out. "Now, Bracken, get all a' yer people back into their own clothes, and be quick about it. We've got to foil us an ambush."

As the Larkin from Clan Two quickly shed their Renegade clothing, Rush turned to Savin and Jay. "Wel-l-l, fellers, this next part of the plan might be a bit tricky. We know that there's a whole army of Renegades between us and the Clan Two stronghold, but we don't rightly know where. We also know that they were plannin' on using the salt detail as a decoy to hold the gates open for 'em, but we don't know how they were to meet up with the Renegade army."

"You can bet the real Renegades will be watching for the salt detail to arrive," Savin said, "since it's the key to the success of their whole plan."

"Well, shore they will," Rush agreed. "They'll be no sneaking through their lines. We'll have to confront 'em some way. So I figured that I'd dress up in one of their varmint suits and pretend to be a Renegade. If that army of heatherns sees one of their own leadin' the salt detail, maybe they won't be suspicious."

"That sounds risky, Rush," Jay spoke up. "I think Savin and I should dress like Renegades and be there with you."

Rush thought on this suggestion for a moment. "I don't think that's the best plan. I'd feel a lot safer if'n you two fellers hung back and hid in the brush to cover me in case I need to make a run for it."

As soon as everyone was dressed and ready, Rush, now dressed as a Renegade captain complete with mask, led them on a hurried march toward the stronghold of the Second Clan of Larkin.

After another half hour on the trail, they were suddenly stopped by a group of five Renegade warriors who stepped out of the brush in front of Rush. At the appearance of the Renegades, Savin and Jay, who had been trailing the salt carriers, hid themselves in the brush.

The warrior who was obviously in charge stepped up and, after looking over the Larkin carrying the salt, turned to Rush. "Yous guys took your own sweet time getting' 'ere. Now yous gots 'da chiefs all mad 'cause 'da attack's been delayed."

"Well, we had a little trouble," Rush growled back, "but we're here now. So do I go ahead and send my guys in?"

"I don't think we're gonna need 'em," the Renegade shot back. "Da chiefs figured dat you goons messed up an' got yerselves thumped, so 'dey came up wid anudder plan."

"Another plan?" Rush snapped. "What're they gonna do?"

"Dey camouflaged some of our best scouts an' sent 'em crawlin' toward da Larkin's gate wif' deir bows. When dey gets close enough, dey're gonna shoot da guards and rush da gate. So it looks like you guys missed yer chance."

"Well, I ain't havin' it!" Rush yelled. "We worked hard to get these Larkin suits, and thunderation, we're gonna use 'em. Let me tell my people where I'm a goin', then yer takin' me to talk to the chiefs."

Without waiting for an answer, Rush turned and walked over to Bracken and the others. "Listen up, fellers!" Rush whispered urgently. "They've already got archers crawlin' up to kill the gate guards. We've got no time to lose. As soon as I get these rascals turned around, you guys take your salt and sprint for the gate. Maybe they'll think the original plan's still on, and you may get through in the confusion. Now get ready to run, and don't stop fer nuthin'!"

Whipping back around, Rush marched hotly back to the Renegades. "All right!" Rush snarled threateningly. "Take me to the chiefs, all of you, and I mean NOW! I'm mad enough to knock somebody's head clean off!"

As soon as he saw Rush and the small group of Renegades turn into the woods to walk away, Bracken, who was leading, looked at the others and said, "Let's go!" The group of Larkin started running along the path in front of them, heading straight for their stronghold.

"Hey!" shouted one of the Renegades beside Rush, "where are they goin'?"

Rush and the five Renegades all turned in time to see the Larkin salt detail running up the trail. "Why, those numbskulls!" Rush shouted. "I said I was goin', not them!"

"Oh no!" spat the Renegade leader. "We've got to stop them before they ruin everything!"

As the Renegade war party began sprinting back toward the trail, Rush, who had dropped to the back, was following closely behind. As he drew near the last Renegade, Rush dropped him with one swing of his club. Sprinting forward, Rush swung at the next enemy warrior. The Renegade emitted a loud groan as he, too, dropped unconscious to the ground.

At this sound, the three Renegades in front looked back and realized what Rush was doing. "Treachery!" screamed the Renegade captain, and the three of them charged after Rush.

"Oops," Rush said as he saw the angry, charging warriors. "Gotta go." Rush turned and began sprinting back down the trail the way they had come.

The screaming Renegades had attracted the attention of others, and when Rush looked back, he saw not three but eight warriors hot on his tail.

This ain't good! Rush said to himself as he ran toward Savin and Jay. He hadn't run twenty more strides when out of the brush on either side of the trail in front of him rose his two friends with bows in hand.

"There's too many of 'em, fellers," Rush yelled as he sprinted toward them. "RUN! RUN!"

At that moment eleven more warriors appeared out of the nearby grass and leaves and stood beside Savin and Jay, all with bows at the ready. The sudden appearance of thirteen archers stopped the charging Renegades in their tracks.

"If you drop your war clubs and run back the way you came, we won't shoot you," shouted one of the new warriors that Rush didn't recognize.

Instantly eight clubs hit the ground, and eight Renegades raced each other to get as far away from there as possible.

"Boy, that was timely," Rush said as he walked up to his friends. "Where'd you get the reinforcements?"

"Rush," Jay said with exaggerated formality, "I would like for you to meet Sir Comfrey and Makerian Ranger Troop Six."

Bracken and the others in the Second Clan of Larkin let nothing stand in their way as they raced for their home. Their stronghold was located in a large outcropping of limestone rock resting in a small open area of thin grass and smaller rocks. At the bottom of this rock formation was a small opening almost two Larkin high. This was the only entrance into the Larkin's stronghold and was protected by two stout ironwood doors. These doors were kept open during the day but were guarded by four gate sentries.

Bracken's crew burst out of the woods and into the small clearing. They had heard several of the Renegades shout at them as they raced along the trail, but now that they had reached the clearing, no one tried to stop them. The gate was only a short distance ahead. The sentries had already spotted them and were awaiting their approach. As Bracken and his troops raced for the entrance to the stronghold, he thought he spotted one of the Renegade scouts behind a clump of low grass very close to the gate guards.

"Drop the salt and run for it!" yelled Bracken.

Tossing their loads aside, the Larkin charged straight into the unsuspecting guards and carried them along with them. Too late, the Renegade scouts discovered that they had been tricked. Leaping to their feet, the enemy warriors launched their arrows, which only stuck harmlessly in the heavy wooden doors as they were being pulled shut.

CḥAPCER FiVE

RANGER TROOP SIX

"Is everybody tucked in nice and secure, Eldan?" Hawthorn asked as he saw his friend appear out of the brush.

"The ropes are good and snug on our other guests," Eldan answered, "but it really doesn't matter right now. All five of those guys are still floating on a cloud in the land of good Renegades."

"Are they going to be all right?" Hawthorn asked with concern. "You don't think we hit them too hard, do you?"

"No worries, Chummy," the redheaded Makerian returned. "I looked at their beady little eyeballs to make sure they were doing okay. Except for five rather large headaches, they'll be as nasty as ever in a couple of hours."

"So how are you getting along with our friend Pox? Did you tell him about Jehesus?"

"His name's Pike," Hawthorn corrected, "and yes, I tried to tell him about Jehesus. But I don't think he was listening to me."

"Now that's a fine thing," Eldan said, addressing Pike. "Here we are trying to tell you the greatest news you'll ever hear, and you aren't paying attention."

"Listen here, Red," Pike growled, "you and the Chummy here are just wasting your time. Why should I care about the Maker's Son when I don't even believe in the Maker?"

"Shame on you, Plunk. You sound just like a Renegade."

"I AM a Renegade!"

"Now don't get your tunic all in a bunch," Eldan shot back. "How can you NOT believe in the Maker? Just look around you. Where do you think all of this came from?"

"I don't know," Pike answered offhandedly. "I've never thought about it."

"Well, think about it!" Eldan challenged. "Look at all of these towering trees and the beautiful flowers and the birds and that butterfly over there and the sky and the clouds and the sun. Where did all of this come from, I ask you?"

Pike sat there for a moment and then shrugged and said, "I guess I figured that it's always been this way."

"Well then, tell me this," Eldan persisted, "where does an oak tree come from?"

"An acorn," Pike shot back.

"Right," returned Eldan. "And where does a bird come from?"

"An egg," Pike answered impatiently.

"Right again!" Eldan said enthusiastically. "See, Plank, everything has a beginning. It all had to start somewhere."

"And you think some god made it?"

"Not just some god," said Eldan, "the one and only God . . . the Maker!

"Just look around you, Prank. There are birds of all shapes and sizes and colors that actually fly through the air! And then there are land critters from the tiniest mite to the towering deer. There are plants and trees of all sizes, some of which produce food, and from some we get medicine.

Then there are the clouds that bring shade and rain, not to mention the sun, the moon, and the stars which move through the heavens so precisely that we can tell the times and seasons and get direction by them. Does it honestly make any sense that all of this stuff just happened? Face it, Pink. You know as well as I do that something doesn't come from nothing.

"When you actually take the time to look closely at it, even the tiniest mite or grub is amazingly complex, and just look at how everything all works together so perfectly. From the sunshine and rain down to the plants and animals, everything feeds and provides for everything else. It's just too perfect, Spud. Somebody had to make all of this, and that somebody is the Maker."

For several long moments Pike sat quietly considering Eldan's words. Finally he looked up. "So what if a great and powerful Maker did all of this? What does that have to do with me?"

"It has to do with you," Eldan answered, "because the Maker loves all of us—you included, and He made all of this for us to use and enjoy."

"Now I know you're nuts," Pike laughed. "You're sayin' that the Maker loves ME? I could care less about Him; how could He love me?"

"He made you, Spurt. Even though you don't know Him, He knows everything about you. And in spite of the fact that you're a no good scumbag, He does, indeed, love you. That's why He made sure that we got a chance to talk to you about Him. The Maker worked this whole thing out so that you could hear about Him and His Son Jehesus."

"Oh yeah," Pike said, cutting Eldan off. "That's the guy that the Chummy was blabberin' about. So how does He fit into all of this?"

"Funny you should ask that," Eldan started again. "You see, Pog, it's like this. The Maker loves all of us so much that He wants us to live with Him forever in the perfect place where He lives. He tells us about it in His book."

"The Maker's got a book?" Pike asked with a confused look on his face.

"Yeah, He's got a book," Eldan shot back, annoyed at being cut off again. "But don't get ahead of me.

"The place where the Maker lives, it's really wonderful, Purge. The Maker says that there will be no pain or sorrow and no enemies. It's a place where there will be plenty to eat and where you are loved.

"The problem is," Eldan continued, "that the Maker is so good that He can't stand being around evil."

"So you're sayin' that lets me out," Pike spoke up.

"It lets us ALL out, Purse. None of us are good enough to live with Him."

"Heh, heh, heh," Pike chuckled. "So I guess that makes you a no-good-scum-bag, too."

"Now you got it, Pike," Eldan smiled.

"Hey, Eldan," Hawthorn laughed, "you finally got his name right."

"Well, of course I did, Chummy. How could I forget his name? But there you go getting me off course. You're just as bad as Pug here. Can't you see that I'm trying to wrest this pestilent fellow from his heathen ways?"

"Don't worry about it," Pike said with a smile, addressing Hawthorn. "Even a blind squirrel finds an acorn once in a while."

"What are you two palaverin' about?" Eldan interjected. "Can we just get back to what I was saying?"

"Just hold on a minute, Red," Pike said, cutting him off again. "I've got a question for you."

"Here we go again," Eldan groaned under his breath. "Okay, Puce, what's your question?"

"If none of us are good enough to live with the Maker, then why are you even telling me about this?"

"Because," Eldan answered as his big smile began to spread across his face again, "you had to know the bad news before I could tell you the good news."

"Good news?" Pike questioned.

"Yep," came Eldan's reply, "the good news about Jehesus."

"I'm shor' glad you fellers showed up when you did," Rush said with relief as he stood before the eleven Makerian Rangers.

"Well, actually, we've been here all day," Comfrey returned. "Our troop has been trailing this Renegade army since early this morning to try to determine their intentions. My scouts saw your detail coming in. They noticed that your two friends slipped away from the others and hid when you were stopped by the Renegades. When we confronted your friends and discovered your plan to try to warn the Larkin of the Second Clan about the Renegade attack, we decided to be available to support these two fellows.

"Your companions tell me," Comfrey continued, "that the three of you are not members of the Second Clan."

"That's right," Rush agreed. "As a matter of fact, we're from the Third Clan. We're a detail sent to collect equipment that was left at the old Bee Tree about a three hours' march north of here."

"Really?" Comfrey responded, somewhat confused. "If you were so far north, how did you get involved in all of this?"

"Wel-l-l," Rush drawled, "the truth be told, we had gotten ourselves into a kinda sticky sitchiation. You see, there was so much honey spilt around there from the day before that the place was crawlin' with ants. Literally! We'd probably still be stuck up in that tree if Floppy hadn't a come along when he did."

"Floppy?" Comfrey questioned.

"Well, yeah," Rush agreed. "You know, Ol' Floppy Hair—he's one of you guys."

"He's talking about Eldan," Jay explained.

"Eldan!" Comfrey growled. "He was with you?"

"That's what I'm tryin' to tell you," Rush shot back. "While we were trapped up in that tree, Eldan showed up and did that thing you people do to talk to the ants. After he convinced the ants to leave us alone, he said he needed our help to rescue some salt miners from the Second Clan who were being attacked by Renegades."

Rush, with help from Jay and Savin, spent the next several minutes relating the story of the rescue of the Larkin miners and stopping the disguised Renegades.

"So where is Eldan now?" Comfrey asked.

"We left him and another from our party to keep an eye on our Renegade captives," Rush explained. "They're holdin' 'em 'til we let 'em know that the Renegade attack has been foiled."

"Your plan certainly stopped the ambush," Comfrey observed, "but there is still a Renegade army surrounding the Second Clan's stronghold."

"If you've got a nifty plan for fourteen of us to fight a whole army of Renegades, I'm all ears," returned Rush, "but the odds look a little lopsided to me."

"We don't actually have to fight them," the Makerian leader answered. "We only need to run them off."

"Oh, is that all?" Rush said sarcastically.

"Yes, it is," Comfrey countered confidently, "and I do have a plan for accomplishing it. We were in the process of working out the details of that plan when you and your miners arrived."

"Well, don't let us get in the way. Just tell us what you need us to do."

Comfrey turned and addressed one of his Rangers, "Mallow, lead us to the tree."

The Ranger named Mallow immediately turned and led them cautiously through the woods. They quietly worked their way back toward the Renegade army until their appointed leader suddenly stopped before a red cedar tree.

At this point Comfrey took charge. In hushed tones he gave his orders, "We are very close to the rear of the Renegade army, so we must be quiet. Mallow, you and Nimbus will be in charge of working the nest. Bream and Galamor will ascend with you and position themselves so as to protect you from the adults. The rest of us will fan out under the tree and be ready to take over once you have accomplished your task."

The four Rangers who were to climb the tree quickly unslung their packs and pulled out their climbers. The climbers consisted of two hand pieces and two foot pieces. The foot pieces were made of oak splits that had been lashed together into a boot-shape that could be firmly tied around each foot. On the toe of each foot piece was mounted a fire-hardened thorn. The person climbing would forcefully kick the toe of a boot into the bark of the tree. This would stick the thorn deep enough to support his weight. The wooden hand pieces were short, parallel rods with a cross piece on one end, wrapped with leather for a hand grip. Firmly attached to the end of each hand piece was another hardened thorn angled sharply downward like a hook. By swinging the hand pieces hard against the tree in a downward direction, the thorn would be impaled in the tree bark deeply enough to support the weight of the climber, but not so imbedded that it could not be pulled back out. Anyone who was skilled in the climbers' use could literally walk up a tree.

Once the climbers were securely strapped in place, the Rangers began their ascent up the bark of the evergreen. They started at different places around the trunk so that the falling bark would not hit their companions. It took several minutes of hard climbing for the four to reach the first limb of the tree. Pausing only briefly to rest, the four climbers continued their ascent until they had reached the second limb. Again the four paused for a short rest. As Mallow and the Makerian named Nimbus began removing their climbers, the other two continued their climb on up the tree.

The Rangers and Larkin below watched intently as the two tiny figures of Mallow and Nimbus moved away from the trunk of the tree and began to travel along the limb. As they neared the end of the branch, they came to a fork in which was built a snug blue jay nest. The two Rangers crept cautiously toward the nest. As they drew near, they could see three baby birds in full plumage huddled together in the bottom of the nest.

Suddenly there was a loud fluttering of wings, and a full grown blue jay dropped onto the edge of the nest. Instantly the young birds began screaming and stretching their necks up to the parent. With their mouths agape, the three fledglings competed loudly for the small cricket that the male jay held in his beak. When the insect was deposited down the throat of the noisiest baby, the parent immediately turned and flew away to hunt for more food.

After carefully scanning the sky for more adult birds and finding none, Mallow jumped to his feet. "Now, Nim! Quickly!"

Running forward and hopping into the nest, Mallow pulled a coil of rope from his belt and tossed one end to Nimbus. As the startled baby birds began to squawk, the two Rangers stepped on either side of the birds and dropped the rope behind the one closest to the outside edge of the nest. Tugging hard on each end of the rope, Mallow and Nimbus pulled the fledgling to the edge of the nest and shoved it off.

By this time the squawking babies had attracted the attention of the parents, who with angry screams dove for the nest. Mallow and Nimbus bolted from the nest and sprinted back down the limb.

WRESTLING THE BABY JAY

As the male blue jay landed on the nest, he found himself suddenly peppered with tiny arrows being launched at him from the limb above where Bream and Galamor had stationed themselves. They were able to distract the angry jay long enough for Mallow and his companion to strap on their climbers and begin descending the tree.

Squawking for all it was worth, the baby jay that had been pushed from the nest flapped and fluttered to the ground. As soon as the bird landed clumsily, two Rangers, each holding different ends of a long lance, ran up behind the baby and began to herd it rapidly through the woods in the direction of the Renegades.

By now the mother jay had appeared and, hearing the cries of its baby, released an angry scream and dove for the ground. In response to her cries, the male blue jay turned his attention away from the Makerian scouts in the tree and darted after his mate.

"You better run, fellers!" Rush yelled at the baby bird herders. "They're gonna get'cha!"

Two more Rangers caught up with the others and began pushing the baby jay even faster. Suddenly they came up on a line of Renegades who had been crouching behind some brush and watching the Larkin stronghold. On hearing the noise of the approaching Rangers, many of the Renegades turned just in time to see the baby jay, who was twice as tall as they were, being rushed into their midst.

As the Rangers turned and began to run back the way they had come, the one who held onto the lance took a moment to prick the baby bird in the rear before escaping. This caused the fledgling to scream even louder. At that instant the parents arrived looking for the source of their baby's torment. Seeing the baby jay among the startled Renegades, the adult jays immediately attacked.

"Thunder and skyfire!" Rush exclaimed as he and the others watched the army of Renegades running terror-stricken in all directions, trying to escape the raging birds. "That should get the job done."

"Well, it didn't have to happen," Comfrey returned. "We captured one of their perimeter guards earlier today and sent him back with a message to the Renegade chiefs telling them that they either needed to go back home or risk being attacked."

"It looks like they didn't listen to you," Savin observed.

"They usually don't," answered Comfrey.

He continued, "We had best be moving along ourselves before those jays come after us. We'll give you Larkin an escort back to where you left your friend and Eldan."

It took them almost three hours to get back to the salt lick due to a large black snake curled up on the trail, causing them to make a wide detour.

"Hey there, fellas," Eldan said with a wide grin as the Ranger troop with the Larkin came marching into their clearing, "and lookee there! If it isn't Ranger Troop Six! Greetings, fellow troopers! Did you miss me?"

"Eldan!" Comfrey snapped. "I'm very upset with you! You were supposed to be a part of this troop, and you left us!"

"Well, I guess that's one way of looking at it," Eldan answered thoughtfully, "but technically, Chief, you guys left me."

"That's because I gave the order to march south to look for the Renegade army—which we found, by the way—while you wanted to go north, and last time I checked, I was in charge of this troop."

"I wanted to go north," Eldan explained, "because I found the trail of a bunch of Renegades hurrying after a Larkin work detail, and I knew that the Larkin were going to need some help. Since you weren't willing to help them, that left it up to little ol' me.

"So what happened?" Eldan asked, addressing Rush. "Were you able to stop the ambush?"

Rush briefly related the series of events that led to preventing the ambush and the dispersing of the Renegade army.

"Well, there you have it!" Eldan said enthusiastically. "So you see, Chief, it was a team effort."

Sir Comfrey sighed and shook his head. "I'll admit," he finally said, "that if you hadn't have done what you did that we might not have been able to stop the ambush in time, but that's still no excuse for you disobeying orders!"

"You look angry right now," Eldan smiled, "but deep inside, I know you really love me."

"So do we let these Renegades go now?" Hawthorn asked from where he stood next to Pike.

"That we do, Chummy," Eldan answered as he walked over to stand behind their captive. Eldan pulled out his knife and began to saw at the ropes holding Pike.

"All right, Puke ol' buddy," Eldan said, addressing their captive. "It is now the moment of truth. Are you going to come with us and follow the Lord Jehesus, or are you gonna go back to being a savage?"

Pike just stood there rubbing his wrists and moving his arms to get the blood flowing back into them. "I can't believe you're just lettin' me go," Pike finally said.

"Red, I'm convinced that you and the Chummy believe that everything you told me about the Maker and His Son is the truth. Maybe it is. But it's just too much for me to believe that the Maker would care enough for somebody like me to send His own Son to die a horrible death to pay for all of my mistakes."

"It's the truth, Pook," Eldan said encouragingly, "and all you have to do is trust Jehesus enough to . . ."

"I know, Red. I know," Pike cut him off. "I just need to trust Him enough to make Him chief in my life. I'll admit that He would probably do a better job at runnin' my life than I do, but to be honest with you, I like being my own chief. Besides, being a Renegade is all I know, and I don't think I can be anything else."

"I think you're making a terrible mistake, Pike," Hawthorn spoke up.

"Maybe so, kid, but it won't be the first . . . or, most likely, the last.

"Now listen up. I want to ask you guys somethin'," Pike continued. "Since you're letting us go anyway, if you don't mind, could you let me release the other Renegades without them seeing any of you? It might help me in the long run if it looks like I escaped and saved them."

Eldan picked up the knife that they had taken from Pike and handed it to him. "Two of your friends are tied to a bush about a stone's throw in that direction," Eldan said, pointing north. "The others are about the same distance to the right, over by the salt lick."

Pike stared at the knife in his hand with an expression of disbelief. He then lifted his gaze, looking Eldan and Hawthorn in the eyes. Giving each of them a brief nod of thanks, he trotted into the woods to the north.

chapter six

THE HIGH PLACE

The Larkin and the Makerian Rangers remained hidden for several minutes until they were convinced that Pike and the rest of the Renegades had gone.

"Say there, friends," Rush finally said, addressing the Makerians, "we're in a bit of a bind. The sun's setting, and my companions and I are still a good three hours hard march from home."

"Yeah," Eldan said, looking through the woods to the fading sunlight in the west, "it would be well past dark before you fellas could make it back to the Keep."

"Even if we did make it back tonight," Rush continued, "the gates would be shut, and they wouldn't let us in before daylight. So I was wonderin' if we could hang out with you guys tonight. You know, safety in numbers?"

"How about it, Chief?" Eldan asked, turning to Comfrey. "There should be plenty of room in the High Place."

Comfrey thought for a moment and then spoke to the Larkin, "Yes, I agree. It would not be safe to leave the four of you in the woods tonight. Come with us, and we'll send you home in the morning.

"Eldan, lead the way,"

"Right you are, Chief! Right you are! Good food, good friends, and a soft bed, that's my motto. I think I even know a shortcut to get there."

"I don't trust your shortcuts, Eldan," Comfrey interrupted. "Just get us there safely."

"You don't trust my shortcuts? How can you say that, Chief? It's ME!"

"ELDAN, MARCH!" the Ranger captain yelled.

"I'm going; I'm going," Eldan said as he turned quickly and led them into the woods to the west. "Whew, what a grump."

For the next hour they followed Eldan as he led them through the brush and forest litter. Eventually they came to steep, moss-covered ridge which they climbed.

"Cheer up, Troopers," Eldan said cheerily as he stood on top of the ridge, waiting for the others to join him. "We're almost to Granny's house."

By now the sun had set, and the light was fading. When everyone had arrived on the crest, Eldan turned north and followed the ridge for almost another half an hour. Finally they arrived at a small clearing. Cutting across this open area toward the northwest, Eldan brought them all to the base of an immense oak tree. A very thick and very old wisteria vine grew around the massive trunk and spiraled up into the heights of this great tree. Marching up to the base of this grand oak, Eldan stopped and turned to address the others, "Mission accomplished, oh great Chieftain," Eldan announced, saluting with a ridiculous grin on his face.

"So is this it?" Hawthorn asked as they stood beside the enormous oak looming above them.

"We call this tree the North High Place," Comfrey explained. "There is another one to the south. Whenever our Ranger troops are spending time on this side of the Meadow, we use the High Places as outposts."

"Yeah, Chummy," Eldan added, "it's like our home away from home."

"We're not going to have to ride one of those load lifter things like you have at that tree at Stillwaters, are we?" Hawthorn asked with some concern.

"No worries, Chummy. We're going to walk up." As he said this, Eldan and the rest of the Makerians took off their packs and began to search through them. "Here, Chums. You're going to need this." Pulling his hand out of his backpack, Eldan handed Hawthorn a vial carved out of resin attached to a loop of cord.

"Oh," Hawthorn said as he recognized the object, "a light stick." Hawthorn shook the vial and a strong pale green light began to radiate from it. "I love these things."

The light stick was another Makerian invention. They carved the vials out of hardened pine resin and filled them with a mixture of juices from glow worms and special mushrooms. When the solution was shaken, light was produced.

Extra light sticks were handed to each of the Larkin. "Wear them around your neck," Comfrey told the Larkin. "It's dark now, and the trip up the tree will be extremely dangerous if you cannot see where to put your feet."

When everyone had a light stick glowing around his neck and each Ranger was again wearing his backpack, Eldan led them over to the tree and stepped onto the wisteria vine. The thick vine grew in a gradual incline as it encircled the trunk of the massive tree. After circling the tree twice, they came to a place where the vine had grown more steeply up the tree. Here the Larkin found that notches had been cut into the bark of the vine, allowing them to climb up the short distance to where the wisteria vine returned to its gradual incline again. They traveled up the vine for quite some distance and were almost a league above the ground when Eldan hopped off the vine onto a very large limb. This limb was so large that it made a wide thoroughfare on which to march.

Light reflecting off the leaves in the distance caused Hawthorn to look back over his shoulder for the source of the light. He saw through the distant limbs that a three-quarter moon was rising into the sky. By this Hawthorn realized that they were traveling west along the branch. After several minutes of walking, he noticed that the limb began to slope upwards. After a quarter of an hour's worth of hard walking up this incline, Hawthorn's leg muscles began to burn from the exertion. All of them were sweating and blowing hard when they finally reached a place where the limb leveled out again. As Hawthorn reached this level place, he stopped for a moment and bent over to catch his breath.

"Welcome, friend," said a voice nearby. Looking up, Hawthorn saw two Makerians standing guard on either side of the limb.

"Uh, thank you," Hawthorn huffed.

"You're almost there," the smiling guard said. "Just a little farther, but you won't have to climb anymore."

Hawthorn nodded a thank you and followed after his companions. Half a bow shot further they came to a place where the limb abruptly came to an end. Built onto the end of this still very thick limb was a wooden building that was almost six-Larkin high.

The structure was constructed of oak poles, each as thick as two Larkin's waists. These thick poles were laid horizontally and notched on the ends so that they fit tightly into the logs that formed the side walls. Great oak beams formed the solid foundation of this building. These foundation beams were firmly set into grooves cut into the thick limb and pegged deeply into place. It was obvious that this house was built to withstand strong winds.

Two more guards stood beside the building's heavy oak door. Hawthorn followed his friends through this doorway and found himself standing in a narrow, dark room that extended from one side of the building to the other. This room was only about two-Larkin high, and using the greenish glow of his light stick, Hawthorn could see slits cut at frequent intervals in the ceiling.

THE NORTH HIGH PLACE

Hawthorn had seen those slits before at the Makerian fortress at Stillwaters. The young Larkin realized that this room was for the defense of the blockhouse. If enemies broke through the door and got into this room, then archers in the room above could shoot down upon them through those slits.

These guys think of everything, he thought to himself.

Once the entry way was closed behind them, Comfrey gave a knock on a solid-looking door in the opposite wall. When the door swung open, a warm and cheery light streamed in on them. When it was Hawthorn's turn to enter the large room, he was met by wave of delicious smells.

Centrally located in this spacious chamber was a circular stone hearth that was open on two sides. The big stone chimney disappeared into the ceiling above. A stocky Makerian was standing next to the fire, carefully tending a large steaming pot from which the mouthwatering smells originated.

As the Larkin looked around the room, they saw a dozen Makerians, some of whom were busy setting up wooden supports and laying long boards across them to make several tables on both sides of the room. Others were carrying benches from where they had been resting against the walls and were placing them next to the tables.

"Something smells really good!" Jay said as he stood next to Rush, Savin, and Hawthorn.

"You're tellin' me!" Rush shot back. "I'm over here 'bout to drown in my own slobber."

"Perfect timing, eh, Chums?" Eldan asked from just behind the four Larkin. "Ol' Barkus and his wife set a mean table."

"Who's Barkus, Eldan?" Hawthorn asked.

"Look over there by the fire," Eldan returned. "You see that big round guy stirring the soup? That's him. He's the warden here."

"The warden?" Savin asked.

"Well sure," Eldan answered. "We have two High Places on this side of the Meadow—this one here and one further south—close to the Renegade Lair. We use them a lot. Ranger troops are always coming and going. So there has to be somebody staying at the High Places all the time to take care of everything and to make sure we have plenty to eat, and that somebody is the warden and his family.

"Barkus there is the North High Place Warden. He, his wife Peony, and his son take good care of us. Ol' buddy Barkus may be a little rough around the edges, but he and his wife know how to cook."

Eldan then led them across the large room and showed them a storeroom where they could put their packs and weapons. Next he showed them an area in the back of the spacious chamber with a long shelf on which were bowls of water and clean towels. It felt good to wash the dirt and sweat from their hands and faces.

"I'd sure hate to have to haul water all the way up here," Hawthorn said as he dried his hands.

"None of that is necessary," said Eldan. "Rain water is collected in a cistern up on the roof. We even have a platform up here connected with ropes and pulleys that raises and lowers so it's not very hard to get the supplies hauled up either."

"This place is amazing!" Rush said.

"Oh, you don't know the half of it, Wretch," Eldan said offhandedly. "After we eat, I'll give you chums a tour of the place. For now though, let's stay close to the food."

Eldan led them back into the middle of the Great Hall where the tables were now set with wooden spoons, bowls, cups, and pitchers of water. Woven dry-grass baskets containing loaves of fresh baked seed bread were just being brought out to be placed on the tables, as well.

"Gather round, friends!" boomed the deep voice of Barkus as he waved his long cooking spoon in the air to get everyone's attention. "We're ready to eat. The missus has baked us up some fine seed bread, and Little Bark and I will be dishin' up the soup. I see we have some Larkin guests tonight. The rule is: Don't be shy. When the time comes, grab yerse'f a bowl an' come get yer soup. Then park yer carcass wherever you want. After ever'one gets served, you can come back and get as much as you want, but if'n I catch one of you hollow-bellied rascals slippin' back to the pot afore we get ever'body fed, I'll plant this here spoon betwix yer eyeballs. And don't think I won't! SAVY?"

"I'll bet he used to be a Renegade," Rush whispered to Eldan.

"It still shows, doesn't it?" Eldan whispered back.

"Now bow yer noggin heads," Barkus ordered. "We're gonna thank the Maker for this fine feedin' we're 'bout to commence."

Barkus bowed his head, lifted his cook spoon toward heaven, and began to pray, "Uh . . . hello, Your Honor . . . Sir. It's me again, Barkus. We're all together here in the High Place, and uh, we're about to eat our dinner. But before we get to eatin', we just wanted to speak with You a moment. You know, Sir, that we . . . uh . . . well . . . ah bugs, Sir! You know I ain't good with words. It's just that, well, all of us here, we think You and Your son Jehesus are the best! An' we're really glad that we're in Your family! It's because of Jehesus that we can even come an' talk to You like we're a doin' right now. We want to thank You, Your Honor, for givin' us such a fine day, and for helpin' the Rangers to do some good things today. I want to thank you also for keepin' all these knuckleheads safe. Now, Sir, we're 'bout to sit down an' eat this here food, and we wanted to say that we know that it all comes from You. Thank you, Sir, for all that You do for us! Thank you very much!"

With that, Barkus lowered his spoon and addressed everyone in the room, "Awright! Grab a bowl and come an' get it! And make sure our Larkin guests get fed!"

A bowl was shoved into Hawthorn's hands, and he and the other Larkin were pushed up to the front of the line. As Hawthorn stepped up beside the cooking pot, a brimming ladle full of deliciously smelling soup was poured into his bowl. As he looked up to the server to say thanks, Hawthorn saw the face of a young Makerian not much older than himself but who was over twice Hawthorn's size.

"Thank you," Hawthorn nodded.

"Sure," the young giant smiled back.

As Hawthorn started to walk away, Barkus was standing in front of him.

"When'd you eat last, young fella?"

"I had a good meal early this morning, sir," Hawthorn returned as his rather plump host gave him a doubtful look.

"Baby Cakes!" Barkus called over his shoulder. Peony, Barkus' short, round wife, was quickly by his side with a basketful of bread in her arms.

"What is it, Honey Lump?" Peony asked sweetly.

"I thought this young Larkin fella looked a bit underfed to me, and I wanted to know what you think."

"Land sakes, but you're right, Darlin'!" she exclaimed. "There's almost nothing to the poor dear. He's as thin as a vine."

"That's what I thought," Barkus returned, nodding in agreement. "Little Bark," Barkus called out to the young giant attending the pot, "put another scoop of soup in this fella's bowl. We need to put some meat on his bones."

"Yes sir, Pa," Little Bark replied and, with a smile, filled Hawthorn's bowl to the brim.

"Thank you, sir . . . and my lady," Hawthorn said, trying very hard not to spill any of his soup.

As Hawthorn started to leave, Barkus leaned down and spoke in his ear. "When you finish that, come back, an' we'll fill it up again."

Hawthorn followed his friends over to one of the long tables and quickly found a place to sit. Nobody said a word for several minutes. They were all too busy eating. Finally Jay leaned back and, through a mouth full of warm seed bread, said, "This stuff is amazing!"

"I had forgotten how good Makerian food is," Hawthorn agreed.

"You got that right!" Rush said as he wiped his mouth with the back of his sleeve. "These folks sling some serious hash!"

"Hawthorn?" called a voice from nearby. "Hawthorn, is that you?"

Looking up from his bowl, the young Larkin saw a Makerian Ranger just a few seasons older than himself approaching him with a surprised look on his face.

"Raken!" Hawthorn exclaimed as he jumped to his feet and ran around the table to greet his friend. Raken had just enough time to set his bowl of soup down before he was engulfed in a hug from the excited young Larkin.

"I haven't seen you in two years," Hawthorn laughed, still holding his friend by the shoulders. "It is so good to see you!"

"It's really good to see you, too," Raken returned. "I almost didn't recognize you."

"So you're still serving as a Ranger?" Hawthorn asked.

"I actually finished up last year, but then they made me a lieutenant and asked me to stay on."

"Wow . . . an officer now," Hawthorn said with a smile and a nod. "I'll wager your family is proud of that, especially your little brother Robbie."

"Yeah," Raken answered, laughing, "Robbie thinks it's great, but he still runs around fighting pretend Renegades, telling everyone that he's 'Hawtorn da Larkin!'"

Hawthorn laughed hard at that news. "That little boy is so funny!" Hawthorn said, still laughing. "Please tell him for me that I miss him and would love to see him. I would love to see your whole family. How are the rest of them, by the way?"

"They are all doing very well. I was with them all just three days ago. Father's the same. He's still working much too hard, trying to keep everyone healthy. Carineda is quite the graceful young lady now."

"That's how I would have described her two years ago," said Hawthorn.

"My other sisters, Clarea and Nollie, are just as sweet and fun as when you were there," Raken continued, "but every time I come home from patrol, those two and Robbie seem to have grown another hand breadth."

"Well, please tell them all that I said hello and that I would love to see them."

"Oh, you can count on that," Raken said with a laugh. "We heard how all of you stopped the Renegade army today. Robbie will be beside himself when he finds out that 'Hawtorn da Larkin' has had more adventures!"

It had been a long time since Hawthorn had enjoyed a meal as much as this one. The food was wonderful and plentiful, and the conversation with his friends was enjoyable. Finally after his second heaping bowl of soup and his third large helping of bread, Hawthorn leaned back with a deep satisfied sigh.

"Are you finally done, Chummy?" Eldan asked with a look of concern.

"I'm so ha-a-appy!" Hawthorn smiled as he rubbed his tight stomach.

"You could have fooled me," Eldan shot back. "You look like you're about to give birth to twins. Why don't you pull your fat self up off that bench, and I'll show you and your buds around the High Place?"

As Eldan led them toward a large wooden door at the far end of the room, he pointed to a smaller doorway on his right. "That's where the warden and his family live."

"So Barkus and his family live here all the time?" Jay asked.

"Usually," Eldan answered, "a warden serves in a High Place for six months, but Barkus and his family have been here for the last two years. They say they really like it. All the Rangers certainly enjoy their cooking."

By now they had reached the doorway at the end of the room. Eldan swung open the door, and they all marched out onto a spacious open-air deck. They could clearly see the vast grassy Meadow in the moonlight and the shadowy shapes of the distant trees beyond it. Several small wooden structures were built around the edge of the deck at regular intervals. These structures consisted of a set of ten steps going up to a small platform about three-Larkin high above the very edge of the deck. A short ladder extended from this platform to another one directly above it. About head-height above this second platform, an upright beam supported a wooden arm.

"Hey," Hawthorn called out as he saw the structures, "I know what those are. Those are those things from which you launch those flying, whirly-bug contraptions."

"Right you are, Chummy! Right you are!"

"Whirly-bugs?" Savin asked with a questioning look. "Were those the things with the spinning blades on top that you told us you flew on?"

"Yes," Hawthorn answered. "They have six large maple seeds on top. The end with the seed is firmly attached to a wooden spool so that the large wings of the seeds are sticking outward. The spool is mounted on top of a long pole so it can freely spin around without flying off. The central pole hangs down with three cross pieces of wood attached to it. One person stands on the bottom cross piece and hangs onto the central pole. The person who flies the thing stands on the second cross piece directly above the first person. He hangs onto the third topmost cross piece and uses his hands and feet to steer the machine as it flies. Oh, and there's a frame that sticks out behind it that has a cloth tail. They hang the whirly-bugs up on those structures over there so that the riders can climb on and get their safety harnesses hooked up."

"So how do they fly?" Jay asked.

"Chummy's description was correct except he left out two important points," Eldan said. "The six maple seeds on the top are firmly set at the top of the spool in such a way as to allow the wings of the seeds to stick out at the perfect angle. That way, when they spin, they catch the wind and lift the whirly bug and its riders into the air. We spin them by taking a rope and winding it around the spool at the top. When the riders are ready, an assistant pulls the rope very hard, which spins the wings of the seeds. Those spinning maple seed wings create a lifting force that keeps the whole thing in the air. As you travel forward, the wind keeps the wings spinning. You can easily fly one from here across the Meadow to our home at Stillwaters. In fact, we do it all the time when someone needs to get from here to there in a hurry.

"We keep them hanging in the storeroom back here," Eldan said as he walked back toward the building to a large set of double doors. "Come on; I'll show you what they look like."

Eldan opened the storeroom doors and disappeared into the darkness. A few moments later a bright pale-green glow erupted as Eldan had shaken a larger version of the Makerian light stick which was hanging from the ceiling in the middle of the room. The Larkin were amazed at the finely crafted machines suspended from wooden racks located around the room.

"All of the racks have wheels on them," Eldan pointed out. "That way we can just push the whole thing, rack and all, out to the launching platforms to load."

After several minutes of studying the flying machines in complete fascination, Rush finally voiced all of their thoughts, "Floppy, how in the world did you fellers ever come up with somethin' like this?"

"Prayer," Eldan answered matter-of-factly.

"Prayer?" Rush questioned.

"You know how it is with the Makerians, Rush," said Hawthorn. "Whenever they have a need or a problem, they all start praying, and eventually the Maker shows them an answer."

"Wel-l-l, some of His answers are purdy wild," Rush returned as he stared at the hanging whirly-bugs.

"He's a great Maker," Eldan responded with a smile. "Now if you chums are finished playing with the big toys, I want to show you something else."

After ushering everyone out of the large storeroom and closing the doors, Eldan led them back into the building. Retracing their steps, they followed their Makerian friend back toward the Great Hall. Just before they reached the warden's living quarters, Eldan turned to the left and took them up some curving steps. When they reached the top, they found themselves standing in another large room, around the edges of which were sacks, boxes, and crates, all neatly organized in stacks. The room itself was brilliantly lit by seven large candles made of bee's wax. These candles were each as big around as a Larkin's leg, and they were all placed closely together in the center of the room, anchored firmly onto a raised stone hearth. Smoke and some of the heat from the large candles escaped the room through a flue constructed in the ceiling. Behind the candles was a wall of large, thick mica plates that had been polished so much that they reflected the light like a mirror. A Makerian was standing nearby with a long-handled tool and was using it to remove dripping wax away from the base of the burning candles.

"This is the Light Room," Eldan announced proudly, "but we also use it for storage."

"I understand why you call this the Light Room, Eldan," Hawthorn said, "because those candles make it so bright. But why do you need all that light in here?"

"Now there you go, Chummy! There you go! You're always thinkin'. Yessir, you've got a mind like a teapot! I don't care what other people say about you. I know you're a thinker!"

"That's nice, Eldan," Hawthorn returned, his frustration beginning to show, "but why do you keep it so bright in here?"

"I was just getting to that, Chums," Eldan shot back, "and if you used that brain of yours more for thinking rather than talking, you wouldn't be interrupting me.

"Now, as I was saying, this is the Light Room. We need it to be really bright in here because of what happens in the next room." As he said this, Eldan pointed to his left. Following Eldan's pointing finger with their eyes, the Larkin saw a solid wooden wall with a closed door on the left-hand side of the wall. In the middle of the wall was a large round hole that disappeared into a dark tunnel.

Eldan waved for them to follow him as he walked over to the door in the wall. Knocking three times, Eldan waited for several moments until the door finally opened and a hand motioned to them to enter.

As Hawthorn followed his friends through the doorway, he was struck by the contrast. The Light Room was so bright that the place he had just entered was completely black by comparison. It took several moments for his eyes to adjust to the darkness, but he finally came to realize that he was again standing on a deck-like structure with a roof. The far wall of the deck was a waist-high wall. Beyond the wall, moonlight revealed the vast Meadow many leagues below them, stretching out into the distance.

"Over here, chums," called Eldan. Turning, Hawthorn and the others saw that their friend was standing with two other Makerians beside some sort of long mechanism. One of the Makerians was seated at a small desk and was using a light stick to view some papers on the desk in front of him.

"I want you to meet a couple of friends of mine," Eldan continued when all of the Larkin were standing near. "Chums, this is Fud and Bud."

The Makerian who was seated stood up and, with a smile, extended his hand to each of the Larkin. "That's just what Eldan calls us," he said with a chuckle. "My name is Gosper, and this is Drake."

After shaking hands all around in the typical Makerian way, Hawthorn turned to his redheaded friend, "Eldan, why don't you just learn their names?"

"I do learn their names, Chummy. Can I help it if they don't like the names that I learn? Besides, you got to admit, he looks more like a *Fud* than a . . . a . . . whatever."

"So what is this place, Floppy?" Rush asked impatiently.

"I'm glad you asked, Wretch. This is the Message Deck, and our two friends here are running the communication station. By using the devices you see in front of you, we can send and receive messages from our friends in a High Place on the other side of the Meadow. They, in turn, can send the messages that we send them either to Stillwaters or to the Southern High Place. We can do it all without the Renegades knowing what we're doing."

"Thunderation!" exclaimed Rush. "How could you possibly do that?"

"I shall explain," Eldan said loftily. "Observe the long hollow cane that is mounted into the wall of the light room."

What they saw was a long straight stem of a cane that was almost twice as big around as a Larkin's head. A wooden support frame was built underneath this long hollow pipe so that it was held firmly in place horizontally at about chest height. One end of the cane pipe extended to the end of the deck and rested securely on a support structure attached to the short wall that overlooked the Meadow. The other end of the pipe was firmly attached to the wall of the Light Room which they had just left. A box-like structure was built around the middle of the cane near to where they all were standing.

"Is that cane running into the hole in the wall that we saw in the other room?" Hawthorn asked when he saw the location of the end of the cane.

"Indeed it is, Chums," Eldan answered. "You see, the shiny mica plates behind the candles in the other room focus all of that bright light into this cane tube, which is aimed straight at the Message Deck that's on the West High Place on the other side of the Meadow."

"So the light from those bright candles shines through this tube, and the people in the High Place across the Meadow can see it?" Jay asked.

"They could see it except for one thing," Eldan returned.

"And what's that?" Jay responded curiously.

Eldan patted the box-like structure surrounding the middle of the cane pipe. "This is the control box. My ol' pal Bud will stand right here next to the box, and by pulling down on this handle built into the side of the box, he can let the light through or shut it off. We have different patterns of light flashes that represent the different letters of our written words."

"Oh, wow!" Hawthorn exclaimed. "So if someone just knows how to read the light flashes, you can talk to each other over a long distance."

"Now you got it, Chums," Eldan answered, smiling.

"But Eldan," Savin said, speaking his thoughts out loud, "the other side of the Meadow is so far away. How can anyone see a small beam of light at that distance?"

"You're right as rain, sir. To see even a bright beam of light from that far away, you're going to need some help, and that's why the Maker gave us the idea of building a long eye."

"So what's a long eye?" Jay asked.

Stepping to the side, Eldan pointed to another smaller tube device that was attached to the side of the long cane pipe. This smaller tube was about as long as a Larkin's leg and was lying in a frame that connected it to the long messaging pipe. The device was actually two tubes connected together, one sliding inside of the other. The end pointing toward the Meadow was about as big around as a Larkin's thigh. The opposite end had tapered down until you could only put three or four fingers in the small opening.

"This is a long eye. It's just a couple of hollow tubes made from reeds where one is slid inside the other. You can't really see much through it until we put a drop of water in each end. Then when you slide the two tubes together or apart to focus it for your eye, you can see for a really long ways. We can easily see the light flashes from the West High Place when they send us messages. So ol' Bud here looks through the long eye and calls out the letters that the guys on the other side of the Meadow are spelling out to him with their light flasher, and Fud writes them down. And there you go—instant message!"

"What kind of messages do you send?" Savin asked.

"Well, for example," Gosper answered, "while the rest of you were eating, Drake and I were sending over the field reports for the Ranger troops. We told them all about you and Troop Six stopping the Renegade attack on Larkin Clan Two. We also told them about you spending the night with us. They then sent that information on to Stillwaters and to the South High Place so that they know what's happening on our end of the woods. They should be sending us troop reports from the south end of the woods any minute now."

"They are asking if we're ready to receive their messages now," Drake announced as he peered through the long eye at the woods on the far side of the Meadow.

Gosper grabbed some paper and his writing stylus. Dipping the stylus in ink made from pokeberry juice, he told Drake he was ready.

While looking intently through the long eye, Drake began to work the handle on the control box, flashing the signal to their friends that they were ready to receive messages. Shortly after that, Drake began to call out letters in succession as they were flashed to him from the West High Place.

"Why don't we slip out of here and let these guys do their work?" Eldan whispered to the Larkin. Very quietly so as not to disturb the concentration of Gosper and Drake, Eldan led his friends back down to the Great Hall. They spent the next two hours drinking mugs of cool sweet blackberry nectar and sharing news and telling stories with their friends.

After the cooking fire was banked for the night, Barkus bid all of his friends and guests a good sleep, and he and his family retired for the night. Shortly after that, thick mats with thistledown stuffing were pulled out from where they were kept stacked in one of the storerooms. These were spread out along the floor of the Great Hall, and the Larkin were invited to take their pick. Hawthorn, lying on his soft mat, was just starting to dose off when suddenly he was shaken back to wakefulness. Looking up, he saw a smiling Eldan kneeling over them.

"Sorry to wake all of you chums up from your beauty sleep, but I got news."

"What's up, Floppy?" Rush asked with some concern.

"Fud and Bud got a message not too long ago that concerns you fellas," Eldan answered.

"What is it?" inquired Rush.

"Well, it seems that when the elders and nobles at Stillwaters found out that you guys were here, they decided that they needed to get a message to you before you left to go back home."

THE GREAT GATHERING

"So what's the message?" Rush asked again.

"Let me put it this way," Eldan returned. "It's important enough that my brother Tobin is coming over here first thing in the morning to tell you in person."

CHAPTER SEVEN

THE EASY WAY

It was still dark when Hawthorn was stirred from his sleep by the sounds of Little Bark as he uncovered the coals in the fireplace and stirred them into life. As the light from the resurrected fire filled the room, the Makerian Rangers began to rise from their mats to start their day. Hawthorn sat up and, after a rather noisy stretch, pulled on his boots and cinched his belt around his waist. Following the example of their Makerian hosts, the Larkin shook out their sleeping mats and carried them to the storeroom to be stacked. When they returned from the storeroom, Hawthorn saw that the great room was busy with activity. Barkus and his hefty son were lifting the large cooking pot up onto the hearth to start preparing the morning meal. The Rangers were washing up and reconstructing the tables in anticipation of breakfast.

"I thought supper was delicious," Jay said when he eventually sat down with his food and took his first bite, "but this is amazing!"

"Wow! It is good!" Savin agreed.

Breakfast consisted of a bowl of hot porridge made of finely ground briar root, millet seed, and honeysuckle nectar. To go along with the porridge, Peony had baked stacks of flatbread made of cattail flour and honey. As they were finishing their meal, Barkus came around and made sure Hawthorn got a second heaping bowl of porridge.

"Eat up, young friend," Barkus said as he slapped Hawthorn on the back. "If you could stay with us for a spell, the missus and I could put enough good food in you that we'd soon have you lookin' like Little Bark."

"Hee hee, yes sir," Hawthorn acknowledged as he shoveled the delicious soup into his mouth.

When the meal was finally over, the Larkin helped their Makerian friends put away the tables and benches while at the same time saying their goodbyes. Afterwards, the Rangers got their packs together as the captains gave them the instructions for the day's patrols. The Larkin used the time to get their own weapons and backpacks ready for the march home.

"Hello, friends," called a nearby voice.

"Tobin!" Hawthorn cried as he recognized the newcomer.

Tobin the Flyer was a Makerian noble whom the four Larkin knew well from their last adventure with the Makerian people. A quiet, unassuming warrior, Tobin had a stocky build and a long thick crop of curly red hair. Add to that Tobin's thick curly red beard, and he resembled a bright red bush. Though he was Eldan's older brother, the two were nothing alike, except for the flaming red hair.

Each of the Larkin took turns greeting Tobin, shaking his hand in the typical Makerian way. Tobin in turn then released each one's hand and grabbed their forearm as the Larkin greet each other. "I'm very glad to see all of you again," Tobin began. "When the message came in last night that you were here, the council of elders asked me if I would meet with you."

"We heard you were coming," Rush spoke up. "What's this all about?"

"Tobin, are we in some trouble for coming here?" Hawthorn asked with concern.

"No, of course not, young one," Tobin chuckled. "You should all know by now that you are always welcome with us anytime, anywhere. But there are some very special plans afoot that we need to let you know about."

"What kind of plans?" Jay asked.

"Is this not the year that you will be having the Great Gathering of all the Larkin clans?" Tobin asked.

"It is indeed," Rush returned. "Every five years most of the members of each of the five remaining clans will gather at the Steps, the ancestral home of all the Larkin. Once there we will spend two weeks feasting, spending time with friends in the other clans, and listening to the Shaman teach and lead the grand worship times."

"When will the Great Gathering occur?" Tobin inquired.

"Quite soon," Savin joined in. "We've already begun gathering the extra food and supplies for the trip."

"What we've heard," Rush interjected, "is that all of the clans are s'pose to arrive at the Steps by next month's full moon. So we should all be makin' the journey in a little over a month from now. The clans farthest away from the Steps will be startin' their trip a day or so before our clan will. But why is that important to you guys?"

"Two reasons," Tobin returned. "We try to put out a few extra patrols when we know the Larkin are traveling. You are especially vulnerable to attack by the Renegades when traveling in large caravans with lots of supplies and having your wives and young ones with you as well."

"You're right," agreed Rush. "It'll be good to know that you fellers'll be lookin' out for us while we're atravelin'."

"There's also another reason we need to know the details about the Great Gathering," said Tobin. "After much prayer and fasting, we believe that the Lord Jehesus wants us to send a secret delegation disguised as Larkin to join you at your Great Gathering."

"But Tobin," Hawthorn exclaimed, "why would the Makerians do that? You've said yourself that if the Shaman discover any of your people, they might have you killed."

"As faithful followers of the Lord Jehesus, you run that risk every day, young one," Tobin answered. "Our risk would be small compared to what our Larkin brothers and sisters face daily.

"Quite a few Makerians have been greatly burdened with trying to do more to give the Good News of Jehesus to the Larkin. The idea of sending a special team of teachers to secretly work among your people was suggested a couple of months ago, and after a lot of prayer, plans for accomplishing it were drawn up. Over the last month we have been trying to communicate with the followers of Jehesus in the different Larkin clans to see if you would be willing to support us in this work if we actually do it. Obviously, if our people are discovered, there is a good chance that those who help them may be discovered also. We certainly don't want to put any of our brothers and sisters at risk, but the team would have a much greater chance of successfully accomplishing the mission undiscovered if there were Larkin at the Great Gathering prepared to help them."

The four Larkin just sat there for a moment trying to grasp the full meaning of what Tobin had just told them.

"This is a really big thing," Savin said, speaking his thoughts out loud. "The risk to all of us who help in this plan will be great. We could lose everything . . . maybe even our lives. But if it is successful, the rewards would be enormous!"

"If it's successful," Jay added, "then it would be worth the risk."

"I think so, too," Hawthorn felt compelled to say.

"We're fergettin' somethin'," Rush spoke up. "It don't really matter if'n it's successful. The bottom line is: Does the Lord Jehesus want us to do it or not?" Rush turned and looked at Tobin, who was nodding his head in agreement.

"Friend Tobin," Rush said after looking at the other Larkin, "before we can give you an answer, my three friends and I need to do some serious prayin'."

"That's exactly what you need to do," the redheaded Makerian agreed. "Come with me."

Tobin led them across the length of the Great Hall until he stood before the door that opened onto the large area where they launched their flying whirly-bugs. Opening the door, Tobin beckoned them through. "The Flight Deck is empty right now. You can pray out here without being disturbed. Take as long as you need. I'll be waiting in the Great Hall to hear what the Lord tells you."

It was over an hour later before the door to the flight deck opened and the four Larkin marched back in to join Tobin.

"Well, friends, has the Lord made His will known to you?"

"We spent most of the time just cryin' out to the Maker, beggin' Him to show us His will," Rush began. "We all took turns pleadin' with the Maker to tell us what to do. Finally it sort of dawned on all of us that we already knew what He wanted us to do. Jay reminded me of a conversation that he and I had last week about how we could teach more people about Jehesus. Then Hawthorn remembered a verse from the Maker's Book where Jehesus was speakin' to His followers just before He went back up to the heaven place.

"How did that verse go, Thorn?"

"It was a part of the Maker's Book that I have been trying to memorize, so it's been on my mind a lot. It goes like this: '*And Jehesus came and spake unto them, saying, "All power is given unto Me in heaven and in earth. Go ye therefore, and teach all nations, bapatizing them in the name of the Father and of the Son, and of the Holy Ghost; teaching them to observe all things whatsoever I have commanded you; and, lo, I am with you always, even unto the end of the world."*

"Jehesus taught his first followers to go wherever they had to go to teach people about Him, and then they were supposed to teach us to do the same thing."

"Those words reminded me of a verse that I read just the other day," Savin added. "I can't quote it like Thorn did, but I do recall the point of it. The believer named Paul was writing to a friend of his and told him that the Lord Jehesus gave Himself for us to redeem us and to purify for Himself a people of His own who are zealous for good works."

"It just seemed to all of us," Rush began again, "that the Lord has been showin' us for the past week or two that this is what He wants to do. We just didn't realize it until you spelled it out for us. We're all agreed that this is a good work that the Lord Jehesus wants us to be busy adoin', so count us in."

"That's great news!" Tobin smiled. "All of the followers of Jehesus in the other Larkin clans to whom we have talked have all come to the same conclusion. I'd say that's confirmation that we have found the Maker's will."

"So what will you want us to do?" Hawthorn asked eagerly.

"Well, first and foremost," Tobin responded thoughtfully, "all of you need to be calling on the Lord Jehesus to lead and bless this mission. We all need to ask Him to show us the ones He has chosen to be a part of the team. Then we need to ask Him to prepare not only the team and each of the Larkin believers but also all of those whom the Maker is drawing to Himself. In addition to that, you should make plans to let some of the team members stay and eat with you during the Great Gathering, and you should be looking for Larkin who might be interested in listening to the message of Jehesus whom you could introduce to members of the team."

"We will need to know how we will recognize the Makerians on the team," Jay spoke up, "since they will be looking and acting like Larkin."

"And," Rush added, "we'll need a way to communicate with them that won't arouse suspicion."

"There are a lot of details that will need to be worked out," Tobin admitted. "Eldan and I will try to keep a regular presence near your stronghold. We will be using the callers when we have information, and when you are free to meet with us, call to us, and one of us will come to where you are."

"If this is the Maker's will, then He will work out all the details," Savin said confidently. All of the others nodded in agreement.

"Well, fellers," Rush said, looking at the others, "we've dee-layed our departure long enough. I figure we've got us at least a three-hour hard march ahead afore we can get home, so we'd best have at it."

"Maybe I can help you there," Tobin offered. "I knew that I was going to delay your march home, so I came prepared to give you a lift."

"You want to fly us home on your crow?" Hawthorn asked with surprise.

"No, young one. Nightwing can only carry one other person besides myself at a time, and so many back and forth flights carrying the extra weight might be too much for him. So I brought Chatter with me."

"Oh no!" Hawthorn gasped. "Not the squirrel!"

"Yeah, Tobin," said Jay, "I only rode on him a short distance last time, and that was pretty rough."

"Well, I will admit that riding with Chatter takes some getting used to, but compared to a three- to four-hour march with all the predators in these woods, believe me, this is the easy way. I'll tell you what, if you friends let me take you home on Chatter, I'll make him go as slow and easy as we can."

"I don't know," Hawthorn returned doubtfully.

"Listen here, fellers," Rush spoke up. "I ain't any more excited about climbin' onto the back of that furry critter than any of you are. But as far as we've got to march, in my mind the chances of the four of us runnin' into danger is fairly high. If we do, we've got a much better chance of gettin' away from it if the squirrel is doin' the runnin' for us. So I think we should take Tobin up on his offer."

"Ah, bugs," Hawthorn sighed. "All right. If we're gonna do this, then let's get it over with."

Shouldering their weapons and backpacks, they followed Tobin out the front entrance of the High Place. They passed the guards by the door and traveled a short distance out onto the wide limb. Finally Tobin stopped and pulled a carved whistle out of the leather pouch on his hip. Placing the whistle in his mouth, he blew a long shrill call. Almost immediately there was a loud rustling in the leaves of a large branch above them. With a powerful bound a muscular grey squirrel came diving off the branch and landed lightly on the limb in front of Tobin. The four startled Larkin quickly jumped backward at the sudden appearance of the huge forest creature, but Tobin stepped forward and began rubbing the beast on the nose.

"Come near, friends," Tobin called to his apprehensive companions. "He's as gentle as can be."

Hawthorn decided that he should be the leader in this since he had had more experience with Tobin's squirrel than any of the rest of the Larkin. Taking a deep breath, he strode boldly over to stand beside Tobin.

"Load up, friends," Tobin called. "We need to get this trip started."

As the Larkin approached the squirrel, they noticed that Chatter had a long wooden saddle strapped to his back. There were seats for six people.

"I'll be sitting in the first seat," Tobin continued. "Rush, you climb into the seat just behind me. Jay, you sit behind Rush and show him how to tie himself in and where to put his hands and feet. Savin, you take the next seat. Hawthorn, you show your father what he needs to do and then take the seat behind him."

Just at that moment the scream of a hawk reached their ears, and all of them jerked around quickly, trying to spot the dreaded sky killer.

"That hawk was close," Jay said to the others in a nervous whisper.

"It scared Chatter, too," Hawthorn said as he watched the squirrel doing a nervous little dance beside them.

"We need to get out of here quickly," Tobin announced.

"Guards! Can you help our Larkin friends get into their seats? We need to leave before that hawk spots us." The two Makerian guards by the door came running over and began to boost the Larkin up onto Chatter's back. Rush and Jay quickly took their places in their seats, but Savin was having trouble figuring out where to put his hands and feet. Hawthorn untied his strap around his waist and had just leaned forward over his father's shoulder to show him what to do when another, much nearer scream froze their hearts. Looking up and to their left, they saw their worst nightmare diving straight for them. An involuntary cry burst from each of their chests.

"Chatter, fly!" yelled Tobin.

The terrified squirrel exploded off the limb in response to his master's command just as the killer bird with talons extended dove past the place where he had been. Bark flew in all directions as Chatter tore along the limb with more speed than he had ever used in his life. Hawthorn had just enough time to grab the back of his father's seat before Chatter leaped away. The young Larkin resembled laundry flapping in the wind as he held on for dear life while the frightened squirrel bounded from limb to limb. Hearing his son's cry, Savin turned and desperately grabbed Hawthorn's arm.

THE EASY WAY

The hungry young hawk quickly corrected her course and darted after the escaping meal. Hearing the piercing cry of the angry red tail, both Tobin and Chatter took a quick glance behind them just in time to see the killer rapidly closing in. Without waiting for a command from his master, Chatter launched himself and his screaming passengers sideways off the limb on which he had been running, sailing out into space as once again the savage bird shot past, snatching only at empty space where the squirrel had been.

Chatter leaped for the trunk of a nearby tree, and fortunately his aim was good. As they slammed against the bark of the tree, Chatter was able to grasp it with his sharp claws and hang on. The hard landing slammed Hawthorn into the back of his father's seat and momentarily knocked the breath from him. The young Larkin took this moment to shove himself into his own seat and to grab the handles in front of him. By this time Chatter had started a rapid climb up this new tree. Quickly, the squirrel scampered around the tree, trying to keep the trunk between them and the hungry hawk, but the sharp-eyed red-tail would not be so easily fooled. Already she had spotted them and was circling the tree. She was hovering only a short distance above them as Chatter pulled himself onto a limb. Suddenly death-on-wings dropped for the kill. Once again the powerful squirrel shot forward as the hawk's sharp talons embedded into the bark where he had been. Hawthorn felt the hawk's hot breath as the bird took a desperate snap at their retreating forms. Unable to tie himself in his seat, Hawthorn did manage to shove his feet in the footholds just as Chatter took off again.

Ripping its talons free of the bark, the determined hawk renewed the chase. Chatter's sides were heaving hard now as he strained to outrace the relentless killer bird. He sprinted along the narrowing limb until the small branch began to bend under his weight. In a flash he threw himself into space and, sailing a short distance in the air, managed to grab the small branches and leaves of the limb of another tree.

Just as Chatter was approaching the tree's trunk, the hawk dove for another attack. Knowing that the squirrel must pause for a moment as he jumped from the limb to the trunk, the intelligent hawk had timed her attack to arrive at the trunk at the same time her quarry did. Spotting the hawk's new tactic, Chatter, in desperation, leaped from the limb, flying past the trunk rather than landing on it. They fell for some distance before they crashed into a thick mat of small branches covered with leaves. Heroically, Tobin's squirrel pulled himself out of the tangled mat, clawed his way back up onto a limb, and raced off as the hawk once again screamed her challenge.

"Here it comes again!" Rush yelled as he looked back at the rapidly approaching red tail.

"I don't think your squirrel can keep this up much longer!" Savin added.

"We can't either!" yelled Hawthorn as he desperately tried to hold himself in the violently bucking seat with aching arms and legs.

"Let's try for that old snag!" Tobin yelled back.

They were very near the ground now, and just below and in front of them was a broken off, hollow tree that was still standing upright. The leap would be a long one for Chatter, but Tobin felt he had enough strength left in him to make it. As they swiftly approached the end of their limb, Tobin directed the exhausted squirrel to jump for the snag. The screaming hawk's rapid advance gave Chatter a little extra incentive. They sailed through the air toward the open top of the hollow tree, providing the hawk with the opportunity for which she had been waiting. Launching herself at the falling squirrel, she raced to intercept him. Hawthorn saw the hawk dropping rapidly toward them and knew it was going to be close. As she shot past, the red tail snatched for her victim but came away only with rotted pine bark as Chatter and his riders disappeared into the top of the tree.

The big squirrel had some trouble getting a solid grip on the rotted wood on the inside of the dead tree, and he found himself slipping to the very bottom of the snag. There was a large rotted hole in the base of tree at ground level, and just as Chatter started to stick his nose out of the hole, the angry hawk's face was there snapping at them.

"THAT'S IT!" Rush yelled as he untied himself and slid off the back of the squirrel. "I've had a bellyful of this!" Tossing off his shield and backpack, Rush unslung his bow and notched an arrow to the string. Marching up to the snapping jaws of the great bird, Rush launched a feathered shaft into the back of the screaming hawk's gaping mouth.

"Eat THAT, you squirrel-chasin' featherduster!"

With a painful squawk, the killer bird jumped back, took several hard swallows, and flew away.

CHAPTER EIGHT

INGATHERING

"So then what happened?" Sycamore asked as he sat in his chair in his living quarters, sipping some feverfew tea and listening to Rush and Jay.

"We-l-l-l," Rush drawled, "it was purdy easy pickin's after that. Tobin had his squirrel take us back to the Bee Tree where we gathered up all the honey buckets and rope. Then he helped us get it all back close to the Keep. He dropped us off before the guards could see him. After sayin' goodbye, we grabbed all of the stuff and marched up to the gate guards."

"Word spread quickly through the Keep that you fellas didn't come back when you were supposed to," Sycamore offered. "They sent some search parties out to try to find you."

"We actually saw one of the search parties as we were traveling to the Bee Tree," Jay returned. "but because we were on top of Tobin's squirrel creeping along a tree limb, they never noticed us."

"Is Tobin that guy with the bushy red hair and beard?" Sycamore interrupted.

"Yeah," Rush answered with surprise. "Syc, your memory IS comin' back!"

"So how much about the Makerians do you remember?" Jay asked.

"Some of it is fuzzy," their friend began, "and there are a lot of gaps in the things that I do remember, but I know that those people saved all of our lives and that they were very kind to me. I also remember that every one of them prayed to the Maker like they were all Shaman."

"Me an' Jay were kinda' hopin' you'd 'member that part," Rush said with a smile. "Ya see, Syc, there was a whole heap a stuff that happened over there at Stillwaters that, because of your injury, you didn't hear about."

For the next hour, Rush and Jay told their friend the history of the Makerians. Sycamore sat fascinated as he heard how Larkin the Great's ancient journal was translated and it was discovered that the Maker in heaven was not distant and uncaring. Larkin explained that while the Maker was all powerful and must be approached with reverence and awe, he was also a God Who cared deeply for His created ones as a father cares for his children. They shared with Sycamore that the Maker revealed Himself to His creatures in a Holy Book that Larkin had found, read, and copied. In that book the Maker had explained what it takes to please Him. Sycamore's eyebrows knit together with concern when he heard that no one can be good enough. When Jay explained what the Maker's Book said about sin, Sycamore had to admit that he also had done things that the Maker said should not be done. A few moments later Sycamore's eyes flew wide in amazement when he heard that the Maker's Son Jehesus had come into the world to pay the terrible price for the sins of God's creatures.

"An' all ya gots to do to get yer sins taken away, Syc," Rush concluded, "is to trust in the Lord Jehesus enough to accept His death as full payment for your sins."

"That sounds pretty easy," Sycamore said suspiciously.

"Wel-l-l-l," Rush drawled, "there's a bit more to it. For Him to count your faith as genuine, you have to trust Him enough to make Him yer Lord."

"My Lord?"

"Yep," Rush answered. "Ya cain't have Him as Savior if yer not willin' to have Him as Lord."

"Making Him your Lord means that you stop living for yourself," Jay explained, "and start living for Him. Instead of doing what you want, you start letting Him tell you what to do."

"Well," Sycamore finally said after some thought, "what does He want me to do?"

Rush and Jay looked at each other and smiled. "If you believe in the Lord Jehesus," Rush answered, "He wants you to repent of yer sins. That means that He wants you to feel so sorry fer the thangs you've done to hurt Him that yer gonna' stop doin' 'em and start livin' the way He wants you to. The next thang yer gonna' do is to confess Him . . . tell someone that you believe in Him."

Sycamore looked both Rush and then Jay in the eyes. "I'm telling you two right now that I believe that Jehesus is the Maker's Son, and I want Him as my Savior and as my Lord. What else do I need to do?"

"If that's the way you feel," Jay said with a big grin, "then you should get bapatized!"

When Rush saw Sycamore's questioning look, he explained that being bapatized was something that Jehesus did and had all of those who wanted to be His followers do. Rush described being bapatized as being buried in water. "This is the way it was tol' to me: Since Jehesus died FOR our sins, we die TO our sins, and like Jehesus was buried in the ground, you get buried in water. But just as Jehesus rose up from the dead to live a new life, you rise up out of the water to live the new life that Jehesus gives you."

"So it's like some kind of ceremony," Sycamore said thoughtfully.

"Well, I reckon it is," Rush returned, "but it's a heap more'n that. There is a place in the Maker's Book where it says: For as many of you as have been bapatized into Christ have put on Christ."

"Put on Christ?" Sycamore questioned. "That sounds like you're wearing Him like a tunic."

"In one sense it is like that," Rush answered as he struggled to explain, "but in another sense it's like He's wearing you."

"It's like this, Syc," Jay added, "when a person who wants Jehesus to be his king trusts Jehesus enough to do what He says about being bapatized in water, then that person is joining Him in His death, burial, and His resurrection. Not only does your old sinful self die with Christ, but you get a brand new life, and that new life is Jehesus in you. All of the things the Maker wants you to think and do and be, Jehesus is able to do in you, if you let Him.

"That sounds like real powerful water!" Sycamore exclaimed.

"There ain't nothin' magical about the water, Syc," said Rush. "This is all about your faith and His grace. When you have faith enough to obey Him when the Lord tells you to do somethin', then He pours out His grace on you. When you obey the Lord, all yer doin' is showin' Him yer faith. On t'other hand, you can think all the good thoughts you want to about the Lord Jehesus, but if'n He tells you to do somethin' an' you ain't willin' to do it, then Jehesus ain't yer Lord—and if He ain't yer Lord, then He cain't be yer Savior."

Sycamore thought about all that Rush and Jay had said for several moments. Finally he spoke, "The Shaman claim to know the Maker better than anyone, and as a group they are arrogant and prideful, and they show little interest in the cares and hurts of the individual Larkin. To be completely honest with you fellas, I have never had any desire to have anything to do with the god they represent.

"But the Makerians risked their lives to save ours when they didn't even know us! Then they spent an enormous amount of time, effort, and resources to care for us and to get us home safely. The reason they gave for all of their sacrifice was that the Lord Jehesus wanted them to do it for us.

"All my life I have been dreaming of a God like that. I want Him, fellas. I want Him in my life, and I'm willing to do whatever He says."

"Okay, then!" Rush said with enthusiasm. "Let's go get you bapatized!"

"Wait a minute," Sycamore said with a confused look. "Rush, you said that when you're bapatized, you get buried in water. So where are we going to do that?"

"Funny you should ask," Rush answered with a sideways grin. "Me an' Jay was just thinkin' of makin' a personal inspection of the water cisterns just below the Watch Deck. If you'll slip into some old clothes that you don't mind gettin' wet, I think this would be a great time for you to join us."

"Yeah," chuckled Jay, "and I wouldn't be surprised if you didn't find yourself bapatized by the time we finish that inspection."

It was almost an hour later when Rush, Jay, and a wet Sycamore returned to Sycamore's living quarters. Their happy banter was suddenly cut short as the door jerked open, and a very upset Poke confronted them.

"Father, where have you been?" Poke barked. "I've been worried sick about you! And what happened to you? You're soaking wet!

"What did you two do to my father?" Poke snarled at Rush and Jay.

"Son," Sycamore said in a calm voice, "it's okay. I just went out with our friends to inspect the cisterns, and I got wet." As Sycamore spoke the last phrase, he turned to look at Rush and Jay, and all three of them burst out laughing.

"Stop it!" Poke screamed. "It's not funny! My father's not well, and you two take him out and let him get wet. Haven't you done enough? It's like you want him to die!"

"Poke!" Sycamore shouted sternly. "That's enough!"

"No, it's not!" the angry youth shouted back. "They keep coming around here acting like they're our friends, and they don't care about us! They just feel guilty for how they've ruined our lives!"

"That's not true, Son," Sycamore began.

"Yes, it is!" Poke shot back. "Yes, it is! Get them out of here, Father, and don't let them come back!"

Sycamore winced and put a hand to his head.

"Are you okay, Syc?" Rush asked with concern.

"It's just a headache," he said with a smile. "Stress brings them on. I think you fellas better go; Poke and I need to talk."

With an understanding nod, both friends turned to leave.

"One more thing, fellas," Sycamore called out. "Thanks for everything, and I mean that with all my heart."

The next day almost the entire clan turned out for nectar collecting. Teams of workers traveled to a nearby honeysuckle vine and began cutting blossoms and hauling them to the work area beside the Keep. As blossoms were brought in, they were lifted onto one of several long work tables which had been set up near the gate path. Three Larkin would grab the blossom to steady it as two other workers with sharp flint knives carefully cut all the way around the honeysuckle flower until its base was severed from the rest of the blossom. Care had to be taken in the cutting process to cut around the bottom of the flower without cutting the stamens growing out of the base and extending up through the middle of the blossom. A large wooden cask was then moved underneath the cut end of the flower, and the lid of the cask was removed. Two other workers walked up holding carved wooden hooks to which were tied long ropes. When the hooks were firmly set into the base of the blossom, a signal was given, and four or more Larkin grabbed each of the ropes and began pulling. As they pulled the base away from the flower, the stamens which were still attached to the base were drug through the flower. When the heads of the stamens were drawn near to the cut opening in the bottom of the flower, a large drop of sweet honeysuckle nectar was pushed out of the opening. With the help of two more workers with wooden paddles standing beside the end of the flower, this drop of nectar was directed into the cask. When this process was completed, the lid was replaced on the cask, the flower and base were discarded, and another blossom was lifted into place.

To protect the workers, guards were stationed at close intervals around the work area a short distance from the Keep to watch for ants or other dangerous creatures which might be drawn there by the strong smell of the nectar. It was now the middle of the afternoon, and the whole collecting process had gone quite smoothly. The only interruption to the work was the occasional fly or bee which, being attracted by the fragrance, had to be driven away by the archers.

Hawthorn was on guard duty. He had spent the morning in the brush nearby scouting for enemies. The afternoon watch had been sent to replace the morning watch, so Hawthorn and his companions had been called in to get lunch and to stand guard in the work area.

"Well hey there, Hawthorn!" called an excited voice from Hawthorn's right. "I didn't think I was going to get to see you today."

"Hello, Juni," Hawthorn returned with markedly less enthusiasm.

"You can help me seal up the full nectar casks if you want to," Juniper said with wide expectant eyes.

"Uh, thanks, Juni, but since I've finish eating, I need to grab a lance and watch for enemies."

"I understand," Juniper responded with a hint of disappointment in her voice. "At least you'll be guarding here in the work area, so we'll get to look at each other once in a while."

"Uh, like I said, Juni, I'll be looking for enemies. Oh, there's Rush over there. I guess I'd better go check in with him and get my orders. Talk to you later." Hawthorn quickly trotted over to where Rush and Jay were standing.

"Hey, guys," Hawthorn said as he trotted up.

"Hey, Thorn," Jay answered. "Have you eaten your lunch?"

"Yeah, I just finished. What are you two talking about?"

"When we was standin' guard out in the brush this morning," Rush began in a low voice, "I was sure that I heard a Makerian caller. But Jay said he never heard a thing. How about you? Did you hear anything?"

Hawthorn thought for a moment and then finally shook his head. "No, I didn't."

"Wel-l-l," Rush said, shaking his head, "maybe I'm jus' goin' crazy."

"Oh, you've been crazy for some time," Jay said with a smile. "Now you're just hearing things."

"Where do you want us positioned to guard the workers, Rush?" Hawthorn asked.

Rush was in the process of answering Hawthorn's question when some loud yelling was heard coming from the brush to their left. As everyone turned toward the source of the noise, they saw one of the guards run out of the grass and leaves, racing to the Keep and yelling, "Dragon! Dragon!"

A moment later a very large grey lizard burst through the same grass and gave a fierce roar. Seeing all the panic-stricken Larkin scrambling for the Keep gates, the hungry lizard charged forward. Several of the Larkin guards managed to shoot their arrows at the beast, but the missiles just bounced off the thick knobby skin.

Hawthorn saw the creature coming and tried to intercept it with his lance, but the dragon was on him before he could get his long spear lined up. The charging lizard broke his weapon and knocked him over one of the work tables and into a stack of empty casks. Hawthorn quickly pulled himself out of the pile of casks and viewed the scene before him. Most of the Larkin were streaming through the gate into the safety of the Keep. Only one person remained in the huge lizard's path, and that person was Juniper. She was standing frozen in fear behind one of the lidless casks and was staring at the beast as it charged straight for her.

"Juniper!" Rush yelled as he ran towards the girl. "Jump in the cask—quick!"

Rush's powerful voice shook Juniper from her paralysis, and she rapidly climbed up onto the edge of the barrel of nectar and dropped her small frame inside. Just as she did so, the great beast ran into the casks, knocking many of them over, including Juniper's. Large quantities of sweet nectar spilled out on the ground. As the hungry lizard tasted the nectar, he stopped and began to lap up the delicious liquid. Running up with sting in hand, Rush stabbed at the dragon's neck. This did little more than irritate the beast, who quickly jerked his large head around and knocked Rush quite a distance back the way he had come. By now other Larkin guards were running up and launching arrows at the lizard's mouth, eyes, and nose. As some of these missiles found their mark, the dragon decided that it was time to get away from these irritating creatures.

Reaching down, the beast grabbed the nearest cask in its mouth and ran for the brush. The lizard hadn't taken three steps before a scream was heard coming from the barrel in the beast's mouth.

"It's got Juniper!" Hawthorn yelled. He and Jay both arrived beside the fallen Rush at the same time.

"Rush, are you hurt?" Jay asked as he knelt beside his friend.

"Don't worry 'bout me," Rush said urgently as he painfully pulled himself up into a sitting position. "Grab whoever you can and go after Juni!"

"Let's go, Thorn!" Jay called as he turned and sprinted after the retreating lizard.

"Rush," Hawthorn said, "why don't you use your caller just in case you really did hear Eldan or Tobin?"

"Good idear," Rush shot back. "Now get goin'!"

Rush watched Hawthorn as he and three other warriors raced after Jay and the dragon. With a groan Rush rolled over onto his knees so he could get to his backpack. After rummaging through it for a few moments, he finally pulled out his Makerian caller. Struggling to his feet, he stepped on the cord coming from the back of the caller and began drawing the rosin up and down the tight string.

As the croaking roar of the caller sent Rush's message out into the woods, another Larkin guard came trotting by and stopped, looking questioningly at Rush. "What 'cha doin', Rush?" the guard asked with a confused look on his face. "Is that some kind'a dragon mating call?"

"It does sound like one, don't it?" Rush returned. "I figure it cain't hurt to try."

The guard just shook his head and ran off as Rush continued to work his caller.

Hawthorn followed Jay and two other Larkin as they raced after the retreating dragon. The big lizard couldn't move very quickly carrying the barrel in its mouth, so the Larkin warriors were able to catch up to him after he had traveled about a bow shot.

Jay quickly launched an arrow that struck the beast just behind the left front leg. The lizard's skin was so thick and knobby that the arrow did little more than scratch him, but the sting of the blow did cause the reptile to whip around to face his enemies. Dropping the barrel, the lizard placed one clawed foot on it to make sure that it stayed in his possession and bellowed a challenging roar to his approaching enemies.

Jay and the others moved cautiously toward the angry beast, spreading out as they slowly advanced. At this point Hawthorn realized that he was only holding the shaft of his broken lance. Jay noticed this as well. "Pepper his face with arrows, mates," Jay called out. "If we can get him to move away from the cask, then Hawthorn, you run in there and get Juni!"

Hawthorn nodded his understanding and looked at the cask under the lizard's claws. He could see the terrified Juniper curled inside.

"Juni!" Hawthorn called. "You be ready to run when I come after you!"

"I'll try!" the girl nervously called back and then screamed as the dragon roared angrily at hearing her voice so near.

"All right, make 'em count, fellas!" Jay announced as he and the other two warriors began launching arrows at the nose, eyes, and mouth of the fierce reptile.

As the feathered missiles struck the beast in the soft, unprotected places, he began to bellow angrily. The creature started to back away but then immediately stepped back over the barrel. When he saw that the dragon wasn't going to leave his cask of nectar, Jay ran closer and began yelling at the beast. When the lizard saw Jay's threatening move, he lunged forward to the attack.

"Now, Thorn!" Jay screamed over his shoulder as he turned and ran from the charging brute.

Hawthorn raced to the abandoned barrel and grabbed Juniper by the arm as she was trying to crawl out.

When the dragon was almost on him, Jay dove under some nearby leaves and began crawling frantically to his right under other leaves in the small pile. The lizard charged into the spot where he had seen the Larkin disappear but did not spot his prey. As soon as the reptile lifted his head to look for his victim, more arrows struck his nose and lips.

By now Hawthorn had Juniper to her feet, and they were just starting to run away when another roar from close on their left stopped them in their tracks. Suddenly a second dragon leaped down from a log behind them and landed between them and their friends. Hawthorn noticed that this lizard was slightly smaller than the first.

"Another one?" Juniper screamed as she saw that this dragon was staring straight at them with hungry, determined eyes.

"That must be the big one's mate!" Hawthorn spoke his thoughts out loud as he held the broken end of his lance shaft threateningly toward the lizard. "Look out!"

Abruptly the hungry dragon lunged for them. Hawthorn shot his lance forward, and the jagged, broken end stabbed into the tender, soft skin just inside the dragon's nose. With a painful scream, the injured lizard jumped back and began pawing at her snout.

"Run, Juni, run!" Hawthorn shouted as he grabbed the scared girl's arm and dragged her along while sprinting to his left into the woods.

They had only raced a short distance when they heard the angry female dragon charging after them.

"It's coming after us, Thorn!" Juniper cried breathlessly as they sprinted. "What are we gonna' do?"

Hawthorn was desperately searching for a way of escape when he heard a voice calling to him, "Over here, Chums!"

Glancing to his left in the direction of the voice, Hawthorn saw Eldan standing on top of a low outcropping of moss-covered rocks, waving at them with both arms. "This way, and you better hurry!" Eldan called again.

Hawthorn with Juniper in tow turned and raced towards the anxiously waving Eldan. As they ran, the young Larkin stole a quick glance behind them and instantly regretted it. He saw that the determined dragon was very near and charging fiercely straight for them. As they reached the bottom of the rock outcropping, Hawthorn knew that there was not enough time for both of them to climb up before the lizard would have them, so he grabbed Juniper around the waist with both hands and tossed her up the rocks as high as he could. "Climb fast, Juni!" Hawthorn yelled. Snatching up his broken lance, he whipped around to face the vicious predator.

Immediately the lizard was there and lunged for the young warrior. Once again Hawthorn stabbed with his broken lance, this time pricking the dragon's lip just under its nose. This caused the beast to draw back, shaking its head.

As Hawthorn held the reptile at bay at the base of the rocks, Eldan climbed down and assisted Juniper to ascend to the top of the small ledge.

The dragon, protective of its injured nose, decided to try a new tactic. She slashed at her enemy with her claws. Hawthorn saw the movement and dove quickly to the side. A large, jagged tear instantly appeared in the side of Hawthorn's tunic as the claws whipped past. The young Larkin hit the ground and rapidly rolled back to his feet just as the lizard turned to face him. Quick as lightning, Hawthorn jabbed the pointed splinters of the broken lance hard into the side of the creature's jaw. Again the beast drew back, shaking its head. A deep growl rolled from her chest as the dragon locked eyes with her prey.

Suddenly a rock thudded against the top of the lizard's head. Another painful roar bellowed from her throat as she jerked her head around to discover the source of her pain. She was just in time to see Eldan standing a short distance above her in the act of flinging down another stone. As the dragon began to angrily climb up the rocks toward Eldan and Juniper, Hawthorn started to move toward the beast, looking for an opening.

"Just stay back, Chums," Eldan called cheerily as he lifted what appeared to be a large brown bag, "and hold your nose." As he said this, the redheaded Makerian flung the brown bag at the approaching dragon with all of his strength. The object struck the lizard solidly on the nose and exploded into a huge thick brown cloud. Immediately the large repile was convulsed with violent fits of sneezing and coughing.

Hawthorn watched with amazement as the fierce dragon now rolled helplessly on the ground, clawing frantically at its face and eyes as it continued to sneeze and cough.

"If I were you, Chummy," Eldan called down, "I'd take this opportunity to shinny on up these rocks so we can beat a hasty retreat before our dragon friend snorts all of that puffball dust out of her nose."

CHAPTER NINE

JUNIPER AND ELDAN

As Hawthorn reached the top of the short bluff, he saw Juniper sitting on the ground and grimacing while Eldan was kneeling in front of her, examining her knee.

"What happened?" Hawthorn asked as he got to his feet.

"I hurt my knee," Juniper answered painfully.

"It seems that in her haste to escape the dragon, our little lady friend smacked her knee against a rock," Eldan added.

"Are you hurt bad, Juni?" Hawthorn asked and then added, "'cause we really need to get moving!"

"Is that your name . . . Juni?" Eldan asked as he smiled broadly and looked into his patient's eyes.

"Well, actually it's Juniper," Juni returned with a wide-eyed grin.

"That's a lovely name, Miss Juniper. One of the loveliest I've ever heard. Yessiree! And it fits you, too. I was saying to myself when I first laid eyes on you, 'Eldan,'. . . that's me . . . 'Eldan', I says, 'a girl as lovely as that has got to have a lovely name.' And sure enough, YOU DO."

117

"So you're Eldan?" Juniper returned, her big expressive eyes fixed on her redheaded companion.

"That's me, Miss Juniper. I'm Eldan, son of Ripgood, Special Scout for the Makerian Rangers."

"Oh, yes," said Juniper excitedly. "I remember! My friends told me that the last time they saw you that you were in Ranger Troop Six."

"Well, uh . . . right! Right you are, Miss Juniper! Right you are! I was in Ranger Troop Six, but they, uh . . . well, I'm not in Troop Six anymore. No, siree! They now realize my unique abilities, and they, sort of, gave me my own position. You might say I'm a Ranger-At-Large now . . . in a manner of speaking."

"Oh, Sir Eldan," Juniper gushed, "I can't tell you how excited I am to finally make your acquaintance!"

"I hate to interrupt this touching scene, but we really need to get out of here!" Hawthorn exclaimed.

"Calm your fretful self, Chums, and show a little compassion. I am providing needed aid to the injured Miss Juniper."

Turning to their injured companion, Eldan addressed Juni, "I think Chummy's right, Miss Juniper. We do need to be moving away from here. Do you think you can walk on your leg?"

"I'm not sure, Sir Eldan," Juniper replied coyly. "It hurts ever so much. Could you help me?"

"Why, of course I could! Of course I could! It would be my privilege and an honor to carry you to safety, Miss Juniper."

"Would you two please hurry?" Hawthorn urged anxiously as he looked back and noticed the dragon had locked her eyes on him and was moving toward the rocks on which they were standing.

"No worries, Chums," Eldan said cheerfully as he helped Juniper to her feet. "We're ready to go. I shall sweep the lovely Miss Juniper in my arms, and we'll be off."

"And that's another thing!" Hawthorn snapped. "How come you can remember Juni's name when you can't remember anyone else's?"

"Stick a boot in it, Chums," Eldan shot back out of the corner of his mouth. "I'm trying to be gallant."

At that instant the approaching dragon bellowed loudly, causing all three of them to jump at the startling roar. When Eldan saw the nearness of the enemy, he turned to lift Juniper into his arms, but she was gone. Looking up, he spotted her half a stone's throw ahead of them with her skirts hitched up and running through the woods like a deer. It was several minutes later before Eldan and Hawthorn could catch up to her, and that was only because she stopped to get her breath.

"I don't think the dragon's coming after us," Hawthorn voiced his opinion as he scanned the woods behind them.

"Just the same, Chummy, we need to keep moving," Eldan returned and then quickly added, "that is, just as soon as Miss Juniper feels that she is up to it."

"Oh, I think I can keep going," Juniper said with a big smile directed at the redhaired Makerian. "If I start to feel weak, Sir Eldan, can I just lean on you?"

"Well, sure you can, Miss Juniper! Sure you can!" Eldan answered excitedly. "You know, you might need to lean on me a little right now, 'til you get your strength back. That's right, just lean on me as we walk."

Hawthorn rolled his eyes and shook his head as he followed along behind.

After several minutes of walking, Hawthorn glanced at the position of the sun to get his bearings. "Don't you think we should be bearing more to the east, Eldan?"

"Listen to you, Chums," Eldan answered with a grin. "You're getting to be quite the woods explorer. You're right as rain, Chummy ol' pal. Your stronghold is mostly east and slightly north of where we are right now.

But the reason we can't head straight for it is because the ground is pretty wet between here and there---quite bog-like after all the rain we've had the last month, if you know what I mean. Now bogs are fine for ol' mud muckers like yourself, but we can't have the lovely Miss Juniper traipsing through all that mess, can we? Anyway, I figure that we'll take the longer but drier way to your doorstep."

The truth of Eldan's words was soon evident when they came upon large patches of moss and algae. Also, the smell of damp leaves began to permeate the air.

Suddenly Eldan stopped. "Uh oh," he mumbled under his breath.

"What's wrong, Eldan?" Hawthorn asked. "Why are we stopping?"

"Listen!" Eldan whispered.

Concentrating on the forest noises around them, Hawthorn and Juniper became aware of a low-pitched humming sound that seemed to come from all around them.

"What's that?" Juniper asked.

"Mosquitoes!" Hawthorn answered her question.

"Lots of them!" Eldan added.

"Should we run back the way we came?" Juni queried anxiously.

"I'm afraid it's too late for that, Miss Juniper," Eldan returned. "If we took off running right now, we might get a stone's throw down the trail, but then they'd be all over us, and we'd be caught out in the open."

"So what do we do?" Juniper shouted, near panic as she looked up and saw clouds of the biting insects swarming towards them.

"We're gonna' defend ourselves," Eldan answered confidently. "Follow me." The redheaded Makerian led them in a run toward some nearby low, thick shrubs. The hungry bloodsucking flies zoomed down upon them, looking for an easy meal.

"Oh!" Juni shouted, waving her arms wildly as she ran. "They're all around me!" Each mosquito was about the size of a Larkin's head, and each one had a sharp, stabbing proboscis that was as long as the distance from the tips of Juni's fingers to the middle of her forearm. As she ran, the young maiden felt the wings and legs of several of the terrible creatures brush against her as they swooped in to the attack.

"Keep running!" Eldan called out encouragingly. "It's much harder for them to stab us while we're moving."

"You two keep running!" Hawthorn cried out from behind. "I'll try to hold them off!"

"No, Chummy! Don't do it!" Eldan ordered. "We've got to stay together. Just keep running. I got me a plan."

Eldan led them to a wide bush with lots of limbs covered thickly with small green leaves. "In here!" he called over his shoulder. The wild privet bush that he had chosen had a number of leaf-covered branches that extended all the way to the ground. As Eldan reached the first of the limbs, he ripped off his backpack and, using it as a club, stood there flailing away at the attacking insects as his two companions, ducking under his swings, dashed into the thick foliage of the bush. As soon as Hawthorn and Juniper shot past him, Eldan turned and threw himself into the thick, leafy limbs of the privet.

As he quickly picked himself up, he heard Juniper's voice beside him. "Are we safe under this bush?"

"Well, Miss Juniper," Eldan began as he slipped his pack back on his shoulders, "it's like this. We're not exactly safe, as it were. But I would definitely say that we are safer than we were out in the open."

As he spoke, Eldan was bent over, searching the ground under the leafy limbs. "You see, Miss Juni . . . may I call you Juni? You see, Miss Juni, I personally feel that *safe* is overrated. Yes siree, very overrated. Why, how many times have you been told that you were safe when you really weren't? Gobs of times, I'll wager." At this point Eldan stood up holding two sticks, each one almost as long as his arm. One of these he handed to Juniper. "Instead of referring to something as safe or unsafe, I prefer to talk about degrees of safeness."

At this point they both looked up to spy two of the persistent mosquitoes weaving their way relentlessly toward them through the canopy of leaves.

"There's one or two trying to get through on my side," Hawthorn reported.

"So what degree of safeness are we in right now?" Juniper asked nervously.

Eldan had pulled back a small branch in order to get an unobstructed view of the incoming mosquitoes. With one quick swing, the Makerian clubbed the first approaching insect. The second biting fly saw his victim and sped to the attack. As it did so, Eldan stepped back and released the branch he was holding. With a solid smack, the springing branch clobbered the mosquito and launched it back the way it had come.

"For the moment, Miss Juni, I'd say our degree of safeness is tolerable," Eldan said loftily.

"Tolerable?" Juniper questioned.

"Yes, quite tolerable—," Eldan returned, "—at least for the moment."

Hawthorn had his sting in his hand and was stabbing and swatting at the biting insects as they came filtering through the thick leaves. "There's more coming this way!" he called out.

By now all three of the friends were busy fighting for their lives. Eldan and Hawthorn managed to club, swat, or pierce most of the insects as they came buzzing through the branches. The few bugs that did manage to get past the two warriors were whacked by the alert Juniper.

The battle continued in this way for several more minutes. Just as Juniper noticed that her arm was getting tired from constantly swinging her stick, there was some movement in the branches above her. She took a quick glance up but saw nothing. Immediately a mosquito appeared directly in front of her, hovering to make a strike. Juniper drew back to swat the insect when suddenly it just disappeared.

"Where did it go?" She exclaimed.

"BRAAAAK!"

Juni screamed at the noise and jumped back.

"There's your rescuer," Hawthorn said, smiling as he pointed his sting in the branches above Juniper. Clinging to the branches just above Juniper's left shoulder was a bright green tree frog. Even as she watched the tree-climbing amphibian, the creature leaned down and effortlessly snatched another mosquito out of the air.

"At least he's on our side," Eldan said as he swatted another enemy.

"He's brought reinforcements!" Hawthorn called out. "There are two more tree frogs in the branches above me, and I can hear more of them higher up in the bush."

"It must be tree frog dinner time," Eldan called back. "They're following the mosquito swarm."

"The frogs are helping!" Juniper cried. "There are not as many insects getting to us now. Yaii! What was that?"

Suddenly the constant low hum of the swarm of mosquitoes was interrupted by a sharp, loud drone that went shooting by the edge of their bush. This was quickly followed by five or six more.

"That's some kind of very large bug flying by," Hawthorn surmised.

"It's a lot more than one!" Juniper shouted as the loudly buzzing insects made an almost continuous roar around their privet bush.

"I don't see any more mosquitoes!" Eldan yelled over the noise. "Whatever it is seems to be running them off. You two sit tight right here while I go reconnoiter." With his newly found club at the ready, Eldan cautiously eased through the thick, leafy limbs to the edge of the bush.

"What's going on out there, Eldan?" Hawthorn finally cried out to his friend.

"You should see this, Chums," Eldan returned. "You, too, Miss Juni."

As Hawthorn and Juniper moved through the thick leaves to join Eldan at the edge of their shrub, they were stunned to see almost twenty very large dragonflies zipping back and forth just in front of them, nabbing mosquitoes left and right as they zoomed by.

"Land sakes!" Juniper exclaimed. "There's so many of them!"

"And they're doing some serious damage to that flock of mosquitoes as well," Hawthorn observed.

"Sir Eldan," Juniper asked, "will those big dragonflies try to hurt us?"

"Hmm . . . not likely, I'm thinking . . . . at least, not as long as they've got plenty of mosquitoes to munch. No offense, Miss Juni, but I expect that, to a dragonfly, you don't taste as good as a mosquito. But to be honest, I don't completely trust them. If one of those bigger dragonflies was hungry enough, he'd come after one of us."

"So, Sir Eldan," Juniper questioned, "what would you say our degree of safeness is now?"

"Oh, it's definitely improving," Eldan responded cheerfully. "Yes siree! I would say that our present degree of safeness has moved up from tolerable to almost acceptable."

At that moment a gigantic yellowish-green dragonfly whipped in front of the bush where they stood and hovered there only two paces away with its hundreds of eyes fixed on Eldan.

"Change that," Eldan said as he stood perfectly still, facing the huge aerial hunter.

All three of the friends began to slowly creep back into the bush when suddenly a dark shadow rocketed by, and the dragonfly was gone. An instant later a blast of wind hit them so hard that all three of them were knocked backwards off their feet.

"Sky fire!" Hawthorn cried out. "What was that?"

Instead of standing up, Eldan crawled to the edge of the bush and stole a quick glance. "Whoowee, Chummy! Situations sure do change in a hurry around here!"

"What's happening out there now?" Juniper persisted.

"There are martins swooping all over the place," Eldan called over his shoulder, "and they're taking out mosquitoes, dragonflies . . . anything they can get their little beaks on. And, yes, Miss Juni, a hungry martin might mistake you for a wingless dragonfly—albeit, a rather cute little dragonfly. But still, we don't need to be letting ourselves get caught out there in the wide open spaces, if you know what I mean. Let's move back further underneath this bush. Maybe we can find a back way out of this mess we've gotten ourselves into."

As they came out the back side of their bush, the three friends found themselves in a thicket of privet bushes interspersed with a few red cedar trees. The foliage in all of these plants was so thick that very little vegetation could grow under them. That made the walking easy for the travelers. They moved steadily along for the next hour, only pausing occasionally when a noise was heard nearby.

Finally the plants under which they traveled began to thin out, and Eldan called a halt in order to scout their situation. Finding that they were past the wetlands, he led them due east back toward the great cedar stump that the Third Clan of Larkin called home. It was late in the day when they stopped at the edge of the brush beyond which they could see the Keep.

"Well, here you are, Miss Juni, back home safe and sound. While our degree of safeness has fluctuated through the day, I would have to say that it's looking rather pleasing right now."

"Oh, Sir Eldan," Juniper gushed, "you did it! You saved us and got us back home safe! You are wonderful!"

"It was all in a day's work, Miss Juni," Eldan responded loftily, "all in a day's work. Saving and rescuing is what us special scouts do. I'm just glad that I could be of service to you."

"Now wait a minute!" Hawthorn spoke up. "I helped, too, you know!"

"Don't be self-serving, Chummy," Eldan returned condescendingly. "It makes you look small."

"How can I ever thank you?" Juniper continued, her big eyes flashing.

"Well, now, Miss Juniper, that won't be . . ."

"I know," Juniper said with a coy look. "I'm going to give you a big hug!"

"What? Oh, uh, well," Eldan stammered and began to step backward, "Miss Juni, I don't . . . I don't . . ." Suddenly Eldan tripped and fell backwards into a thick clump of dried grass.

Hawthorn and Juniper stood there with open mouths, staring at two legs sticking up out of the grass clump.

"Uh . . . little help, Chums?" Hawthorn heard the muffled voice of Eldan coming from deep within the grass clump.

It took several minutes of pulling to get Eldan unstuck from the clump, but finally they had him on his feet again. He had mud on his back and neck, and he had bits of dried grass clinging all over his clothes and his thick, floppy red hair.

"Sorry, Juni," Hawthorn said with a smile, "but I don't think Eldan is in any condition for one of your *thank you's* right now.

"We appreciate all your help, Eldan," Hawthorn said to his Makerian friend, "but I think I need to get both of us home."

"LITTLE HELP"

"Well, uh, sure you do, Chummy. That's exactly what I was about to say. You know, all your people must be worried sick about both of you by now. So you two just stroll on up to the gate there, and I'll be moving along."

"Goodbye, Sir Eldan! Goodbye!" Juniper said with feeling as Hawthorn led her away. "I hope you will remember me."

"Goodbye, Miss Juni," Eldan waved in return. "Forgetting you would be more than I could ask my brain to do."

CHAPTER TEN

TURNCOATS

"You mean he's dead?" Hawthorn blurted out with a shocked expression on his face.

"I'm afraid so, Son," Savin returned sadly.

"But . . . but . . . how could he be dead? Rush, you and Jay said that he was getting better and that he had even become a believer in Jehesus."

"I know, Thorn," Rush returned from where he stood in the main room of Savin and Rose's living quarters. "It's the most heartbreakin'est thang! Sycamore seemed better'n he's been in a long time. He was thinkin' clear and 'memberin' stuff. That's why Jay and me told him about Jehesus, and the more we told him, the more he wanted to know."

"He was even remembering things that the Makerians had said to him about Jehesus," Jay added.

"After about two hours of talkin'," Rush started again, "Syc tol' us that he was ready to follow King Jehesus wherever He led. That's when we slipped him up to the water cistern and bapatized him."

"He was so happy, Thorn," Jay remembered. "At least until we got back to his living quarters. That's when we ran into Poke."

"That kid went nuts when he saw us," Rush explained. "Syc tried to calm him down, but he just got worse. Me and Jay finally just had to leave. As we started to go, I noticed Syc grab his head like he was hurtin'. When I asked him about it, he said that stress brings on the headaches. Apparently all of Poke's fit pitchin' really set his headaches off this time. From what I hear, Sycamore was hurtin' all night with his head pains. Sometime this mornin' while all the nectar gatherin' was goin' on, he started havin' some of his really bad spells, one right after another. Finally the Lord just took him."

Everyone in the room was silent for several moments. "How is Poke doing?" Hawthorn finally asked, breaking the silence.

"Not very well," Rush answered, shaking his head slowly. "Flint's wife Fern heard all the commotion and went over to see what was happenin'. She got there as the Shaman were tryin' to help Sycamore. She tol' me that when Syc died, Poke went crazy, screamin' an' hollerin'. She said he started runnin' around the room, smashin' ever'thang he could get his hands on."

"Oh, the poor dear!" Rose gasped.

"He doesn't know the Lord," Hawthorn spoke his thoughts out loud. "He doesn't have any way to deal with the fear and the grief."

"So where is Poke now?" Hawthorn asked.

"Wel-l-l," Rush drawled, "the Shaman couldn't just leave him like that. Once they got him calmed down, they took Poke with them. Fern said that Shaman Castor told her that the Shaman were gonna look after Poke for now."

"I wish there was something we could do to help him," Hawthorn returned sadly.

"It's a purdy fair guess that Poke blames us for his father's death," said Rush. "I doubt if he'll have much to do with any of us for now. The best and likely the only thang any of us can do for that boy right now is to pray for 'im."

So they did.

THE GREAT GATHERING

The day after Sycamore's burial, the departure day for the clan to leave for the Great Gathering was announced. Immediately on receiving this news, the Keep was abuzz with activity. Scouting parties were sent out to find and prepare secure places where the large caravan of Larkin from the Third Clan would stop overnight on their way to the Steps. It was during this time of preparation that Rush was able to contact Eldan and let him know the clan's departure day.

"That's great, Wretch ol' boy!" Eldan responded with his usual enthusiasm. "The whole plan seems to be unfolding nicely."

"So how's all this supposed to work, Floppy?" Rush asked. "We ain't heard what the final scheme is to get yor people into the Steps."

"No worries, Wretch," Eldan returned. "I got all the details right here in my head bone. There's going to be six Makerians in the group going in—two ladies and four males. Rather than try to slip them all in at one time, three of them will try to blend in with the Fifth Clan as they arrive, and three will join your group. Tobin and I will shadow your clan as you travel, and as you get close to the Steps, we will look for a chance to have our three join with your group."

At this point Eldan handed Rush a folded white cloth. "Ask Chummy's mother if she would be willing to wear this white scarf around her neck during the trip. That way our people can recognize her if they need help. They will identify themselves with the word . . . uh . . . with the word . . . well, uh."

"Well, what's the word, Floppy? This is important!"

"Keep your tunic on, Wretch! I'm working on it! Let's see . . . I remember that it was something familiar, or was that the password to the South High Place?"

"I cain't believe you did this," Rush said with an exasperated shake of his head.

"This isn't totally my fault," Eldan shot back defensively. "I told them not to change all the passwords. But nooooo! They had to have all new passwords. So now all of their new passwords are muddling up all my important thinking thoughts."

"Think, Floppy! Think!" Rush barked, grapping his friend by the shoulders. "We need to know that word."

"I'm thinking! I'm thinking!" Eldan yelled back. "Wait! Was it *sunshine*?"

"HOW SHOULD I KNOW?" shouted Rush.

"No, that wasn't it. Oh, it's just no good, Wretch. I've searched every corner of my brain, and it's just not there anymore."

"So what are we supposed to do?" snarled Rush.

"Well, I guess you're just going to have to read it off this note Tobin wrote it on," Eldan returned as he handed Rush a piece of folded parchment.

With a growl Rush snatched the note from Eldan's hand and read the word *Stillwaters*. Flipping the note around, Rush held it up so his friend could read it.

"Oh, yeah," Eldan chuckled. "That was it. Well, you got to admit, I was close."

"Burn yor' hide, Floppy!" Rush barked. "Yo're about the exasperatin'est rascal I know!

"I guess I do put a little stretch on the relationship at times," Eldan returned, his wide grin spreading across his face.

Three days later at first light, the two large doors that formed the gate of the Keep swung open, and the grand caravan of the Third Clan of Larkin marched out on their three-day journey to join the other clans for the Great Gathering. It made an impressive sight, even though a few of the Larkin remained behind. Some were too old or too sick to make the journey. Some families had children too young to go. With these there remained a few warriors to guard the Keep.

Two small scouting parties were sent out ahead of the main caravan to explore the trail and the woods on either side for signs of danger. These had left the Keep an hour earlier and were steadily making their way to a small cave under a mossy ledge that would be the safe haven where the caravan would spend the first night. If they found no dangers along the way, the scouts would secure the cave and guard it until the caravan arrived late that afternoon.

The first day's journey proved to be fairly uneventful for those in the procession. The long column had to stop unexpectedly only twice, once when a dragon and later when a spider were spotted crossing the path in front of them. But nothing came of either event. A small rain shower caused the caravan to stop and take cover under some of the large oak leaves lying about.

Hawthorn marched along near his parents, taking turns with others shouldering the many litters on which were piled the food and supplies the clan would need at the Great Gathering. When he was not carrying supplies, he was listening to a constant barrage of comments and questions from Juniper about everything they happened to see.

They reached the guarded cave late in the afternoon. Immediately everyone set to work preparing the small grotto for their overnight stay. Soft bedding material was gathered from the surrounding forest, and a rotating watch was established to guard the opening through the night. No fires were lit so as not to attract attention to their place of shelter. They would dine on dried meat and fruit tonight.

Hawthorn had just lain down to rest when Rush and Jay appeared. "Don't get too comfortable there, Thorn," Rush greeted him. "You got more work to do."

"What do we need to do?" Hawthorn asked, stretched out on his thistledown mat.

"I've been ordered to take out a scouting party for the next leg of the trip," Rush answered, "and I picked you and Jay to help me do it."

"When are we leaving?" Hawthorn asked, sitting up.

"Right now," came the answer.

"Now?"

"We got a long night ahead of us, Thorn," Jay added with a smile.

"So get yer stuff, an' let's hit the trail," Rush barked.

"Do you need me to go?" Savin asked from where he was sitting next to his son.

"I appreciate you askin', Savin," Rush returned, "but I figure the three of us will be enough. Besides, I don't want to leave yor missus here by herself."

"Keep an eye out for our Makerian friends," Savin said in a low voice.

"That's what I was a figurin' on doin'," Rush nodded back.

Rush considered this the most dangerous part of the trip, because once the caravan started on this leg of the journey, they would be over a day's march to either the Keep or the Steps. The three scouts took their time as they carefully inspected the trail and the surrounding woods for signs of enemies.

It was just at twilight that Hawthorn found himself moving carefully through the woods about a bow shot to the right of the trail. A faint noise caused him to freeze beside a patch of grass, his sting and shield at the ready. As the young Larkin stood there with his back against the grass and staring at the darkening shadows of the woods, a large hairy arm snaked silently from between the blades of grass behind him. Like lightning, the powerful hand grabbed for Hawthorn's face, covering his mouth, and yanked him through the grass before the young warrior could react or cry out.

He found himself held firmly by a very powerful Renegade and surrounded by several others. Just inches away from Hawthorn's face was an enemy warrior wearing a frightful-looking mask resembling a bird's head. "Just keep yer mouth shut, Larkin," a nasally voice ordered from behind the mask. "Don't do no hollerin', an' you won't get hurt. Savvy?"

Hawthorn tried to nod his head with the strong hand still around his mouth.

"Now drop that pokey stick o' yorn so's none o' us gets hurt."

Obediently Hawthorn released his grip on his sting.

"Take it easy with him, you two," came an authoritative voice from behind the bird-masked Renegade. "I told you I don't want 'im hurt."

Suddenly the enemy warrior in front of Hawthorn was roughly shoved out of the way, and a different fighter with a red and black mask took his place. "That is you, ain't it, Chummy?" As he asked this question, the Renegade lifted his mask, and in the fading light of the day, Hawthorn recognized the face of Pike.

"Mumph?"

"Hee, hee. Turn 'im loose, Thug," Pike chuckled. Immediately the strong arms holding Hawthorn were removed.

"Pike," the young Larkin said nervously as he surveyed the small war party of Renegades surrounding him. "What's this all about?"

"I'm sorry about ambushin' you," Pike began, "but I need to talk to you, and this was the only way I could think of to do it. The rest of these slugs are mates of mine.

"You see, Chummy, I been spendin' a lot of time thinkin' about the stuff you and Redhead told me about the Maker and His Son Jehesus. I even started talkin' to my mates here about it all. Well, the bottom line is that we don't want to be Renegades no more. Redhead said that I could go with him and learn more about the Maker and His Son. We was wonderin' if Red would let all of us go with him?"

Hawthorn looked around at the hideously masked faces around him, and they all nodded in agreement. "I'm glad to hear that, Pike, but how do I know that you really mean it? This could be some kind of trick."

"I told you he'd say that," came a voice from behind Pike.

"Button it up, Muckly!" Pike snapped. "Now we talked about all of this. Are we still in agreement?" Again all of the heads nodded.

Pike then turned back to Hawthorn. "Awright, listen up, kid. I'll give you the proof that we're tellin' you the truth, but you've got to give me your word before the Maker that you will protect us, because what I'm about to tell you will get us killed if you double-cross us."

"As long as you're true with me, I will be true with you," Hawthorn returned, looking Pike in the eyes.

Pike once again looked around at the masked faces surrounding him. For a second time they all nodded their heads to show their agreement with what he was about to say.

"I owe you this anyway because you and Red saved my life," Pike began. "The reason that we found you, Chummy, is that we were sent out by our army to watch for the Larkin caravan's approach to the hollow tree that you will be using to spend the night in on your way to your grand Larkin gathering."

"The Renegades know that we are going to camp in the hollow tree?" Hawthorn blurted out with a mixture of shock and anguish.

"Not only do we know it," Pike answered, "but an army of Renegade warriors is already there waiting to ambush you. Our job was to find your advance scouts and to let our army know when you will be approaching so that they will have time to prepare the trap."

"I've got to get back and warn the Larkin!" Hawthorn exclaimed. "They must return to the Keep!"

"If they start back tonight," Pike warned, "as slow as they will be traveling, they'll be at the mercy of the night creatures out hunting for food. If they start back in the morning, they might make it back to your stronghold, but the Renegades will be sending more scouting parties out in the morning to watch for your approach. You can bet that as soon as they see the Larkin heading for home, they'll get word back to the army, and they will come charging in pursuit. I'm thinking that our army will easily catch your caravan before you can get home."

Hawthorn had his head in his hands trying to deal with all that Pike had just told him. Finally he looked up. "I've got to talk to Rush and Jay!"

"All right," Pike agreed, "but remember, you promised to protect us."

Hawthorn moved back through the woods in the direction of the path to rejoin his friends. Following behind him was Pike and his small band of Renegade warriors.

"Thunderation, Hawthorn!" Rush exclaimed. "I just sent you out into the woods to do some scouting, and you convert a whole war party of Renegades!"

"Well, they're kinda converting themselves," Hawthorn returned. "It's Pike, the Renegade that Eldan and I talked with a few weeks ago, and some friends of his. They want us to help them contact the Makerians so they can join them and learn more about Jehesus."

"Do you think we can trust them, Thorn?" Jay asked.

"To prove that they were sincere," Hawthorn answered, "they told me something that would get them all killed if word got back to the other Renegades."

"What did they tell you?"

"I think you fellas need to hear it for yourselves. Follow me," Hawthorn said as he turned and walked toward some thick brush.

"Where are they?" Rush asked.

"They're just right over there in that brush watching us," the young Larkin returned.

"THE WHOLE MUCKAREE OF 'EM?" Rush gasped as he and Jay suddenly stopped short and yanked out their stings.

"Guys," Hawthorn said, turning to face his friends, "if they wanted to kill us, we would already be dead. Now come on!"

There was a nervous meeting of the Larkin and the group of enemy fighters, following which Pike explained the details of the Renegade ambush to Rush and Jay. After getting the Renegade warrior's answers to a few detailed questions, Rush was silent for several moments as he thought the problem through.

"Wel-l-l, fellers," Rush drawled, "I have to agree with Pike that sending our people back to the Keep would probably result in some of our folks getting' kilt or captured. As far as it is to get back home and as slow as they would have to travel with the wives and children, it's a sure bet that that army of gutless varmints would catch 'em from behind. Oh, uh, present company excluded.

"From his answers to my questions, Pike has given me a' idear for how we can fix it so our people can march right past them without being attacked." Rush then took several minutes to explain his plan. "But for this thing to work," Rush finished, "it's got to be done tonight."

"If it's up to you three Larkin to do all of it," Pike spoke up, "I don't think it's gonna' work, and if your plan fails, then me and my mates here are as good as dead. Since our lives depend on your success, I think we had better help you."

For a moment the three Larkin just looked at each other, then Rush spoke up. "Well, here's how she sits. It would definitely improve our chances if'n we had you fellas helping' us out. And I'm willin' for you to work with us on this, but . . . you got to follow orders."

"We'll do whatever you say," Pike returned, "if you will just get us in contact with Redhead and his people."

"It's a deal," Rush shot back. "So if'n you fellers is serious about not bein' Renegades anymore, I'd shor' feel a lot less nervous if you'd get rid of them frizzelin' masks.

"Now let's get movin', 'cause we ain't got much time, an' we got a whole heap a stuff to do."

Although the night had fully come, a half-moon shone with enough light for the three Larkin and seven Renegades to see as they ran along the old path. They maintained a long distance trot for several hours, stopping briefly three times: once to rest and twice to hide from suspicious noises in the woods nearby. Sometime near the beginning of the final watch of the night, they arrived at the hollow tree which the Larkin had intended to use as a place of refuge but which was now inhabited by an entire army of Renegade warriors. Immediately Rush began giving orders, sending small groups of fighters out to put his plan into effect.

This old den tree was actually a large white oak with great spreading limbs that grew right beside the path leading to the Steps. The once grand tree had been struck by lightning years ago, which caused a portion of the center of the tree at its base to rot out. This left a large tree cave in its trunk at ground level. The entrance into this wooden cavern was a small opening just slightly wider and taller than a Larkin.

It was an hour and a half later before the new allies all met back together.

"What's the report from yo'r scouts?" Rush asked Pike as the last of the Renegades arrived.

"It's just like I told you," Pike returned. "The only guards are the two you can see standing beside the entrance of the hollow tree. The rest of the army is asleep in the tree cave."

"Jay," Rush asked, turning to his friend, "did you and your team find some bark?"

"Indeed we did," Jay returned with a smile. "It's the right size, very thick, and it's fresh, too. They won't be bustin' through this anytime soon."

"What about the poles?" Rush asked.

"That was my group's job," Hawthorn called out. "We've got several nice pieces from oak branches that should work very well."

"It sounds like all we have to do now is to figure out the best way to take care of the guards," Pike said his thoughts out loud.

"Hurrrumph." This sound came from the very tall and very large Renegade who had grabbed Hawthorn at their first meeting.

"Thug thinks dat we should just snuff deir candles," said the thin, hawk-nosed Renegade named Buzzard, who was the constant companion and interpreter of the huge Thug.

"We cain't do that," said a small Renegade who was maybe five seasons younger than Hawthorn. "We talked about that in our group, an' the Chummy said that there wasn't to be no killin' unless we absolutely got's to. Ain't that right, Uncle Muckly?"

"Yep, yep, Lil' Snide's right as rain," returned Muckly, who was the larger and much rounder version of his nephew. "That's just what the Chummy said. He told us that King Jehesus wants us to avoid killin'."

"So we's back to da same question," growled the deep voice of the very short but very broad-chested warrior named Stub. "How do we take out da guards if we cain't kill'em?"

"Fellers," announced Rush, "don't worry your purdy little heads 'bout that part of the plan 'cause I got it all figured out."

"So what's yer plan?" Pike asked suspiciously.

"Wel-l-l, I thought we might steal an idear from ol' Redheaded Floppy Hair hisself. We'll take out these guards the same way we took out all of your thievin' buddies the first time we met you."

"That's a great idea, Rush!" Hawthorn exclaimed. "I had forgotten all about Eldan's arrows with the rounded stone heads."

"But I didn't," returned Rush with a big grin. "All we gots to do is to break the arrow heads off two arrows and replace them with rounded pieces of stone. Then we pick our two best archers and send those two guards to dreamland. That's when we put the rest of the plan into action. But we all have to move fast, 'cause droppin' them guards is likely to roust up some of the rest of them sleepin' beauties."

"Mumbles is one of the best archers in our whole army," Pike said, pointing to a lanky, stoop-shouldered warrior nearby.

"An Jay's one of our best," Rush replied. Then turning to Jay, Rush said, "Jay, get with their archer, and you two prepare your stone-tipped arrows as quickly as you can while we start getting the rest of our group into position."

It was almost an hour later before Hawthorn found himself and seven others hidden in the brush directly across from the opening to the tree cave. He could see clearly the two Renegade guards standing on either side of the entrance. They were less than half a bow shot away from where Hawthorn and the others were concealed. The young Larkin could also see the two warriors from Pike's group who had stealthily crept up from behind the Renegades' hiding place and were now waiting on either side of the tree just out of sight of the guards.

With a nod from Rush, Jay and the Renegade named Mumbles drew their bows and took careful aim.

"Ready?" Jay whispered.

"Ye-ye-ye-ye . . . uh, s-sure," Mumbles whispered back.

"Shoot!" Jay said as he released his missile. The second arrow left a split second later.

"Now!" said Rush as he and the remaining warriors hefted the large piece of oak bark and sprinted for the tree cave entrance. Before the bark carriers had cleared the brush, the stone-tipped arrows had struck their marks. Both of the guards were wearing their wooden masks, and the powerfully shot arrows struck them both in the forehead area of their mask with the force of a hammer blow. As the two guards dropped stunned to the ground, the two hidden warriors on either side of the tree raced from their places of concealment and quickly tossed the two guards into the tree cave with the rest of the Renegade army.

Some gruff voices from inside the hollow tree called out to know what was going on, but just then the warriors carrying the slab of bark arrived and slammed it over the opening, completely blocking the entrance. All eight of the allied fighters leaned hard against the bark to hold it in place. A moment later Jay and Mumbles ran up carrying the long oak poles. These were quickly and firmly shoved against the bark slab while the other end of each pole was tightly wedged into the ground. Once he was sure that the opening was securely fixed in place, Rush held his finger to his lips and waved all of them to follow him further away from the trapped Renegades.

When they were a stone's throw away, Rush turned to Hawthorn. "Thorn, I need you to pull out yer climbers."

"Uh, sure, Rush," Hawthorn returned and began pulling the climbing devices from his backpack.

"Now listen up, fellers," he began. "Everybody did a great job, but we still gots to be careful. All of you, uh, former Renegades need to keep your voices down so's you won't be recognized by any of your old mates trapped on the other side of that bark."

"Now that we got 'em trapped in there," Pike spoke up, "it shouldn't be a problem."

"Wel-l-l, Pike ol' buddy, the truth be told, they ain't totally trapped. They're only mostly trapped. You see, there's another way out o' that hole. Now I don't know if'n them varmints have found it yet or not, but they'll definitely figure it out come daylight."

"Where's the other way out?" Pike asked with concern.

Rush lifted up his arm and pointed up the trunk of the huge oak tree. "About a bow shot up the left side of that tree is where, a few years ago, one of its limbs broke off. The center of that limb has rotted out, which has left a hole in the trunk that connects with the tree cave. If'n they have some climbers with 'em, they could climb up the inside of the tree and slip out through that hole. Then it would be easy enough to climb down and either remove our poles and open the cave or slip off and go get more help."

"Then we need to guard that hole," Pike said firmly.

"As soon as Hawthorn here gets his climbers, that's exactly where he's headed.

"Jay," Rush called to his friend, "I need you to run back to the cave where our people are staying and get them moving as quickly as possible. Tell the leaders that they're gonna have to make a long day of it. Tell them that once they get here, they will need to keep going until they get to the Steps. We can keep these Renegades shut up here until they get there. I know it's a long march, but if they get an early start an' only take brief rests, they should get to the Steps before it gets completely dark. Can you do it?"

As Rush was talking to him, Jay had opened his backpack and started searching for something. In answer to Rush's question, Jay pulled out a pair of lace up moccasins with thick soles. "Let me get my runnin' boots on, and I'll be off like an arrow."

"Thanks, Jay. Oh, and by the way," Rush added, "try to send Savin back here ahead of everybody when the caravan gets close to us so's I gots time to hide Pike an' his crowd before any of our people spot 'em."

"You got it," Jay returned as he saluted and then sprinted up the dark trail the way they had come.

Rush now turned back to Hawthorn. "Thorn, your job is to guard that hollow branch up there on the side a' that tree so that none a' our captive bushwhackers can climb up an' slip out. Leave everything here but yer bow an' arrows. That rotted opening in that limb is big enough for you to sit comfortably in while you're a doin' yer guardin'. But now listen here, I know yer tired an' all, but if'n you was to doze off up there, you're liable to get yer throat cut."

"Don't worry, Rush. I'll stay alert."

"See that you do," Rush shot back. "An' if'n any o' them varmints tries to climb up the walls, don't be afraid to discourage 'em with a few well-placed arrows. I'll send someone up to replace you in a couple of hours."

"So now what?" Pike asked.

"Why don't you pick out a couple of yer people to stand the first watch so's the rest of yous can get some rest? While yer a doin' that, I believe it's time fer me to keep my promise. I'm gonna see if'n I can call that redheaded, floppy-haired Makerian friend of ours an' tell him that I got some folks here what needs to talk to him.

CHAPTER ELEVEN

THE STEPS

The sun was just peeking through the trees in the east when a loud croaking roar sounded from the woods just north of Rush and his companions. Rush, who had been dozing, was startled to wakefulness by the nearby noise.

"Hey, Pike," Rush called to the former Renegade, "there's Floppy."

"Floppy?"

"Yeah, you know—Ol' Redhead." Rush was pulling his caller out of his pack as he answered. "He apparently has scouted our camp here, and he's spotted some of yor' crew. He's askin' if'n it's safe for him to come in. If I don't answer him, he'll know we're in trouble."

With caller in hand, Rush quickly sent the message back to Eldan that all was safe. The word was then sent out to the guards that a friend was coming in. It wasn't long before the very short but very muscular former Renegade named Stump came walking in leading Tobin, Eldan, and three others.

"Well, paint me red and call me a strawberry, if it isn't my favorite Renegade, Puke!"

"Red!" Pike barked. "You're a hard guy to find. My mates and I have been tryin' to catch up with you for three weeks."

"No offense, Pork, but I usually try to avoid being caught by you Renegades."

"But we don't want to be Renegades no more, Red," Pike returned. "I been talkin' to my mates here about what you and the Chummy told me about the Maker and His Son, and we all decided that we want to come with you and learn more about Jehesus."

"Well, that's great!" Eldan exclaimed. "But how many of you are there?"

"There's seven of us," Pike said proudly.

At this news Eldan turned and looked with wide eyes at his brother. In reply Tobin simply shrugged his shoulders and said, "It complicates things, but this is the Maker's business, Eldan. We will complete our mission first, and then we will figure out a way to help these fellows."

Rush stepped up to greet his Makerian friends. "So who have you and yer brother got with you, Floppy?" Rush asked.

"Wretch ol' boy, this is Mission Team One from Stillwaters. These are the three who will be joining your clan as they enter the Steps. Allow me to introduce you to Sagamor, Noblis, and I believe you already know . . ."

"Carineda!" Hawthorn shouted as he suddenly recognized his friend. "I didn't realize you would be a part of this mission. It is so good to see you!"

"It's good to see you, too, Thorn," Cari returned. "I was counting on visiting with you and your father again. I'm also looking forward to finally meeting your mother."

"I pity you the hug you're going to get when she realizes that you are the one who saved my life," Hawthorn said with a smile.

"It was the Maker Who saved you, Thorn."

"Oh, I know that," Hawthorn answered, "but He used you and Eldan and Tobin and a whole bunch of other people. I also know my mother, and when she finally meets you, she's going to give you everybody's hug."

146

With their camp now composed of Larkin, Makerians, and Renegades, it was an interesting rest of the day. They shared a meal of dried fruit and meat and rotated the guards and the scouts as they waited for the Larkin caravan to show up. Some rested but most talked. Hawthorn and Carineda used the time to catch up on the doings of each other's families over the last two years. Rush, Tobin, Sagamor, and Noblis discussed the strategy for the Makerian mission to take the truth about Jehesus to the Larkin people. Nearby sat Eldan surrounded by Pike and his Renegade friends.

"All of this stuff you're tellin' us about Jehesus sounds really good, Red," Pike was saying, "but I still don't understand why somebody as good as Jehesus would let people like us into His family."

"Yeah, Red," the plump Renegade named Muckly spoke up. "We's a bunch of thieves and lowlifes. How do you know King Jehesus would even allow us to join Him?"

"If you fellas knew Jehesus like I know Him, you wouldn't need to ask that question," Eldan began. "But since you don't, let me tell you a little story about Jehesus. I've already told all of you that Jehesus died on a cross to pay the price for all of our sins, but did you know that He didn't die alone? Two other fellas were hung on crosses on either side of Him, and both of them were thieves. At first both of them were yelling some pretty bad stuff, and they were even giving Jehesus a hard time. But one of them started having second thoughts about his words and his life when he realized that Jehesus didn't deserve this death. The thief really started feeling ashamed when he saw that while everybody was cursing Jehesus, Jehesus was asking the Maker to forgive them."

A grunt came from one of the Rengades in the circle. "Thug wants to know what the thief did about it," Buzzard interpreted.

"He did something that was probably the only good thing he ever did in his life," Eldan answered. "While his thieving partner was yelling at Jehesus, the repentant thief yelled back at him and shut him up."

"Good fer him," the very short Renegade named Stub nodded his approval.

"B-b-but wh-what did He s-s-say?" Mumbles wanted to know.

"The thief said, '*Don't you fear God, seeing you are in the same condemnation? And we indeed justly; for we receive the due reward of our deeds; but this man has done nothing wrong.*' And then the repentant thief looked at Jehesus and said, '*Jehesus, remember me when you come into your kingdom.*'"

"Now ain't dat just like a thief?" Pike spoke up. "He does one good thing, and then he's trying to get somethin' from Jehesus."

"Maybe so, Peck," Eldan answered, "but listen up. The best part of this story is what Jehesus said back to him. Jehesus said, '*Truly, I say unto you, today shall you be with me in paradise.*'"

"What?" Muckly exclaimed, voicing all of their thoughts. "That sounds like Jehesus was gonna take the thief to the good place with Him!"

"That's exactly what He did," Eldan assured them.

"B-b-b-bu-bu-bu . . ."

Stub held up a hand, cutting off the excited Mumbles, and said, "But the guy was a thief!" Mumbles and the others nodded their heads vigorously in agreement.

"That's the way Jehesus is," Eldan explained. "He loves thieves as much as He loves everyone else, and if they are willing to admit they are thieves and want to change, He is happy to have them in His family. Any person who is ready to give up being their own boss and is willing to make King Jehesus the lord and ruler of their lives will be fully and completely accepted into the Maker's family. That goes for each of you, too." As Eldan glanced around the circle of Renegades, he noticed shocked expressions and open mouths.

"Hurrrumph!" grunted the big Renegade, breaking the silence.

"Thug, you took the words right out'a my mouth," agreed Buzzard.

The sun was still shining through the trees in the west when Savin came trotting up to the hollow tree.

"Over here, Savin!" Rush called from the brush just to the north of the trail. "We've been expecting you."

Savin stood there with his hands on his knees taking some deep breaths. Finally he straightened up. "The Caravan is making good time. They should be arriving here in less than an hour."

"Did Jay tell you about Pike and his bunch?" Rush asked.

"Yeah, he did," Savin returned. "That's just unbelievable!"

"Yep," Rush agreed, "it is hard to believe. But when the Maker starts workin' on folk's hearts, you never know what He'll do."

Rush sent Hawthorn back up the hollow tree to relieve Little Snide, who was guarding the opening into the tree cave. While the young Renegade was descending the tree, Rush and Savin joined the Makerians in a time of prayer to ask the Maker to bless and lead the work of sharing the good news about Jehesus with the Larkin clans.

Rush then turned and called all of them together. "Gather 'round fellers! Based on what Savin told us, the Larkin caravan should be here in less than half an hour. That means that all you Makerians and all you Renegades need to do the traveler's dance an' get on outta here afore the rest of our people get here."

"Hurrrumph!" This sound came from a rather irritated-looking Thug.

"What's he all hot and bothered about, Buzzard?" Rush asked when he saw the look on the big Renegade's face.

"Well," began Buzzard, "he's a bit miffed that we keep being referred to as *Renegades*. We's done made it clear as air that we're through bein' Renegades, an' it's o-fensive to keep hearin' that name applied to us'ns!" Thug and the other former Renegades nodded in agreement.

"Well, all right," Rush returned. "What do ya want us to call ya?"

"Red and Chummy keep talking to us about becomin' Gooders," Pike spoke his thoughts, "but we're all such a rough an' rowdy bunch that I don't think we could fit in. Red could probably give us Gooder lessons, but you can't polish a dirt clod, if you know what I mean." This was met with more nods of agreement.

"Ya know," Muckly added, "we're kinda our own group."

"Red's about the only one who could put up with us for very long," Stub agreed.

"Well then, why don't you call us *Red's Rowdies?*" Pike suggested. Nods of approval from Pike's companions told Rush and the others that the decision had been made.

"Why, Perk ol' buddy," Eldan said with feeling, "I'm honored!"

"All right then," Rush barked. "Now that we've got that settled, would you newly dubbed Rowdies be so kind as to join our Makerian friends and get yer grimy carcasses outta sight before the Larkin caravan gets here?"

"Now yer talkin'!" Buzzard laughed as he and the others grabbed their weapons and packs.

Tobin then gathered all of the Makerians and Red's Rowdies and marched them down the trail in the direction of the Steps.

When the Larkin caravan did arrive, the leaders only allowed the clan a short rest and then pushed on. With a Renegade army that close and intent on attacking them, all of the Larkin warriors were anxious to get their families into the safety of the Steps. They had gotten an early start for that very reason, and the hope was that the caravan would reach the stronghold of the First Clan before it got completely dark. Several of the Larkin warriors relieved Rush, Savin, and Hawthorn in guarding the trapped Renegade army. The Renegades were not to be released until word was sent back to the Larkin guards that all of the traveling clans were safe at the Steps.

This last stage of the trip proved to be uneventful, to the relief of all those in the caravan. The sun had set, and the day was fast fading as they marched along the bank of the swift creek leading to the three-step waterfall which contained the small opening to the cave that was the ancestral home of all the Larkin.

For the last hour Hawthorn had been constantly searching the woods for Carineda and her two Makerian friends. As the Larkin traveled up the path, marching past the first two waterfalls, Hawthorn began to get concerned that something may have happened to the Makerians who were supposed to meet them.

It was twilight when Hawthorn and his family reached the top of the trail that was on the level of the uppermost of the three waterfalls. Up ahead Hawthorn could see that those in the caravan had made the turn and were following the path that led along the ledge behind the cascading water. There was a lot of cheering and excited shouting as the tired but happy people celebrated their arrival at the Steps. Hawthorn was watching all of this when suddenly he heard a voice at his elbow.

"These certainly aren't still waters, are they?"

"Cari!" Hawthorn whispered excitedly. "I was wondering if your team was gonna' make it or not."

"We thought we would wait until it started to get dark before we made the attempt to join you," Carineda answered.

"You timed it perfectly," said Hawthorn. "Everybody in the caravan is so excited about getting to the Steps that nobody noticed you and your friends."

"So, Thorn, aren't you going to introduce me to your mother?"

"Oh, yeah! Hey, Mother, I want you to meet . . ."

Hawthorn never got to finish. As soon as Rose saw the young lady standing beside her son wearing the same type of scarf around her neck that Rush had given Rose, she pushed past Hawthorn and threw her arms around Cari's neck.

"I told you," Hawthorn said to Carineda as he noticed her smiling at him.

"Rose," Savin whispered into his wife's ear, "we must keep moving, or we will look suspicious."

Finally Rose pulled back but held on to Carineda's arm. "I have wanted to give you that hug for two years!" she whispered to Cari.

The three disguised Makerians joined Savin's family as they blended into the happy crowd of Larkin filing along the rock ledge behind the waterfall leading to the entrance to the Steps. The rushing water roared over the ledge of rock above their heads and formed a wall on their right as it crashed continually down to the creek bed below. It was almost dark now as they entered the passageway of the entrance to the Larkin stronghold. Torches had been lit and placed in holes along the rock wall on their left to provide light for the arriving pilgrims. The millions of tiny water droplets covering the wall as well as the misty droplets in the air shimmered in the torchlight like so many diamonds. Even those who had made the trip many times before were amazed at the gorgeous luminescent display.

After walking over a bow shot along this ledge, they arrived at the small rectangular opening in the limestone wall which was the actual entrance to the Steps. Guards and some of the Shaman stood near the entrance, both to protect and to welcome the newcomers. Cari felt a nervous flutter in her stomach as she approached the welcoming committee, but when her turn came to enter, she smiled and nodded thanks to each of the Shaman and guards in turn. She quickly followed Rose and their family through the entrance and down the torch-lit, sloping passage that led into the fortress. She had only taken six steps when she found herself in a very large chamber with a low ceiling. There was a crowd of excited people in this area, all laughing and talking.

Cari started to panic when she found herself in the middle of the crowd of unfamiliar faces, but then suddenly to her left she spotted Rose's shawl and quickly moved to join them. As she pushed her way through the happy throng, she had to move past several of the robed Shaman. Nervously she dropped her head and kept moving. Suddenly she ran right into the chest of a young Larkin who was standing in front of her.

"Oh, I'm terribly sorry!" she exclaimed as she looked up at the person she had bumped against.

"It's all right," the young Larkin answered. For a moment their eyes met, and in that instant Cari recognized the face. It was Polk.

CHAPTER TWELVE

THE SLUMBER PARTY

"**A** ROTTED LOG!" Eldan exclaimed with a disgusted look on his face.

Eldan, Tobin, and Pike were standing on a wooded slope overlooking the upper waterfall of the Steps. In front of them towered a massive decaying log which had fallen across the face of the hillside years before.

"Maybe you didn't understand the plan, Perch. But while brother Tobs and I were getting our people on the mission team secretly connected with our Larkin friends entering the Steps, you and the rest of the Rowdies were supposed to find us a nice safe place to camp out close by for the next ten days."

"That's what we did, Red," Pike returned defensively. "This log will work great. We'll just crawl underneath this front edge. It's mostly dry, and if we move back far enough, there's an open area where the rain won't hit us if we have a shower."

"But a rotted log!" Eldan tried again. "It's nasty under that thing, Punk, and it stinks! There's no telling what's living back under there!"

"You Gooders sure are squeamish," Pike observed. "Now listen, Red. You gave us the job of findin' a camp site, and we found one. Me and my mates camp in places like this all the time."

"Why does that not surprise me?"

"Besides," Pike continued, "it's just about dark, and we ain't got time to find somethin' more fittin' to yer delicate constitution. Now cinch up yer britches an' quit bein' so prissy!"

Turning to his brother, Eldan gave an imploring look and a deep sigh. Tobin's answer was a shrug of his shoulders. Resigned to their fate, the two Makerians each pulled out a light stick and dropped to their knees, following Pike as he crawled under the dank-smelling, rotted log to the place where the others were waiting for them.

They made their way to a place where a section of the underside of the log had rotted and fallen off, leaving a small space in which they could almost stand. As they entered the area, Eldan pulled himself erect and immediately smushed his head into the underside of the log. As it turned out, it didn't cause him any pain at all since his head sank to his ears into the soft decaying surface.

"Nasty, nasty, nasty!" Eldan yelled as he quickly extricated his head and began hopping around, trying to brush the decayed bits of log and mold out of his mop of red hair.

Amused chuckles burst from the Rowdies who were lying about and making themselves comfortable on the pile of spongy, rotted log litter and mold that had covered the ground under the log. When Eldan had finally calmed down, he and Tobin used their light sticks to get a better look at their new home. Above them, the bottom edge of the log was a honeycomb of moist bore holes and worm tunnels. The thought of something crawling out of one of those holes and falling on him during the night made the little hairs on the back of Eldan's neck stand up. Eldan then scanned the decaying material underneath them. "There's no way I'm laying down on this stuff," Eldan whispered to his brother. "I'm getting me a leaf to lie on. You want one?"

"Yep," was Tobin's one-word reply.

As Eldan was out searching for a leaf for each of them, Tobin went around to find out how much food they had with them. He approached each of the Rowdies with his light stick and had them open their packs to show him what food they possessed. The results of his inventory were disappointing. "You fellas are each down to your last piece or two of dried fruit," Tobin announced. "What in the world were you planning on doing for food?"

"We each had three days' worth of food when we left on our scoutin' detail," Pike explained. "That was just about three days ago."

Tobin was thoughtful for a moment. Finally he said, "We should be okay for tonight. If we pool what's left in your packs with all the food that Eldan and I brought with us, we should be able to feed all nine of us this evening. But we'll need to spend tomorrow searching for something to eat."

As Tobin was explaining the food situation to all of them, Eldan returned, dragging two elm leaves with him. Eldan curled his nose up involuntarily as he had to walk on his knees in the soft moldy debris under the log to get the leaves in position. Piled on top of both leaves was a small mound of dried grass to be used as bedding material. Eldan drug the two leaves to the back edge of the rotted log and placed them in the driest spot he could find.

Tobin had Stub and Mumbles gather together all of the food from everyone's packs and then divide it equally among each of them. It wasn't much, but it was enough to get their stomachs to stop growling. When their meager meal was finished, Tobin put Pike in charge of security and had him assign each of them their guard duty for the night. Pike divided them into three watches with three guards in each watch. Buzzard, Thug, and Little Snide were to take the first watch. Then after about three hours, Eldan, Pike and Mumbles were to take over. Tobin, Stub, and Muckley were to take the last watch.

Tobin called Little Snide over and handed the youth his light stick. He then opened his pack and began going through it until he found his spare one. "Hey, Eldan, pull out your extra light stick. We'll give each of the guards one to have on hand in case they need it during the night.

"When the second watch comes on duty," Tobin said, addressing the rest of the group, "you fellas on the first watch hand them the light sticks. Then you second watch guys hand them off to the fellas on third watch. When you use them, don't hold the light in front of your eyes, or the brightness of the light will keep you from seeing past it. Hold it below your eyes or to the side."

It took Pike several minutes to get the first guards positioned like he wanted them. He placed Little Snide almost a stone's throw to the left of where they were camped. He put Buzzard about the same distance to their right. Thug was positioned out in front, close to the front edge of the log. With the guards set, Pike strolled out from under the log to look up at the night sky. He saw that a thick bank of clouds had blown in, obscuring the moon and the stars.

"You'll have to do most of yer watchin' with yer ears tonight, Thug," Pike informed his large friend. "There's heavy clouds tonight, and it's gonna be extra dark."

Thug grunted a response and nodded his head.

"Just stay alert and keep yer ears open," Pike returned. "I'll go tell the others." After checking with Buzzard and Little Snide once more, Pike returned to the camp and let the rest know what he had observed.

With nothing else to do, those who weren't standing guard made themselves as comfortable as possible. Wiggling down into the deep, spongy, mold-covered material that made up the floor of their rotted log lean-to, they each readied a nest for themselves and one by one dropped off to sleep—all except Eldan and Tobin. With a chorus of snores emanating out of the darkness all around them, they both lay there, trying to will themselves to go to sleep. Suddenly a few small pieces of rotted debris fell down on Eldan's face. Jerking up into a sitting position, he began frantically brushing and spitting away the bits of decayed material. "Just look at the mess you've gotten us into, Tobs!" Eldan whispered angrily in his brother's ear.

"Me!" Tobin whispered back. "What did I do?"

"We could have been spending the night in a nice dry cave or in some warm abandoned squirrel's nest, but nooooooo! You had to ask Pinch and his bunch of bottom-feeders to find us a camp site."

"Quit griping and go to sleep, Eldan," Tobin snapped. "It's just for tonight. We'll find something better tomorrow."

"How do you know we'll even BE here tomorrow, Tobs? What if while we're residing in the Fungus Inn a whole army of hungry grubs slides out of those hundreds of holes over our heads and eats us in our sleep? Answer me that, oh Wise One!"

"If they eat you in your sleep, Eldan, then both of our problems are solved. You won't be here anymore, and I won't have to listen to you!"

"You're heartless, Bubs! Absolutely heartless! Instead of lying over there thinking only of yourself, you should be concerned with protecting your poor little brother, who's over here in the darkness wallowing in a sea of rot and mold with a horde of hungry grubs and worms hovering over his head, just waiting for him to close his eyes so they can pounce on him!"

"It's not the worms and grubs that you need to be worried about, Eldan," Tobin shot back in an angry growl. "What you really need to be worried about is what I'M going to do to you if you don't clam up and GO TO SLEEP!"

"Heartless," Eldan mumbled to himself, "absolutely heartless."

It took some time, but they both did fall into a restless, fitful sleep.

Almost two hours later a roll of thunder announced the beginning of a heavy rain. The same time that the rain began to fall in earnest, a scream rang out from the guard on the far left.

"Eeyiiiii! Oh, help! Oh, help! It's a spider, and it's a big one! Somebody help! Somebody pray!"

"Hold yer ground, Little Snide!" yelled Buzzard. "We's a commin'!

"Roust out, you lazy varments!" Buzzard yelled at his sleeping companions. "Fight's on!"

Before the words were out of his mouth, the rest of them were grabbing weapons and moving towards the threat.

The heavy rain had driven the large brown spider to seek shelter under the log. The unsuspected confrontation with Little Snide startled her at first, but the fierce insect decided to fight rather than be forced back out into the storm. Bellowing its roar, the spider showed her fangs and moved forward. Her appearance was terrifying in the greenish glow of the light sticks. By now all of the warriors had joined the guards, and with loud yells and threatening gestures, they were attempting to scare off the large creature, but she continued to move towards them.

"Try throwing something at it!" yelled Pike.

"There ain't nothing to throw!" Muckly yelled back, picking up a piece of spongy wood below him.

"Back up! Back up! Here it comes!"

The spider, annoyed with its lack of progress, began lunging forward, snapping at her antagonists with her fangs.

"Somebody use their bow on that critter!" Pike called out.

159

"That won't work!" Tobin called out. "The arrows won't stop it, and as riled as it is now, arrows will aggravate it enough to make it charge us. Just hold your positions. I've got a plan.

"Eldan," Tobin continued, addressing his brother, "grab some of that dry grass you're using as bedding and twist it up good and tight." Tobin then grabbed his own bow and removed the bowstring. When Eldan handed him the thick roll of twisted grass, Tobin began wrapping it around one end of his bow. "Pull out your fire stones, Eldan. We've got to light this up!"

"I'm way ahead of you, Bubs," Eldan replied. He jerked open his pack and pulled out a piece of flint and a heavy stone with rust on it. Quickly he began to strike the two rocks together. As he did so, a shower of sparks burst from the stones and fell on some of the dried grass just below him. Almost immediately Eldan saw the edges of some of the grass starting to glow red as the continuous shower of sparks ignited it. Blowing gently on this, a flame suddenly shot up. Grabbing his bunch of burning grass, Eldan extended it so that Tobin could apply his improvised torch to the flame. When it caught, Tobin yelled for everyone to get out of his way, and he began hurrying towards the spider.

The approaching flame and its accompanying heat surprised the spider, and she started to draw back. The creature had only taken a few steps backward when she felt rain spattering against her legs. At that point, she decided to renew her attack.

"We need more torches!" Tobin yelled over his shoulder.

"Quick!" Eldan yelled, "use this dry grass to twist around anything you can use for a torch."

As he said this, Eldan followed Tobin's example and twisted a bunch of grass around his own bow. Crawling over to his brother, Eldan lit his torch from Tobin's.

AN UNWELCOME VISITOR

Now the spider was confronted by two dancing flames. When she moved toward one, the other torch would dart in and sear her leg or side. Within a few moments, two more of the painful fire sticks appeared in front of her. As she stopped her attack to consider how to deal with this new dilemma, three more of the fiery enemies appeared. She tried another attacking lunge and got burned in three places at the same time. Conceding defeat, the irritated creature turned and dashed back out into the rain. A cheer of both excitement and relief went up from the defenders when they saw the spider retreat.

As the victorious Rowdies celebrated, several of the burning torches bumped against the underside of the rotted log, and the flames licked up into several of the holes above them. Suddenly a chorus of high-pitched shrieks was heard coming from overhead, and instantly swarms of scorched and terrified roaches, water bugs, and crickets began to pour down on the defenders and scurry out into the rainy darkness. The cheering turned into bedlam as the Rowdies and Makerians found themselves bowled over and trampled by the escaping herd of panicking insects.

When the bug stampede was finally over and all the screaming and yelling began to subside, everyone began to pick themselves up and check for injuries. Just about everyone was scraped, scratched, and bruised, and many had torn tunics and leggings, but surprisingly, no one was seriously hurt.

Eldan raised himself up to a sitting position from where he had been overrun by the fleeing bugs. "You see, Tobs? You see?" Eldan growled as he pulled a water bug that had attached itself to his tunic off his chest. "I told you this would happen! But did you listen to me? OH NO! Instead of taking heed to my prophetic warnings, you chose to disregard them. Oh, foolish, foolish Bubsy! Be sure your sins will find you out!"

"Eldan!" Tobin snapped as he lay on the ground, brushing dirt and bug droppings off his tunic, "I'm in no mood for this!"

The rain was really pouring down now, and they noticed that the ground under the log was getting wet. Suddenly a small river of water began to flow over the top of the log from where the pouring rain on the hill behind them was cascading down.

"Wif' so much rain, all da' water is startin' to seep under da' back side of da' log," Stub announced.

"How are we gonna sleep?" Little Snide asked with concern.

"You prob'ly ain't gonna get much sleep tonight," answered Stub. "You can try sittin' on yer pack and leanin' over with yer head on yer knees. You might get a little sleep that way."

"I sure do feel sorry for all you mud puppies," Eldan said loudly as he stretched himself out on his leaf, "It's a shame you don't have a nice dry leaf on which to bed down. Yessiree, a little forethought could have saved you fellas a night's sleep."

"Red, you're pushin' it!" Pike warned with an irritated growl.

"He, he, he," chuckled Eldan. "Now don't get your feathers ruffled, Pock. This was your choice of a campsite, remember? I'm just trying to make the best of it. Hey! Who's moving my bed?"

The leaf on which Eldan lie began to suddenly rise with the ground underneath it.

"Watch out, everyone!" Tobin called. "The ground's giving way!"

With a gushing surge, muddy water belched from the bottom edge of the rotted log and rushed down the slope, carrying Eldan with it.

"Aiiiiieee!" Eldan screamed as he gripped the sides of his leaf and was launched out into the downpour.

All of the others had heard Tobin's warning and managed to escape the flood. They ran to the sides as the water burst from under the log just at the low spot where Eldan had put his leaf.

"RED!" screamed Little Snide. "We've got to go find him!"

"Humph!" grunted Thug.

"Thug's right, you know," Buzzard called out over the roar of the water and the storm. "As hard as it's raining, whoever goes out there is gonna get washed away, too."

"But we can't just leave him!" Little Snide yelled back.

"We will have to wait until the rain slacks off before we can try to help Eldan," Tobin announced.

"Can't we do anything for him now?" Snide called back, almost in tears.

"Yes," Tobin answered with confidence, "we can pray for him."

So right there in the darkness with the storm raging, Tobin led all of them into the presence of the all-powerful Maker, and they cried out for Eldan's safety.

It was another quarter of an hour before the storm began to ease up. When Tobin felt that it was safe to venture out, he draped his leaf around himself and went out into the steady rain. He returned shortly, dragging two more leaves. "Two of you wrap up in these, and you can help me search."

"But we all want to help," Muckly called out.

"We'll bring back more leaves," Pike said as he and Mumbles covered themselves in the leaves Tobin brought in. "Then we can all look for him."

It was a grim procession that emerged from under the log a short while later. They each had a leaf wrapped around them for protection from the pelting rain drops that were still falling steadily. They spread out the four remaining light sticks along their line, holding them aloft so that those around them could use the light as well. Slowly they began to move down the slope through the woods, looking for evidence of their friend. They followed the newly formed river of runoff water that was now flowing out from under their log. They called Eldan's name as they worked their way closer and closer to the creek. Each step that they came nearer to the creek without finding their friend, the more disheartened the searchers became. They each knew that if the water had washed Eldan into the swollen, raging creek, then their friend was already dead.

The rain had almost stopped when the search reached the bottom of the slope, but there was still no sign of Eldan. The roaring of the swollen creek a short distance in front of them was almost deafening. As they moved out of the woods and drew near to the bank of the now fierce-flowing stream, they saw piles of mud and forest litter heaped beside the path of the flood waters that had carried away their friend.

As the grieving searchers approached the raging creek, they continued to desperately call Eldan's name. A movement in one of the debris piles caught Mumble's attention. Out of the dark shapeless mass of mud and muck, a greenish light began to emerge.

"Loo-loo-loo-loo-LOOK!" he yelled, pointing to the light.

Quickly the friends surrounded the huge pile of debris. "Eldan!" Tobin called.

"Red! Red! Are you in there?" Pike yelled.

"Little help," returned the muffled voice of their friend.

CHAPTER THIRTEEN

NEW FRIENDS

"Did he recognize you?" Hawthorn asked urgently as they hurried down one of the hallways set aside for living quarters.

"I don't think so," Cari returned. "He only saw me for a second, and then I dropped my head and hurried after you."

"But you recognized him," Savin spoke his thoughts, "so we have to assume that he might have recognized you. Or if he didn't remember you at the time, he certainly may recall where he had seen you once he thinks about it for a while."

"Well, we can't do anything about it now," Cari said with resignation. "I'm here, and the mission hasn't changed. I'll just have to be extra careful."

"We will have to come up with some disguises for you when you go out," Rose suggested.

They had been following a stream of pilgrims from Clan Three down the long, wide passageway. Finally they came to a spacious, room-like area that was to be their home for the next ten days. Savin led their group past the families setting up their beds and living areas to the back of the chamber.

Using some sticks and curtains that they had brought with them, Savin, Hawthorn, Sagamore, and Noblis quickly had the three tent-like structures erected which were to serve as privacy and sleeping areas. It was decided that Rose and Cari would stay in one, Savin and Hawthorn in another, and Noblis and Sagamore would use the third one.

By this time everyone in the Third Clan was exhausted from their extremely long day and hard march. After a supper of dried meat and fruit, they all quickly found their sleeping mats. Sagamore and Noblis took turns through the night at the opening of their privacy area, watching for signs of problems.

The next morning the rhythmic booming of the clan drum echoing through the caverns and tunnels of the Steps stirred the inhabitants to wakefulness and informed all that the weather was clear and that the sun was climbing into the sky. Shortly after the throbbing cadence ended, the Larkin began to emerge from their compartments to begin their morning chores.

Most of the tunnels and passageways in the Steps were illuminated by oil lamps contained in box-like structures made of clear mica sheets glued together by resin. These lamps were placed on rock ledges or suspended from hooks carved out of the limestone walls of the cave. Each morning and each evening the lamps were taken down and refilled with plant oils, and the wicks were replaced or trimmed. Some of the larger caverns and chambers in the First Clan's home were lit by torches which were placed in sockets cut into the chamber walls.

When someone entered the Steps through the entrance behind the waterfall, they would descend a short, sloping, narrow tunnel which opened into a wide chamber with a low ceiling. It was known by the members of the First Clan as the Gathering Room. It was primarily used simply as a place for the guards to meet and organize their details, or for hunting and food gathering parties to assemble as they prepared for their tasks. If, after entering the Steps, one stood in the middle of the Gathering Room and looked straight ahead, a tunnel could be seen leading deeper into the Larkin stronghold. But to the left and right were two other passageways, each leading to large open areas which were normally used for storage but which were now cleaned out and were being used as temporary living areas for the visiting Larkin clans.

Clans Two and Three were sharing the wide chamber on the left of the Gathering Room, and the Fourth and Fifth Clans were to have the now empty storage area on the right. The report that was circulating among the Larkin in the Third Clan was that all three of the remaining clans should be arriving today to fill these newly prepared living areas.

There had originally been seven clans of Larkin, each the decendents of the seven sons of Larkin the Great, but over the years tragedy had reduced their numbers. The Sixth Clan had been destroyed by a terrible Renegade attack a century in the past. Also, the Seventh Clan had been so devastated by disease over thirty seasons ago that the few of them who survived were just incorporated into the Fifth Clan.

"Thorn, I need you to come over here a moment."

Hawthorn was sitting on an upturned bucket and was finishing the hot porridge that his mother had prepared for their breakfast when he heard his father's voice. Savin was sticking his head out of the opening of the tent-like sleeping area his mother and Cari had used. Setting down his bowl, Hawthorn walked over to his father, who with a subtle nod of his head indicated that Hawthorn was to follow him into the small chamber.

"What's going . . . Oh . . . uh, who's this?" Hawthorn stood inside the small sleeping cubicle with his father and mother. Sitting on one of the mats in front of him was a mysterious young Larkin with a familiar-looking knitted cap pulled down low on his head.

"Can't you tell?" a smiling Rose asked her son.

"It's me, silly," Cari said as she lifted the front edge of her cap.

"Wow!" Hawthorn laughed. "What a great disguise! Where did you get the clothes?"

"Actually," Rose spoke up, "they're some of yours. Carineda and I just needed to make a few adjustments to them so they would fit her."

"Now if Poke starts looking for you," Hawthorn said his thoughts out loud, "he'll be looking for a girl, but you'll be looking like a boy."

"He may already be looking for her, Son," said Savin. "He and one of the Shaman came into our living area just a few minutes ago. They started going by each of the family groups up by the entrance to our cavern, and they're working their way toward us."

"Cari's new outfit should fool them," Hawthorn observed.

"I doubt it, Son. Our clan is the only one in here right now, and Poke knows everyone in our clan. If he sees someone he doesn't recognize, male or female, he's going to get suspicious."

"So what do we do?" Hawthorn asked with concern.

"The rest of the clans should be arriving this afternoon," returned Savin. "We just need to keep our Makerian friends from being spotted until they get here."

"Don't you see?" Rose joined in. "When the other clans arrive, there will be plenty of Larkin whom Poke will not recognize, and the Makerians will just blend in with everyone else."

"So we just have to keep them hidden for today."

"That's right, Thorn," nodded Savin.

"Any ideas as to how we do that?" his son asked.

"Well, as soon I spotted Poke and the Shaman, I explained the situation to Noblis and Sagamore, and they crawled into that small opening in the bottom of the wall behind our sleeping cubicles."

169

Hawthorn carefully stuck his head out of the tent opening and stole a glace back behind the shelter. The low, small opening of which his father had spoken was now closed up by some rocks that the two Makerians had shoved in place after they had entered the crawlway.

"But what about Cari?" Hawthorn asked as he turned back to his father.

"I've noticed that there are a lot of people coming and going hauling water," Savin explained. "I thought you two could grab some buckets and go off to the pool to get us some, but just don't come back for a while."

"That's good," Hawthorn agreed. "If Poke is looking here, then I need to keep Cari someplace else."

"That will give me a chance to explore the Steps and learn my way around," Carineda added.

"Do you remember how to get to the pool?" Rose asked.

"I think so, Mother. But it really doesn't matter. We'll just wander around until we get there."

"All right then," Savin announced, "you two grab some buckets and get out of here. Try not to come back until you hear that at least one of the other clans has arrived."

Hawthorn reached down and helped Cari to her feet; then both of them quickly stepped out of the sleeping area. Grabbing two empty buckets, he handed one of these to Cari. Hawthorn looked toward the entrance to the large room where they were staying and spotted Poke and the Shaman in intense conversation with some Larkin about halfway from the entrance.

"Cari," Hawthorn said in a low voice, "I think you should walk ahead of me. If Poke looks our way, you just keep walking. I'll try to keep his attention on me."

Obediently Carineda pulled her cap down, lowered her eyes, and started walking with a purpose toward the entrance at the far end of the room. Hawthorn let her get about eight paces ahead of him; then he followed. As they drew close, Poke did look toward them, and Hawthorn lifted his hand to wave at his friend. But as soon as Poke recognized him, Poke quickly averted his gaze. Hawthorn just shook his head sadly and kept walking.

When Hawthorn arrived in the Gathering Room, he found Cari waiting for him. "Do you think he noticed us?" Cari whispered.

"He noticed me," Hawthorn answered solemnly, "but he didn't want to. He didn't pay any attention to you."

"Your mother said that he blames all of you for his father's death."

"Yeah, he does." Looking into Cari's eyes, Hawthorn added. "He'll blame you, too, if he figures out that you're here.

"He was my best friend, Cari. I risked my life for him. I still would! And he hates me."

"I'll tell you what, Thorn," Carineda said with a smile. "Let's make Poke our special prayer project for the next ten days, and we'll see what the Maker will do.

"Now where do we go from here?"

Hawthorn turned left toward the main passageway located in the back of the Gathering Room. There were a few slight turns as they traveled down this short tunnel. Suddenly they found themselves standing in an enormous room with a very high ceiling, the center of which was shaped like a dome. This large room was lit by a number of torches that were resting in sockets carved into the rock wall. From the center of the domed ceiling far above, a small trickle of water fell into a large pond located in the center of the room.

"This is the Dome Room," Hawthorn announced. "This is the largest room in the whole cavern, although the Great Cathedral where the Shaman conduct all the religious ceremonies is really large as well. Water flows out of the top of this room all year round into this pond, which is the main source of water for the clan."

171

"If it flows all the time, why doesn't it flood the room?" Cari wanted to know.

"I've heard that there is a crack in the rock in the bottom of the pond that allows the water to drain out about as fast as it trickles in."

"So where do the people in the First Clan live?" Cari asked, looking around.

"If I remember correctly, the tunnels leading to the living quarters are over on the other side of the Dome Room."

Hawthorn led the way over to the right side of the great cavern until they noticed several openings in the rock wall. As Hawthorn was trying to decide which passageway might lead to the living areas, he suddenly saw a Larkin youth about his own age carrying a bucket and walking towards them out of one of the tunnels. Assuming that the youth was coming from one of the living areas, Hawthorn proceded to head into that tunnel, but before he could, the youth confronted them.

"You two must be from the Third Clan," the youth said with a friendly smile.

"Actually, we are," Hawthorn answered. "We got in last night. We need to get some water, so while we were out, my friend and I thought we would look around a little bit."

"Well, welcome to the Steps," said their acquaintance. "My name's Reed. What's yours?"

"My name is Hawthorn, and this is my friend . . . uh."

"You can call me Quince," Cari quickly broke in, speaking in a lower tone of voice.

"Uh, right," Hawthorn spoke up. "It's good to meet you, Reed. We were wondering if this was the passageway that leads to some of the First Clan's living areas."

"Indeed it does, friends," Reed answered, "and if you'll wait here for two shakes and let me fill my bucket, I'll come back and show you around."

Hawthorn and Carineda stood there watching as Reed trotted off to the pond to hurriedly collect his bucket of water. Finally Hawthorn turned and looked at Cari. "Quince?"

Cari just shrugged her shoulders. "It was all I could think of."

True to his word, Reed returned quickly, lugging his now-full water bucket. "Come on. I'll show you where I live."

"Let me help you with that," Hawthorn smiled as he reached over and grabbed one side of the bucket handle.

Reed took them down a short hallway and into a very large room lit by oil lamps with a high ceiling, though not nearly as high as the Dome Room. Many of the Larkin lived in cave-like living areas that were carved into the walls of the cave. There was even a second level of living compartments further up the walls that were reached by ascending steps cut into the rock that led up to a ledge from which one could reach the doors to these upper living areas. There were also a number of stone houses built in rows along the floor of the huge room, forming streets.

"Wow!" Carineda voiced her thoughts. "There are streets and everything in here!"

Reed led them to a modest stone house close to the middle of the room. "Wait here," he announced to his new friends as he disappeared through the doorway with his bucket. In a few moments he returned, and with him were two others.

"Mother, these are two new friends I just met. Their names are Hawthorn and Quince, and they're from the Third Clan.

"Guys," Reed said, turning to his new friends, "I want you to meet my mother. Her name is Holly, and this little squirt behind her is my sister Marigold."

Holly greeted the newcomers with tired but friendly eyes. Stepping from behind her mother, the energetic Marigold was quick to be included in the introductions.

"I wish my father were here to meet you," Reed added, "but he had to go out this morning with the escort detail to assist the other clans as they arrive."

"I'm sure we'll have a chance to meet him later," Hawthorn returned with a smile.

"Mother, I was going to ask if I could show my new friends around, but you look so tired today that I think I should stay here and help you."

"Nonsense, Reed," Holly responded, wiping her forehead with the back of her hand. "You go with your friends. I'll just finish baking this bread; then I'll rest for a bit."

Reed was reluctant at first, but his mother's insistence finally won out. The young Larkin led Hawthorn and Cari on a brief tour of the living area and then back out into the Dome Room.

"All of the tunnels that lead to the living areas, storage chambers, the Great Cathedral, and the special meeting rooms for the Shaman open into this huge chamber," their personal tour guide began. "You can go everywhere from here. Come with me."

Reed turned left and followed the front wall of the Dome Room around to the far left side of the cavernous room. As they approached the wall on this side of the room, they could see a rounded opening in the rock wall lit by torches on either side.

"Where does this go?" Cari asked.

"This passageway leads to the various living quarters of the Shaman, and a short distance beyond that, it leads to the doors of the Great Cathedral."

"Could we go see the cathedral, Reed?" Carineda said excitedly.

"No one is allowed down this passage unless the Shaman call the people to assemble in the cathedral. So if we go down there now, we'll get in trouble, but there will be several called assemblies during the next ten days. You'll get a chance to see it then."

"Is that all that's down there?" the Makerian girl wanted to know.

"No, there's actually a good bit more down that passageway. Somewhere behind the Great Cathedral is a tunnel that leads down to the Treasure Cave, and I've also heard that there are some prison cells down there, but I haven't seen any of that. I've never been back there. In fact, I don't know of anyone who has actually been back there except some of the Shaman."

At that moment they could see some robed figures moving toward them up the shadowy passageway. Reed turned and led them to the right. As they walked along the wall on that side of the Dome Room, they came to other passageways. They took the time to explore each of the tunnels to which they came. It proved to be an interesting day for Hawthorn and Cari. They found a number of storage chambers, a couple of large trash pits, and several rooms used specifically for the preparation or preservation of foods.

One long tunnel led to a wall with a wooden door built into it. Reed walked right up to the unlocked door and, taking one of the torches from the wall, he pulled open the door and invited Hawthorn and Cari in to explore. What they found amazed them. The room had a ceiling that was only about three Larkin high at the tallest place, but it was so long and wide that the torch would not illuminate all of it.

"Look at all of the mushrooms!" Carineda exclaimed. "I have never in my life seen so many!"

"This is one of the underground farms," Reed responded.

"I remember my father brought me to see one of these farm rooms when I was little," Hawthorn volunteered, "but I didn't remember where they were."

"You could feed every one of the Larkin clans with all of this food and probably never run out!" Cari returned.

"Did you say that there are other farm rooms beside this one?"

"There are two more," Reed answered. "They raise several different varieties of edible mushrooms and fungi."

"I remember some of them are delicious," Hawthorn added, "and I also remember that a few of them aren't so great."

Carineda turned and gave Hawthorn a curious look.

"The grilled mushroom steaks are really good," Hawthorn answered her unasked question, "but if you have a choice whether to eat the spore soup or not . . . don't."

"I would agree with that," Reed said with a laugh.

When they found the tunnels that led to some of the other the living quarters, their guide led them right in. They nodded greetings to several of the Larkin in the First Clan whom they passed on their way. Reed took the time to introduce them to several of his friends and family members. As they stood there visiting with one of Reed's cousins, a friend of his came trotting up, breathing hard.

"Hey, Reed!" the newcomer called out breathlessly.

"What's wrong, Bergie?"

"Your father's back, and he sent me to find you," the young Larkin blurted out, still trying to get his breath. "Your mother's real sick, and they need you now!"

Reed instantly shot from their presence, sprinting up the tunnel the way they had come. Still lugging their empty buckets, Hawthorn and Cari hurried after him. When they rushed out into the expansive Dome Room, they quickly scanned the area.

"There he goes!" Cari called as she pointed toward the sprinting figure of their new friend as he darted into a tunnel in the distance. Running as fast as they could with their burdens, they entered the same tunnel and raced on. Once they arrived in the main living area, it took them a few moments to remember where Reed's home was located. They finally recognized it only because little Marigold was sitting by the doorway crying.

"How bad is she, Marigold?" Cari asked as she knelt beside the young girl.

"I don't know," the girl cried. "She's real hot and weak. She can't stand up."

"Would you ask your father if I could see her?" Cari asked. "I know a lot about treating sickness."

"Father's not here," Marigold shot back.

Just then the curtain covering the doorway pulled back, and an older lady stepped out. "I overheard your request," the older lady spoke, looking down at the disguised Carineda. "That is very kind of you, young sir, but her husband Chirt has gone for the Shaman. They will care for her."

"I really believe that I can help her," Cari persisted.

"That won't be necessary," the lady said with finality and turned quickly and disappeared into the dwelling.

Carineda looked at Hawthorn and sighed. Hawthorn shrugged his shoulders and looked down at the still weeping Marigold. "Then how about we sit here and keep you company until your father gets back?"

The two friends sat beside the young girl, consoling her for over a quarter of an hour, until Marigold suddenly jumped up and pointed up the lane. They saw a bearded Larkin hurrying toward them with a long-robed Shaman right behind him. Marigold ran to her father, who without missing a step scooped up the little girl and carried her quickly to the door of their dwelling. Holding the girl in one arm, he pulled back the curtain of the doorway for the Shaman to enter with the other and quickly ducked inside himself. Marigold gave Cari and Hawthorn a sad wave as the curtain fell back into place.

With nothing else to do, the two friends picked up their buckets and walked back toward the Dome Room. On the way out of the Larkin living area, they heard enough of the excited talk around them to understand that earlier in the afternoon the Second Clan had arrived and that the

Forth and Fifth Clans were marching in now. The two friends stopped by the pool in the middle of the Dome Room and filled their buckets with fresh water.

Hawthorn and Carineda left the pool and took the passageway that led into the Gathering Room to watch the other clans arrive. They actually could not get very far into the smaller chamber due to the great crowd of people. Most of the new arrivals were milling around excitedly, irregardless of the efforts of a delegation from Clan One to get them to keep moving into the cleaned out storage chambers to the right that were to be their living areas for the next ten days. Everyone was too excited and having too much fun.

"The Second Clan should be setting up their huts and cooking places in our large living area by now," Hawthorn whispered in Cari's ear, "so it should be safe for us to go back."

"Why don't you go first, just to make sure?" Cari suggested. "I'll stand here and watch the crowds till you get back."

With a nod of agreement, Hawthorn picked up his bucket of water and started shoving his way through the crowd to get to the passageway leading to their huts.

Carineda watched as her friend pushed through the crowd. Just as she lost sight of Hawthorn's back, she saw another face she recognized moving towards her. It was Poke.

There was now twice as much activity in the living area since the Second Clan arrived. Weaving through the mass of newcomers, Hawthorn made his way to the back of the chamber where his family was located.

"Hey, Mother," Hawthorn said as he sat his water bucket down beside his mother, who was busy working on a stew for their supper.

"Oh, Son, I'm glad you're finally back with the water. I had to borrow some from our neighbors to start the stew."

Leaning down close to his mother and speaking softly, Hawthorn asked, "I left Cari out in the Gathering Room watching the incoming clans. I wanted to make sure it was safe before I brought her in."

"Safe?" Rose asked absently, still absorbed in her cooking.

"You know," Hawthorn prompted. "Are Poke and the Shaman still snooping around?"

"What? Oh, yes . . . I mean, no. They came by about midmorning while Rush was here and asked if we had everything that we needed for our stay. Your father spent several minutes talking with them. The Shaman seemed genuinely interested in our welfare, but the whole time they were talking, Poke was nosing around and looking in the huts. I was afraid he was going to notice that we had one more hut than our family needed. I guess Rush thought the same thing, because he suddenly announced that he was going to take a nap and walked past Poke and lay down inside the hut the two Makerians were using. When Poke tried to look in the hut, Rush invited Poke to join him. I guess Poke didn't care for that, and he and the Shaman left. That was about two or three hours ago, and since then I haven't seen them."

"So where're Father and Rush?" Hawthorn asked, looking around.

"Rush had been staying further up the cave toward the entrance," Rose answered, "but he decided that he had better move down here and stay with the Makerians in their hut in case Poke or the Shaman come back. He hasn't come back yet, so I guess he got caught helping some of the Larkin from Clan Two get moved in."

"What about Father?"

"Well, he was here until just a short while ago. He thought he had better go check on our Makerian friends. So he moved the rocks out of the way and crawled into the low tunnel behind the huts to go look for them. I hope they get back soon. Our soup will be ready shortly."

"Should I go after him?" Hawthorn asked.

"No, Dear. You go get Carineda."

With a nod Hawthorn turned and walked briskly toward the Gathering Room.

Less than a quarter of an hour later, Rose heard some scraping sounds nearby, and glancing over, she saw the head and shoulders of her husband emerge from the low hole in the bottom of the back wall. When he was squatting beside the small opening, he looked over at his wife with a questioning gaze. Rose slowly looked around and, seeing that no one was paying attention to them, she gave her husband a subtle nod. Savin leaned down and said something into the opening, and in a very short time, Sagamore and Noblis were standing beside Savin.

As Rose related her conversation with Hawthorn, they looked up and saw Rush walking toward them with an armload of bedding and supplies. After relating the new situation to the Makerians, they moved some of their things aside and made room for Rush in their hut.

Suddenly Hawthorn came running up breathlessly, "I can't find her!"

"You mean Carineda?" Savin asked with concern.

"Yes! Yes!" Hawthorn answered in a panic. "I went back where I left her and found her bucket, but she was nowhere around. I ran into the Dome Room and went back to some of the places where we went today, but I can't find her anywhere!"

CHAPTER FOURTEEN

THESE ARE NOT OUR PEOPLE

It took only a few minutes for the friends to organize a search party. They recruited Rush and Jay to help, putting one of the Makerians with each of them. Rose reminded each of them that Cari was dressed as a boy. Acknowledging this information with nods all around, the three pairs of searchers left quietly, trying not to draw any attention to themselves.

It was almost three hours later when Hawthorn and Savin returned to their huts. They found Jay and Sagamore already there, sitting with Rose. Hawthorn could tell by the looks on everyone's face that the news was not good.

"Has anyone seen her?" Hawthorn asked. The concern in his voice was obvious.

They all shook their heads in the negative.

"We've all been sitting here hoping that you fellas had better success," Jay voiced everyone's thoughts.

"Have you heard from Rush and Noblis?" Savin asked, looking at his wife.

"No," Rose answered. "I've been right here since everyone started searching, and no one's been back until Jay and his friend showed up right before you two."

"What are we going to do?" Hawthorn sighed.

"I'll tell you what you're going to do," Rose said firmly. "Each one of you is going to sit down and get a bowl of stew and some bread that I've fixed for you and get some strength back in you. Then we're going to pray about this." At the mention of food, Hawthorn suddenly realized that he had had nothing to eat since breakfast. Rose began serving up bowls of a little overly cooked stew along with a hunk of seed bread that was no longer warm. They were all lost in their sad thoughts as they ate their supper. When the bowls were empty, Rose collected them and announced, "We'll deal with these later. Why don't we pray first?"

The five of them crowded into one of the huts so that they could pray without being noticed by their neighbors. For the first few moments, the only sounds that were heard were deep sighs and a few whispered praises as they gathered into the very throne room of heaven. Finally Hawthorn spoke his thoughts. "Most High and Holy Maker," he began in a quiet but intense voice, "Father of King Jehesus, we come to you now because we are desperate for your help! We can't find Carineda, Lord, and we are very concerned for her. Please bring her back to us."

"Hey, everybody! I'm sorry I took so long to get back . . . Oh! Am I disturbing you?"

At the new voice, all five of the Larkin believers looked up and saw Carineda entering the doorway of the hut, followed by Rush and Noblis.

"Thank you, Lord!" Rose exclaimed, throwing up her hands. "I knew You would bring her back to us!"

"Cari, where have you been?" Hawthorn asked with concern. "We've been so worried about you!"

"I'll tell you in a minute, but first, is there anything to eat? I don't know about Rush and Noblis, but I'm really hungry!"

Rose offered to stir up the fire to rewarm the stew, but the three newcomers wouldn't wait. They ate cold stew and bread like it was the best meal they had ever had. In between mouthfuls of food, Rush explained that they had found Cari in the large cave that Clan Four and Five are using as a living area.

"She apparently spotted the other Makerians who had slipped in with Clan Four," Rush volunteered as he swallowed a large bite of seed bread. "That was the last place me an' Noblis had to search. It weren't no easy thing to do, neither, with two clans worth a' folks all millin' 'round in there. We took our time doin' it, 'cause we was tryin' to get a look at ever'body's face. We never did recognize Carineda, at least not at first. We'd been at it for a while when suddenly Noblis grabs my arm and whispers to me that he spotted the other Makerians on their mission team. They were sitting with a few other Larkin in a group. So we went over to make contact with 'em. That's when we found Carineda. She was sittin' right there with 'em."

"Why didn't you let us know where you were?" Hawthorn asked.

"I couldn't at first," Cari answered. "Right after you left, I looked up and saw Poke and his Shaman friend coming straight for me. I couldn't tell if he had recognized me or not, so I ducked my head and pushed into the crowd of people coming in. Eventually I found myself in the other large living area with all the people from the two newly arrived clans. I didn't know where Poke was, so I just kept moving. I was helping one of the families set up their hut when I spotted Jillia. She's one of the Makerians on Team Two. I decided that I would stay with them until I felt it was safe to come back here, but they got into a discussion about Jehesus with some friends of the believers they were with in Clan Four. I guess I lost track of time. I'm really sorry for causing all of you to worry about me."

"It's all right, dear," Rose said, giving Carineda a hug. "The Maker took care of you, and you're safe. That's all that matters."

It took several minutes of digging to extricate Eldan from the pile of mud and debris. When they did get him out, he was unrecognizable. He was plastered with black mud and hundreds of bits of leaves and bark pieces. There was only a small tuft of red hair poking through the mire which covered the young Makerian from head to foot.

By now the clouds were breaking up, and scattered beams from the moon began to illuminate the area around them. Tobin and several of the Rowdies helped Eldan to his feet and supported him as they led him to the bank of the creek. They found a washed out area of the bank that allowed Eldan to descend to the level of the water where he discovered a cluster of rocks that gave him some protection from the swift current of the swollen creek as he cleaned himself up.

"I guess we'll need to find us a new camp site," Pike said his thoughts out loud to Tobin as they waited for Eldan to finish washing himself. "I'll get the boys lookin' for something while you keep an eye on Red."

"NO!" a voice shouted from below the bank of the creek. Suddenly Eldan's mud-streaked face appeared above the rocks. "Thanks anyway, Pug, but that won't be necessary. Brother Tobs and I will find our next camp site."

"Well then, what are we supposed to do?" Pike returned with obvious irritation in his voice.

"Since the moon's out and you can see to find your way around, why don't you Rowdies try to find us a food source?"

After almost half an hour of washing and scrubbing, Eldan had most of the filth off. He was sopping wet and shivering in the cool night air when he climbed back up on top of the bank to join his brother.

"Are you okay?" Tobin asked.

"I-I-I'll b-be a l-l-lot bet-t-ter when we f-find a w-w-warm, dry p-p-place to s-s-sleep. L-let's g-g-get moving."

The two Makerians traveled a little further up the hill and slightly downstream from their first campsite to find the rocky, moss-covered outcropping of limestone that they had spotted earlier as they waited for the Larkin caravan to arrive. They hadn't searched the face of the rocky ledge for very long when they found an opening under a shelf of rock.

"This should do nicely," Eldan announced cheerfully. Though his clothes were still wet, the brisk hike through the woods had warmed him up, and he felt much better. "Let's go track down our underprivileged wards, Bubsey, and we'll show'em how civilized folks camp out."

Within an hour Eldan and Tobin returned to the small cave, and with them were Pike, Muckley, Little Snide, and Stub. Buzzard, Thug, and Mumbles were still out looking for food.

"Now THIS is a campsite," Eldan announced as he stood beside the cave opening, "—a veritable bastion of comfort and security."

"Have you checked it out?" Stub asked as he stepped into the opening, "cuz' it sounds like dere's sumpin' in dere."

"No worries, friends," Eldan returned, his wide grin spreading across his face. "I have the perfect cave-emptying plan. How about a few of you fellas grabbing some of those dry twigs and leaf litter from inside the mouth of the cave and following me'?"

Eldan led the procession a short distance away from the cave opening. After finding a level spot, he gathered all of the dry material and used his fire starting rocks to light a small fire. When he had burned enough materials that he had a collection of hot coals, he implemented his plan. Laying out a wet, dead leaf, Eldan placed a small amount of the dry material on top, and using two sticks as tongs, he set one of the coals on the pile.

"Now roll this up into a bundle and tie it closed with some vine. Toss it into the cave while I make another one," Eldan instructed.

Within a few minutes, the redheaded Makerian had several more of the fire bundles put together, and they, too, were being carried to the opening of the coveted grotto. As the last of the bundles were being tossed inside, they noticed smoke from the first bundles beginning to fill the cave. It wasn't long before a thick cloud of smoke was rolling out of the opening.

"Everyone better move back," Eldan announced. "Whatever is in there should be coming out real soon now."

Almost as soon as the words were out of Eldan's mouth, a lot of scratching and clicking noises could be heard back in the smoky darkness of the cave. Suddenly, with a wheezy roar, a large female scorpion came charging through the smoke and ran out into the night. Right behind her scurried five smaller versions of their mother.

"Good job, Red!" voiced Pike. "I'm glad we don't have to share the cave with that crowd of whiptails."

"It should be all cleared out now," Eldan announced proudly. "How about some of you fellas crawl in there and drag out what's left of our fire bundles? Then all we have to do is wait a little bit for this nice breeze to air out our cave."

"While we're waiting," Tobin added, "let's scout around and see if we can find some dry bedding material."

After searching for half an hour, they finally decided that the rain had soaked just about everything. As Eldan, Tobin, Pike, Muckly, and little Snide stood near the cave mouth waiting for the last of the smoke to be cleared away, they heard a call from the moon-lit shadows. "Hey, mates, look who I found!"

As they turned toward the sound of the voice, they saw the burly form of Stub approaching out of the shadows. Behind him stumbled Buzzard, Thug, and Mumbles.

WORM STEAKS

They appeared to be in a moving fight with a thrashing, snake-like creature.

"Help us out over here, fellas, before breakfast gets away," Buzzard yelled.

"What'd ya catch?" Muckly yelled back.

"Worm," Buzzard returned, "an' he's a biggun'! We can eat off him fer a week!"

"Oh, yes!" Little Snide exclaimed. "Earthworm steaks!"

Tobin and Eldan watched the others as they ran to help bring in the struggling worm. With a look of utter disgust, Eldan leaned over and spoke to his brother, "They eat earthworm steaks? Tobs, these are not our people."

The next day was officially the first day of the Great Gathering. At midmorning a deep booming drum cadence called everyone into the cathedral for the first of several assemblies that were to take place over the next ten days. Carineda was especially interested in this special event. Growing up at Stillwaters, she had heard about the Larkin assemblies but had never had a chance to experience one. What made it particularly interesting to her was that the secret prayer language that the Shaman used when they prayed to the Maker was the same language in which all of the ancient Larkin manuscripts were written, and it was also a language that all of the Makerians were taught to read and write. Of all the Larkin in the Great Cathedral, only the Shaman understood the words the Shaman spoke in their prayers to the Maker, but every Makerian in the room knew exactly what they said.

"So what did the Shaman actually say in their prayers?" Hawthorn whispered to Carineda as they followed the crowd back up the wide hallway after the end of the solemn assembly.

"Oh, they said the right things," Cari whispered back with an irritated look on her face. "They praised the

Maker and thanked Him for bringing everyone together. They asked Him to look with favor on all the activities of the next several days. They even asked Him to protect everyone when it was time to go home. They probably said *reveal to us your will* twenty times, but there was no genuineness."

"What do you mean?" Hawthorn asked.

"They said the words, Thorn, but you couldn't tell by the tone of their voice or the way they said it or by their facial expressions that they really wanted His will."

"You really can't judge their hearts, Cari," Hawthorn responded. "We don't actually know what they were feeling when they spoke their prayers."

"You are absolutely right, Thorn. I have no right to judge their hearts. But you would expect that, if someone were crying out to the Maker for His will and they really wanted to receive it, you could detect at least a little bit of passion, a hint of longing from one or two of the five Shaman who prayed. Did you notice any longing or desire in their voices?"

"To be honest," Hawthorn whispered his answer, "no, I didn't. But maybe that's the way they were all taught to pray. Just because they are products of their traditions doesn't mean that they don't have a genuine heart for the Maker. Remember, Cari, the only reason the Makerians exist is because three of the Shaman with pure hearts heard the truth and accepted it."

Carineda's eyes dropped toward the floor, and she laid her hand on Hawthorn's arm. "Please pray for me, Thorn. I'm not looking at the Shaman the way you do . . . the way Jehesus does. I desperately need His love for them."

By the time that Hawthorn and Cari had reached the Dome Room, they saw a small army of Larkin hurriedly setting up rows of tables in the middle of the large open chamber.

"What's all this?" asked Carineda.

"It's for the welcome feast," Hawthorn returned. "This is the first big feast that we'll have during the Great Gathering. The people of the First Clan have prepared a banquet for all of us in order to welcome us here."

"That's a lot of people to feed," Cari responded thoughtfully as she looked around at the crowd that was still leaving the Great Cathedral. "Isn't that going to be a big burden on the First Clan?"

"I guess it would be except that each of the other clans will host a feast for everyone before we leave." Hawthron gave Cari a big grin. "We eat well during these things."

As it turned out, Carineda had to agree with Hawthorn on that point. There were baskets full of fresh baked seed and pollen bread, steamed green briar shoots, hot roasted tuber cakes, hickory and pine nut pudding, glazed acorn meats, and many large platters of fish. Some of the fish was roasted, some was smoked, and some was dried and covered in spices and seasonings. Carineda also had to admit that the mushroom steaks were delicious. Hawthorn's mouth was so full of food that the only response he could make to her admission was a smile and an *I-told-you-so* nod. The special drink for the feast was cold sumac tea. The bright red berries from the sumac plant were soaked in large clay pots until the red tangy coating from the berries dissolved in the water. This was then sweetened with honey, and the result was very tasty.

Hawthorn was reluctant to drink it at first. "Isn't sumac poison?" he asked Carineda, who was sipping from her cup of the pinkish liquid.

"Poison sumac is," Cari returned as she lowered her cup, "but this isn't."

Hawthorn started once again to take a drink but stopped himself. "How do you tell the difference?"

"Poison sumac has white berries that hang down on the limbs. Smooth sumac has a slick bark and has bright red berries that point upwards on the ends of the limbs. Do you see the pink color of the drink? Well, that shows that it was made from the safe smooth sumac. It's also delicious, so if you're not going to drink yours, then give it to me."

Hawthorn needed no more encouragement. After his first taste, the young Larkin licked his lips thoughtfully and immediately drank half of his mug. "Why have I never had this before?" Hawthorn asked excitedly. "This stuff is amazing!"

"We make it at home sometimes," Cari answered, "but this is some of the best I've ever had."

Everyone took their time. With all of the eating and the visiting, the feast lasted almost three hours. When it was finally over and everyone was as full as could be, all of the clans pitched in to help clean everything up. Just as this work was being completed, Hawthorn saw Juniper approaching.

"Hey, Juni. Did you find enough to eat?"

"Oh, my! Oh, my!" Juniper returned, rolling her large eyes. "My tummy's so tight, it's a wonder I didn't pop my sash clean in two, an' that's a fact! Stars above! The last time I had that much food to eat was when Momma an' Aunt Fanny were tryin' to lose weight at the same time."

"Well good, Juni," Hawthorn returned, trying not to laugh. "I'm glad you enjoyed yourself."

Juniper looked around suspiciously and then leaned close to Hawthorn. "I don't mean to disappoint you, Thorn, but I didn't come over here just to visit," she whispered.

"You didn't?" Hawthorn returned softly.

"No. I need to find your friend from you-know-where."

"Oh, you mean Carineda."

Juniper nodded her head rapidly as she took another look around them.

"She's standing right here next to me, Juni," Hawthorn smiled and pointed to his Makerian companion.

191

Juniper stared hard into the face of the person standing beside Hawthorn, and after several moments, a large grin spread across her face. "Well, bless my buttons! Miss Carineda, is that you under all those boy clothes? Who'da thought it! I never dreamed that was you! Here I was thinking you might be some spy fella from the Shaman tryin' to steal our secrets, and then when I looked under that floppy cap of yours, who did I seek peakin' back out but Miss Carineda? Who'da thought it?"

"Hello, Juni," Cari laughed. "It's good to see you!"

"And you too, Miss Cari, but I'm not here on pleasantries." Again Juniper took a suspicious look around them. "I'm here on secret business," she whispered.

"What's going on?" Cari whispered back.

"I've been talking with a couple of friends of mine about the Maker and His Son, and they've started askin' me more questions than I can answer. Would you come an' help me talk to them? They're real interested, and I think there's a good chance that they might become believers."

"I would be happy to, Juniper, but are you sure that it's safe?"

"Well, about as near as I can be," Juni returned seriously. "They didn't come to me. I'm the one who brought up the idea to them. One of the girls I've known for a long time, and I trust her. The other one is a cousin of hers from a different clan, but she seems all right to me."

"Maybe I should go with you," Hawthorn suggested.

"No," Carineda was firm. "I trust Juniper's judgment about these girls, but if it is a trap, the fewer of us who get caught the better. I'll go with Juniper; you start praying."

"So, Red, how'd you like yer worm steak?" Pike asked as he patted his own full stomach.

192

Eldan paused for a moment, looking down on the remnants of the recently cooked meal, the majority of which was still lying on the leaf he had been using as a platter. "Well, Pudge, I can honestly say that that was the best worm I have ever eaten."

Pike nodded his agreement and walked over to join the others.

Once no one was looking, Eldan turned toward his brother, crossed his eyes, and puffed out his cheeks. Tobin, for his part, looked down at his own half-eaten worm steak and just shook his head sadly back and forth. "It's going to be a long ten days," Tobin muttered from behind his bright red beard.

"I know what we'll do!" Eldan said, voicing his thought. "You and I will volunteer for guard duty tonight. Then while our rowdy bunch of worm eaters are blissfully snoozing away, you and I will slip out of here."

"Eldan, you know we can't do that," Tobin protested.

"And why not?!" Eldan almost shouted.

"We would be leaving them defenseless. Without guards something could come along and eat all of them before they had any warning."

"Seriously, Tobs?" Eldan shot back. "They live under rotting logs! They eat worms! What self-respecting creature would possibly want to eat them?"

"We can't leave them," Tobin said with finality.

"All right, have it your own way. But mark my words, Bubs, if we live through this experience, you and I are both going to need a major purging after spending ten days eating worm steaks with these guys."

"It's daylight now," Tobin responded. "Maybe you can find us some seeds or fruit to eat."

Eldan stood up, eager to pursue his new assignment, when he and Tobin heard some noise behind them. They had both been sitting in the opening of the small cave that Eldan had found. As they turned and looked back into the cave to see the source of the noise, the morning light reflecting off the limestone walls revealed that the very short Rowdy named Stub was moving some of the debris in the back of the cave.

"Well, look at 'dis!"

Something was moving in the leaf litter next to where Stub was standing. As he bent down and picked up the struggling creature, they could hear a lot of hissing and angry snarls.

"What is it, Stub?" Little Snide called out excitedly.

"It's a baby whiptail," Stub answered, "an' he's hurt! His family must'a trampled 'im when they ran outta here last night. Neither one of his pinchers is workin' right, an' his stinger got broke off his tail."

By now Stub was standing in the opening of the cave, holding the furious creature in the light for all to see. Both front claws were broken and mangled. The little whip tail could grasp small things with his mangled claws, but he couldn't do much damage with them. Also, while the entire tail was still intact, the creature's venomous stinger on the end had been torn off.

As they crowded around to watch, they saw the young scorpion grabbing angrily at Stub's beard and snarling loudly. "Ahh, ain't he cute?" Stub smiled.

"W-w-what are y-y-you gonna' d-d-do with him?" Mumbles asked curiously.

"Well, he can't take care of hisself, hurt like he is," Stub reasoned, "so I figure I'll keep 'im."

"You can't keep a whiptail, ya bone head," Buzzard shot back.

Why not?" Stub countered. "Tobin's gots a bird an' a squirrel, so why can't I have a whiptail?"

Eldan rolled his eyes at his brother and said, "How can you argue with logic like that?"

By now the furious little creature realized that he wasn't getting anywhere with his deformed claws, so he began smacking Stub in the side of the head with the nub at the end of his injured tail. Every time the whiptail hit him, it made a *doink* sound.

"Hey, look!"

Doink, doink, doink.

"He likes me!"

Doink. . . snarl, hiss. . . doink, doink.

"So what are you gonna' name him, Stub?" asked the excited Little Snide.

"I been standin' here thinkin' 'bout dat . . .

Doink . . . snarl . . . doink . . . doink.

". . . and a name just came to me.

D*oink . . . doink.*

"I think I'm gonna call him *Doink*."

"That's a great name!" Little Snide returned enthusiastically. Then he turned to the angry whiptail. "Hey, Doink! Hey, little buddy!"

S*narl . . . snap.*

"Yeow!"

Snarl . . . snap, snap.

CHAPTER FIFTEEN

REALLY GOOD NEWS

Over the next two days, Hawthorn saw very little of his Makerian guests. Carineda and Juniper had been so successful in their discussions with Juniper's two friends that the two girls had wanted to include their families in the talks. At that point Carineda felt that it would be best to bring Sagamore and Noblis into the discussion as well.

From the reports he had heard, Hawthorn understood that the other Makerians on Team Two were being just as successful in establishing several of their own discussion groups with Larkin in some of the other clans. Much prayer was being offered by the believers for the success of these talks.

On the evening of the fourth day after their arrival at the Steps, Hawthorn was at the pool in the Dome Room filling his family's water buckets when he looked up and saw his friend Reed from the First Clan approaching carrying water buckets. "Hello there, Reed!" Hawthorn called cheerfully to his new friend. "Do you remember me? I'm Hawthorn from the Third Clan."

"Oh, hey," Reed returned sadly.

"What's wrong? Is your family okay?"

"No, they're not," Reed answered with tears welling up in his eyes. "Do you remember when we last met that my mother got sick?"

"Yes, I do," Hawthorn responded with concern. "How is she?"

"I think she's dying, Hawthorn." Reed could no longer conceal the tears. They were streaming steadily down both cheeks when he spoke again, "Over the past several days, the Shaman gave her a bunch of herbs, but it didn't help. This morning she's much worse, and when the Shaman came to look at her just now, they said that there was nothing more to do."

"Listen, Reed," Hawthorn began, "I have friend who is really good at treating sicknesses like your mother's."

"But what more can your friend do than the Shaman?" Reed cried.

"Maybe a lot," Hawthorn reassured his friend. "I'm going to go find her, and then we are both coming to your home. We will see what can be done."

Hawthorn lugged his heavy water buckets back to their living area just as fast as he could. Depositing the bucket, he took off the find Carineda. He knew the general area where the Makerians were having their talks about Jehesus, but even so, it took Hawthorn nearly half an hour to find them. After apologizing for interrupting their discussion, Hawthorn quickly explained to Carineda the desperate condition of Reed's mother. Without hesitation Cari jumped up and raced with Hawthorn back to their living area to grab two of her packs.

They were both sweating and breathing hard when they came trotting up to the stone house where Reed's family lived. Reed and his father were standing outside waiting on them.

"You told my son you could help my wife," Reed's father said bluntly with red swollen eyes. "What do you think you can do that the Shaman cannot?"

"I honestly don't know if I can help her or not," Cari said forthrightly, "but I have treated a number of severe fevers like hers before. Would it hurt just to let me look at her?"

The sad-faced Larkin thought on those words for a moment and then pulled the curtain back and allowed Carineda and Hawthorn inside. They followed Reed's father till they came to a back room where the sick lady was lying on a mattress full of thistledown. She was covered with two thick robes so that only her face was exposed. Carineda drew a lamp near so she could examine her. Carineda tried to talk to her, but she could only mumble incoherently. Reed's mother had brightly flushed cheeks which were very hot to Carineda's touch. Cari saw that her lips were dry and cracked and that her eyes seemed to be slightly sunken.

"She's way too hot!" Cari announced urgently. "The fever is cooking her! We must cool her down!" As she said this, Carineda began to yank away the heavy robes lying on top of the stricken lady.

"But the Shaman said to keep her covered!" the husband announced.

"They were mistaken," Cari returned confidently. "Hawthorn, I need Reed's bucket of water! We've got to get her fever down quickly!"

Hawthorn laid down the pack he was carrying and disappeared from the room. He had only been gone a moment when he swiftly returned with the water. Cari found an apron lying near the bed, and grabbing it, she plunged it into the bucket of cool water. She used the dripping apron as a wash cloth to bathe the fevered lady's face, arms, and legs.

"Sir Chirt," Carineda called to Reed's father standing near the foot of the bed, "can you find two more towels that you and Hawthorn can use to help me cool her down?"

Without answering, Chirt quickly left the room, returning momentarily with a towel and a woven shirt. Tossing the towel to Hawthorn, they both soaked them in the water and began to wipe down Holly's limbs and face. Not satisfied with the results, Carineda began to wring out her wet apron over the body of the sick lady, soaking her dress. After doing this for several minutes, Holly gave a faint moan.

"Now fan her with your towel, Thorn, while I try to get her to drink some water."

The bathing and the fanning continued as sip by small sip, Cari was able to get cool fluids past those parched lips. After repeating this process again and again for almost an hour, Cari finally stopped to check on her patient. Bending down and laying her cheek against Holly's, she stood there for a moment. Finally she stood back up and smiled at Chirt. "It's working," she said encouragingly. "Her fever is coming down."

"So what do we do now?" Chirt asked with concern.

"Well, for now we'll get Hawthorn here to take over my job of pouring small sips of water into her mouth.

"Not too much at a time, Thorn. We don't want her to choke."

Nodding his understanding, Hawthorn took the wooden cup Cari had been using.

"Sir Chirt, if you can find some dry bed clothes, we will lift her up and get rid of all the wet bedding. That should make her more comfortable. And while you are getting that, I shall be putting together some herbs that should help even more."

It was very late when Hawthorn made his way back to his family's living area. "Did Carineda come with you?" his father asked when he saw his son.

"No, Sir. She felt that she needed to stay with Lady Holly."

"How is she, Thorn?" Savin asked with concern.

"Well, her fever is down, and she's resting right now. When I first saw her, Father, I thought there was no way she was going to make it. She looked awful! But Cari knew just what to do. Lady Holly's fever was so high that Cari said that a lot of the water in her body had been cooked out of her. After we got her fever down, we took turns pouring little sips of water into her. We did that for hours. Then later, when she started looking better, we gave her sips of Cari's herb mixtures. Every once in a while Lady Holly's condition seemed to change a little, but each time Cari knew exactly what to do. All I could do was just pray."

"It sounds like we need to do some more praying right now," Savin announced as he and his son dropped to their knees and began to earnestly petition their Heavenly Father in the name of King Jehesus to save Holly's life.

For the next two days, Carineda remained by Holly's bedside, tending her illness with teas of feverfew, cone flower, and burdock leaves. Cari also gave her patient a few drops of klamath weed extract several times a day. When not administering medicines, monitoring Holly's condition, or taking short naps, Carineda spent a lot of time praying openly for the Maker's healing.

On the morning of the third day, Holly opened her eyes and weakly asked for a drink. Chirt and the children were beside themselves with relief and joy when they saw how Holly was responding. When Hawthorn arrived later that afternoon, he joined in the quiet celebration. By that evening Holly was doing well enough that Cari left her in the care of Chirt and the kids so that the young Makerian healer could go back to the living area and get some sleep.

"I promise I will come back and check on her in the morning," she assured the family as she and Hawthorn left the house.

The next day when Carineda and Hawthorn returned, they brought Rose with them. After hearing all that the First Clan family had been through, she had cooked up a pot of her delicious spurge and primrose soup. She insisted on coming to deliver it as well as some fresh baked pollen bread.

On entering the sick room, they were all surprised at Holly's remarkable recovery. They found her sitting up in bed and eager to try some of Rose's soup.

"Her fever is gone!" Chirt said excitedly. "She is still weak, but she is so much better! Those herbs you gave her really worked!"

As Chirt gave his enthusiastic report, Cari leaned over to examine her patient. She looked into Holly's eyes, felt her cheek, and even placed her head against Holly's chest and listened to her heart. Finally she stood up and looked at the others. "The herbs certainly helped," Cari began, "but to be completely honest, they don't work this fast. This is the Maker's work. My friends and I have all been praying for Lady Holly, and her quick recovery is evidence that the Maker has granted our request."

Chirt was silent as he considered what he had just heard.

"We've got a hot pot of some of the best soup you've ever tasted sitting on the table in the other room," Rose spoke up, breaking the silence, "and it looks to me like there are a number of folks in this house who could do with a bowl of it. If someone can show me where you keep your dishes, I'll start serving it up."

It had been several days since any of Chirt's family had eaten a hot meal, and all of them consumed the soup and the bread with great enthusiasm. Holly seemed to enjoy her food as much as any of them.

Finally, when everyone was full and Rose began cleaning the dishes, Chirt turned to address Cari and Hawthorn, "My wife and I have some questions we'd like to ask you."

Hawthorn and Cari looked at each other and smiled. "We thought you might," Hawthorn returned. "Why don't we take some chairs into Lady Holly's room where we can talk?"

"I'll join you when I finish up in here," Rose said over her shoulder.

When they had taken their seats beside Holly's bed and Hawthorn had placed a chair for his mother, they sat there in silence for a few moments. Finally Chirt spoke, "I really don't know where to start."

"I think we should start by saying *thank you,*" Holly interrupted.

"Oh, yes!" Chirt agreed. "Yes! Thank you! My wife was dying . . . very near death . . ." Tears had begun to well up in Chirt's eyes as he spoke, "but you . . . what you did . . . you saved her!"

"Sir Chirt, my medicines didn't do what you saw," Carineda answered gently. "Our Great Maker in Heaven heard our prayers and granted Lady Holly her life. He is the one you should be thanking, not me."

"Neither of you are Shaman," Chirt returned, wiping his eyes. "How can you speak to the Maker? And where did you learn so much about treating fevers? And why do you dress like a boy when you are obviously a girl?"

"Who are you?" Holly asked.

"Before we go any further with this, you need to know something," Cari began. "My answers to your questions will change your lives forever and may put you in real trouble with the Shaman. Knowing that, do you want me to continue, or should we just leave?"

Chirt and Holly looked at each other for a moment. Finally Chirt rubbed both hands through his hair and looked at his guests. "The Shaman did nothing for my family," he began. "They came here and said some words I couldn't understand, burned some leaves, and blew the smoke over my sick wife. When she got worse, they told me that the Maker had decided that Holly should die! If it had been totally up to them, she would be dead by now! So displeasing the Shaman is of no concern to me."

"We want to know," Holly agreed earnestly.

With a nod of agreement, Carineda of Stillwaters began to tell them about herself. She told them about the origin of the Makerian people. It was the same story Hawthorn had heard two seasons before when he first met them. Hawthorn was even able to add a few points to Cari's history lesson. Chirt and Holly gave expressions of surprise when they heard that the Maker had a Son.

"I don't understand why the Maker would send His Son Jehesus to live here with us," Chirt asked with a confused look on his face. "Was Jehesus in trouble with the Maker?"

"No, Sir Chirt," Carineda answered, "the Maker sent Him because we were the ones who were in trouble. Remember that I told you that our forefather, Larkin the Great, found the Maker's Book? In those writings the Maker tells us what it takes to live a life that pleases Him. As Larkin read the Maker's Words, he discovered that no one can be as good as the Maker. No matter how hard we try, we can't be good enough to earn the right to live with the Maker and His Son in their home. Because we have not kept His words and because we have each done our own will instead of His will, then we are traitors to Him. When we die, we have to face Him in judgment. Instead of being able to welcome us into His beautiful kingdom to enjoy peace and joy with Him forever, He must condemn us because of our guilt and send us into eternal punishment."

"But we didn't know!" Chirt protested.

"Sir Chirt," Cari returned, "have you ever done anything in your life that you knew was wrong?"

At this question, Chirt dropped his eyes and answered, "Well . . . yes. I think everybody has."

"Then you knew," said Cari.

"So everyone is guilty before the Maker?" Holly asked with concern.

"Once you are old enough to know the difference between right and wrong and you decide to make that wrong choice, you're guilty."

"That's the bad news," Hawthorn said jumping into the conversation.

"That's very bad news," Chirt agreed.

"But there is also good news--," Rose spoke up with a smile, "--really, really good news!"

"The good news is the reason the Maker sent His Son Jehesus to live with us," Cari said, taking up the message again. "The Maker is perfect and completely just, so He must punish wrongdoing. But He also loves us very much. He doesn't want to punish us; He wants us to live with Him forever. So He came up with a plan. Since we couldn't save ourselves, He sent His Son to save us. The Maker took all of our wrongs and put them on His perfect Son Jehesus. Then the Maker put Jehesus through the punishment that we deserve, so that all of us who believe in Jehesus as the Son of the Maker and accept Him as the complete sacrifice for our wrongs can be forgiven."

"Why would Jehesus agree to such a plan?" Holly asked with dismay.

"He agonized over it for several hours as He talked about it with His Father, the Maker," Carineda explained. "Those hours were very hard on Jehesus. The Maker's Words say that the sweat that fell from Jehesus was like great drops of blood."

On hearing this, Holly's hand flew up to her mouth. "Oh, my!" she gasped.

"But Jehesus is no ordinary person," Cari continued. "He loves the Maker, and He loves us more than He loves His own life. His final words to the Maker were '*Not my will but Yours be done.*'"

Cari, Hawthorn, and Rose took turns describing the terrible suffering that Jehesus endured, ending in his death by being nailed to a wooden cross. As they finished this part of their story, Cari noticed that Chirt looked shocked, and Holly was weeping softly.

"Remember we told you that there was really good news in this?" Carineda smiled. "Well, here's where it starts: After Jehesus died and had been buried for three days, the Maker raised Him from the dead!"

"What?" Holly gasped.

"How could Jehesus have survived all that they did to Him?" Chirt blurted out.

"He didn't survive, Sir Chirt," Hawthorn added. "He died on that cross. The soldiers were even ordered to make sure He was dead, so they ran a spear through His side before they took Him down and buried Him. Then they put a guard over His tomb so that no one could steal the body. They wanted that to be the end of Jehesus."

"But the Maker had other plans," Rose said cheerfully. "Three days after being buried in that tomb, the Maker raised His Son back to life again, strong and healthy, to show us what will happen to us if we trust in His Son and follow Him."

When Rose had finished, there was silence for a moment. Finally Chirt spoke his thoughts, "Did that really happen?"

"All of that really happened," Cari answered as Rose and Hawthorn nodded their agreement, "and telling you about Jehesus is the reason why we're here."

CHAPTER SIXTEEN

CARI'S SACRIFICE

The next few days were very exciting for all of the followers of Jehesus. Both Makerian mission teams had been successful. Not only had they found a number of Larkin interested in talking with them about Jehesus, but after numerous discussions, they had eleven people who wanted to be bapatized and become followers of Jehesus. Actually getting them bapatized took a little creativity.

Since there were eleven of them, it was decided that they would form an herb gathering party with a few of the Larkin believers. As the group left the Steps with their baskets in hand, they headed upstream to find a quiet pool on the edge of the swift stream. They also wanted to locate a secluded spot where they would not be noticed by any of the guards.

Eldan and Tobin had spotted the procession as it left the Larkin stronghold. As soon as they recognized some of the Makerians and some of the Larkin believers, they slipped out of the woods and joined the happy group. Since the Rowdies had been asking a lot of questions about what it means to follow King Jehesus, the two brothers decided to let the Rowdies come to the ceremony.

Before they had reached the place where the Larkin were to be bapatized, Eldan turned and gave the Rowdies a stern lecture. "Now listen here, fellas," Eldan began in his most serious tone of voice, "you guys are a bit rougher than these good folks are used to, and we don't want to overwhelm all of these new believers getting bapatized. So be on your best behavior! Understand?"

"Don't worry, Red," Stub returned confidently. "All of us remembers . . . . King Jehesus don't want us killin' nobody."

"No!" Eldan exclaimed. "That's not what I mean! . . . Uh, I mean, yes, that's good . . . not killing is good, but that's not what I was talking about. What I'm trying to say is, don't do anything that might upset these folks."

"No problem, Red," Buzzard said cheerfully, "we'll just be ourselves."

"NO!" Eldan almost shouted. "You can't do that! Not to these nice people!"

"Well, who are we supposed to be?" Pike asked what they were all thinking.

"I don't know!" Eldan exclaimed in frustration. "All right, here're your orders: I want each of you to stand where you can see and hear what's going on and watch and listen. Have you got that? All I want you to do is watch and listen."

"Watch and listen . . . watch and listen," they all said, repeating the order.

"That's good," Eldan said with some relief as he heard them repeating the order. "Now follow me, and we'll go down closer to these folks so you can do what?"

"Watch and listen," they all returned, following their leader down close to the people at the edge of the creek.

As each of the new believers were led down into the water, they were asked if they believed that Jehesus was the Son of the Maker and that He died for their sins and that He was raised from the dead. After each one had made their

207

confession before the others, they were submerged in the water in obedience to the Maker's Words and to show that they had become united with the Lord Jehesus in His death, burial, and resurrection. There was much hugging, laughing, and joyful celebration as new followers of Jehesus were welcomed into the Maker's family.

Several of the Larkin hunters wore backpacks in which they carried dry clothing for those who had gotten wet in the bapatism ceremony. They hung all of their wet clothing up in the lower branches of some brush and spent the rest of the day gathering herbs and praising the Maker and His Son.

The Rowdies were quiet as they walked back through the woods toward their camp. Finally Mumbles spoke up. "Hey, R-R-Red."

"What is it?" Eldan answered, looking back over his shoulder at Mumbles.

"How come w-w-we can't d-d-do that?"

"Do what?"

"Get b-b-bapa, b-b-bapa . . ."

"Bapatoose, or whatever it was," Stub said to help his friend.

Eldan and Tobin stopped and turned to face the others. "Anyone who believes that King Jehesus is the Son of the Maker and who is willing to trust in His death as the full payment for their sins and who trusts King Jehesus enough to allow Him to be King of their life can and should be bapatized," Tobin answered.

"Getting' all m-m-my w-w-wrongs made r-r-right s-s-sounds good," Mumbles responded with a big grin.

"It sounds good to me, too," Buzzard agreed.

"Hurrumph!" Thug added while all of the others nodded their agreement.

"But there's more to it, fellas," Eldan spoke up. "Jehesus didn't come here just to give you what you wanted. He came to give the Maker what He wanted."

"And what's that?" Pike asked.

"The Maker wants you," Eldan returned. "The Maker has set up a kingdom—a kingdom filled with the Maker's own children, children who are willing to let His Son Jehesus be their King. So that's the big question. Jehesus is willing to be your Savior, but are you willing to let Him be your Lord and King?"

"I've heard that speech before, Red," said Pike. "Last time I wanted to be my own king, but I've finally seen where that leads. I'm ready for a new king, and Jehesus is the best one I've ever heard about. I don't know about the rest of you slugs, but I'm for following King Jehesus."

"M-m-me, t-t-too," grinned Mumbles.

Not quite an hour later, Eldan and Tobin were standing back by the creek, smiling at seven very wet and new followers of King Jehesus.

The next day when Hawthorn and Carineda told Holly and Chirt about the new followers of Jehesus, they were excited. They had decided that they wanted to become followers of the Maker's Son as well, but Holly was not well enough to risk getting wet yet.

"I'm feeling almost normal today," Holly responded excitedly. "With two more days of rest, I should be strong enough to be bapatized like the others."

"We've been talking to our son Reed," Chirt added, "and he believes in the Maker's Son also. As soon as Holly is recovered, the three of us want to be bapatized together."

"That's wonderful!" Hawthorn smiled. "Cari and I will let the others know, and we will begin working on a plan to do it."

Later that evening Hawthorn and Carineda related the happy news to the Larkin and the Makerian believers. "Yessiree, that there's great news!" Rush spoke up. "But, ya' know, it ain't gonna be as easy as it was last time."

"Why not, Rush?" Hawthorn asked. "We'll just take out another herb gathering detail."

"What do you figure those guards at the gate are gonna think when they see most of the same crowd of folks headin' out to look for more herbs just three days after they done brought back in ten baskets full? We got away with it once, but there's no way we'll fool 'em twice. No, we'll just have to come up with a different plan."

After several ideas were discussed and rejected, Jay suddenly sprang to his feet with a big grin on his face. "Listen up, everybody. I think we're looking at this wrong. Instead of trying to figure out ways to sneak all of us out to the creek, why don't we bapatize them in here?"

"You mean in our sleeping quarters?" Rush asked incredulously.

"No, not *in here* in here," Jay returned. "Let's bapatize them inside the Steps. There's plenty of water in the Dome Room."

"Well, sure!" Savin agreed enthusiastically. "We'll just have to do it when no one will see us."

"The middle of the night," Jay responded with a nod of agreement.

Rush was thoughtful as he considered this new idea. "Wel-l-l, I rec'on that's about the best plan we got," Rush finally agreed. "The tricky part will be getting' all of us out there to the pool and back in the middle of the night without makin' noise enough to get us spotted. But if'n we're careful, we should be able to do it."

Two days later, about suppertime, Hawthorn and his mother left their living quarters carrying a pot of stew and a couple of loaves of warm seed bread. They made their way through the Gathering Room, around the Dome Room, and into the large cave that was the living quarters for many of those in the First Clan. When they reached the doorway for the home of Chirt the Hunter, they gave a greeting and were quickly welcomed into the small stone house.

Everyone was very excited and a little nervous. Rose set her pot of stew on the table, and Holly quickly laid out the bowl and spoons. As they shared a happy meal together, Hawthorn reviewed the plan for the evening. "My mother will be spending the night with you," Hawthorn explained. "When our group gets to the pool, then I will come back here to get you. While the three of you are being bapatized, my mother will stay here with Marigold while she's asleep. Be sure to bring some blankets with you to wrap up in after the bapatism, because the water's going to be cold. Any questions?"

Looking around at each face and seeing they all understood the plan, Hawthorn spoke again. "We usually ask the new believers to confess their faith in Jehesus as they are being bapatized, but the biggest danger is that someone may hear us tonight. In order to try to make the actual event as quiet as possible, I'm going to ask each of you to confess your faith in our King now, in front of each other and my mother and me."

Right there, sitting at their supper table, Hawthorn asked Chirt, Holly, and Reed if they believed that Jehesus was the Son of the Maker. He asked them if they believed that Jehesus died on the cross to pay the full price for their sins. Finally he asked them each if they were ready to make Jehesus Lord and King of their lives.

"That never gets old," Rose said with a smile after she had finished listening to each of the family members speak their faith.

After leading them all in a prayer of thanksgiving to the Maker for each of these new believers, Hawthorn rose to leave. "I will be back to get you sometime in the middle of the night when everyone should be asleep," Hawthorn said to his friends. "Remember, when we go to the pool and when you return, we must not speak or make any noise."

As Hawthorn said this last statement, he looked at Reed, who returned a smile and an understanding nod.

After Hawthorn returned to his living quarters, he relayed to his friends that Chirt and his family understood the plan and would be ready when he went back to get them.

"It's gonna be a while before people around here get done with their evening chores and visitin' an' finally get to sleep," Rush observed. "To keep it from bein' such a long night fer all of us, why don't we pick two or three of us to rotate a watch, and the rest of us can get a little sleep? As soon as it looks like everyone's sound asleep, then whoever's on watch can get the rest of our group up, an' we can slip outta here quiet-like."

"That sounds like a good plan to me," Jay responded. "All of you go ahead and sack out while I take the first watch. In a couple of hours, I'll get Sagamore to take the next watch. If after two more hours Sag gets sleepy, he can wake you up, Rush."

"All right," Rush agreed. "That'll be the plan. Whoever's not on guard, try to get some rest."

As excited as he was, Hawthorn didn't think he would be able to sleep at all, but hours later he suddenly found himself shaken from his sleep by his father's hand. As his foggy mind tried to understand what was happening, Hawthorn saw his father hold a finger up to his lips for silence. In that instant Hawthorn remembered the secret ceremony which they had planned.

When everyone was awake and ready, Rush led the way toward the Gathering Room. Next in line came Jay, Carineda, and Hawthorn, and Savin brought up the rear. They thought it best to have Sagamore and Noblis remain behind to keep the group smaller.

Rush led them slowly along the open walkway through the large cave where the Second and Third Clans had made their temporary home. The only light was the glowing coals of several of the smoldering cooking fires.

When a voice suddenly called out close by, they froze. When more murmuring and muttering was heard coming from the same location, they realized that it was only someone talking in their sleep. Rush kept them there, unmoving, for several more minutes until he was sure that the noise had not caused others to awaken.

After what seemed to Hawthorn like an hour, Rush began to move forward again. Twice more they halted when noises were heard around them, but eventually they made it safely out of the living area and into the Gathering Room. Rush halted the small party until he had scouted the room to find where the guards were. There were four oil lamps hung from the walls located around the large room to provide a small amount of light for those coming and going on guard duty. Finding no guards in the Gathering Room, Rush scouted the small passageway that was the exit of the Steps and carefully glanced up the tunnel. Satisfied that the guards were all outside along the ledge behind the waterfall, Rush quickly returned to his group. With a wave of his hand to indicate that the others should follow him, Rush used the dim light of the oil lamps to lead his group around the edge of the chamber to the opening that led into the expansive Dome Room.

Again Rush called a halt as they studied the great cavern before them. Most of the huge room was shrouded in darkness. They listened a long time in silence for the sounds of other Larkin but heard no one. Finally Rush waved them forward.

They moved soundlessly around the edge of the great room, staying in the dark. When they eventually arrived at the opening to the tunnel that led to Chirt's family's living area, Rush pointed at Hawthorn and then at the opening. Nodding his understanding, Hawthorn moved purposefully down the darken tunnel to contact their friends.

Hawthorn had to move very warily in the dim lighting. It seemed to him that it was taking much longer to reach his friend's house than he had expected, and he was beginning to think that he might be lost, but he slowly pressed on. Just when he was about to stop and retrace his steps, he found it. He cautiously pushed aside the curtain covering the doorway and stepped inside.

"Chirt," Hawthorn whispered.

"We're all here and ready to go," the whispered answer came from the darkened room.

Lifting the curtain once more, Hawthorn allowed Chirt, Reed, and Holly to walk past him before he carefully replaced the curtain and followed the family back up the poorly lit path. It seemed to Hawthorn that the trip back out seemed to take much less time. As Chirt stepped out of the tunnel into the cavernous Dome Room, a hand suddenly grabbed his shoulder.

"Glad you made it," he heard Rush whisper in his ear. "We were startin' to get worried."

Rush gathered the family close to him so that they could all hear. "We need to do this quickly, 'cause there's been some guards movin' through here. They came close to spottin' us once. It seems quiet enough right now, so let's get this done. " He cautiously led the group over to the edge of the pool. Noiselessly Rush stepped into the water, followed by Savin, Chirt, Holly, and Reed. Jay, Hawthorn, and Carineda stood at the edge of the pool, holding the dry blankets. They hadn't waded far out into the pool until the water was above their waists.

"This here should be deep enough," Rush whispered as he stopped the group. "You first, Chirt."

Savin moved over and stood on one side of Chirt while Rush stood on the other. Holding firmly to Chirt's shoulder and arm, Rush said, "Chirt, because you believe in the Lord Jehesus and because of yo'r confession which you already done made, me an' Savin are now gonna bapatize you in the name of the Maker an' His Son Jehesus an' the Holy Spirit."

With that, Rush and Savin lowered Chirt under the water and quickly brought him back up.

"Yes!" Chirt hissed excitedly as he came up. He waded over and gave his smiling wife a wet hug.

"Now you, Holly," Rush whispered urgently. "Quickly!"

After repeating the ceremony with Holly, it was Reed's turn. As Reed hurried to take his place, he suddenly slipped and fell into the water with a big splash. From the far side of the Dome Room, they heard a voice call out of the darkness, "They're over there! Guards, move in!"

As Reed struggled back to his feet, Rush quickly grabbed him and said, "In the name of the Maker, Jehesus, and the Spirit!" and shoved the boy back under the water. Snatching Reed back up, Rush drug him back to the shore as fast as he could.

"Run, all of you!" Rush whispered urgently as he hurried the boy into Jay's waiting blanket. "Jay, Hawthorn! Help them get back and stay there!"

"It's too late, Rush!" Jay cried out. "They'll catch all of us before we get there!

"Savin and I will hold 'em! Now run!"

"Wait!" Hawthorn cried out. "Where's Cari?"

At that moment they heard Carineda's voice a short distance away. "Oh, help me!" she screamed loudly as she ran through the dark shadows to meet the approaching guards. "Please, someone help me!

"Cari, no!" Hawthorn started to yell when he realized what Carineda was doing, but Rush quickly slapped his hand across the young Larkin's mouth.

"We cain't help her if we get caught," Rush whispered. "She's givin' us a chance to get away, so run!" It took all Hawthorn could do to turn his back on Cari and obey Rush's order.

As Carineda ran screaming up to the approaching guards, she continued to play the part of the terrified victim. "Help me! Oh, please help me!" she exclaimed as she threw herself into the arms of one of the nearest guards.

At that moment more figures came running up; one was carrying a torch.

"Something may be after me!" Cari exclaimed excitedly. "I'm so glad I found you!"

"We're glad we found you, too," said the voice behind the torch. "That's her all right. I remember her face."

Cari's heart sank when she recognized that the voice behind the torch was Poke's.

CHAPTER SEVENTEEN

DESPERATE PLANS

"Quickly, everyone," Chirt whispered urgently, "come with us! They don't know who we are. We can hide all of you in our house."

"That won't work for us," Rush answered. "There's folks here who thinks we're ahelpin' the Makerians. If they send some guards back to our camp site and don't find us, they'll know fer sure."

Chirt quickly turned to his wife and son, "Holly, you and Reed get home quickly but try not to be seen. I've got to get our friends back to their living area. Go now!"

Holly and Reed turned obediently and hurried toward the tunnel opening leading to their home. There was no time to lose. The heavy footfalls of the guards were hurriedly approaching from the dark shadows of the Dome Room.

"Follow me," Chirt whispered as he sprinted into the darkness to their left. Chirt didn't bother trying to be quiet as they ran. He wanted the guards to follow them rather than his wife and son.

Jay, Rush, Savin, and Hawthorn raced after Chirt, following the sound of his running feet in the darkness ahead of them. After several minutes of hard running, they heard Chirt speak, "Follow my voice!" he whispered. "Come to me quickly!"

Behind them they could see a torch and could hear the running guards fast approaching. Within a few seconds the friends were standing beside Chirt.

"Now join hands and follow me as quietly as you can!" Chirt announced as he grabbed Jay's hand and pulled him into the black shadows to their left. As they moved along in the darkness, they each tried to lift their feet as they walked, trying not to stumble or make any scrapping sounds that might betray their presence. As the light of the torch in the hands of one of the running guards drew near, Chirt had his friends lie down on the cave floor among some of the rocks and small bolders that littered this part of the cave. Almost immediately they could hear the running guards rush past where they had been. Chirt had led them far enough to the side of the great cave that the light from the guards torch didn't quite reach to where they lay.

As soon as the guards were past them Chirt whispered the order for everyone to rise and follow him. With hands again joined, Chirt hurriedly led them through the inky darkness. He obviously knew where he was going. After a few moments he stopped. Standing quietly, Hawthorn heard a door opening just in front of them.

"Inside, all of you!" they heard Chirt's quiet voice command them. Again they were moving forward. Hawthorn felt for and found the frame of the door as he followed his friends through the opening. He was aware of a dank, earthy smell close all around them. Again there was the sound of a door moving on its hinges. This time Hawthorn deduced that Chirt was closing the door behind them.

As Chirt joined them again, he spoke briefly, "This is one of our mushroom farms. We're on a long passageway that leads to another door on the other side of the Dome Room. While they're looking for us on this side of the room, we will be slipping around behind them to the other side. Now follow me."

Chirt stuck out his left arm until his hand rested on one of the large mushrooms growing in the room. Then he began trotting down the path with his left hand brushing against the large fungi growing along the edge of the trail. In this way he was able to keep them on the trail as they trotted along in the darkness. Eventually, when they reached to doorway on the other end of the long room, Chirt called a halt.

"I'm going to open the door," Chirt whispered. "Everyone be very quiet."

They heard the wooden door being swung open and Chirt's quiet steps as he scouted the area. He returned shortly with his report, "It's quiet on this side of the Dome Room. They're still looking for us on the other side. Let's go, but stay in the shadows."

Passing out of the long farm chamber, they quietly moved into the large open Dome Room. They could hear some occasional shouts in the distance coming from the other side of the cavern, but all seemed quiet where they were. The guards had not thought to light up more of the torches and lamps around the great cave chamber, which was an advantage for the friends as they crept cautiously toward the room's entrance.

When they reached the opening which led to the Gathering Room, they heard running and some voices coming from the tunnel to the Shaman's quarters just a short distance to their right.

"There's more of 'em comin'!" Hawthorn hissed.

"Chirt, we got to go!" Rush ordered as he shoved Jay and Chirt through the opening.

The five friends hurried through the Gathering Room and shot into the cave that was their own living quarters. Trying to make as little noise as possible, they rapidly tiptoed through the sleeping Larkin until they came to their huts in the back of the cave.

"Is everything okay?" Noblis asked as he scanned the nervous faces of his friends.

"We got 'em bapatized, but we got spotted," Rush said as he took an anxious look back toward the opening of the cave.

"They captured Cari!" Hawthorn blurted out.

"An' we expect a posse of 'em to show up here any second," Rush added. "You two better scoot back into that hole of yorn 'afore they get here."

Without another word Nobis and Sagamore darted to the back wall of the cave, moved the rocks out of the way, and slid into the small, low hole in which they had hidden before. Savin followed them and put the rocks back in place.

"Here they come, Savin," Rush whispered just loud enough for his friend to hear. Savin quickly crawled into the nearest hut. The friends had just enough time to pull off their boots, outer garments, and throw a blanket over themselves before they heard the approaching footfalls.

"This is it," they heard Poke's voice just outside their huts. "This is where they camp. If they're not here, you'll know it was them."

Suddenly the cloth opening of the hut was thrown back, and someone stepped in with a torch.

"Hey! What's the meaning of this?" Savin shouted at the intruders. Hawthorn sat up from the bedding next to his father, yawning sleepily.

The guard stepped out and made his report. "There's two of 'em in there. I woke 'em up."

"Well, check the other hut," snapped an authoritative voice.

The guard shoved his torch into the other hut. As he did so, Jay and Chirt sat up. "What do you want?" Jay demanded.

"Settle down," the intruder answered. "I got orders to look in here."

As he looked around the floor of the hut, he saw Rush curled up on his side, pretending to still be asleep. The guard grabbed Rush by the shoulder and rolled him over, holding the torch close to get a look at Rush's face.

"Fire! Fire!" Rush shouted and began flailing around with his arms, smacking the Shaman's trooper in the head as he did so.

"Calm down, you bonehead!" the irritated guard shouted as he drew back, rubbing the side of his face. "It ain't no fire. I just needed a look at you."

"What's this all about?" Savin snapped as he stepped out of his hut. He saw four guards, one of the Shaman in his long robes, and Poke.

"How . . . how'd you get back here so fast?" Poke blurted out, his frustration clearly showing.

"You come barging into our sleeping huts in the middle of the night, waving torches in our faces, and you want to know how we got here?" Savin shouted back. "What are you talking about?"

"Don't give me that . . ." Poke snapped back but was suddenly cut off by the Shaman's upraised hand.

"Please accept our apologies to all of you," the Shaman said, smiling and giving a slight bow. "The guards thought they saw something suspicious, but they were obviously mistaken."

"That's not . . ." Poke started to protest but was again cut off.

"We will let you return to your sleeping," the smiling Shaman continued. "We are sorry for disturbing your rest." Quick orders were given, and the guards and the Shaman left, shoving Poke ahead of them.

Jay, Rush, and Hawthorn had joined Savin outside the huts and stood there watching the retreating guards. Chirt thought it best to stay out of sight.

"That was close," whispered Jay.

"Chirt, that shortcut of yorn saved our beans this time, an' I don't mean maybe!" Rush addressed their friend.

"Well, there's no doubt about it now," Hawthorn spoke up, "Poke's working for the Shaman."

"Yeah," Rush added, "an' he's told 'em at least some of what he knows about us."

"They've got Carineda!" Hawthorn whispered urgently. "What are we going to do about her?"

"We're gonna pray," Rush shot back, "right now!"

After Poke identified her, rough hands grabbed Carineda and held her tightly. Poke wanted to question her right then, but the Shaman was more concerned with catching the others who were at the pool with her. While the Shaman and the guards were searching in vain to find her companions, Strong arms grabbed Cari and led her to the other side of the Dome Room. They walked purposefully past the opening leading to the Gathering Room until they arrived at the mouth of a dimly lit tunnel that Cari remembered led to the Shaman's quarters. Without hesitating, her captors drug Carineda down this dark tunnel, which was occasionally lit by oil lamps. The guards hauled their captive past the great wooden doors that led to the Larkin Cathedral. About a bow shot further down this passageway, they passed a large opening on their right that revealed a well-lit tunnel which, Cari assumed, was the entrance to the Shaman's living quarters.

"Where are you taking me?" Carineda finally asked one of her guards.

In response, the guard gripped her arm even tighter and jerked her to a stop. "Don't say another word," the guard snarled as he shot a finger under her nose. "You got that?"

With wide eyes Cari nodded her understanding of the bully's command, and the procession began again.

to the cells

She was forced to march down the shadowy tunnel for some distance. There were a number of twists and turns, but she observed no side passages. Eventually she became aware of an increased dampness to the cave. The floor was wet, and there was evidence of moisture on the walls. Almost at the same time, Cari noticed that cave began to widen and the ceiling rose.

What had been a subterranean tunnel now grew into a large cavern. A number of large rocks and boulders littered the floor, as well as a few pools of water. Occasional dripping could be heard in the darkness around them.

The path was dimly lit by more of the oil lanterns. As they followed the path around a particularly large boulder, Carineda saw two torches protruding from holes cut in the wall about a stone's throw ahead of them. These two torches lit up a heavy wooden door built into the wall of the cavern. Two more guards stood on either side of the doorway.

"What's this?" one of the guards at the door asked.

"Another prisoner," barked the bullying guard. "This one's a spy, most likely. The Shaman will be down later to find out what she knows."

The door guard turned and lifted a heavy wooden bar from where it lay across the face of the door. This allowed him to push open the entry to the cells. Then the guard took one of the torches from the wall and walked into the dark room. Cari was shoved after him.

The room was just tall enough to walk in. It was only about four paces wide and no more than ten paces long. On either side of this small room, holes had been carved into the walls to form prison cells. The doors to the cells were a lattice framework of stout ironwood poles held against the mouth of the cells on both sides of the room by a heavy oak beam, both ends of which were wedged tightly against the frames.

These holes that created the cells came up to Cari's waist and only went in a short way. It was obvious to Cari that you couldn't stand up in these dirty cells, and it didn't look like you could fully stretch out in them either. As nasty as they were, she wasn't sure she wanted to.

While one guard kept a firm grip on Carineda's arm, two others walked over and began to knock the beam up and out of its place. The other guard stood to the side with his sting drawn. It was then that Cari noticed that she was not the only prisoner. As the heavy beam was removed, the guard with the sting leaned against the bars covering the cells on the right, behind which was another captive who was squinting painfully at the torchlight. The lattice work of bars on the left was allowed to fall to the floor, which opened the cells on that side.

Carineda was drug forcefully over to one of these holes and shoved in. By the time she got herself turned around so she could see out of her cell, the bars had been lifted back into position, and the beam was being replaced. With the bars to the cells secured, the guards walked out of the small room, taking the torch with them.

"Won't you leave us a light?" Cari yelled at them as the door slammed shut, engulfing the prisoners in blackness. With a deep shuddering sigh, Carineda took stock of her situation. Fear began to tighten its terribly cold fingers around her heart as she considered the overwhelming hopelessness of her situation. She was trembling involuntarily as feelings of panic, dread, and abandonment seemed to engulf her.

Carineda didn't know how long she sat there in the dark, clutching her own arms closely about her and rocking back and forth as she thrashed in a sea of despair, but slowly she became increasingly aware of another idea. It was a thought which was completely foreign to her miserable circumstances, and it was nudging its way into her consciousness. As this new awareness began to take shape in her mind, it brought with it peace and hope and resolve. A smile came to her as she realized that the meaning of that beautiful, irresistible concept was expressed in the very words from the Maker's Book that she had been thinking about that morning.

"'Where shall I go from your Spirit?'" Cari began to say out loud as she remembered the verses. *"'Or where shall I flee from Your presence? If I ascend up into heaven, You are there: if I make my bed in hell, behold, You are there. If I take the wings of the morning, and dwell in the uttermost parts of the sea; even there shall Your hand lead me, and Your right hand shall hold me. If I say, "Surely the darkness shall cover me; even the night shall be light about me." Yes, the darkness hides not from You; but the night shines as the day: the darkness and the light are both alike to You.'"*

"Actin' crathy ain't gonna work, lil' missthy," came a voice from the cell on the other side of the room. "I know, cuth I'm crathy as a loon, an' it ain't done nothin' fer me."

"I'm not crazy," Cari answered, smiling to herself, "at least, not yet. And I wasn't acting. I was just remembering a beautiful truth that is very comforting to me. I was really scared, and I was starting to panic. But then I realized that the Lord Jehesus, the Son of the Maker whom I worship and serve, knows exactly where I am. Those were some of the words from His book that I was saying a moment ago. I could not be in a pit too deep or too dark that the Maker and His Son Jehesus could not see me and know what is happening to me."

"What differenth doeth it make if He can thee you or not? You're thstill thstuck in this here hole," the voice answered back.

"Oh, it's very encouraging to know that the One Who made everything and Who has all power and all knowledge and Who loves me as He loves His own Son can see me and my situation. He even made me a promise. He said, *'I will never fail you or forsake you.'"*

"Well, at leasth one thing you thaid waths true," the voice answered. "You're not actin'. You're definitely crathy. No doubt about it—you've lost it, thister."

"Crazy or not, we're stuck in here together. So we might as well get to know each other.

"What's your name?" Cari asked.

"Oh, them guardth have lotth of nameth fer me, but the one I generally go by ith Pothum."

"I'm glad to meet you, Possum. My name is Cari.

"Why do they have you locked up down here?" Cari asked.

"Hee, hee" Possum chuckled. "Well, uh . . . I thupposth the besth anther ith that I really annoy the Shaman. I'm what'th known ath an *unthavory character*.

"How about you?" Possum continued. "Don't those goonth have anything better to do than arreth young girlth?"

"Actually," Cari began, "there's a very good reason why I'm here, and I want to tell you about it."

For several hours Rush, Chirt, Savin, and the other concerned followers of Jehesus poured out their hearts to the Maker. They prayed for wisdom. They prayed for deliverance. They prayed for a miracle.

When Rush was convinced that the guards were not going to come back, he had Hawthorn crawl over to the small opening in the cave wall and call for Noblis and Sagamore to come join them. After the two Makerians returned, the friends spent a long time trying to come up with a plan. They asked Chirt question after question about possible ways into the cells where the Shaman would have taken Carineda. His answer was always the same.

"I don't know," Chirt answered. "The prison cells are somewhere in the caves behind or below the Dome Room. None of the clan members are allowed past the Great Cathedral. Only the Shaman can go there."

"They've got to have guards that go back there," Rush spoke his thoughts out loud.

"Back there the Shaman do their own guarding," Chirt returned.

"We all knew there were risks in doing this," Sagamore spoke up.

"Yeah, we knew the risks," Rush growled, "but I'm 'bout to do some more riskin'! The Great Gatherin' is ending in two days, an' there ain't no way I'm leavin' here without her!" A quick glance around told Rush that Savin, Hawthorn, and Jay all felt the same.

"Just tell me what I can do to help," Chirt joined in.

"Listen up, fellers," Rush began. "We done asked the Maker fer wisdom, an' I believe He's given it to us. So let's put our heads together an' see what He's provided."

"I don't know if this will help or not," Noblis spoke up, "but you know how the tunnel that leads to the Great Cathedral and where the Shaman live runs parallel to the cave we're in right now?"

"You think we can tunnel through all of this rock to get to her?" Hawthorn asked incredulously.

"You may not have to tunnel," Noblis answered, "at least not very far. The first time Sagamore and I hid in that small hole in the wall, we got bored and decided to look around."

"We also thought we might need to know our way around in there if our hole was discovered," Sagamore added.

"Well, anyway," Noblis began again, "we pulled out our light sticks and started moving back further into the tunnel. It opened up enough for us to crawl around, but we couldn't stand up. We went for quite a ways back in there, but eventually we heard voices. We figured that it must lead to another part of the main cavern. I decided that it might be important for us to know where it went, so I had Sagamore stay put while I eased forward to scout it out. The tunnel eventually got so small that I was afraid that I'd get stuck if I went any farther, so I stopped. But I could see light, and I could hear the Shaman speaking to one another a short distance ahead of me."

"How do you know they were Shaman?" Rush asked.

"Because they were speaking in their secret language."

"Heh, heh, heh," Jay chuckled. "Their *secret* language that every Makerian in the world knows?"

"Could you tell where your tunnel came out?" Rush asked.

"No, I couldn't get close enough to see, but as far back in there as we crawled, we had to be a good ways past the Great Cathdral."

"If we could make the passageway bigger," Hawthorn spoke up, "we could slip in there, get Cari, and then crawl back here."

"There's a lot of unknowns in that plan, Thorn," Rush returned. "But if'n we did get her back here, then what? They'd figure out purdy quick that she was missin', an' with Poke on their side, the first place they'd come lookin' would be right here. An' even if we did hide her, they'd have the entrance guarded so tight, they'd spot her going out, disguise or not."

"So what do we do, Rush?" Savin asked what they all were thinking.

"I ain't rightly sure yet," Rush answered thoughtfully. "With that small passageway goin' where we need to get, we definitely got somethin' to work with, but I'm figuring we need some help. I think I need to join up with one of the wood gatherin' details leaving the Steps this morning an' try to talk this over with our friends on the outside."

"Wretch, how did you let her get caught?" Eldan exclaimed, throwing up his hands in frustration.

229

Rush had found his friends in the nearby woods and was explaining their predicament. "You ain't listenin' to me, Floppy," Rush shot back. "We didn't let her get caught. She slipped away from us in the dark and let herself get caught to protect the new believers and the rest of us."

The three friends were sitting on rocks in front of the small cave that Tobin, Eldan, and the Rowdies were using as a campsite. Pike, Stub, and Muckly were standing nearby, listening with concern about Carineda's capture.

"It really doesn't matter how it happened," Tobin spoke up. "It's happened. The question now is: what can we do about it?"

Tobin and Eldan began to ask questions about the layout of the Larkin stronghold and the possibility of reaching their captured friend. Rush spent a lot of time explaining in detail where they believed Carineda was being held and the difficulties of getting to that part of the cave.

"We'll be happy to help if we can," Pike offered.

"Yeah," Stub added. "We could sneek up to 'da gate in 'da middle of 'da night, take out 'da guards, charge in, get her, an' fight our way back out."

"That won't work, Stub," Tobin answered. "As much as we want to help our friend Carineda, we don't want to do anything that might get somebody killed."

"Sorry," Stub shrugged. "I keep fergettin' dat part. Dis Gooder stuff is still new to me."

"They think she's just a helpless girl," Eldan was speaking his thoughts. "They probably won't have but one or, at most, two guards at her cell. If we could get enough of our people down there, we could overpower them with little or no fight at all."

"Right," agreed Rush, "but there ain't no way to get 'em in and back out again without causin' a stink."

"Maybe there is," Eldan said with a smile.

"Floppy, yer little army is gonna have to march through the whole length of the cavern, down the Shaman's private hallway, down to the cells, and then, if you get that far, you got to march all the way back out past all of the Larkin guards leading up to the entrance."

"But what if we can get our rescue party in and out without using the entrance?" Eldan asked, still smiling.

"What are you talkin' 'bout, Floppy?" Rush growled. "There's only one entrance."

"I beg to differ, Wretch ol' buddy," Eldan nodded knowingly. "There's two."

Rush sat there for a moment with a confused look on his face.

"How soon we forget," Eldan said loftily. "Don't you remember the story of how Micah, Jasper, and Linden found Larkin the Great's journal and learned all about Jehesus for the first time? They found the chest containing his journal hidden in a small tunnel, and when Jasper and Linden followed that tunnel, they discovered that the small passageway led from the Treasure Cave out to an opening behind the lowest waterfall."

Oh yeah, that's right!" Rush exclaimed. "An' after they an' their families got kicked out of the clan for findin' out about Jehesus, they were able to crawl back into the Treasure Cave to make copies of the journal and some of the Maker's Words."

"Now you've got it, Wretch ol' boy," Eldan grinned, patting Rush on the head. "If they could crawl in that way, we should be able to as well."

"But there's a problem with that," Rush said thoughtfully. "The door to the Treasure Cave will be sealed shut. Most likely it'll be wedged from the outside of the Treasure Cave, and you fellers'll be on the inside."

"Is there any way you can get someone down there to open it for us?" Eldan asked.

"Wel-l-l, maybe," Rush drawled. "Noblis and Sagamor found a small crawlway that leads back to the cave where the Shaman live, but there's another problem. Noblis said that the crawlway gets so small that he couldn't get through it. He could see light ahead, an' he could hear the Shaman talkin', but he couldn't get close enough to see where it came out."

"Could you widen it?" Eldan asked.

"Not without lettin' every Shaman and guard in the whole place know where we were an' what we was doin'."

Everyone was thoughtful for a moment. Finally Muckly spoke up. "Did your friend say how small the opening in the crawlway was?"

"It's purdy small," Rush assured him. "Noblis said maybe a kid might get through, but a grown person couldn't."

"I'll bet Lil' Snide could do it," Muckly said confidently.

"Hey, yeah!" Stub agreed. "Der ain't no hole dat kid cain't push hisself t'ru, an' dat's a fact."

"Hold on a minute," Rush protested. "I ain't too keen on askin' a kid to do somethin' like that."

"Once he hears about it," Muckly returned, "I don't think yer gonna be able to keep him from tryin' it. Crawlin' through holes is all he lives for, an' if he could do it to help rescue that purdy lil' girl, well, that would just about make his life."

CHAPTER EIGHTEEN

ROWDIES TO THE RESCUE

"**R**ush, have you lost your mind?" Jay whispered urgently when he saw Rush's small companion standing next to him with an armload of wood. Rush and Little Snide were standing in front of the huts that Hawthorn's family were using as living quarters. Both had their arms full of wood.

"It's a wonder the guards didn't stop you at the front gate!" Savin snapped.

"He's a Renegade, Rush," Jay started again.

"Former Renegade," Little Snide corrected.

"Well, former Renegade or not," Jay shot back, "you both should have been arrested and put in the cells! And every second you stay here increases the chances of that happening to all of us!"

"What were you thinking, Rush?" Hawthorn asked with concern.

"If all of you nervous Nellies will pipe down and get our young friend here hidden in one of the huts, I'll explain what he's doin' here."

They all crowded into the largest of the huts, and Rush spent the next quarter of an hour explaining Eldan's plan.

"I don't know, Rush," Hawthorn spoke up. "You said my idea had a lot of unknowns in it. It seems to me this plan has at least as many." Savin and Jay nodded their heads in agreement.

Rush looked around at his friends before he spoke. "You're all right as rain. This here plan's got more holes in it than a den tree, but the reality of the sitchiation is that we're leavin' day after tomorrow. That means whatever we do to save Cari has got to be done quick, and the way I sees it, as holey as it is, Floppy's plan is our best option."

"So when is all of this going to take place?" Savin asked.

"Floppy and his bunch are gonna cross the creek tonight and slip up the opposite bank till they get to the lowest waterfall. Then they will crawl behind the falls until they come to the opening that Micah, Jasper, and Linden used years ago to get into the Treasure Cave. We will give them all day tomorrow to get into position. When everybody starts settling down in here tomorrow night is when we send Little Snide through the crawlway to open the door to the Treasure Cave and let our people in."

Rush looked around at his skeptical friends. "If any of you fellers can come up with a better plan, let's hear it. But considerin' what we got to work with and the short amount of time we have, it appears to me that Floppy's plan is the best one on the table." The nods Rush got this time were more of resignation than of approval.

As soon as it was dark, Tobin and Eldan put their scheme into effect. Since Muckly couldn't swim, it was decided to leave him behind. His job was to stay hidden close to the entrance to the Steps and to prepare some of the rock-tipped arrows, being ready to help anyone trying to get out the front gate if the plan failed. The rest of them grabbed their gear and followed Eldan down to the creek.

The opening they needed to find which led into the Treasure Cave was located somewhere behind the lowest waterfall. They considered trying to crawl behind the falls from their side of the creek, but the rushing water had washed away so much of the rocky ledge over which the water flowed that the strong torrent of water made that impossible. Because the creek itself had settled down considerably since the last storm, they decided to cross the creek on rafts and attempt to crawl in from that side.

After Rush left to return to the Steps with Little Snide, Eldan and Tobin supervised the construction of two rafts to ferry them and their equipment across to the other bank. They found several large oak leaves to use. Dragging two of these down to the edge of the creek, Tobin pulled out his knife and cut several slits into the body of the leaves close to the edges.

While he was doing this, Eldan had taken the Rowdies with him further down the bank until he found a stand of reeds. Finding four dead reeds that had fallen over, they drug these back to where Tobin was working on the leaves. After plugging the ends of the reeds with clay dug out of the bank nearby, they passed the reeds through the slits that Tobin had cut in the oak leaves to serve as floats.

"Now let's set another leaf on top of the ones with the reed floaters," Tobin directed, "then we'll move them into the water."

When the double-layered leaf rafts were floating in the water, they began to load their equipment and weapons. With several people standing on both rafts, Tobin and Eldan checked to make sure that the reed pontoons would support the weight. Satisfied that the rafts were safe, Tobin gave the order to launch the floating platforms. Stub and Pike pushed the leaf raft on which Tobin, Mumbles, Buzzard, and Thug rode out into the water while Eldan stood on the shore and held on to the other one.

RAFTING THE CREEK

After Pike and Stub had climbed on the second raft, Eldan joined them and used a long stick he had found to push their leaf boat away from the shore.

Buzzard and Thug found several pieces of bark that they could use as paddles, so they were able to make good time across the creek. Landing their ungainly crafts proved to be more of a challenge. Though the flow of water through the creek was diminished, it was still enough to push them down the creek. They bumped and twirled their way along the far bank, unable to hold the leaf rafts against the shore.

"How do you stop this frizzlin' thing?" Stub cried out in desperation as the raft on which he, Pike, and Eldan rode spun out of control.

"A little help, Bubs!" Eldan called to his brother on the other raft. Eldan was extending the long stick towards Tobin as they spun past. The red-bearded Makerian grabbed Eldan's stick and hung on. This stopped Eldan's raft from spinning, but it caused both rafts to begin a slow rotation as they were pushed further down the bank.

"Eldan!" Tobin growled. "You've got all of us spinning now!"

"Maybe so," Eldan returned cheerfully, "but we're not spinning nearly as much."

"Well, that's fine an' dandy fer you, Red," Buzzard snapped, "but we weren't spinnin' at all!"

"Hummph!" grunted Thug.

"Do I want to know what he just said?" Eldan asked, still smiling.

"Let's just say that Thug ain't real happy with you right now."

"Cheer up, chums!" Eldan said. "It looks like help is on the way." Eldan was staring into the darkness further down the creek. In the dim light of the stars, he could just make out the shape of an outcropping of rocks extending out from the creek bank which they were approaching.

"If we can paddle our rafts behind those rocks," Eldan explained, "we should get enough protection from the current to land."

Quickly taking up their pieces of bark, they all began paddling furiously toward the back side of the rocks as they passed them. Once both crafts were in the protected cove behind the rocks, they had no trouble landing their rafts and unloading.

Tobin had them pull the leaf rafts up onto the bank and lay their bark paddles on top of them in case they needed to launch them quickly when they returned. When everyone was ready, Tobin gave the signal to march.

They traveled along the bank of the creek toward the waterfalls, using the faint light of the stars and the now-rising quarter moon to find their way. The current had pushed them further down the creek than they had realized. It took them almost an hour of hard marching to finally reach the lowest waterfall.

"We'll take a rest here before we crawl in," Tobin announced as they stood beside the small cascading cataract. While the Rowdies munched on strips of worm jerky, Eldan and Tobin pulled out some seeds Eldan had found for their supper.

After several minutes Eldan whispered something to Tobin, and shedding his backpack, the young red-haired Makerian walked over to the bottom of the waterfall. The lowest fall of the Steps was only about two- Larkin high. As the water cascaded over the short rocky ledge, there was a small space behind the falling water just tall enough for a Larkin or, in this case, a Makerian to crawl behind. Eldan dropped to his knees and disappeared into the watery cave.

Tobin turned from watching his brother and walked over to the others. "Eldan has gone to scout the entrance to the cave. He will return in a few minutes. Mumbles and Stub, I'm leaving both of you here. If we get into trouble and have to run for it, I want you two ready to cover us when we come out. It will be late tomorrow night or the next morning before we get back. Spend the time making some stone-tipped arrows to use."

"No killin', right?" Stub winked at Tobin.

"Right," Tobin returned. "No killing.

"Pike, you, Buzzard, and Thug will go with Eldan and me into the cave. We don't know where the Shaman guards will be posted, so it is most important that all of us stay as quiet as possible when we get in there. And remember . . ."

"Yeah, we know," Pike interrupted, "no killin'."

"Hey, Bubsy!" Eldan called as he hurriedly crawled out from behind the waterfall "We got problems!"

"Couldn't you find the opening?" Tobin asked with concern.

"Oh, I found it all right," Eldan shot back, "but as soon as I stuck my head in to check it out, a huge water bug took a serious snap at me! And let me tell you, that rascal meant business!"

"Could we use your smoke bundle trick like we did across the creek?" Pike asked.

"It would probably work," answered Eldan, "but the smoke escaping up through the cave might give away our presence."

"We could use torches," Stub suggested. "Dey don't smoke very much."

"I've already thought of that," Eldan returned, "but torches won't work this time because it's too wet behind the falls to keep them lit."

"They'll stay lit if'n you stick a ball of pine sap on the end of em," Buzzard put in.

"Why didn't I think of that?" Pike exclaimed. "That's a great idea, Buzzard! You're a whole lot smarter than you look."

"Well, thanks . . . Hey!"

"Spread out, mates," Eldan called to the rest. "We need to find some pine sap speedy quick!"

It took some time to find the sap and prepare the torches. Tobin and Eldan used their fire stones and a piece of flint to start a small fire and lit the torches in the fire. Since the pine sap was going to burn hot and bright, they kept the torches well below the rocky ledge so as not to be noticed by the guards at the entrance to the Steps.

"All right, hand me two of those torches," said Eldan. "I'm going to need one of you intrepid Rowdies to help me with this."

"I'll go with you, Red" Pike volunteered.

"Good for you, Pork," Eldan smiled back. "Now grab those other two torches and follow me. Time's a wasting!"

Eldan led the way back behind the waterfall. He tried to keep the burning torches as close to the rock ledge as possible, but they still hissed and sputtered as mist and drops from the cascading water hit the flames. Pike crawled close behind carrying two more flaming torches.

"Not too close, Pink," Eldan called back over his shoulder. "I don't want you setting my pants on fire."

After several minutes of difficult crawling, Eldan came to a stop. "Okay, Pint, we're here. The opening is just in front of me. I'll go in first. When I'm ready, I will call for you to follow me. Don't crowd the opening too closely. If this bug comes after me, I may have to dive back out."

"I'll stay back 'til you call," Pike answered.

Cautiously Eldan pushed the flaming torches through the small opening in the rocky ledge. Suddenly there was a hiss and a snap as the large water bug went for the torch, knocking it out of Eldan's hand. There was shrieking roar as the burned insect withdrew from the torch.

"Yikes!" Eldan shouted. "He was waiting for me."

"He was probably attracted by the light," Pike suggested.

"I'm going to try it again," Eldan announced.

With a tight grip on his one remaining torch, the young Makerian pushed it into the opening. A hissing snarl could be heard from further back into the dark opening, but the insect did not attack this time. As Eldan drew his head and shoulders into the opening, he heard more of the angry growls.

"Be warned, Prank," Eldan called back to his friend. "There are at least two more of them in here with ol' Grumpy."

"Watch yerself, Red!" Pike answered.

Eldan reached down and picked up his fallen torch, which was barely flickering on the damp cave floor. He quickly relit it from his burning torch and continued to crawl into the cave. The passage he was in was very low with a rocky floor. Eldan could only crouch in the small grotto. As the young Makerian lifted his torches, he could see three of the large, flat, leaf-like insects further back in the cave. They were very upset that their home had been violated by an intruder, but they were also very wary of the flaming source of pain that Eldan waved in each hand.

"They're staying away from me now," Eldan called out to Pike. "I think Grumpy must have told his girlfriends about the torches. Scurry on in here, Puce, and we'll herd them out of the opening."

Within a few moments, Pike was crouched next to his red-haired companion.

"All right, Purge ol' boy, here's the plan: you back up a few steps so that the cave opening is clear and hold up your torches so that the waterbugs won't run past the opening and go further up into the cave. I'll get behind them and scare them your way. With you blocking the way up into the cave, the only escape they will have is out the way we came in."

When Pike was in position, Eldan started working his way around the three large grey creatures. After he had flanked the water bugs, he began to approach them from the rear, waving his torches as he came. The three insects became extremely agitated at this maneuver and began striking at Eldan with their mantis-like forelegs. For a moment it looked like they might charge, but as the redheaded Makerian continued to approach them, the nearest one reluctantly began to retreat. When the first one turned away from the heat of Eldan's torches, the other two quickly joined him.

"They're coming your way, Pock!" Eldan exclaimed. "Hold your ground and wave your torches! I'll crowd them toward the exit."

The roar of the waterfall covered all of the yelling. Tobin and the others stood there anxiously watching the opening behind the waterfall. The only sign they could see of Eldan or Pike's presence was the occasional glint of light flashing through the cascading water. Tobin was beginning to get concerned when suddenly three large, dark forms came charging out from behind the falls. In their mad dash to escape the torches, the waterbugs ran right through the midst of Tobin and the Rowdies. The friends had to quickly dive out of the way as the angry insects came barreling into their midst. Mumbles didn't see them coming and was savagely knocked aside by the first raging insect. Fortunately for Mumbles, the water bugs were trying to get as far away from the torches as possible and kept running.

"Is everyone all right?" Tobin asked in a low voice.

"It's Mumbles!" Stub answered back. "One of da beasts knocked 'em into some brush, an' e' ain't movin'!"

Quickly the others rushed over to Mumbles as Stub was dragging him out of the tangle of branches.

"Hurrrumph?"

"Thug wants to know if'n he's hurt bad," Buzzard translated.

"I cain't see nuthin' in dis dark," Stub shot back.

At that moment a greenish glow engulfed all of them as Tobin pulled out his light stick. As Tobin held the light close to Mumbles, Stub began to examine his unconscious friend.

"Dis ain't good!" Stub voiced his thoughts.

"He ain't kilt, is he?" Buzzard asked with concern.

"Naw," Stub answered. "He got knocked out when 'e hit his head on a limb over dere. He'll come to directly. But, see, dat ain't his problem. When he got flung into da bush, a piece of one of da sharp limbs speared his leg. I don't t'ink da leg's broke, but its bleedin' real bad."

"Can ya bandage it?" Buzzard suggested.

"Not 'til I gets dis stick outta 'is leg, an' even den I ain't so sure da bandage will stop dis kind of bleedin'."

"Go ahead and remove the stick before he comes to," Tobin ordered.

"Yeah," Stub agreed. "I guess dere's no sense lettin' 'im come to and den pullin' it out when he can feel it."

After the stick was removed, Tobin tied a leather strap tightly around the injured leg above the wound, which greatly slowed the flow of blood.

"Well, look at dat!" Stub exclaimed. "Tyin' dat strap tight around his leg stopped the bleedin'! I wish I had known dat trick when I had dat bad nose bleed last year."

"Stub, yer brain must be made outta rock," Buzzard declared. "Ya cain't put one of them thangs around yer neck."

"Well," came Stub's embarrassed response, "at least it fixed Mumbles' leg."

"His leg's not safe yet," Tobin joined in. "We can't leave that strap on his leg for very long, and as soon as we take it off, it will start bleeding again unless we can get the bleeders to close up."

"How do you do that?" Stub asked.

"There are actually several ways to do it, but what I'm going to do is take this vial of liquid and pour it into the wound."

"What is it?" Buzzard asked as Tobin uncorked a long resin vial he had pulled from his pack and began pouring the clear liquid into the leg wound.

"It's an extract from the leaves and bark of the Hamamelis bush," Tobin answered. "It sort of causes the torn muscles, skin, and bleeders in the wound to contract. If they shrink up enough, then the bleeding stops. It should at least slow the blood loss enough for a bandage to control it."

"Hey! What's going on out here?"

"Red!" Buzzard snapped as he saw Eldan and Pike approaching. "Dem crawlers you and Pike skeered outta dat cave ran smack over Mumbles. It knocked him colder'n a crawdad an' messed up his leg."

"Glad you made it back," Tobin said as he saw his brother and Pike walk over to join them. "Do you have any yarrow leaf with you?"

"I believe I do, Bubs," Eldan returned as he looked with concern at the injured Rowdy. "Are you going to make a poultice?"

"I thought we'd crush up some yarrow leaves and bandage them against his wounds."

"What does that do?" Pike asked curiously.

"It helps keep the festerers away," answered Eldan.

As Tobin and Stub were bandaging the injured leg, Mumbles began to moan and stir.

"It looks like he's starting to come around, but there's no way he's going to be much use to us," Pike announced.

"We'll have to find a safe place for Stub to look after him until we get back," said Tobin.

It didn't take very long to find a secure spot for Stub and Mumbles to camp. There was a small outcropping of rocks very near the creek a short distance from the end of the waterfall. An easy climb up these rocks revealed a small crevice that would provide some protection for the two Rowdies while still giving them a clear view of the opening behind the waterfall.

It took a little work to get Mumbles up the face of the rocks, but by this time he was conscious and able to help with the climb. After getting their injured friend settled on a bed of soft grass up in the crevice, Tobin pulled a small brown package out of his pack and handed it to Stub.

"What's 'dis?"

"That's an Aralia thorn," Tobin answered.

Stub looked down at the small bundle in his hands. "Uh . . . what does I do wid it?"

"When Mumbles' leg starts hurting him, you can get that whole packet soaking wet and then pound it with a rock to crush the thorn inside. Squeeze some of that juice into his wound, and it will stop the pain for a short while. Do it as often as you need to in order to keep him comfortable."

"It'll really do dat?" Stub asked incredulously.

"Yep," Tobin answered.

"Wow!" Stub exclaimed, looking at the small package. "It kinda makes you wanna get hurt just to try it out."

"Now listen up, Stub," Pike said firmly. "I know you're gonna be looking after Mumbles, but be alert! When we come out, if somebody's after us, you've got to cover us; so be ready. You got that?"

"I got it."

"Let's shake a leg, troop," Eldan encouraged from below the rocky ledge. "We need to get in the cave before Grumpy Waterbug comes back with his two sweeties."

When everyone had their packs and was assembled beside the edge of the falls, Eldan and Pike crawled back into the space behind the cascading water and led the others into the cave.

CHAPTER NINETEEN

LITTLE SNIDE

"What's he doing?" Hawthorn asked with concern. "He's been hanging around here all day."

He and Jay were lying in the entrance of one of the huts watching as Poke wandered aimlessly around the large cave which served as their living quarters.

"Yeah, you're right," agreed Jay. "He just keeps moving through the camp looking at stuff and talking to a few folks. He never comes back here, but he never gets far away either."

"He's watchin' us," Rush answered from inside the hut.

"Cari obviously hasn't told the Shaman about us," Hawthorn reasoned out loud, "or they would have already taken us to the cells."

"And we made Poke look pretty bad when he led the Shaman back here the other night and we were here waiting on them," Jay added.

"The Shaman may not be convinced that we're in cahoots with the Makerians," returned Rush, "but Poke's a different story. He knows that we're friends with Carineda, an' I'll bet he figures we're gonna try to free her."

"Of course!" Hawthorn exclaimed. "That's exactly what he's doing! He knows we only have a day before we pack up and leave, so if we try to free her, he knows it's got to be today or tonight."

"That little sneak is tryin' to figure out our plans," Jay agreed.

"So what are we going to do, Rush?" Hawthorn asked with concern.

"Wel-l-l," Rush drawled, "Poke knows we're gonna try somethin', but he thinks we'll be makin' our move by slippin' out of the main entrance to our cave. He don't know we got us a backdoor. So I think we should do just what he expects. We'll send some of our people out the front entrance of our cave to wander around a bit and give ol' Poke something to fret about while we send Lil' Snide into the small tunnel the Makerians found."

"Rush," Jay chuckled, "that's brilliant! If we do what he expects, he will watch us like a hawk."

"So who should be the diversion?" Savin asked.

"Well, think about it for a minute," Rush answered. "Of all of us, who does Poke trust the least?"

"That's easy," Jay shot back. "He trusts you and me the least."

"Exactly!" Rush returned with a smile. "So you and me and maybe Savin will take a little stroll here in a bit and let Poke think he's got us all figured out. But first let's go over the plan with everyone and make sure we all know what we're gonna do."

It was well past supper when they decided to put their plan into effect. Rush, Savin, and Jay stepped out of their huts and started an easy walk toward the entrance of their cave. Rush picked up a bucket, and Jay grabbed a coil of rope and threw it over his shoulder just to make Poke more suspicious. Hawthorn lay in the opening of one of the huts watching his father and friends as they made their way to the far end of the long cave.

"Perfect!" Hawthorn whispered to himself as he saw Poke jump up from where he was sitting against one of the walls and follow cautiously after the others. Hawthorn waited until he was sure that Poke wasn't coming back before he gave Sagamore, Noblis, and Lil' Snide the sign to move to the entrance to the crawlway.

To hide their three friends' movements from the view of others nearby, Hawthorn and Rose drug some bedding material out of one of the huts and pretended to be airing it out. As they lifted up the large blanket between them, Noblis carefully crawled out of the hut and behind the blanket to the small hole in the wall behind the other hut. The other two quickly followed. Once the three had disappeared into the opening, Hawthorn and his mother folded the blanket and returned it to its place.

They had just settled down for the long wait when a small, slim form approached their camp. "Hey, Thorn! Hey, Lady Rose!"

"Well hello, Juniper," Rose answered with a smile when she saw their friend. "How come you're not getting ready for bed?"

"Land sakes, Lady Rose!" Juniper whispered excitedly. "How is a body supposed to sleep knowing that poor Carineda is locked away in the Shaman's prison and sufferin' who knows what? Why, I would have plum fretted away to nothin' if Momma hadn't kept reminding me that the Lord Jehesus was taking care of all this! I know she's right, but I just want to do something about it! Momma said, 'Now, Juniper,'—when she's about to get on to me she always calls me Juniper—'Now, Juniper,' she says, 'If there was some way I could help the poor girl, I'd do it, even if it meant risking my life. I would expect you to do the same. It would be what Jehesus would want us to do for a sister. But as it stands right now, there is nothing you or I can do to help her except pray and trust in the Maker's power to save her.'"

"How is your mother, Juni?" Rose asked with concern.

"Momma? Oh, she's fine, Lady Rose. She's as fine as mole fur. Momma's got a lot more faith than I've got. After she said all of that and we prayed for Carineda, she lay down and went right to sleep. Now isn't that just like Momma, Lady Rose? Once she turns something over to the Lord, she's done with it. She figures it's His concern now, and she's completely at peace. I sure do wish I was more like her, but I reckon my belt is cinched a little tighter than Momma's. I couldn't sleep, so when I looked down here and saw that you two were still up, I decided to see if you and Thorn might want to pray some more."

Rose walked over and threw both of her arms around the young girl's neck. "I understand what you're going through," Rose said as she stood back and held Juniper by the shoulders. "I don't think my faith is as strong as your mother's either. But, you know, she is right. The Lord Jehesus seems to be working in all of this. Sit down here with Hawthorn and me, and we'll let you know what's happening. Then the three of us will do some serious praying."

Noblis led the way through the small rocky tunnel. Next crawled Little Snide, followed by Sagamore. The greenish glow of the light sticks suspended around the two Makerians' necks illuminated the tiny passageway. The squat opening they were crawling through was really no more than a crack in the limestone rock that was just large enough at the bottom to allow a Larkin-sized person to squeeze through.

For the next half hour, Noblis led them through the twisting, snake-like passageway. They finally arrived at a place where the lower part of their tunnel widened out, which gave them a little more space. At this point Noblis stopped and waved for his companions to join him.

"Why are we stopping'?" Little Snide asked.

"The crawlway narrows just ahead," Noblis returned in a whisper. "This as far as I was able to crawl the last time we were in here. Take my light stick and see if you can make it through." Noblis lifted the cord from around his neck from which the light source was suspended and placed it over the head of the young Rowdy.

"Be as quiet as you can," Sagamore warned, "and when you think you're getting close to the Shaman's cave, you better stick the light stick inside your shirt so no one will notice."

"Remember, young one," Noblis reminded, "we don't know where you will come out in their cave. That means that you won't know where the door to the Treasure Cave will be."

"Yeah, I know," Little Snide shot back. "I'll have to hunt for it."

"Just be alert, and don't get spotted."

Little Snide nodded his understanding and turned to follow the shrinking passageway. As he reached the constricted area, the young Rowdy had to turn his body sideways to fit into it. It was indeed a tight fit for him, but he managed to continue inching forward. At one point the space through which he crawled was so tight that he had to breathe all of the air out of his lungs and deflate his chest to get enough room to keep going. He crept forward as far as he could until his lungs screamed for air, then he stopped and took a moment to breathe. Then he again let all of the air out of his lungs and crawled some more. He had to repeat this process ten times before he finally reached the opening into the Shaman's cave. He noticed that the crawlway he was in connected to the Shaman's cave near the ceiling. Little Snide lay there in the opening for several minutes, watching and listening for anyone who might be in the passageway into which he was about to drop.

The cave before him was dimly lit by occasional oil lamps resting on holders mounted on the walls. Cautiously

Little Snide worked his way out of the tunnel opening and let himself quietly down to the floor. He took some time to study his surroundings so he could find the opening again when he returned. Turning to his right, the young Rowdy made his way along the wide tunnel searching for a sealed doorway.

He had been moving forward for several minutes when he heard voices. He halted immediately and listened. The voices seemed to be some distance away but did not come closer. He crept forward more cautiously till he reached a curve in the tunnel. Peering around the corner, he could see an opening in the side wall up ahead out of which the voices came. As he watched, suddenly two figures in long flowing robes appeared out of the darkness further down the cave and turned into the lighted opening Little Snide was observing.

That must be their living quarters, the young Rowdy thought to himself. *I've gone the wrong way!* At that moment two more Shaman dressed as guards came walking out of the opening and strode purposefully toward Little Snide. *Oh Bugs! Oh Bugs!* his thoughts yelled at him. *I got to go!*

The young rescuer's short little legs beat a path back the way he had come. He was relieved when he spotted the place where his crawlway opening was located. Leaping up, he grabbed at the rocky prominence behind which he knew was the opening to the small tunnel that led back to his friends. He had just slid into the opening when he heard the steps of the Shaman guards. He held perfectly still, hardly daring to breathe as the jailors walked past him. Little Snide waited until he could no longer hear their footsteps before he crawled out of his place of concealment.

Quietly dropping back down onto the cave floor, the young Rowdy followed after the Shaman sentries. He moved as quietly and as quickly as possible. He really wanted to get close enough to the two guards so that he could at least keep an eye on them. After several minutes he peered around a turn in the cave and spotted them a short distance ahead of him. *Maybe they'll lead me to the cells,* he thought. *At least by keeping them in sight, I'll be able to tell when they start to head back toward me.*

Little Snide had not been stalking after them for very long when he spotted something that caused him to stop in his tracks. He saw an old wooden door on his right built into the wall of the cave. He crouched quietly beside the old door, watching after the retreating jailors until they disappeared around a corner. Placing his ear against the door, Little Snide tapped his finger against it softly. Hearing nothing, he tried tapping a little harder. Still there was nothing. Finally the young Rowdy looked both directions down the cave and, seeing no one, cupped his hands around his mouth and whispered as loudly as he dared, "Hey! Are you guys in there? It's me, Lil' Snide!"

He quickly pressed his ear against the door to listen. This time he thought he heard a muffled sound. Finally a voiced whispered back, "Kid, is that you?"

"Yeah, Pike! It's me, Lil' Snide."

"Can you get this door open?" Pike called back.

"Give me a minute," returned Little Snide as he pulled out his light stick and began studying the door.

There was no bar locking the door like Little Snide was hoping. Instead the boy saw that two wedges had been driven into grooves in the door frame near the top and the bottom of the door to seal it shut. He pulled and tugged on them, but they would not move. He tried to loosen the wedges by rocking them, but even with all of his strength, he could not budge them.

"I can't do it, Pike!" Little Snide called through the door. "The wedges are in too tight!"

"Can you find a rock to knock them out?" This voice sounded like Eldan's.

"I don't think that will work," Little Snide answered after studying the wedges. "There's no head or edge on the wedges to hit against. There's only a hole drilled in the side of both of them."

There was silence for several moments; then Little Snide heard Eldan's voice again, "Listen up, bub. That hole is how they get them out. You have to put a rod in the hole and then hit the rod with a rock or a hammer to drive out the wedges."

"But I don't have anything like that!" Little Snide almost shouted at the door, "and besides, someone would have to hold the rod in the hole for me to hit it with a hammer."

Again there was silence. "You'll have to go back and get help," the answer finally came.

"But Red, I'm the only one who can get through the tunnel."

"The Maker must have someone else who can help you," Eldan encouraged. "You've got to go back and find them."

After hearing this, Little Snide smacked his hand hard against one of the wedges in frustration. "How am I supposed to do that?" the youth snapped.

"The Maker has an answer to this," Eldan returned. "He will help you find it. Go back and tell Chummy what you need. I know he and his people are praying. We will be, too."

"Okay, I'm goin'," he called back, then turned and ran back up the cave to the opening of the small crawlway. Nimbly the young Rowdy slid into the tunnel and hurried back the way he had come.

Hawthorn, Rose, and Juniper were still praying when an urgent whisper interrupted them, "We got big trouble!"

Looking up, Hawthorn saw Little Snide crawling in the doorway of the hut with Noblis and Sagamor right behind him.

"Calm down, young one," Rose said gently, "and tell us what's happened."

Little Snide quickly related the difficulty with removing the wedges from the door to the Treasure Cave. "But the real problem here is gettin' somebody back in there to help me," Little Snide added. "That tunnel is really small! It was all I could do to snake through it myself. There's no way you could get through there, Chummy, and you're the smallest one here!"

"Well now, I don't mean to be inserting myself into somebody else's conversation, but your last comment wasn't entirely correct."

All eyes turned to the speaker. It was Juniper.

"I think just about everybody here would admit that small is my specialty," Juni said with her big eyes flashing.

"Juni," Hawthorn said, "he's talking about someone crawling back through that small passageway to help him open the sealed door."

"I've been sitting here listening, Thorn," Juniper returned. "I know what our little friend's talking about, and I'm saying that I'm the one to go with him."

"But, Juni, you don't know what you're getting into," Hawthorn pleaded. "You've never done anything like this before!"

"Now you're right as rain when you say that," Juniper smiled back. "You sure are. But that doesn't mean that I can't do it. My Mama says that you don't know what you can do unless you try."

"Juni girl," Rose spoke up, "this is dangerous! What would your mother say about you doing this?"

"She'd say that since there is no one else who could fit through that tunnel but me, that I must be the Maker's answer to all of our prayers.

"Now I really think we've talked enough. We're going to run out of time if we don't get started."

With a resigned nod of agreement, they set about getting a hammer and rod for Little Snide and Juniper to carry with them for removing the wedges in the door.

"If you fellows will step out of the hut for a moment," Rose announced, "I will see if I can get Juni in some cave-crawling clothes."

"Well," Hawthorn said with resignation, "there goes another pair of my pants."

CHAPTER TWENTY

JUNIPER'S MISSION

The crawl back through the tunnel was much slower this time. Juniper kept up a good pace with Little Snide and the Makerians until they got to the narrow spot in the small cavern. Little Snide went first to show Juniper how to do it, but the crawlway was so tight and twisty that the young Rowdy had to coach her along almost every inch of the way. Juniper was scared and scraped in a number of places, but she didn't give up.

Eventually they reached the real tight spot in the crawlway. Before he went through, Little Snide tried to explain to Juniper what she had to do. "You're doin' just great," Little Snide whispered back, "but this part is kinda tricky. It's real tight, see . . . but you can do it. You got to blow all the air out of your chest to make yourself as small as you can and then crawl forward. Keep crawling until you got to breathe again, then stop and get your breath. When you're ready, blow out all of your air again and crawl some more.

"Okay, here I go," Little Snide announced and began working his way through the tiny passageway.

After several minutes Juniper heard her friend's voice whispering back down the tunnel, "I made it through. Now it's your turn."

Using the Makerian light stick hanging around her neck, Juniper surveyed the tiny crack into which she was supposed to crawl.

"I . . . I don't think I can do this," she stammered.

"Oh yes, you can," Little Snide whispered back.

"No . . . no, it's much too small! I'll get stuck!"

"It'll be okay," came the answering call. "It's big enough to get through. I did it."

"What are you talking about?" Juniper snapped. "I can't even get my head in that hole."

"Start with your arms," Little Snide encouraged her, "then you have to turn your head sideways to get it through the opening. When your chest gets to the opening, that's when you let out all of your air and crawl in. Now hurry up! Our friends are counting on you!"

Those last words provided Juni with the motivation she needed to move forward in spite of her fears. "Oh Lord Jehesus," she prayed out loud as she moved into the tiny crack, "somehow get this scared little girl through this worm hole!"

Once her arms were in the tiny crawlway, she turned her head sideways and discovered that she was able to move forward. It took an enormous amount of courage to blow all of the air out of her chest and push herself further into the small opening. By the time she got her hips into the opening, she felt like her lungs were going to burst. She stopped and gasped in great gulps of air.

"You need to keep moving," Little Snide called to her.

With her heart pounding, Juniper tried to move forward, but she wouldn't budge. She clawed at the rocks ahead of her and pushed hard with her feet, but she couldn't dislodge herself from that spot. "Oh no!" she cried in panic. "Oh no! This is bad! This is very bad!"

"Be quiet!" Little Snide whispered urgently. "What's wrong?"

"I'm STUCK!"

"Just calm down. It'll be okay."

"Okay? OKAY?!" Juniper called back in complete panic. "It won't be OKAY! Didn't you hear me? I'm stuck! I can't move! I won't budge! I'm jammed in here tight as a stopper! I know what *okay* looks like, and THIS ISN'T IT! Maybe you people define *okay* differently than we do, so let me tell you something, moleboy: being stuck in here is NOT OKAY!"

"Would you please calm down?!" the young Rowdy hissed back. "I know what's wrong. You're stuck because you're breathing. If you will stop yelling and let all of your air out, you will be able to crawl forward again."

"Oh," Juniper said with some embarrassment as she realized that that was exactly what she was doing. Once again willing herself to blow out all of her air, she discovered that she was no longer stuck and began to crawl forward. It took all the strength she had and more coaxing from Little Snide, but eventually Juniper made it to the end of the crawlway.

"We made a lot of noise back there," the young Rowdy announced as they rested at the end of the small tunnel. "You stay here for a minute. I'm going to climb out of the opening and have a look around to see if we attracted any attention. If it's safe, I'll come back and get you."

Juniper was starting to get nervous at her companion's delay when she heard a voice close at hand. "Everything's clear. Climb on out."

With some help from Little Snide, Juniper made her way out of the tiny crawlway, slid over the rocks at the exit of their small tunnel, and dropped down to the floor of the large passageway that led to the cells. "Where do we go from here?" Juniper asked as she dusted herself off.

"Follow me . . . and keep quiet," came the answer.

JUNI AND LIL' SNIDE

Leading the way, Little Snide trotted down the passage, staying close to the left hand wall. He stopped regularly to listen for sounds of approaching guards.

"Do you know where you're going?" Juniper asked with some frustration after several minutes of the trotting and stopping.

"Shhhh!" Little Snide hissed. "There could be guards all around here! You've got to be quiet!"

"Well, with all of our starting and stopping, it seems to me that we aren't getting anywhere," Juni shot back.

"The door we're looking for is up ahead a little farther. We're almost there; just be quiet and follow me."

Little Snide continued cautiously down the shadowy passageway with Juniper close behind. After several more minutes they stopped again. "That's it over there," he said, pointing to an old wooden door in the side wall of the passage and immediately trotting over to it.

Little Snide slapped the surface of the door several times lightly with his hand. He then leaned next to it and whispered as loudly as he dared, "Hey, we're back!" Without waiting for an answer, the young Rowdy pulled out the stone-headed hammer that he had tucked into his belt and turned to Juniper. "We need that rod you brought with you."

"Oh . . . uh . . . right," Juni answered as she began to pat around the middle of her tunic.

"You lost it?" Little Snide hissed in a panic.

"No, not exactly," Juniper answered, still searching her tunic. "It's here someplace. I stuck it inside my tunic so it wouldn't get caught on anything, but I guess it kinda got moved around a bit with all of the crawling. Oh, bother!" In exasperation the young girl untied her belt and began jumping up and down. After the third jump, the wooden rod fell at her feet. With a smile Juni picked up the rod and handed it to her companion.

Little Snide placed one end of the rod into the hole in one of the wedges sealing the door. The hole had been drilled at an angle in the wedge so that the rod actually pointed more toward the frame of the door. He turned to his companion. "I need you to hold the rod in this hole just like this while I hit the end of it with my hammer."

"Excuse me for sayin' so, but won't that make a lot of noise?"

"You're right; it will," Little Snide returned thoughtfully. "I know! I'll muffle it with my tunic." Rapidly untying his belt, the young Rowdy slid his tunic over his head, folded it a couple of times, and wrapped it over the end of the rod. "Now you hold onto all of that," he told Juniper, "whiles't I smack it!"

Little Snide began with easy taps, increasing the force of each blow as he realized that the tunic was doing its job. With every hard blow, he would stop and listen for approaching guards. Suddenly, after the seventh hard swing of his hammer, the wedge flew out.

"Quickly!" he whispered. "Put the rod in the hole of the bottom wedge." As soon as Juniper had it in place, Little Snide again began pounding it with his hammer. Once again the wedge popped out, and in the next instant, strong hands began to shove the door open.

The first one through was Pike. "Hey, kid," Pike smiled. "We were starting to worry."

The next one out was Eldan. "We're glad you got that open, but you took your own sweet time getting back here. What were you doing?"

"I got back here as fast as I could, Red. Honest!" Little Snide answered. "It took some time to crawl back out and find someone to help. My friend here did the best she could, but it was a tough crawl."

At this point Eldan looked over at Little Snide's helper. His mouth dropped open as he recognized her. "Miss Juni?!"

"Well, hi there, Sir Eldan!" Juniper said, her eyes wide and smiling. "I guess you didn't expect to find little ol' me out here, did you? What a special blessing this is.

Not only do I get to help poor Miss Cari, but I get to see you as well! Now isn't the Maker good?"

"Why . . . uh . . . yes," Eldan finally answered. "Yes, He is! And speaking of the Maker, we need to get busy doing what He sent us here to do."

"Oh, Sir Eldan, you are such a leader!" the young girl gushed. "I just love a person who can take charge."

Eldan, Tobin, and Pike spent several minutes talking to Little Snide. The young Rowdy told them everything he had seen when he first scouted the Shaman's cave.

"That's not much to go on," Pike announced after he heard Little Snide's report.

"At least we know which direction not to go," Eldan said encouragingly.

"Eldan's right," Tobin spoke up. "We'll head deeper into the tunnel, but let's be cautious. Eldan, you scout ahead of us. Make sure we don't run into trouble. The rest of us will be right behind you."

"Can we go, too?" Little Snide asked hopefully.

"I don't think so, kid," Pike answered. "You've been a big help, but I think you've done enough. Muckly would skin me if I let anything happen to you."

"You two young ones had better stay here till we return," Tobin ordered. "Hide inside the doorway to the Treasure Cave."

With expressions of disappointment, Juniper and Little Snide stood to the side as the rescue party trotted down the tunnel toward the cells.

Because it had taken so long to get the Treasure Cave door open, Eldan knew they were running short on time. He wasn't sure when the next set of guards would show up, so he moved quickly. He would sprint down the tunnel until he came to a turn, stop, listen, and then ease his head around the corner. Seeing no one, he would wave to the others behind him and sprint to the next turn. The fact that, so far, there had been no side passages to worry about had made the journey much easier.

Eventually Eldan came to the place where the tunnel enlarged into the wet cavern. Creeping forward cautiously, Eldan led the way along the lighted path. When the redheaded Makerian glanced around the large boulder and spotted the two guards standing beside a door in the wall, he knew they'd found the cells. He waved to his friends to join him. After they arrived, Eldan signaled for them all to be quiet, pointed at Tobin, and nodded toward the edge of the boulder.

Tobin crept quietly to the side of the large rock and took a look. After a moment's consideration, he squatted down and began to sketch a plan in the dirt on the cave floor. Pointing to individuals and to his drawing, Tobin made each of them understand his idea. With nods of understanding all around, everyone but Tobin and Eldan moved quietly into the darkness around them. After waiting quietly for several minutes for the others to get into position, Tobin nodded to Eldan, and they both stood up and walked around the boulder and approached the two guards.

"Hey!" one of the guards called out, "Halt right there and tell us who you are."

Tobin and Eldan continued forward without answering. Eventually the two Makerian brothers were close enough that the guards could see them quite clearly.

"Answer me! Who are you?" Both sentries had their stings in their hands and were on their guard.

"We're here to keep you from getting hurt," Tobin said calmly as he and Eldan continued walking towards the guards.

"What are you talking about?!" one of the guards snapped.

"It's really quite simple," Eldan said with a smile as he and Tobin stopped a short distance in front of both guards. "Both of you put your weapons on the ground and lift up your hands, and our friends who are hidden in the darkness on either side of you won't attack."

"There's nobody else here but you two," the first guard sneered as they pointed their stings at the Makerians.

"I wouldn't be too sure about that," Pike called out of the darkness on their right.

"That goes ditto for our side," Buzzard added from the shadows on their left.

Both guards looked at each other, then back at Tobin and Eldan.

"So what's it gonna be, fellows?" Eldan said with a large grin. "We can leave you in the cells till the next guards show up, or you can wake up several hours from now with a splitting headache."

Both guards dropped their stings and raised their hands.

"Open the door," Tobin ordered, and both guards jumped to the door and lifted the bar.

By now the Rowdies had joined them and surrounded the guards. The door was opened, and Eldan rushed in with one of the torches.

"There she is—over there!" Eldan cried as he spotted Carineda's limp form lying in one of the cells. "Miss Cari! Miss Cari!

"Tobs, she's not moving!" Eldan called to his brother.

"They worked her over pretty bad the lasth time," said a voice from the cell across from her.

"Quickly!" Tobin snapped at the guards. "Get these cells open!"

The Rowdies shoved the guards forward, and the two sentinels grabbed the beam holding the bars and lifted it out of the way. As they did so, the latticework bars fell to the floor. Eldan ducked into the hole to get Carineda and gently drew her out into the light. A groan escaped her swollen and bruised lips as he laid her down.

Tobin already had his water pouch out of his backpack and handed it to Eldan. Eldan yanked the stopper out with his teeth and began to pour a small amout of the cool liquid over her lips. As the water trickled into her mouth, Cari swallowed and began to lick her lips.

Tobin knelt down beside them, and taking the water pouch from Eldan, he poured some water into his hand and gently began to wash Carineda's face with it.

"Thank you," Cari whispered as she began to respond. ". . . very thirsty," she said weakly.

Eldan lifted her head, and Tobin began to pour more of the water into her open lips. She took several swallows before she opened her eyes. Tears of relief began to well up in her red swollen eyes as she said, ". . . hoping you'd come . . . wasn't doing very well."

As Tobin and Eldan worked on Cari, Possum crawled out of his cell to join them. "She wath telling me about the Maker and His Thon Jehethuth when the Shaman came back to question her," Possum volunteered. "They wanted her to tell who helped her get into the Stepth and who elth came with her. Each time they asthed her, all she would thay is how much the Maker loved them. I guesth they got fruthrated with her not antherin' their questionth, tho they began thlapping her and hitting her. One of them even kicked her. Each time, when she would recover enough to thpeak, she would sthart telling them about the Maker and His Thon Jehethuth again. The lasth time they justh beat her till she pasthed out. At firsth I thought they had killed her, but after they locked uth back up in here, I heard her groan a few timeth.

"I'm gonna be honesth with you fellowth," Possum continued. "I ain't never really put much faith in the Maker mythelf, but she thure doesth. She took a horrible beatin' to tell thosth heartlesth rathcalth that Jehethuth wanted to thave 'em. There she wath tellin' 'em how much the Maker wanted to thave their worthlesth hideth, and all the while them just a beatin' her. It made me thick to my sthomach. I wanted to kill 'em, but not her. The lasth thing she thaid before she pasthed out wath a lil' prayer athkin' the Maker to forgive 'em. Can you believe it?"

"Yeth...I mean, yes," Eldan said, still holding Cari, "I can believe it."

"Well, before the Shaman came in thisth lasth time," Possum continued, "she wath telling me that I could pray to the Maker if I wanted to, and He would listhen to me. I thought that wath crathy when she told me, 'cuz I wathn't no Shaman, but then after I thaw how they treated her and how she reacted, I stharted prayin', askin' the Maker an' Hith Thon to help her."

"Thank you, friend," Tobin said, looking Possum in the eyes. "The Maker sent us as an answer to those prayers."

"Quiet, Girl!" Little Snide hissed as he cut Juniper off in the middle of her telling about her favorite meal, where her name came from, how to put a pleat in a dress, and that honeydew made her lips itch.

"My name is not *girl*," she returned. "It's Juniper, and it's a very nice name."

"Just be quiet!" he whispered urgently. "I hear someone coming!"

"Well, maybe it's our people coming back," Juniper said encouragingly.

"No! They're coming from the wrong direction to be our people. Now shush up!"

Little Snide pulled the doorway to the Treasure Cave completely shut and held it tightly, hoping that the guards would not notice the missing wedges that were supposed to be sealing the door. Gruff voices could be heard through the thick wooden door as the guards passed. As the voices died away, Little Snide cracked the door back open. "There's four of 'em!" the young Rowdy whispered over his shoulder. "They're headed to the cells. One of them said that this time she would talk or die."

"Oh, mercy!" Juniper shot back. "That bunch will come up on our people from behind and spoil everything!"

"You're right, Girlie," Little Snide agreed with a look of determination. "We've got to do something! Come on!" With that, he pushed open the door and ran after the guards.

"My name is not *GIRLIE!*" Juniper snorted. She took the time to push the door closed before she sprinted after her companion.

CHAPTER TWENTY-ONE

THE WAY OUT

Tobin pulled a leather pouch from his backpack and handed it to his brother, who was still supporting the injured Carineda. "Give her some of this nectar to drink, Eldan. We need to get some strength back into her."

Eldan took the offered pouch, and removing the carved wooden stopper, he offered the sweet drink to Cari. Carineda understood her need for strength, so she tried to take in as much of the nectar as she could.

Tobin took the water pouch from Eldan and handed it to Possum, who began to drink greedily from it. He finally lowered the pouch and wipped his mouth. "Ahhh! That there ith good sthuff," Possum said with a smile, "esthpecially when you ain't had it fer a while."

When Cari had finished with the nectar, Eldan handed this to Possum as well. "Take several big swallows of that," Eldan encouraged. "You'll need it before we get out of here."

"Um-um!" Possum said with enthusiasm after lowering the nectar pouch. "Thath about the moth delithiouth sthtuff I ever did drink. None of you fellowth happen to have any real food, do ya?"

"I got a piece of jerky you can chew on," Buzzard answered as he threw down his pack and began searching through it. "Ah, here it is." The Rowdy pulled out a piece of dark brown leathery meat. He wiped it across his pant leg a couple of times to wipe the dust off it and handed it to Possum.

Possum took the offered jerky and sniffed at it suspiciously. Sticking the dried meat between his teeth, he yanked off a piece and began to chew. Suddenly he stopped, and his eyebrows went up. "Hey," he exclaimed, "ith thith worm?"

"It shore is," Buzzard beamed proudly.

"Leapin' leafhopperth! I ain't had me a good piece of worm jerky thince I wath juth a little thquirt!"

"Hurumph!"

"Excuse me, friend," Buzzard said, "but my buddy Thug wants to know why a nice feller like you got hissef locked up in this here hole?"

Possum looked up sheepishly. "I ain't gonna lie to you fellowth. I'm not a nithe perthon. To be completely honeth, I'm a thief an' a robber, an', uh, thumtimeth I take thtuff that don't belong to me."

"Why, he's one of us!" Buzzard exclaimed and began laughing and slapping Possum on the back like a long lost cousin.

"We need to hurry up and get out of here, Red," Pike spoke up. "No tellin' when the next set of guards will show up."

"He's right, Eldan," Tobin agreed.

"All right," Eldan shot back. "We'll have to carry her. Some of you fellows help me get her up."

"Hurrumph," Thug grunted as he walked over and lifted Carineda like she weighed nothing.

"Okay, then," Tobin announced, "let's move out."

The rescue party had just stepped out into the cavern when a gruff voice called out, "It looks like we got here just in time."

Tobin and the others looked up to see four Larkin guards just in front of them with their stings at the ready.

"Now start talkin'," the guard in front said with a threatening gesture of his sting, "who are you, and how did you get down here without being seen?"

"They caught 'em!" Little Snide whispered into Juni's ear as he pulled back behind the boulder a short distance behind the four Larkin guards.

"What are we going to do?" Juni whispered back anxiously.

"We're gonna' help our people, but we gots to do it fast." As Little Snide explained his plan to Juniper, he quickly untied his sling from where he kept it around his waist. When Juni nodded her understanding, the young Rowdy reached down at his feet and grabbed three rocks. After seating one of the stones in the pocket of his sling, he nodded to Juniper.

"I don't have any patience for this!" the lead guard snapped at his captives. "Either tell us what we want to know, or you'll feel our stings, an' that's a promise!"

"Oh, yoohoo!" called a female voice from behind them. Turning and looking into the darkness, the four guards saw a smallish girl walking out of the gloom.

"I'm sorry to bother you," Juniper said as she continued approaching the sentinels. "I really don't mean to be a pest, but I'm lost, and I desperately need to find the little girls' room."

"Hey! How'd you get down here?" one of the warriors snarled as he started walking briskly towards the girl.

Suddenly Little Snide jumped from where he had been hiding behind Juniper and, with a quick twirl of his arm, sent the stone flying into the front of the approaching guard's acorn cap helmet. With a groan he dropped unconscious to the ground. Instantly Tobin, Eldan, Buzzard, and Pike lunged for the remaining three sentries. The two closest went down in a heap, but the third saw what was happening and managed to sidestep Buzzard's attack. The Shaman warrior brought the pommel of his sting down hard on the back of the Rowdy's head, and Buzzard dropped to the ground.

Turning quickly, the lone remaining sentry sprinted back up the trail for help. Little Snide tried to use his sling, but the escaping warrior was on them too quickly. Without stopping, he ran past Little Snide and Juniper, shoving them both aside as he passed.

"That one got away, Tobs!" Eldan exclaimed.

"That can't be helped," Tobin answered. "Throw these two in the cell room and bolt the door. Leave the unconscious one where he's laying. We've got to get to our way of escape before that guard gets help, or we're done!"

"How's Buzzard?" Pike called over his shoulder as he, Eldan, and Possum shoved the captives into the small prison room.

"Hurrumph," returned Thug, who was kneeling over his sitting companion while still holding Carineda.

"Quit fussin' over me, Thug!" snapped the irritated Buzzard.

"Hurumph."

"I'm okay, I tell ya! I jus' messed up an' let that frizzlin' yahoo get the drop on me. Now he's done got clean away, an' we're in a fine bucket of muck, thanks to me!"

"We're not caught yet," Eldan said encouragingly, "but we do need to shake a leg. Can you run?"

"I expect so," Buzzard answered. "Just help me up on my feet and point me in the right direction."

"What about me . . . poor ol' Pothum?" the Larkin thief called out. "You can't juth leave me here to the merthy of thethe worthleth thcoundrellth!"

"Yer a comin' with us," Buzzard announced. "Yer sorta' fambly anyhow. How'd you like to be a Rowdy?"

"A Rowdy? Ith that what you guyth are?"

"Yep!" Buzzard said proudly, putting his arm around Possum. "We're Red's Rowdies. That there feller over there is Red."

"Well, thure!" Possum answered. "What do I got to do to be one of Redth Rowdieth?"

"We're all kinda learnin' as we go along," Buzzard answered. "For right now you just got to follow King Jehesus and don't kill nobody."

They all ran as fast up the cavern path as they could. They were slowed a little by the stunned Buzzard, who was being helped by Possum and Pike, and by Thug, who was carrying Carineda.

"You an' the girl done good, kid," Pike smiled at Little Snide and Juniper as they ran up the passageway.

Thanks, Pike," Little Snide returned proudly.

"I am NOT *the girl*! My name is Juniper!"

"Hurrumph!" Thug called out as they ran.

"Miss Juniper," Buzzard spoke up as he ran nearby, "Thug says that we's all most grateful for what you an' Lil' Snide done did to get us outta that there scrape we was in."

"Oh, Sir Thug," Juni gushed, "that is so sweet!"

"Hu, hu, hu," Thug chuckled to himself.

"The door . . . to the Treasure Cave . . . is just ahead," Eldan panted as he ran up the tunnel. When Eldan stopped in front of the doorway, he could hear a lot of shouting from the passage further ahead of them.

"Do you want me to stay behind and hammer the wedges back into the door so they won't know where you've gone?" Little Snide asked as he stood beside the doorway getting his breath.

"There's no time!" Eldan shot back. "The Larkin guards will be here any second!"

"You two will have to come with us," Pike said, addressing Little Snide and Juniper.

"Quick, everyone!" Tobin ordered. "Down the tunnel! We've got no time to lose!

"Eldan, you lead!"

Holding his light stick up to light the way, Eldan ran down the narrow, winding passageway leading into the Treasure Cave. Tobin was last to follow. He took a quick glace up the main tunnel and saw the first of the guards round the corner.

"We got to thop thoth guyth!" Possum said as he looked over Tobin's shoulder at the approaching guards.

"We can't stop them," Tobin answered.

"Thure we can," Possum answered. "Juth leave it to Pothum. I got thith."

At that moment Possum jumped from behind the door out in front of the approaching guards. Thowing up his arms, he gave a terrifying scream. In response, an arrow came flying by his head. A second later another arrow stuck into the door.

"Come on!" yelled Tobin as he grabbed the dumbfounded Possum and drug him into the Treasure Cave.

"I don't underthand it," Possum said as he was hurried down the passageway. "That always worked when my thithter was tryin' to get me."

"They're right behind us, Eldan!" Tobin called ahead as he hurried down the tunnel dragging Possum.

Eldan led the way through the large room of the Treasure Cave, past the memorials and slabs containing the bones of the famous Larkin leaders. At the far end of the cave were two slabs containing the bones of Larkin the Great and his wife Lily. As he approached these two slabs, Eldan turned to his right and sprinted to the cave wall. Near the bottom of the wall was a Larkin-size hole. He stopped by this hole and held his light stick up so that those behind him could see the opening. Eldan stood there hurrying the others into the small hole until Tobin arrived with the other light stick. Eldan then shot through the opening and took the lead again.

Because of the darkness, everyone had waited until Eldan joined them with his light. Eldan led them down the sloping tunnel to another opening in the wall on the left side of the passage.

"Keep going, Eldan!" Tobin called as he crawled through the first opening. "They're in the Treasure Cave and coming quickly!"

"Follow me, all of you!" Eldan called as he dived into the small hole low in the wall that led to the way out.

The tunnel they were now entering was very small, and there was only enough room to crawl along. The large rocks on the floor of the tunnel made the way even more difficult, but they pressed on as rapidly as they could. The Thug had the hardest time as he crawled along using two legs and one arm while he held Carineda with his other arm.

They hadn't been crawling very long when the shouts from behind told Eldan that the guards had entered their small crawlway and were coming fast.

As Eldan hurried forward, he noticed that he was now crawling over a lot more sticks and leaf litter which had been washed into the cave from the last rain that had flooded the creek. "Keep coming, everyone!" Eldan called back over his shoulder encouragingly. "We're getting close to the entrance!" The redheaded Makerian hadn't crawled much farther when he noticed that the small crawlway was becoming wider and taller.

Tobin, who was bringing up the rear of their party, had heard Eldan's call and had himself just reached the spot in the cave where the flood rubbish had accumulated. As Tobin paused to find the best spot to place his hands to negotiate the debris, he suddenly felt his feet jerked out from under him.

"I got one of 'em!" Tobin heard a gruff voice yell from behind him.

"They're here!" Tobin shouted a warning to his friends up ahead.

"You need some help?" Pike called back.

"Keep crawling!" the Makerian answered. "Get our people out!"

"I'll help you," said Possum, who was on his knees just in front of Tobin.

"Just get out!" Tobin yelled.

"No can do, my hairy friend. *Never leave a friend behind.* Thath my motto!"

Possum reached down and picked up a long stick that was lying on the floor of the passageway. Looking at this stick with wild eyes, Possum exclaimed, "I know just what to do!"

"I hope this idea isn't like your last idea," Tobin said as he tried kicking his legs but failed to break free of the Larkin guard's grasp.

"Oh, no," Possum answered as he gripped the heavy stick with both hands. "This idea ith nothing like that one. Watch yer head!"

As Possum shouted these last words, he threw the stick butt first with all of his might, straight at Tobin's forehead.

"Yiii!!" Tobin yelled and dropped flat on the floor. The stick shot powerfully through the space where Tobin's head had been. There was a solid "thonk" and a groan as the butt of the stick smacked hard into the forehead of the Larkin guard who had grabbed Tobin's legs.

Pulling his legs free, Tobin began moving forward as fast as he could, pushing Possum ahead of him as he crawled. After several moments of hard work, they managed to catch up to their friends in the more spacious part of the tunnel.

"What's wrong?" Tobin asked urgently. "Why aren't we crawling out?"

"Red says there's a problem," Pike returned.

Tobin looked past Pike and saw his brother quickly searching through his backpack.

"Eldan, the guards are right behind us! We don't have time for this!"

"Don't yell at me, Tobs!" Eldan shot back, still digging in his pack. "It's not my fault! Grumpy Waterbug and his sweeties are back in the cave ahead of us, and he's grumpier than ever.

"We need those torches, Purk, RIGHT NOW!" Eldan called to Pike.

"I've only got one of 'em, Red," Pike returned. "I lost the other one climbing in here."

"Tobs, get his torch lit pronto," Eldan barked at his brother.

Possum was now standing next to Thug, who was still holding Carineda. Turning to the injured girl, Possum said, "I'm kinda new to thith Rowdy buithneth, Mith Cari. Should I pray now?"

"Yes, you should," Carineda answered with a weak smile. "Followers of Jehesus pray all the time."

"All the time?" Possum responded.

"Yes, siree!" Juniper added. "'*Pray without ceasing.*' That's what the Maker's Book says."

By now Eldan had pulled his two torches and some tender from his pack and was using his flint and fire-starting rock to shower sparks onto the tinder.

"Better hurry, mates," Buzzard said anxiously. "I can hear the guards just behind us."

"I left one of them unconscious in the narrow part of the crawlway," Tobin said without looking up from his effort to light the torch. "It's going to take a few moments for them to move him out of the way to get to us. HERE!"

As Tobin shouted this last word, he lifted the torch, which now contained a growing flame, and handed it to Pike. Pike in turn held this flame close to Eldan so he could light both of his torches.

"Follow me, Punk," Eldan called as he turned and hurried forward into the larger passageway. "The rest of you follow us!"

As Eldan's torches illuminated the small room before him, the familiar snapping and hissing began to be heard from the dark shadows in the far end of the cave.

HERDING WATERBUGS

"I can see them!" Eldan called to Pike. "All three are against the far wall. Help me keep them back there until our people get out."

Pike quickly moved up closer to Eldan, and the two of them held out their torches threateningly towards the three insects.

"Okay!" Eldan called to the others. "All of you get out of the hole as quickly as you can!"

Those words weren't necessary. Tobin already had the others scambling toward the opening that led to the ledge behind the low waterfall.

"They're coming, Eldan," Tobin announced as he crouched in the opening. "I can hear the guards in the passageway."

"Is everyone out?" Eldan called over his shoulder as he and Pike faced down the huge waterbugs.

"Except for you two," Tobin answered.

"Pitch, take one of my torches and join Tobs on the ledge. Wave the two torches back through the cave opening."

Without asking any questions, Pike moved quickly to obey. By now Eldan could easily hear the yelling of the approaching guards. As soon as he saw Pike crawling though the cave entrance, Eldan began moving, torch first, towards the nearest waterbug. The big male lunged threateningly as Eldan approached, but the heat from the torch swiftly changed his mind, and he began moving quickly away.

Once Eldan got the insects moving along the wall ahead of him, he began yelling and throwing rocks at them to hurry the bugs along. They began scurrying quickly along the wall towards the exit to the cave. Just as they drew near to the opening, Pike's two torches appeared, blocking their way. Eldan hurriedly advanced his torch from behind, and the terrified waterbugs took the only way left to them . . . back up into the cave toward the approaching guards.

"Now let's get out of here!" Eldan yelled as he dove for the opening.

Crawling along the ledge behind the small waterfall, Eldan could hear screams and yells as well as fierce hissing roars echoing from the cave opening behind them.

"What happened?" Little Snide asked with wide eyes as Eldan crawled out from behind the waterfall and on to the bank of the creek to join his friends.

"Well, I think it's fair to say that the Shaman guards have other things on their minds right now than chasing us," Eldan answered with a big smile. "As it turned out, His Royal Grumpiness Sir Waterbug and friends decided to have a word with our recent pursurers.

"All the same," Eldan said, addressing Pike, "I think we would be wise to guard the opening behind the waterfall until we're ready to head to the rafts."

"Good idea," Pike agreed.

"Buzzard, you and Thug get some of Stub's stone-tipped arrows and stand guard over the opening behind the waterfall. Call out if you see anything."

Now that they had time to take stock of their situation, Tobin and Eldan spent several minutes evaluating Carineda's condition. Thug had laid her down on a nearby leaf, and Juniper was kneeling beside her holding her hand.

"Can you sit up, Miss Cari?" Eldan asked.

"I can, Eldan . . . but I'm still a little dizzy," Carineda answered with some labored breaths. "For right now . . . lying still is more comfortable."

"How badly are you hurt?" Tobin asked.

"Ever since my big friend put me down . . . I've been trying to examine myself. I've got some broken ribs, a mild head injury, and lots and lots of bruises. I can't tell for sure, but I might have a punctured lung."

"We'll let you lie here for a few minutes," Tobin returned, "but we can't stay very long. We aren't safe yet. We will put together a litter on which we can carry you. Then we will start toward the rafts that we left downriver.

We have a safe place on the other side of the creek where we can decide best how to handle your injuries."

"Oh, Miss Cari, Miss Cari," Juni exclaimed with tears streaming down her face, "what they did to you was awful . . . just plain awful! I am so sorry that happened!"

"I think I'll be all right, Juniper," Cari smiled up at her friend. "It's actually an honor to be counted worthy to suffer for the name of Jehesus, and I will cherish that thought the rest of my life. But I've got to be honest with you, Juni. I've discovered that I'm not a brave person. I wasn't thinking about the honor of suffering for Christ while it was happening. I screamed and cried terribly. I spent the whole time just begging God to make it stop. I'm very ashamed of myself. But I also know that as poorly as I handeled it, Jehesus never left me the whole time"

At that point Cari look up at Thug and smiled. "Thank you for carrying me out. You're my hero."

Thug lowered his eyes and said, "Hurrumph."

"Ol' Thug said that he was honored to do it," Buzzard interpreted.

"Hurrumph!"

"In fact," Buzzard continued, "Thug sez that if you or the lil' Missy here ever need anything, he'll do it fer ya."

"Thank you!" Carineda answered with a smile.

"Oh, Thuggy," Juniper gushed, "you just say the sweetest things!"

"Huh, huh, huh!" Thug chuckled with embarrassment.

CHAPTER TWENTY-TWO

A NOT-SO-SMOOTH EXIT

"How could this happen?!" screamed a very angry older Shaman with a long grey beard. He and the other High Seven Shaman had just been informed of the escape of their prisoners, and they weren't handling the news very well.

"You said that they got out through the Treasure Cave," the Shaman snarled at the captain of the guard standing before them, "but how did they get in?"

The captain looked very uncomfortable as seven pairs of angry eyes glared at him, waiting for his answer. "Uh . . . well, Your Eminence, since nobody came in through the front gate, I guess they came in the same way they got out."

"You guess?" sneered the old Shaman leader. "Did they have help?"

"We don't know, sir."

"Was the Treasure Cave door damaged?" the Shaman shot back.

"Well, uh . . . no sir," the guard answered. "It's fine."

"Then if they didn't break down the door, they had to have help on the inside to open it. Who helped them, Captain, and where are they?"

"We don't know, sir. It possibly could have been the boy and the girl who came up behind us when we confronted the warriors. I guess they, uh . . . got out with the others," the guard stammered.

"We are getting sick of your guesses, Captain!" the old Shaman snapped. "We want answers!"

The captain of the Shaman guard was standing in front of the seven leaders of the Larkin clans. They were each seated in their high-backed, throne-like chairs on one end of the Hall of Judgment. There were several moments of uncomfortable silence before another of the Shaman leaders spoke.

"The gall of these people is unbelievable! It's not enough for them to try to brainwash our hunters while they are out providing for the needs of their clans, but now these fiends are brazenly marching into our homes with their perverted teachings! They are doing everything in their power to undermine the authority of the Shaman and to destroy the very framework of our society!" The furious Shaman had leaped to his feet and was glaring fiercely at the other Shaman leaders.

"We have been challenged, my brothers," the passionate speaker continued, "and the future of the Larkin clans depends on our meeting this challenge with terrible retribution! I say we declare war on them!"

"Excuse me, Your Eminence, but aren't we always at war with the Renegades?" the captain asked.

"These are not your regular Renegades, Captain," the first speaker explained. "These are the followers of an evil and diabolical former Shaman named Micah. This all happened over thirty seasons ago. This Micah always acted kind and helpful, but inside he was jealous and ambitious. He wanted honor and power. He wanted to be one of the High Seven, and when he didn't get what he wanted, he became bitter and vengeful. He claimed that he had discovered some secret teachings while doing an inventory of the Treasure Cave."

"What kind of teaching?" the captain asked.

"He said that he had discovered ancient documents that declared that anyone can speak to the Maker anytime that they wish."

"What?" the captain shouted. "That's . . . that's . . . heresy!"

"Yes, Captain, it is," the Shaman continued. "If Micah could not be one of the High Seven, he decided that he would come up with a plan to destroy the Shaman. He reasoned that if everyone thought that they could speak to the Maker on their own, then the Shaman would not be needed. Fortunately his devious plan was discovered before he got too far, and he and all those he had deluded with his lies were banished."

"And even after thirty years this Micah person is still trying to destroy the Shaman?" the captain asked incredulously.

"His followers seem to have a fanatical devotion to his lies," the Shaman explained.

"It's a shame you didn't execute Micah thirty years ago when you had the chance," the captain observed.

"We're all in agreement on that point, Captain. Rest assured that if we ever get our hands on him or any of his leeches, we will not make the same mistake again."

"So it's war, right?" the second Shaman asked sharply.

"Yes, Balsam," the first Shaman answered, "it is most definitely war. But I think it had better be our secret war for now. I don't want to announce to the clans what these devils are trying to do. Otherwise we will have to deal with a lot of questions about their false teachings, which in turn might cause some of the people to want to know more about them."

"So how do we conduct a secret war, Shaman Guggool?" the captain asked with a confused look.

"That is where you will come in, Captain," Guggool, the first Shaman, responded. "With your help we will select and train a brigade of Shadow Warriors that no one but us will know about. They will be sent on special undercover missions, both to discover those of our own people who sympathize with these Micah followers and also to spy out the haunts of these snakes and make them pay for their wickedness."

"And when we catch some of them, what do we do with them?" the captain asked with a sneer.

"You will gather all the useful information that you can, and then, Captain, you will execute them—no exceptions." As Shaman Guggool said this, he looked at his fellow Shaman leaders, who all nodded their agreement.

"Captain," Guggool continued, "it will be your job to find and recruit Larkin who are completely loyal to the Shaman to be our Shadow Warriors. I think you can start with that young Larkin whom Shaman Rah brought with him from the Third Clan."

"You mean the one who identified the girl spy we caught?"

"Yes, that's the one. I believe his name is Poke. I want you to get him now and bring him here to us. It's time we find out all that he knows about these people."

"Are you sure they got away?" Jay asked as they all crowded into one of the living huts. Noblis and Sagamore had made it back through the tunnel and were telling their friends what they had been able to hear through the narrow passageway Little Snide and Juniper had used to enter the Shaman's cave.

"No, we're not sure," Noblis answered, "but it sure sounded like it. I heard one of the guards shout that the prisoners were escaping. Then later we heard someone yell something about the Treasure Cave."

"Prisoners?" Rush asked.

"Yes," Noblis returned. "He definitely said *prisoners*. Apparently Carineda was not the only captive they had."

"But what about Juni and Lil' Snide?" Hawthorn asked with concern.

"We don't know for certain, but it sounded like our people were discovered in the process of rescuing Carineda, and they all had to make a run for it," Sagamore reasoned. "With as much activity from the guards as we could hear, there was probably no chance for the two young ones to get back to us."

"Most likely Tobin and Eldan would have taken everyone out through the Treasure Cave," Noblis added.

"So what do we do now?" Hawthorn asked.

"Wel-l-l-l," Rush spoke up, "since we ain't got no information to the contrary, I say we trust that the Lord answered our prayers an' got 'em out.

"Lady Rose," Rush continued, "it would most likely be a big help to Juniper's momma if'n you was to slip up to their hut an' let her know where Juni is and what we think has happened. Tell her not to worry, 'cause I figure that Tobin and Floppy will get her back to us while we're a travelin' back home to the Keep."

With a nod of her head, Rose quickly left the hut and hurried to find Juniper's mother Verbina.

"So that means it's all over with, right?" Hawthorn asked with a smile.

"Not yet, it's not," Rush returned. "We've still got to get our two Makerian friends out of here safe, an' that's liable to be a might trickier with all the hubbub we stirred up rescuing Carineda."

"At least it's just us," Noblis spoke up. "I'm glad the other team got out yesterday."

"Yeah, that was pretty slick," added Jay. "They joined up with the afternoon wood gathering party yesterday and then just slipped away from their group and didn't come back. They're probably at Tobin and Eldan's camp right now."

"I shore wish you two had gone with them," Rush said, addressing the two Makerians.

"None of you knew how to get through the cave we found," Sagamore answered, "and Noblis and I weren't leaving until we had done all we could to help rescue Cari.

We will handle this challenge just like we did before. We will pray our way through it."

"The clan's starting to stir, Rush," Savin announced as he looked toward the far end of their cave. "We need to grab a bite to eat and start breaking camp. They'll be lining all of us up to march out of here in a couple of hours."

With a nod of agreement, they all set to work getting a quick breakfast and packing up their belongings. After Rush and Jay finished getting their packs ready, they both went up to Lady Verbena's hut to help with her packing. They were just finishing up when the announcement was made for the Second and Third Clans to line up to march out.

They stood in line with their packs for quite some time while the line moved forward very slowly. "Why is this taking so long?" Rose asked Savin as they continued to creep toward to entrance to their cave.

"I don't know. We should have all been out by now. There must be some hold up at the entrance."

"Here comes Jay, Father," said Hawthorn. "Maybe he knows what's going on."

As Jay came trotting up, he subtly glanced around to make sure no one else around them was listening. "It's not good," he whispered. "I went up to see what was slowing us down and saw that the Shaman are standing at the entrance looking at everyone as they leave. They have selected someone from each of the clans to identify any unfamiliar faces with their clan."

"That's bad," Savin agreed.

"It gets worse," Jay added. "They've got Poke with them."

"What'll we do?" Hawthorn exclaimed under his breath.

"There's nothing we can do now," Savin answered.

"We knew something like this might happen," Sagamore whispered over Savin's shoulder. "It's in the Lord's hands now. Noblis and I will move ahead of you a ways so that if they spot us, we will not be standing with any of you."

As the two Makerians started to walk past their friends, Rose reached out and grabbed each of them by the hand and squeezed. "The Maker be with you," she said earnestly.

"And with you," Noblis said with a smile.

As Rose released her grip, both Makerians shouldered their packs and began to move further up the line. Jay walked with them a short distance. When they arrived at where Rush was standing with Lady Verbina, Jay stopped and joined his friend. The two Makerians went a little farther and stood with the others in the Third Clan waiting to leave.

The slow approach to the entrance to the Steps was beneficial in one way. It gave everyone time to let their eyes adjust to the bright sunlight streaming through the cascading waterfall and into the guarded doorway to the cavern.

Everything went fine until Noblis and Sagamore stepped out of the cave and onto the walkway behind the waterfalls.

"Wait a minute," a voice spoke up. "I don't know this guy or the one behind him." The speaker was Poke.

"What are your names?" asked one of the Shaman standing beside Poke.

"My name is Noblis, and this is my friend Sagamore," the Makerian answered congenially.

"They aren't members of the Third Clan," Poke volunteered eagerly.

"So just who are you?" the Shaman asked with a crafty look.

Turning so that his voiced carried to the crowd still in the cave behind him, Noblis answered this question loudly, "We are followers of the great Lord Jehesus, the Son of the Maker, and He has sent us to tell you . . ."

"SILENCE HIM!" screamed the Shaman. Immediately one of the guards standing beside Noblis hit the Makerian with his fist.

From a few steps away, Rush and Jay watched in agony as their friends were roughly grabbed by the guards.

"I'm sorry, Jay," Rush said, turning to his friend and handing him a pack he had been carrying for Verbina, "but I cain't let this happen."

Before Jay could respond, Rush charged forward up the slope to the opening. With fists flying, Rush knocked the first guard down and then the other before they even realized that they were being attacked.

"Now jump for it!" Rush yelled at his two friends. Without hesitation, Noblis and Sagamore turned and dove through the wall of water cascading down behind them. At that same moment Poke leaped on top of Rush and began yelling for help. Rush began flailing around, trying to pull Poke off, but he could not get a grip on his attacker.

"Help him catch that traitor!" ordered the furious Shaman.

through the waterfall

Just as the two guards were regaining their feet, Jay came flying forward. He hit the first guard he came to, knocking him into the other. The next instant Jay rammed full force into Rush and Poke, driving all three of them through the wall of water.

CHAPTER TWENTY-THREE

HOMELESS

The force of the water cascading over the falls drove the three Larkin to the sandy bottom of the creek. Jay felt himself being forcefully rolled along the bottom by a giant invisible hand. Finally both the roaring sound of the falls and the pressure from the current began to lessen as he was pushed further away from the bottom of the waterfall. Eventually he could feel himself rising to the surface of the creek. Just as it seemed like his lungs were about to explode, his head broke above the water. He greedily gulped in great lungfuls of air.

"Rush! Rush!" Jay yelled as he bounced along the surface of the swiftly moving creek, twisting all around in search for his friend.

"Swim fer the bank, Jay!" he heard Rush yell back from nearby. As Jay rose up on to the crest of a wave, he caught a glimpse of his friend's head bobbing in the water a short distance to his right. "Swim hard! We're a'headed fer two more waterfalls!"

Fear suddenly gripped Jay's heart as he remembered that the Steps were built behind the uppermost of three cataracts, and the swiftly flowing creek was rapidly rushing them toward the next two. He struck out toward the nearest shore, swimming with all of his might. Every time he crested a wave, Jay took a glance ahead to make sure he was still swimming toward the shore. With his last look he saw that he had closed the distance between himself and Rush. The closer they drew to the bank, they could feel a lessening of the current's pull on them. Jay was just beginning to feel that they would make it when he heard a voice yelling behind him.

"Help me! I . . . can't . . . make it!"

Looking back, Jay and Rush saw Poke flailing his arms as he topped a wave not too far away. The two friends turned and looked at each other. "You know what Jehesus wants us to do, don't chu?" Rush said as he started swimming after Poke.

"Yeah, I know," Jay answered with a sigh as he followed his friend.

Poke continued to splash and yell as Jay and Rush chased after him. Jay drew even with Rush as they both topped the crest of a wave. They spotted Poke just ahead of them, but he was already very close to the edge of the next waterfall.

"Jay!" Rush yelled above the roar of the water. "We won't reach him in time! Swim for the bank!"

As Jay looked ahead, it was clear that Rush was right, but Jay also saw something else that gave him hope. "Poke!" he screamed as loud as he could. Poke jerked around when he heard his name. "Swim for that branch! Hurry!"

A large limb had fallen from a tree on the bank, and its branches extended out into the creek just above the falls. Poke saw it, too, and began thrashing towards it, but he was making poor headway.

"We better swim for it, too!" yelled Rush as he began stroking hard for the bank.

Jay took one more look at the struggling Poke and said, "Lord Jehesus, have mercy on him."

It suddenly became clear to Poke that his efforts were not going to get him to the coveted limb before he was swept over the falls. Just as he approached the brink of the waterfall, he felt himself sucked under water as he passed over a rolling hydraulic caused by water rushing swiftly over submerged rocks. The powerfully churning water grabbed Poke, whirled him around and around, finally launching him out of the torrent. With a painful thump Poke landed hard on the bough that was extended over the creek. He lay there gasping for breath and hanging on to the small branches close by.

Rush and Jay reached the main trunk of the limb where it lay close to the shore. Using the smaller branches extending down into the water, the two friends were able to climb out of the water and make their way to where Poke was stranded. With a lot of coaxing and help from both of them, they were able to finally get the young Larkin to shore. For the next several minutes, Poke did nothing but cough water from his lungs and gasp for breath.

"Are you okay?" Jay asked, placing a hand on Poke's shoulder.

With a fierce swat, the young Larkin knocked the hand away and glared at Rush and Jay with hate-filled eyes.

"What do you care?" Poke snarled at Jay. "You're the one who tried to kill me!"

"I didn't try to kill you, Poke," Jay countered. "I was trying to keep Rush from being captured. You just wouldn't turn loose, so you came with us."

"I didn't turn loose because he's a traitor! You both are! I told them you were, but they wouldn't believe me. They said they needed proof. Well, you just gave them the proof in front of the whole clan. They'll believe me now!"

At this point Poke stood up on unsteady legs and began backing away from Jay and Rush. "You two think you've gotten away, but you haven't. You think that all you've got to do now is to join up with your little traitor friends and go live all comfy and cozy in their fort on that lake. But the Shaman have had it with all of you! They have decided to get rid of all of you, and I get to be on the team that does it!"

"What are you talkin' about?" Rush growled.

"Oh, don't you wish you knew? You'll figure it out eventually, but by then it will be too late. Watch your backs, boys, 'cause my friends and I are gonna be comin' for you!" As soon as he said this, the young Larkin turned and sprinted along the bank upriver, heading back toward the Steps.

"What do you think he meant by that?" Jay asked as he and Rush stood on the bank of the creek watching Poke hurry away from them.

"I'm not entirely sure," Rush answered. "Poke has been constantly with the Shaman, and they had him stand with them to identify any Makerians in our group."

"He's definitely workin' for the Shaman now," Jay agreed.

"It's more than that, Jay," Rush said, speaking his thoughts out loud. "Poke was so mad at us that I figure he wound up shootin' his mouth off to us mor'n the Shaman wanted him to. It sounds to me like they're gonna put together a group of warriors to come after anybody associated with the Makerians."

"How can the Shaman declare war on the Makerians and their friends without letting all of the Larkin know about the Makerians and what they teach?"

"They cain't," Rush returned, "unless the group of warriors that they send after us is a bunch of secret assassins."

"Do you think the Shaman would actually do something like that?" asked Jay.

"Yeah, I do."

"Well," Jay responded thoughtfully, "thanks to good ol' Poke, we at least know they're coming, and we know who one of them is."

"Hey!" came a shout from nearby. "What are you two doing here?"

Looking up, the two Larkin friends saw Noblis and Sagamore approaching them from upriver.

"I was wonderin' if'n we was gonna be able to find you fellers," Rush said with a smile. "I'm glad you survived yer jump through the waterfall."

"After we surfaced, we both swam for shore," Sagamore explained. "Right after we climbed out of the water, we heard some shouting from out in the water and we saw some folks getting swept down the creek."

"We thought we'd hurry down here to see if anyone needed help," Noblis added. "When we got here, we saw the three of you talking. Everybody looked all right, so we thought we'd keep out of sight until we could tell what the situation was."

"Well, here's the sitchiation," Rush returned. "Based on what that young feller let slip out while he was yellin' at us, it appears that all of us might be in some danger. We need to find Tobin and his brother purdy quick."

Rush led the way up the bank and through the brush in the direction of the Makerian camp that he had visited two days before. As the four friends disappeared into the grass and brush beside the creek, another figure slipped from his place of concealment behind a large oak leaf further upriver and began to cautiously follow.

Rush and his group hadn't traveled far when they drew near to the trail that led to the Steps. The last of the caravan from the Second Clan of Larkin was passing, so Rush and his three friends remained hidden in the brush until the clan was gone.

"The Third Clan should be coming along any time now," Rush announced when he saw the path was clear. "Let's scoot across before they show up so we don't get spotted."

The four companions darted quickly over the trail and up into the woods on the other side. Rush wasn't sure where the exact location of the Makerian camp was since he was approaching it from a different direction from his last visit, but he knew the general area where it could be found, so he headed there. They hadn't been hiking but a quarter of an hour when they were suddenly halted by a warning shout. It was Stub. Once Rush let the Rowdy know who they were, they were escorted into camp. Noblis and Sagamore were relieved to see that the three Makerians who were with the Second Clan and who had slipped out of the Steps the day before with a wood gathering party were there.

"Well, lookee there! It's my ol' buddy Wretch!" Eldan called from the outcropping of rocks where they were camped. "Say, friend, you came from the wrong direction. Tobs and a couple of our delinquents are waiting for you fellows in the woods near the entrance to the Steps. I'm surprised that you were able to slip by him unnoticed."

"We had a little trouble," Rush began as he told his friend about their escape.

"Oh, no!" Eldan said with concern. "That means that the Larkin Shaman know that you and your friend here are supporting the Makerians. You can't go back to your clan!"

"That's about the size of it," Rush returned.

"Yeah," Jay agreed with a brave smile, "we're homeless!"

"Oh, fellas," Eldan said with deep concern, "I am so sorry!"

"Well-l-l, it cain't be helped," said Rush. "That little sneak Poke turned your people in, an' I wasn't gonna' stand there an' let 'em get caught."

"And I wasn't going to stand there and let you get caught," added Jay.

"I hate that it happened," Rush added, "but you know, with all He's done fer us, givin' up yer home is small price to pay fer follerin' King Jehesus.

"Hey, Floppy, I've been meanin' to ask you. What happened down in the cells? Were you able to get everybody out safe?"

Eldan briefly recounted their rescue adventure. "We got Miss Cari out all right, but she's hurt. The guards beat her badly. She's not in any shape to walk for very long yet. We've got her resting in the cave under the ledge right now. Miss Juni is in there with her."

"So you got both of the young ones out with you?" Rush asked.

"Once the guards got after us, there wasn't time to send them back the way they came," Eldan explained. "After what you had to go through to get our other team members out, it's a good thing. It sounds to me like the little Rowdy would likely have gotten himself nabbed."

"Listen, Floppy, me an ol' Jay here have found ourselves in a kind of needy sitchiation, if you know what I mean. An' since we've got no place to hang our hats, so to speak, would it be all right if'n we tag along with yor crew?"

"Wretch," Eldan said with a hurt expression, "you have to ask? As far as I'm concerned, you fellows are family! My cave is your cave.

"Why don't you two find yourselves a sunny spot and try to dry out while I hike up to where Tobs is waiting for you? He's in the edge of the woods near the entrance to the Steps. Hee, hee, hee! I think I'll rag him about falling asleep on watch and letting you fellows walk right by him."

Almost an hour later Rush, Jay, Eldan, Tobin, and Pike sat in a circle near the front of the small cave in the ledge. Rush and Jay had just recounted all that they had been through that morning. Several questions were asked about Poke's comments.

"I'm tellin' you fellers," Rush said as he finished, "I think we're in some danger. I'm convinced the Shaman are cookin' up somethin'."

"Rush," Tobin said, "after your conversation with Poke on the bank of the creek, what happened next?"

"Well-l-l, after Poke got mad and ran back up toward the Steps, that's when Noblis and Sagamore showed up."

"Did Poke see them walk up to you?" Eldan asked.

Rush looked at Jay, who just shrugged. "Ah reccon he could have," Rush answered. "He acted sort of afraid of us, so once he ran off, I didn't take any notice of him."

"When you traveled from the creek to the camp here," Tobin questioned, "did you think to cover your back trail?"

"Me and Jay always take a glance behind us once in a while when we travel through the woods, but that's all. We didn't scout the back trail. Do you think Poke might have followed us here to your camp?"

"He seemed pretty scared," Jay offered. "I don't think a scared person would do that."

"You're right," Tobin agreed. "A scared person wouldn't do that, but an angry person would. Was Poke more scared or angry?"

Rush and Jay looked at each other and answered at the same time, "Angry."

"So what do we do?" Pike asked.

All were thoughtful for a few moments. Finally Tobin spoke, "I believe we have to assume that Poke did follow you and that our enemies now know where our camp is."

"That means that we need to leave here as quickly as possible," Jay said his thoughts out loud.

"We can leave," Eldan spoke up, "but it won't be quickly. Mumbles has a leg wound, and Miss Cari is pretty banged up. They can walk some, but they'll be going slowly."

"Could we make a litter to carry Carineda?" asked Rush.

"That would work fine if we were traveling on a trail," Eldan returned, "but we will be traveling through the woods . . . at least for a while. There's no way we could climb over rocks and logs and carry her on a litter."

"We'll carry her out of here the same way we got her out of the cave," Pike spoke up. "But we can make it a little easier if we rig a sling she can sit in with straps that we can wear over our shoulders. We can each take turns carrying her on our backs till we get her someplace safe."

"What about Mumbles?" Rush asked. "You cain't carry him."

"Just p-p-point me in th-th-the r-r-right dir-r-rection, an' I'll g-g-get there," Mumbles said cheerfully from where he lay nearby.

"Any better ideas?" Tobin asked, looking around at his companions. "Then that will be the plan. Rush, how about you and Jay putting together a sling with which to carry Carineda?

"Pike," Tobin continued, "you and Eldan get some scouting parties out quickly in every direction from camp and give us warning if you see anyone heading our way. Tell all of the scouts that I will give a blast on my caller when we are ready to leave."

As it turned out, the most time consuming part of breaking camp was the construction of the sling for Carineda. Several of the Makerians donated their cloaks to use in its making. Buzzard announced that, when Thug heard that Miss Carineda was to be carried out, Thug demanded to be the one to carry her. "He's done made his mind up on the subject," Buzzard added, "an' he won't hear no other option. Thug's stubborn like that."

"Hurrumph!" Thug added for emphasis.

When the sling was completed and everyone was ready to leave, Carineda was called. With Juniper's help on one side and Jillia from Makerian Team Two on the other, Cari was able to crawl out of the cave and walk over to a level spot where Rush and Jay had the sling. Carineda stepped into the leg loops, and the sling was slid up into position.

"Here, Cari," said Noblis as he handed his injured friend an armload of white fluff that they had collected from some milkweed seeds. "Hold that against your chest to pad your injured ribs while you are being carried."

When she was ready, Rush and Jay lifted Cari up so that the large Thug could slide his arms into the arm loops of the sling. Once Thug had the padded loops seated comfortably, Carineda was gently lowered until she was sitting in the sling with all of her weight on Thug's powerful shoulders. She took a moment to adjust the pile of milkweed fluff so that it was between her injured ribs and Thug's back.

When everyone was ready to travel, Tobin sounded his caller. "Rush," Tobin said to his friend, "the scouts should be back here soon. I need you to stay behind and make sure Eldan and the Rowdies know which direction we're traveling. We will be traveling slower than all of you will, so you should be able to catch up with us soon. Our group will be heading west. My goal is to try to get Cari to the High Place where she will be safe and where we can properly care for her."

"All right," Rush nodded. "Why don't I keep Juniper with me, and I can try to slip her back into the Third Clan's caravan?"

"Now just hold it right there, Sir Rush," Juniper spoke up. "Miss Cari has risked her life to help bring the good news of Jehesus to our people, and she got seriously hurt doing it. Yes, she did. I won't be leaving her side until I'm as sure as I can be that she's safe. My mama wouldn't have it any other way, an' that's a fact!"

"I guess she's going with us," Tobin added.

"Sagamore," Tobin ordered, "we're going to the nearest High Place. You and Beech lead. Head due west for now. Jay, you and Raynor watch our back trail. All right, let's head out!"

CHAPTER TWENTY-FOUR

ON THE RUN

Rush had been waiting for about a quarter of an hour when he heard the first of the scouting parties returning. Little Snide was the first one to come in.

"I watched a big group of Larkin march by on the trail down by the creek," Little Snide reported, "but nobody came our way."

"That would be the last of the Third Clan's caravan aheadin' home," Rush answered a little sadly. "I sure wish I was agoin' with 'em."

Pike came trotting in next. "I stayed in the woods and followed the trail back north for a couple of bow shots, but other than the Larkin clan that's moving along the trail now, I didn't see anybody else."

A short time later Stub came walking into their old camp sight.

"Did you see anything suspicious?" Rush asked.

"Naw," Stub returned, "nothin' to the south."

"And nothing to the west either, Chums," Eldan called from where he suddenly appeared, standing on the ledge of rock above the cave.

"Your brother said to let you know that he was takin' his group west," Rush said, addressing Eldan. "He's headed to the High Place to get help for Carineda."

"That makes sense," Eldan answered.

"Who are we missin'?" Rush asked, looking around.

"Muckly," Pike responded. "He went further north, toward the waterfalls. I figured he'd be back by now."

"Maybe we should go look for him," Little Snide said with concern.

"Wait a minute," Stub interrupted. "Here he comes now."

As they all turned to look to the north, they could see their fat friend running quickly towards them. When he reached his companions, he pointed over his shoulder and began trying to speak excitedly, "Hey! Hey! Hey!!"

"Did you see someone?" Stub asked, trying to help his excited friend.

"Yeah!" Muckly called breathlessly.

"Who was it?"

"War (huff . . . huff . . . huff) war (huff . . . huff . . . huff)—them!" Muckly yelled, pointing behind him.

Immediately six warriors came charging after Muckly, bursting out of the brush with their stings in their hands and holding shields. At that same moment an arrow shot from Eldan's bow slammed into the center of the shield of the first Larkin warrior.

"Down!" cried the attacking warrior, and all of the other fighters dropped to the ground with their shields in front of them.

"Wretch," Eldan cried, "get our people moving! I'll give you a head start by keeping our unwelcome guests pinned down!" As he said this, another arrow was leaving his bowstring.

"Move it, fellers!" Rush ordered, and they all grabbed their packs and sprinted south away from the attackers.

305

There was no path in the woods, but Rush, who was in the lead, tried to pick the easiest way through the leaf litter and brush. He hadn't been running for five minutes when he heard a voice calling to him from his right.

"This way, Wretch!"

Looking to his right, Rush saw Eldan standing on a low rise a stone's throw away. Immediately Rush and the others turned and raced to join their friend. Behind them they could hear the yells and crashing of the Larkin warriors in hot pursuit.

"Follow me!" Eldan called when the others arrived on his hill. Eldan led them at a fast pace through the brush in a northwesterly direction.

"Where are we goin'?" Rush huffed as he ran beside his friend.

"East is the creek," Eldan answered. "South is the Third Clan caravan. West is Tobs and his group. We don't want to lead these rascals to them. North is our only other direction."

"So what's north of here?" Rush asked.

"Nothing that I know of," Eldan shot back, "which is why we're leading them that way. We'll run north a spell, and then we'll cut back west. Once we've lost our little group of angry hornets back there, we can try to meet up with Tobs."

"All right, everyone," Tobin announced, "we'll rest here."

They had been hiking due west for several hours, and everyone was looking tired. The weary group of Makerians and Rowdys had been steadily moving uphill since they had started, and they had just completed a difficult trek up a steeply sloped, rock-strewn hill. Amazingly, Mumbles had pushed himself on his injured leg to keep up, even though the thick brush and leaf litter had not made the climb easy. When they finally arrived at the top of the hill, they discovered a broad, flat limestone surface covered with patches of carpet moss. At Tobin's direction, they all dropped their packs and began to stretch out on the comfortable moss.

"Buzzard," Tobin called out, "you and our new friend Possum help Carineda down from Thug's back."

"How'ya doin', Thug?" Buzzard asked when they had relieved the burden from their friend's back.

"Hurrumph."

"Whad he thay? Whad he thay?" Possum asked eagerly.

"Why, ol' Thug says he ain't tired at all," Buzzard interpreted. "He says he hardly even noticed that she was back thar."

"I with I was sthrong like you, Thug," Possum said with admiration. "Then I would juth tote people all over the plathe."

"How about 'chu, Miss Cari?" Buzzard asked. "How are you holding up?"

"Oh, my ribs are a little sore, but Thug has been so gentle and careful with me."

"He's an amazing feller," Buzzard said proudly.

"Thug is my hero!" Cari added from where she lay on a nearby patch of moss.

"Huh, huh, huh!" Thug chuckled as his cheeks turned red.

"Uh, excuse me, Sir Tobin," Juniper asked. "I really don't mean to be a bother, but I'm curious about something, and once my curiosity's been peeked, I just have to unpeek it, if you know what I mean."

"What would you like to know, Miss Juniper?"

"Well, you know we've been at this hiking business for quite some time now, and I was just wondering, shouldn't Sir Eldan and the others have caught up with us by now?"

"If everything had gone the way it was supposed to," Tobin answered, "then yes, I would have expected them to have joined up with us an hour or two ago. But Miss Juniper, when it comes to Eldan, nothing ever goes the way it is supposed to. Over the years I've learned to make sure he knows where he's supposed to be and then just not worry about when he shows up."

"So I guess all we can do is just pray for them," concluded Juniper.

"That's a good plan," Tobin returned. "As far as Eldan is concerned, that boy needs all the prayer he can get."

After their brief rest, Tobin kept them moving the rest of the afternoon. A few beetles and a millipede crossed their path along their march, but there was no threat. Shortly before sundown Sagamore and Bracken came in. They had found a good place to spend the night and were going to lead the rest of their group to it.

The top of a large oak tree had been broken off by the storm a few nights back. This huge cluster of branches had fallen down to the ground and was leaning against some other trees. When Tobin's group arrived at the leaning treetop, they discovered that the main trunk was lying at such a flat angle that they could easily walk up it. A short climb up the thick branch, and the tired group found a wide area where several smaller branches split off the trunk. A slight bend in the main trunk created a relatively flat area which would make an acceptable place to camp for the night. There were still enough leaves attached to the dead treetop to provide them with some cover from night preditors.

They shared the meger rations that were available and settled down to sleep. Unfortunately for Carineda, Buzzard, and Thug, Possum wasn't sleepy. Now that there was time to talk, their new friend had lots of questions. For the next several hours, they had to explain to him who the Makerians were, who the Rowdies were and why they were no longer Renegades, and who King Jehesus is. Possum was especially excited when Buzzard told him the story about how Jehesus saved the thief who was on a cross with Him.

"Wow! That'th Great! A God for thieveth!"

"He's a God for thieves and Makerians and Renegades and for Larkin," Cari explained. "Jehesus is for everyone who is willing to trust in Him and make Him their Lord and King."

"You guyth are followin' King Jehethuth, right?" Possum asked.

"Me an' Mumbles an' ol' Thug here have been learnin' about the King for over a week now," Buzzard returned. "The more we hear about Him, the more we like Him. It took a bit of thinkin' about, but eventually all of us made up our minds that King Jehesus is fer us." Thug and Mumbles nodded their agreement.

Possum thought about this for a moment. "Well, if you follow King Jehethuth, what doeth He want chu to do?"

"Well, fer one thang," Buzzard answered, "we've figured out that He don't want us actin' like Renegades no more . . . killin' an thievin' an ambushin'.'"

"No thievin'?" Possum asked with concern.

"Nope, no more thievin'."

"But thievin'th all I know!" Possum shot back.

"Well, Renegadin' is all we know," Buzzard returned, "but Red was tellin' us that the King not only forgives all of that, but He has a whole new life fer us now. Instead of causin' harm an' hurtin' people, He gives us a life where we do good an' help folks."

"I justh don't think I can do it," Possum said after some thought. "I mean it justh ain't in my nature, if ya know what I mean."

"It's not in any of our natures, Possum" Carineda added. "The Maker wants His followers to be like His Son Jehesus. Well, you don't have to be a thief or a Renegade to know that none of us are that good. But the Maker has taken care of all of that, too.

"On the last night of His life, Jehesus was eating with His closest followers. At the end of that meal, Jehesus told all of them that they were going to forsake Him. They were shocked and upset when Jehesus said this. The follower of Jehesus known as Peter said that even if he must die with Jehesus, he would never forsake Him. Jehesus told His dear friend Peter that he would deny three separate times before morning that he even knew Jehesus.

"Well, they were all very distressed about what Jehesus had just told them, but Jehesus' next words were amazing. He said, '*Let not your hearts be troubled, neither let them be afraid.*'"

"That sounds like He wath thayin' *don't worry about it*," Possum said with surprise.

"I believe that was exactly what He was saying," Carineda answered.

"I don't get it," Possum returned. "Why would Jehethuth thay thomethin' like that?"

"Because of what He said next," Cari answered. "After telling His followers not to worry about failing Him, Jehesus said, '*Believe in God, believe also in Me.*' Jehesus was telling His followers that they weren't able to be faithful to Him. Try as they might, they were going to fail Him. And we will fail Him, too, if we rely on our strength or character. But Jehesus is strong enough to be faithful for us. Later on, all of these fellows who failed Him endured persecution, suffering, and even death for the name of Jehesus—not because they got stronger or tried harder, but because they learned to trust Jehesus enough to let Him live His life through them.

"You see, Possum, once you become a follower of King Jehesus, He comes and lives in you. If you are a true follower of His, then you will make sure that you live in Him as well."

"What doeth that mean?" Possum asked.

"That means that you're always aware that you are with Him and He is with you. Jehesus is always trying to help you see other people and the situations you face the way He does. If you just ask Him, Jehesus will help you see things the way He does, then it usually becomes clear what He wants to do through you. Your job is simply to say *Yes, Lord* and then let Him do it."

"Do you really think that King Jehethuth would come to live in thomeone like me?"

"I am absolutely sure of it," Carineda said confidently.

"So what do ya think about that?" the grinning Buzzard asked, punching his new friend in the shoulder.

Possum sat in thoughtful silence for several moments. Finally he looked at his friends. A large smile spread across his face as he exclaimed, "'Awthum!' thaid the Pothum."

Rush and Eldan had kept their group moving through the woods with only brief rests. Eventually Eldan thought it was safe to turn west, and they began moving in the direction of the Meadow. Having to dodge all of the forest litter kept their pace much slower than they desired, but Rush and Eldan took comfort in the fact that, if their Larkin pursuers were still on their trail, the Larkin couldn't travel any faster than they were traveling.

"Whoa!" Eldan shouted over his shoulder as he came to a sudden stop.

"What is it?" Pike asked.

"Red ant mound," Eldan answered. "It's right in front of us. I almost ran into it."

"You can talk to 'em, Floppy," Rush called from the rear of their group. "Just tell 'em we're friends, and we can move on across."

"It's not that easy, Wretch," Eldan returned. "I would have to give that message to every ant moving on

311

the mound. That would take all day, and besides, if we met up with two or three of them at a time, there would be no way that I could get the word to all of them before they decided to attack us. No, the only way is to backtrack and find a way around them."

Rush thought on this for a moment. "All right then," he finally said, "let's get goin' 'afore them Shaman guards catch up to us."

"You lead, Wretch," Eldan called back.

Turning around, they all followed Rush as he quickly retraced their steps. When he felt they were far enough away from the ant mound, he decided to lead them south. He hadn't gone five paces when two figures jumped from behind leaves in front of them with their bows drawn. Rush jerked around quickly, looking for an escape route, but saw that they had been surrounded.

"Hold it right there, all of you!" snapped a voice from behind. "The first one to reach for a weapon gets an arrow."

"Hey, Slate, they got a kid with 'em!" one of the Larkin reported as he spotted Little Snide.

"Well, that's just too bad," the one called Slate answered with his bow still drawn. "We got orders from the High Seven, an' I aim to make sure they get carried out. But first we're gonna get as much information as we can from these spies.

"All right, you spies," Slate shouted at his captives, "toss all of your weapons on the ground, an' I mean all of 'em." The Shaman guard leader had Poke and another guard collect the weapons.

"Now," Slate spoke again, "shuck them backpacks an' step away from 'em." While four of the guards kept the prisoners covered with their bows, two others came forward and bound each of the captives' hands securely behind their backs. Slate then gave the order for his warriors to stand at ease.

312

"In a minute we'll interrogate the prisoners," the Shaman captain sneered, "an' I think we'll start with the kid. Once we slap him around some, I figure one or two of the others'll be a little more willin' to tell us what we want to know. But first let's search their packs. Let's see what our spies have stolen from us." Eager hands began rippin open the backpacks and searching their contents. Poke approached Stub's pack.

"Ya better be careful wid dat pack, kid," Stub cautioned.

"Why?" the young Larkin shot back with a sneer. "What are you gonna do about it?"

"I'm just warnin' ya," was Stub's answer.

Poke thought he felt a movement when he started to untie the flap covering the pack but dismissed it. As he flipped open the covering, an angry whiptail lunged straight for his face. "Snarl, snap, snap, doink!"

"Aaaiiihhh!!!" Poke screamed in a rather high-pitched voice and threw himself backwards into one of the other guards, knocking both of them to the ground.

"Don't chu hurt him!" Stub roared as he struggled at his bonds.

Poke managed to tear the enraged young whiptail from his face and fling it away. Doink wound up landing on the neck of another guard, who screamed almost as loud as Poke when he realized what was attacking him. As Slate and one of his warriors ran to help, Rush kicked the legs out from under one and Muckly tripped the other.

At the same moment, Pike and Eldan jumped on the pile of downed enemies, followed quickly by Rush, Muckley, and Little Snide. Although their hands were bound, Rush and the others used their bodies and legs to hold the Shaman warriors down.

Rolling over, Eldan snatched a knife from the boot of one of their capturers. "Give me your hands, Pork!" he yelled and quickly cut the bonds that held Pike.

POKE MEETS DOINK

Pike, in turn, grabbed Eldan's knife and quickly returned the favor. With their hands free, both of them sprang up and waded into the thrashing pile of guards.

Stub didn't wait to be untied. With his hands still bound behind him, he charged full speed into an enemy who was trying to get to his feet, sending him flying into the trunk of a nearby bush.

The lone remaining Larkin guard had been watching all of this with stunned disbelief. Finally realizing that he should do something, he launched his arrow at Stub and ran off through woods.

Rush, Muckly, and Little Snide were still trying to hold down the remaining fallen guards. One of the Shaman warriors managed to pull himself free. He grabbed for his knife in his boot, but before he could use it, Muckly head butted him.

By now Eldan and Pike had the remaining adversaries covered with a couple of Larkin stings that they had managed to grab. After freeing their friends, Eldan and Pike ran over to check on Stub while the others tied up the Shaman guards.

They found Stub lying face down on the ground with an arrow protruding from his back.

"Stub! Stub," Pike cried anxiously as he rolled his friend on his side, "are you all right?"

"No, I ain't all right!" Stub said with some frustration. "I got a' arrow stuck in me. Cut me loose, will ya, an' then help me find Doink. The lil' guy is probably scared to death."

"I'll find him for you, Stub," Little Snide volunteered enthusiastically.

"Yeah, you just take it easy, partner," Pike said, putting his hand on Stub's shoulder. "We got to get you patched up."

CHAPTER TWENTY-FIVE

BIG TROUBLE

Tobin had his entire group up at dawn the next morning. There was no food left, but everyone was able to get a good drink from the dew that had collected on the leaves around them. When they had all descended from their perch, Tobin sent out his advance scouts and started his troop west again.

They had been steadily climbing through the woods since they left their camp by the creek, but now they found themselves in a more level part of the woods, and consequently, they discovered the march was not nearly as difficult. There were more open patches through which to travel, and they were able to make much better time.

About midday they came to a rotted log beside which was growing a small patch of edible mushrooms. Tobin halted the march and allowed them to pick a few for their lunch. While the mushrooms were being gathered, Tobin pulled out his fire-starting rock and a piece of flint and very shortly had a small fire going on which their lunch could be roasted.

The red-bearded Makerian allowed his group a long restful meal before he ordered them back to the march. Tobin was pleased to discover that both Carineda and Mumbles were holding up reasonably well on the difficult march. Carineda's occasional cough concerned him, but she was not running a fever, and she didn't seem to be in very much pain.

The sun was nearing the wooded horizon when Tobin, who was leading their band, heard the noise of someone or something approaching through the woods from the west. He quickly signaled the others behind him to take cover. With weapons at the ready, the Makerians and Rowdies tensed for an attack. Suddenly out of the brush in front of them charged Sagamore and Beech.

"We're here!" Tobin called to his two scouts as he stood up from behind a dried hickory leaf. "I'm glad you two found us."

"There's big trouble ahead!" Beech huffed as he and Sagamore bent over to catch their breath.

"Yeah . . . really big trouble!" Sagamore panted.

Eldan, Rush, and their Rowdies had been on the move most of the day. After defeating the Larkin guards and treating Stub, they tried to put as much distance between them and their enemies as possible. Stub pushed himself bravely. The short but powerful Rowdy had not lost a lot of blood when the arrow was cut out, thanks to Eldan and his bag of medicinal herbs; but the pain from the wound occasionally become so great that Stub had to stop and rest. During these times Eldan would take the pouch containing a crushed aralia thorn from his pack, pour more water on the pouch, and then squeeze this over the wound to deaden the pain.

"Do ya think the Larkin guards are back after us?" Little Snide asked as Eldan and Rush were treating Stub's wound for the fifth time.

Rush took a quick glance at the setting sun and responded to his little friend's question, "There ain't much doubt about it now. Even if'n the guard what got away didn't come back, the one that yer uncle took out would have come to by now and untied the ones we left all trussed up."

"So what are we gonna do?" Little Snide wanted to know.

"Well-l-l, the first thang we're gonna do is finish treatin' yer buddy Stub's back wound. Then as soon as he feels up to it, we're gonna make tracks."

"Do ya think the guards will catch up to us again?"

Rush looked down and saw the worried look on the young Rowdy's face and gave him a gentle smile. "I ain't gonna lie to ya, Lil' Snide; they might. But I figure we got us a purdy good headstart on 'em. Ol' Stub here is quite a trooper. He's been pushin' hisself hard to keep our pace up, even with this here hole in his carcass. It seems to me that them rascals a'follerin' us are gonna have to do some high steppin' through these woods to catch up with us."

"We also took most of their weapons," Eldan added as he finished rebandaging Stub's back. "That means that fear of running into enemies should make them more cautious."

"An' ya cain't travel fast through the woods when yer cautious," Rush finished.

Suddenly a faint croaking roar echoed through the woods from the south. Rush and Eldan both perked their ears up. "Hey, ain't that yer brother?"

"You're right as rain, Wretch ol' boy," Eldan answered, "and it sounds like something has happened. He wants us to join up with them speedy quick."

"Hey, fellers!" Rush called to all of their compainions. "That there was Sir Tobin callin' to us. Somethin's happened, an' they need us there pronto."

"We'll be pushing south as quickly as we can to meet up with our friends," Eldan explained.

"Are you up for it, Stub?" Pike asked with concern.

"Don't worry about me," Stub answered, rising to his feet. "I can do it."

"But if the guards are trailin' us, won't we be leading them right to our friends?" Little Snide asked with a little panic in his voice.

"Not if we can help it," Rush answered. "Lil' Snide, you an' yer Uncle Muckly will go with Floppy an' help Stub if'n he needs it. At the same time, me an' ol' Pike will stay behind. We'll cover yo'r trail a ways so the guards won't know yer a headed south. Then we'll lay a false trail towards the west to make 'em think we're still agoin' that direction. Then we'll double back and head south to meet up with you fellers. Now let's head out. Tobin wouldn't a called us if'n it weren't important."

It was into the second watch of the night when Eldan halted his tired followers once more to give them a rest. Eldan had been using his light stick to help them find their way through the dark woods. The Makerian scout knew that they had to be getting close to their friends, so while Stub, Little Snide, and Muckly rested, he pulled out his caller and sent a message through the woods to try to locate Tobin. After several minutes Eldan used his caller again, but still no answer came.

"Do you think we've passed them?" Little Snide asked.

"No," Eldan answered. "I don't think we passed them, but we ought to be getting pretty close to them. I'm a little concerned about continuing forward until we hear from them, so I think we'll stay put and just keep calling."

After a quarter of an hour, Eldan tried his caller again, but once more he was answered by silence. Another quarter of an hour had almost passed when Stub broke the silence. "I hear somethin' comin' through the woods behind us!" he whispered urgently.

Everyone grabbed for their weapons and ducked behind available cover. Eldan grabbed his light stick and dropped it inside the neck of his tunic, plunging all of them into darkness. They waited breathlessly, tensed for an attack. By now all four of them could hear the faint rustling and crunching of movement through the brush behind them. They each held perfectly still as the approaching creature drew so near that they could hear it breathing.

"Well-l-l, are you just gonna' sit there in the dark like a bunch a toadstools, or are you gonna tell us where you are?"

"Wretch ol' buddy!" Eldan exclaimed as he pulled out his light stick. "I was wondering if we were ever going to see your ugly face again."

"You fellers certainly didn't let no moss grow on ya," Rush growled back. "Me an' ol' Pike here have been runnin' through the woods like two stung mooflon, tryin' to catch up with you birds. We'd probably still be chasin' after you if'n you hadn't a stopped here to use yer caller."

"Have you heard back from yer brother?"

"No, I haven't," Eldan answered. "This has to be close to where his call came from, but apparently he's busy and can't answer."

"Then ah recon we'll just have to wait," Rush returned.

"Hey!" Little Snide called out, pointing into the dark woods to the south. "What's that?"

When they all turned to look, they saw a green dot floating through the woods, moving towards them.

"Is it some kind of a firefly?" Muckly asked.

"Not dat low to da ground," Stub answered. "It's got to be a glowworm."

"It's neither firefly nor glowworm," Eldan said with a big grin. "It's Bubsy!"

By now he was close enough that the greenish glow of the light stick around his neck revealed the familiar features of their friend Tobin.

"I appreciate you coming and all that," Eldan addressed his brother after everyone had greeted him, "but couldn't you have at least returned my call and tell us you were on your way rather than let us sit out here in the dark like a bunch of puffballs?"

"I couldn't," Tobin answered. "I was out scouting when I heard your message, and I didn't have my caller with me. I could tell where you were, so I decided to come get you."

"So what's all the big hubbub?" Rush asked.

"Yeah," Muckly added, "why'd you call us?"

"We'll talk about it when we get to our camp," Tobin returned. "Follow me; it's not far from here."

Tobin led them through the woods to a small outcropping of rocks emerging from the floor of the forest. A shelf of limestone created an overhang under which Tobin and his group had made their camp. As Tobin led them into the encampment, the noise of their arrival awoke the sleepers. A small fire was stirred to life, and after placing a guard, Tobin called them all to a council.

"So what's this all about?" Rush asked.

"I'll let Sagamore explain what he and Beech discovered," Tobin answered, nodding to Sagamore.

"Beech and I were scouting west of here ahead of our group when we heard some voices in front of us. We slipped up on them quietly to see who it was. What we found was a Renegade war party."

"There were probably twenty of them," Beech added.

Sagamore nodded his agreement and took up the tale again. "We were close enough that we could plainly hear what they were saying. They had been scouting the Third Larkin Clan that is traveling on the old trail south of us. They were laughing about how that they were going to take the whole clan as slaves. After several minutes of resting, they formed ranks and marched off to the west."

"The whole clan!" Rush almost shouted. "How could they take the whole clan?"

"Just wait till you hear the rest of this," Tobin shot back.

321

"When we heard that, Beech and I knew that the Renegades had something big planned," Sagamore continued, "and we figured that we had better find out what it is. We followed the Renegades from a safe distance for most of the morning. Eventually they came to the clearing where the Third Larkin Clan's home is."

"The Keep?" Rush asked.

"Yes," Sagamore continued, "the Keep, as you call it. We thought that, with most of the clan gone, they were just scouting its defenses. But to our shock, the whole war party marched across the clearing right up to the gate. After yelling something to those inside, the gates swung open, and the Renegades marched in."

"WHAT!!" Rush yelled and sprang to his feet. He was pacing back and forth and saying more to himself than to the others, "No! No! The guards would never have let them in!"

"No, they wouldn't have," Tobin agreed. "We don't know how, but it's clear that the Renegades have taken the Keep. They probably have an entire army hidden inside."

"And when the rest of the clan shows up at the Keep tomorrow," Rush returned angrily, "they're gonna march right into a perfect trap! I ain't gonna let that happen!"

"I've sent Jay and Raynor to find where the Third Clan is camping tonight," Tobin explained. "They left just before sundown. When they get back, we will move all of our people near to the Third Clan and try to contact them in the morning before they begin their march."

"Hey, Tobs," Eldan spoke up. "While Wretch and the rest are doing that, how about you and your favorite brother taking a few of the Rowdies with us and head west?"

"What do you have in mind?" Tobin asked.

"When we get to the Larkin Keep, we can leave some of the Rowdies to keep an eye on things there. That way they can warn the Larkin and our people of any more devilry the Renegades might have up their sleeves. Then you and I can make quick tracks to the High Place and see if any of the Ranger troops might be available to help."

"I really appreciate that, Floppy," Rush said, turning to his friend, "I shore do. But retakin' the Keep from them heathern varments is likely to be one hard war. I figure a bunch of folks are gonna get hurt or kilt doin' it. I don't think you fellers should be riskin' Makerian lives fer somethin' that ain't really yor fight."

"Well, Wretch, since you got yourself kicked out of the Third Clan, it's not technically your fight either. And don't forget, we haven't asked the Maker for His help yet."

"Oh, yeah," Rush said with a rather dumb look on his face. "What a meat-head I am! I plumb fergot about askin' the Maker fer help. He's got plans and idears that we haven't even dreamed about. Let's commence to prayin' right now while we're awaitin' fer Jay and Raynor to get back."

"Great idea, Wretch," Eldan returned, "and while all of you are praying here, Tobs, Yours Truly, and a few of the Rowdies are going to make tracks. We'll do our praying on the run."

A hand placed on his shoulder woke Hawthorn from his sleep. He was wrapped in a blanket and lying on some dry grass in a shallow cave under a moss-covered ledge with the rest of the Third Clan. Opening his eyes, he could just make out the features of his father looking down at him in the faint grey light of the early dawn.

"Something's going on," Savin answered his son's questioning look. "Get up and come with me."

"Do you know what it is?" Hawthorn asked as he pulled on his boots and belted on his sting.

"One of the guards heard someone calling from the brush near the front of the cave opening. "They're trying to find out if it's a friend or enemy. All of our warriors are to be ready just in case."

When Hawthorn and his father arrived at the front of the shallow cave, they joined the formidable group of Larkin warriors.

"Well, if you're a friend, then why don't you step out of the brush so we can see you?" shouted the Larkin warrior who was in charge of the detail of guards protecting the entrance of the cave.

"'Cuz I don't wanna get skewered with a bunch of arrows from you nervous nellies. Flint! Is that you?"

"Who wants to know?" Flint answered with his bow drawn and pointed in the direction of the voice.

"Flint! It's me, Rush!" the voice called back. "I got to talk to you! It's important!"

"He's a traitor! He's a traitor!" shouted Shaman Rah, who was standing beside Flint. "If he shows himself, kill him!"

"Now wait a minute!" Savin shouted so all could hear. "All of you know Rush. He's risked his life countless times to protect our clan.

"Flint, we've stood shoulder to shoulder with Rush fighting Renegades. You even owe him your life. I think we should at least hear what he has to say. He deserves that much."

"You dare to oppose the Shaman?" Shaman Rah growled angrily.

"Yes," Savan returned, meeting the Shaman's angry eyes with his own determined gaze, "if it will keep us from killing someone unnecessarily."

Flint lowered his bow. "You're right, Savin. Knowing Rush like we do, none of this makes any sense. We should at least hear what he's got to say about it." As he said this, Flint looked around at the other Larkin warriors standing near. Most were nodding their heads in agreement with him.

"Okay, Rush," Flint shouted at his friend. "We won't shoot! Come on out!"

There was a movement in the grass across from where they stood, and Rush walked into the open with his arms extended to show that he held no weapons. As soon as he appeared, Shaman Rah snatched the bow and arrow from Flint's hands and quickly took aim and shot. The arrow cut a deep slice across Rush's neck as he dove to the ground.

"WHAT ARE YOU DOING?" Flint screamed furiously at the Shaman. "I gave him my word!" Flint grabbed the bow from the Shaman's hand and held the end of it threateningly against the tip of the Shaman's nose. "If you ever do anything like that again, I will put an arrow through you myself!"

Turning, Flint joined Savin and Hawthorn who were running over to check on their fallen friend. "Rush! Rush!" Flint yelled as he arrived at Rush's side. "I'm sorry! I didn't know he was going to do that! Are you hurt bad?"

"Aww, Flint," Rush said with a smile, "I didn't know you cared."

"We need something to bandage this wound with . . . quick!" Flint called over his shoulder to the other Larkin guards. Within a few minutes, Rush's wound was treated with some crushed goldenseal root and bandaged.

"All right, Rush," Flint spoke up when they had Rush treated and back on his feet, "all any of us know is that you and Jay did something that made the Shaman mad enough to want to kill you. So what happened back at the Steps?"

"Well, I ain't no traitor," Rush said, speaking loud enough for all to hear, "an' neither is Jay. But listen here, fellers, we can talk about that later. We got bigger fish to cook." Rush quickly told the Larkin all he knew about the Renegade ambush. Immediately cries and gasps were heard from the ladies and the children.

"And you believe this report?" Flint asked suspiciously.

"I got no reason not to," Rush returned.

"He's lying!" Shaman Rah yelled from further back in the cave where he was standing with two other Shaman. "He's a traitor, and trying to lead us into an ambush!"

"It sounds to me like he's trying to keep us out of an ambush," Savin responded.

"Have you got some proof of this?" Flint asked.

"Nope," Rush answered. "But we could take a scouting party to the Keep to check it out before you expose your families."

"Does that sound reasonable to everyone?" Flint asked, looking around.

"I definitely think that we should send the scouts," said an older warrior named Hickory, "but let's keep most of the fighters here to protect our wives and children, just in case it is a trap."

They had just begun the process of choosing the members of the scouting party when they heard a cry for help further up the trail. Looking up, they saw Jay approaching. Behind him were two others who were carrying a litter on which lay an injured Larkin. The wounded warrior was lying face down on a makeshift bed with a Renegade arrow protruding from his back and another from his hip.

"Help us out, fellows!" Jay called again. "This is Spruce, and he's hurt pretty bad!" Several of the Larkin warriors ran to help carry their friend back to the cave.

"Spruce was one of the party we sent out last night to scout the trail to the Keep," Flint said to Rush.

Spruce was in a bad way when they finally got him in the cave, but he was still conscious. He kept trying to lift himself up off his bed, but his companions were holding him down and trying to convince him that he was with friends.

"Just rest easy, partner," one of the tending warriors was saying to the struggling Spruce.

"No time . . . ," Spruce grunted with obvious pain. "Must tell you what I know!"

"What is it, Spruce?" Flint asked, kneeling down so Spruce could see his face. "What do you know?"

"Flint! It's the Renegades . . . They're in the Keep! We made it back home . . . during the night. We called to the Watch Deck to let 'em know who we were. The guards told us to wait at the gate. Suddenly the gates flew open, and out charged a bunch of Renegades. They grabbed Cedar and Moss. I was in back . . . and managed to run for it. They hit me with a couple of arrows, but I made it to the grass and hid. I tried to make it back to warn all of you, but my strength gave out, and I collapsed."

"We found him a ways back on the side of the trail," Jay added. "He told us what he just told you, so we brought him back here."

"That arrow in his back looks to be pretty deep," Hickory observed as he examined Spruce's wounds. "It's gonna be difficult getting that out without him losing a lot of blood."

"We've got some folks with us who are excellent with wounds like that," Rush volunteered. "If'n it's all right with you fellers, I'll go get my healer friends to work on him."

"You can bring 'em in, Rush," Hickory said as he looked at the other warriors who were tending to Spruce, "but you come in one at a time and no weapons. Got it?"

"You still don't trust us?" Rush asked with a smile.

"Well, it looks like you were right about the Renegades, but let's just say that a lot of us still have questions."

"I understand," Rush nodded. "We'll do it your way."

CHAPTER TWENTY-SIX

ANSWERED PRAYER

"All right, you birds, listen up!" Rush barked when he came bursting through the brush to where his Makerian and Rowdy friends were hiding near the Larkin camp. "Oh . . . uh . . . no offense, ladies.

"Here's how she sits: the Larkin believe me about the Renegade ambush. Right now they're discussing among themselves what to do about it. Jay, Raynor, and Sagamore just brought in one of their scouts with two Renegade arrows stuck in him. Miss Cari, if you feel like you're able, it would sure help our cause if you would try to help him."

"I will be happy to do what I can," Carineda said with a weak smile. "Jillia has assisted me before. She can help."

"Are we all goin' in, Rush?" the injured Stub asked.

"Well-l-l," Rush drawled thoughtfully, "we're still in a kinda' ticklish sitchiation with the Larkin. While they believe us about the Renegades, they don't totally trust us. Jay, Raynor, and Sagamore saved their injured scout, which has generated some positive feelin's among the Larkin about them three. The ladies shouldn't be no threat to 'em, but I ain't so sure that the Third Larkin Clan is ready to be introduced to Red's Rowdies yet, if ya know what I mean.

"The Larkin have made it clear that we're to come in one at a time without any weapons, so I figure we'll just leave our weapons here with all of you. Stay hidden, but keep an eye on the Larkin camp in case things turn against us and we need yer help getting' out. And if it comes to that, I want all of you to remember . . ."

"Yeah, we know," Stub interrupted, "King Jehesus don't want no killin'."

"But what about Stub and Mumbles?" Little Snide said with concern. "They've got bad injuries, too! Somebody needs to stay and treat them."

"They are both doing fine right now," Carineda answered. "They just need their bandages changed each day and new herbs applied. Noblis and Beech will be here to help you with that."

"That'll have to be the plan until we find out what's gonna happen," Rush announced. "Noblis, why don't you take charge of this camp until you hear from me, Tobin, or Floppy?"

"What about me, Sir Rush? Should I go with you?"

"I've been thinkin' about you, Juniper. What with all the intermingling that goes with a clan march, I'm hoping that you haven't been missed. I would love to slip you back into the Third Clan without them knowin' that you've been with us. Why don't you stay here for now? When things calm down a bit in the Larkin camp, they will start sending some of the ladies out to gather wood. I'll try to whisper to Lady Rose and your Mother to come out with them to gather, and Noblis can help you try to secretly join up with them."

Hawthorn and his family felt a silent rush of joy when they saw Carineda appear out of the brush and begin slowly walking toward the Larkin camp. Their joy was quickly turned to concern when they saw her bruised face and her weak condition. She was being helped along by Jillia. Rose immediately pushed two of the Larkin warriors aside as she walked out to lend her assistance to the injured

Makerian girl. "You're hurt!" Rose exclaimed with concern.

"I'm doing okay for now," Carineda returned and then whispered, "don't let on that you know us."

When Carineda with Jillia and Rose's help was almost to the cave, Rush stepped out into the open holding a large backpack. "This here's a pack that the ladies need to treat Spruce," Rush called. "It's got a bunch of herbs and special healin' stuff in it. Can I bring it across, or do one of you fellers want to look in it first?"

"Just bring it over, Rush," Hickory called out. "We'll look in it over here."

Once the Larkin had thoroughly searched the pack, it was taken over to Carineda and Jillia who were kneeling beside the makeshift bed on which the injured Spruce lay. Spruce's tunic and part of his legging had been cut away, exposing the terrible wounds. After talking with Spruce for a moment and reassuring him that they were there to help him, Cari began her examination of the injuries. She finished by leaning down and placing her ear against the wounded Larkin's back and listened carefully to his heart and his breathing. "Well," she said as she rose back up, "the arrow in his back will be difficult to remove, but the good news is that his lungs are clear so far.

"We're going to need some hot water," Cari added, looking at Rose.

"I can take care of that," Rose said and hurried off.

As Rose was heating the water, Carineda had Jillia bathe the wounds with the juice of a crushed aralia thorn to deaden the pain. Cari also spread a blanket beside Spruce's bed and began laying out the contents of the backpack that she expected to need. All the time a number of the Larkin hovered nearby, watching closely as their companion was being treated.

In a short while Rose returned, carrying a fired clay bowl containing hot water. With a mug that she had procured, Cari dipped out some of the hot water. Into this she poured some crushed dried leaves from a dark brown pouch. This she set aside to steep. From the blanket she lifted a bottle made of carved resin which was about as big as her fist. She carefully removed the wooden stopper from the flask and poured some of the dark liquid into a small wooden cup. "I have a couple of things that I want you to drink," she said to her patient. "They will make you sleep so that removing the arrows won't be so painful for you."

Eager to escape the coming pain, Spruce raised up enough to drink the dark liquid. After several more minutes, Cari had him begin drinking the skullcap tea she had prepared. Even after Spruce became so groggy that he could no longer drink the tea, Cari had Jillia pour the rest of the hot brew into a shallow bowl and place this close to Spruce's head so he could breathe the steam.

When she was satisfied that her patient was under the strong influence of the herbs, the Makerian healer began to probe the wound on the back. She had Jillia continue to drench the wound in the aralia juice as Cari cut through the layers until she was finally able to remove the deeply embedded arrowhead.

As this drama was being played out under the rocky shelf of the shallow cave, Jay, Raynor, and Sagamore were standing near the entrance and relaying to Hickory, Flint, and the other Larkin warriors what they knew about the situation at the Keep.

"If we attack the Renegades holding the Keep," a middle-aged warrior named Moss was saying, "it's as sure as sunrise that a whole bunch of us are gonna get killed." His words were met with somber nods of agreement from many of the other warriors standing around.

"Well, we could lay siege to it and starve 'em out," a younger Larkin suggested. Several calls of approval could be heard in response.

"It'll take a while," the older Hickory said thoughtfully. "There's enough stores left in the Keep to feed an army well for several months."

"What about our families?" someone called out. "How do we take care of our wives and children with no more food than what we have with us and no safe place to protect them?"

"We'll have to try to make it back to the Steps," the Larkin named Fennel said.

"As soon as the Renegades at the Keep figure out that we're doing that," Flint shot back, "they'll send most of their army after us. As slow as we'd be going with the wives and little ones, those murderers would wind up catching us out in the open."

"Then what do we do?" came a frantic cry from one of the warriors, followed by loud cries and shouts from many others.

"Now hold on . . . all of you!" Rush yelled above the noise. He stood there with his arms raised and waited until everyone quieted down. "Things ain't as dark as they seem. We've got a very powerful friend who can help us. All we need to do is to ask Him."

"Who is this powerful friend of yours?" Hickory asked.

"He's yo'r friend, too," Rush returned. "I'm talkin' about the Maker."

"Get serious, Rush!" Fennel barked. "Religion can't help us with this!"

"Religion has nothing to do with it," Rush shot back. "This is the All Powerful, All Knowin', All Seein' Maker of Ever'thing we're talkin' 'bout. He not only knows about the problem, He knows what the enemy is doin' right this moment, AND He knows what we need to do to fix this. So before we make some panic-driven decision that could get us all hurt or kilt, we need to stop and ask the Maker what He wants us to do."

"And once we ask Him," Jay added, stepping up next to Rush, "we need to trust that He will answer us." Rush nodded his agreement.

There was silence for a moment as Rush and Jay's comments sunk in. Finally Hickory spoke up, "I reckon it can't hurt.

"Shaman Rah," Hickory called to the three scowling Shaman standing under the ledge, "We need you and the other Shaman to ask the Maker to tell us what to do."

"You disrespect us and then expect us to pray to the Maker for you?" Shaman Rah snapped. "You can't treat us like this! We are the Shaman, and we have the ear of the Maker! What would all of you do if we just decide to go back to the Steps with our brothers and leave you here with all of your traitorous new friends? But we are not like you. We will not neglect our duty. Since you have asked us to pray, then I will pray."

With that the Shaman began to use the ancient prayer language by which they communicated with the Maker. Their prayer only lasted for a few minutes before the Shaman lowered his eyes and his hands and looked in anger at the people in front of him. "There!" he snapped in anger. "I have prayed."

"Oh, he prayed all right," called Sagamore, "but he didn't ask the Maker to help you."

"What do you know about it?" snarled the Shaman.

"That was no prayer for help," Jillia spoke up angrily.

"That's right," Raynor added. "All the Shaman did was to ask the Maker to curse us."

"How do you know that?" Shaman Rah demanded in stunned disbelief.

"Because all of us know your prayer language," said Carineda as she stood up from treating Spruce, "and they are right. All you did was ask the Maker to curse us."

"And what if I did?" the furious Shaman growled. "That's all you deserve!"

"They just saved my husband's life!" Spruce's wife shot back in anger. "I don't think they deserve cursing!"

"And what about your own people?" Rush demanded. "They just lost their home! Don't they deserve to be prayed for?"

"No one who disregards the wisdom and guidance of the Shaman deserves to be prayed for!" a second Shaman named Agnus spoke up in agreement with Shaman Rah. "If you will not accept our leadership, then we will give you no blessing!"

At this the third Shaman stepped up beside his religious brothers and, with his arms folded, spoke his stern agreement, "Unless you get rid of these traitors and their evil conspirators, there will be no more prayers for this clan!"

"Hey, just a minute," Flint spoke up. "Didn't these people on their own warn us of the ambush that the Renegades planned? And didn't they bring Spruce back for help when they found him severely injured? And didn't their healers just remove those arrows with less pain and less blood loss than any of us have ever seen for wounds like that?

"I don't know who they are or where they come from, but they've done nothing but good since they've come here, while you Shaman have done nothing but spew hate at them. Then when you have the opportunity to help the clan by praying for us, you refuse to do it.

"I agree that there's evil here, but I don't think it's these people."

"We will not tolerate this rebellion any longer!" screamed Shaman Rah. "The Shaman are leaving! We are returning to the safety of the Steps. Any of you who are loyal to the Shaman, get your things and come with us. We are leaving immediately. The rest of you we leave to the wrath of the Maker!"

There were seven families in all who packed up and followed the Shaman down the path back towards the Steps.

"So what do we do now?" one of the Larkin warriors asked.

"The same thing we started to do a few minutes ago," Rush answered. "We still need the Maker's help."

"But all Shaman just left," one of the ladies spoke up. "Who will pray for us?"

"I think we can help you with that problem," Sagamore said with a smile.

"Yes, that's right," Hickory said. "All of you understand the Maker's secret prayer language. You can pray for us."

"We could do that," said Sagamore, "but I think that the Maker would like it better if you prayed for yourselves."

"But we don't know the prayer language," Hickory returned.

"You don't have to know it," Sagamore responded. "The Maker made everyone and everything. He is all powerful and all knowing. He speaks to the birds, the animals, and the insects. He even knows the very thoughts of our hearts. The Maker speaks all languages. If he couldn't understand all languages, He wouldn't be much of a God."

"When you put it that way, it makes a lot of sense," Flint agreed, "but I still feel really uncomfortable praying to the Great Maker. I wouldn't know what to say to Him."

"Oh, it's as easy as talkin' to yer best friend," Rush coaxed. "You just tell 'im what's on yer mind."

"If it's so easy, then why don't YOU do it, Rush?" Hickory shot back.

"Oh, I get it," Rush chuckled. "If the Maker don't like us prayin' to Him, then I'M the one He's mad at and not you. Is that it? He, he, he."

Hickory lowered his head and looked a little sheepish. "Something like that," he finally said.

"Wel-l-l-l, that ain't no problem," Rush returned, still smiling. "I'll be happy to talk to Him fer you."

Rush pulled off his acorn cap helmet and lifted his eyes to the brightening sky. "Uh . . . hello, Your Highness, Sir. It's me again, Your ol' friend Rush. You've been awfully good to us today, Lord. Thank you fer a'lettin' us find poor ol' Spruce. All of us here allows that you saved his life, Sir, by getting' him found and back to us and then givin' Miss Cari and Miss Jillia the strength and the wisdom to get them arrows out of 'im without 'im bleedin' to death. All of us want to thank you very much fer that, Sir. But we gots us another problem.

"It's the Renegades again, Sir. By them rascals takin' the Keep like they have, that leaves the Third Clan without a home. It's terrible enough for the fellers to have no shelter or protection, but it's heartbreakin' to think about what's gonna happen to the ladies and the young ones. We know that this ain't what You want to happen to all of these folks, but attackin' the Keep to run out the Renegades is liable to get a bunch of folks kilt, and that ain't good either. We're at a loss to know what to do.

"Lord, my Larkin friends here don't know about Yer Book, but I heard someone read out of Yer Holy Book that if anyone comes to You in faith an' asks fer wisdom, You give it to 'em. Well, Sir, I'm a'askin'. We're in bad need of You a'showin' us Your plan for getting'the Keep back without killin' a bunch of folks. If You wuz to do that for us, Lord, it would also show my Larkin friends here that You care about 'em and that they can pray to You just as good as I can.

"Well, Sir, I reckon that's it. Thank you for listenin' to me, and we'll all be a'waitin' fer Your answer. I know that most of my friends here don't know about King Jehesus, but I do. I know that He's the One who gives us the right to pray to You like this, so before I quit, I want to thank you fer Him and fer what He means to me."

There was silence for several moments after Rush finished his prayer. Finally Flint spoke up, "So what happens next?"

Rush thought for a moment before he answered, "Well, the Maker's Book said that when you ask the Maker for wisdom, you have to believe that He's gonna answer you. I believe that the Maker's done answered our prayer. That means that we just need to figure out what He's given us.

"How about it?" Rush called loudly so everyone could hear. "Has the Maker given any of you an idear for takin' back the Keep?"

"I believe He gave me one!" a voice shouted from the brush across from the opening of the shallow cave where they all stood. All eyes turned to look in the directon from which the voice had come. At that moment out strode a thin young warrior with a great mop of floppy red hair and a large grin that was spreading across his face.

"Floppy, is that you?" Rush asked with surprise.

"It's as me as you can get, Wretch ol' boy."

"I thought you and your brother were goin' to get help."

"Well, the plan changed a little bit when Tobs and I ran into Ranger Troop Six. It seems that the Rangers discovered that the Renegades had taken the Third Larkin Clan's stronghold, and they were keeping an eye on things to be sure the Larkin didn't fall into a trap. So after all of us did some praying, Tobs, Sir Comfrey, and Yours Truly discussed the problem, and eventually the Maker put a plan in my mind. Personally I thought it was a great plan, but Bubs and Sir Comfrey aren't the visionaries that you and I are, Wretch. They felt like my plan needed some adjustment to tone down some of the danger, but what's the fun in that? Well, we finally agreed on a plan that would get the job done and satisfy the fuddy-duddies, so I got sent back to coordinate with all of you what we need to do."

"Let me introduce you to all these folks in the Third Clan," said Rush, "and you can tell all of us what we need to know."

Rush introduced his Makerian friend to Hickory and the others, who received Eldan cordially but with more than a little bit of suspicion. In the end it took not only Rush but Jay, Savin, and Hawthorn to come forward to vouch for Eldan's trustworthiness.

"Well, then," Hickory finally asked with some lingering skepticism, "why don't you tell us your plan for getting the Renegades out of the Keep?"

Eldan spent the next several minutes explaining in detail the plan that the Makerians had come up with. When he finished, there were several more minutes of questions from a number of the Larkin warriors.

"You've explained everything except how we're supposed to get our warriors on top of the Keep when it's full of enemy fighters," Hickory challenged.

"Trust me, Sir Larkin Leader, Sir," Eldan responded cheerfully, "that will be the easy part of the plan. But for this to work out, we've got to get moving. All of us have to be in position before Ranger Troop Six gets there, or we could have a disaster!"

"You'll need to leave some of the warriors here, Hickory, to guard the ladies and the little ones," advised Rush.

After thoughtfully considering Rush's suggestion, Hickory gave his orders, "All of you who were on guard duty last night . . . all three watches—you will stay behind and guard the families until we return. The rest of you draw what supplies that you will need from our stores and grab your weapons. We are leaving for the Keep immediately!"

"If it's all right with you, Hickory," Rush appealed, "I'll slip over and let the rest of our people know what's going on. I've got a couple of wounded fellers over there who I would like to leave here so our healers can look after them, too, if'n it don't ruffle your feathers none."

CHAPTER TWENTY-SEVEN

ELDAN'S PLAN

"There's no doubt about it, Hickory," Flint said as he and two other Larkin returned from scouting the Keep. "Our home's been taken over by the enemy. We crawled up as close as we dared without being spotted by the guards on the Watch Deck, and we could tell that they weren't any of our people."

"We even saw one of 'em with his Renegade mask on as he walked up to the wall," said another scout. "He jerked it off real quick when one of the other guards said something to him."

"Yeah," Flint added, "they're trying to make it look like nothing's wrong. They want us to think that Larkin are guarding the walls."

"This just makes me sick!" Hickory snapped. "I can only imagine what has happened to our people we left there!"

"Well-l-l," Rush drawled, "you can put it in yer bag o' truth that they've had a rough go of it, but chances are that they're still alive."

"How do you figure that?" Hickory asked.

"Some of our scouts overheard a war party of Renegades say that the reason they're adoin' this is to get more slaves. They wouldn't want to kill any more of their slaves than they absolutely had to."

"I hope you're right," Hickory returned.

"I hope I'm right, too."

Most of the warriors of the Third Clan of Larkin were spread out in the brush on the south side of the Keep. They had carefully scouted the area as they approached their captured home, looking for Renegade sentinels, and they had found some.

A guard of three Renegades was posted near the old trail so that they could spot the Larkin caravan as it approached the Keep and give warning to their friends inside the captured stronghold. Suspecting this, the Larkin warriors avoided the old trail and advanced through the woods. By doing this, the Larkin spotted the enemy guards in time to cut them off before they could get back to the Keep.

"So where's that redheaded friend of yours, Rush?" Hickory snorted impatiently. "We're all here and in position, but he's nowhere to be seen."

"He's out in the woods contacting his brother," Rush answered. "He'll let his brother Tobin know that we're here and ready to go. For this thing to work as planned, it all has to be executed at just the right time, and Tobin is the one who knows what the right time is."

They had to wait another quarter of an hour before they heard Eldan rapidly approaching through the woods from the south. By the time he ran into the small clearing where they were waiting for him, a strong breeze began blowing from the west.

"We were getting' worried about you, Floppy," Rush said as Eldan labored to get his breath.

"Okay . . . (huff, huff)," Eldan began, "everyone listen up . . . (huff, huff). No time to say this twice . . . (huff, huff). I found Tobs . . . and let him know we are here. He's gone to give the signal to the Rangers; then they will be on their way. As soon as Tobs sees them coming, he will rush back here and pick up five warriors from this group to go with him to secure the top of your stronghold before the Rangers arrive. This all has to be done quickly in order to protect the Rangers when they arrive."

"So when your brother gets here, we'll need to pick five people to go with him, is that it?" Hickory asked suspiciously.

"No," Eldan answered, still breathing hard, "there won't be time to do it then. When Tobs gets here, whoever is going has to be ready to leave right then. So we need to pick them now."

"I don't like the way this is sounding," Hickory scowled back. "It all seems too rushed."

"Well then, Sir Larkin Leader, Sir, you're going to like this next part even less," Eldan said with a smile. "There's no easy way to tell you this other than to just say it. When my brother arrives, he won't be running up like I just did. He will be racing in here riding on the back of a very large, very intimidating grey squirrel. There is a wooden saddle on the squirrel's back that will hold five more warriors behind my brother. The five we pick will ride with him on the squirrel to charge the top of the Keep and secure it before the Rangers arrive."

Hickory stood there listening to Eldan with his eyes wide and his mouth half open. Slowly he turned to face Rush. "This guy is crazy! He is an absolute nut!"

"Well . . . he, he, he . . . that may be," Rush chuckled, "but what he just said is what's gonna happen. Like it or not, we need to get ready for it."

"You're both crazy!" Hickory declared. "Even if what he just said was true, who in their right mind would volunteer for something like that?"

"Crazy or not," Eldan said with some urgency, "we're going to need five warriors for this plan to work. I can be one of them."

"I'll be another one," smiled Rush. "Hey, how about you, Jay?"

"Yeah," Jay called from a short distance away. "You can count me in."

"I'll go, Rush," called Savin from where he stood near Jay.

"Now we're cookin'!" Rush called. "We only need one more."

"I can go if you need me," Hawthorn called from where he stood near Savin.

"Thanks for offerin', Thorn, but we're countin' on you an' your group to deal with the vents."

"How about you commin' with us, Flint?" Rush continued.

"I don't know, Rush," Flint answered cautiously. "Do you think it's safe?"

"Well, o'course it ain't safe!" Rush shot back. "We're goin' to fight Renegades!"

"I meant the part about riding on the squirrel," Flint returned.

"Oh, him? He's all right. You just have to hang on, that's all."

"Here he comes!" called Eldan.

"We're outta time, Flint," Rush snapped. "We need you! But we need you NOW!"

At that moment Tobin, riding his big squirrel Chatter, came bounding into the small clearing and slid to a stop in front of the Larkin. Most of the stunned warriors dove for cover, including Flint. By the time Flint poked his head around the leaf behind which he was hiding, he saw Savin and Eldan seated in the wooden saddle on the back of the great beast and Jay climbing up, each with a large coil of rope slung over his shoulder.

"Come on, Flint," Rush called to his friend. "You were born for greatness, and THIS is the TIME!"

"You said that last time," Flint shot back as he crawled out from behind the leaf and began walking toward Rush.

"Oh, yeah, I did, didn't I?" Rush said with a sheepish look. "Well, that was not the time."

"No!" Flint agreed. "It wasn't."

"But THIS is the TIME!" Rush proclaimed confidently with his finger in the air.

"I can't believe I let you talk me into this," Flint grumbled as he received the large coil of rope that Rush was handing him. Flint slung the rope over his shoulder and stepped up to the huge squirrel.

"Well, don't just stand there grinning like a deer eatin' briars, help me up onto this four-legged furball!"

Once Rush had the very nervous Flint in his seat, he quickly climbed up into the seat behind him. Rush leaned over Flint's shoulder, showed him how to tie himself into the seat, and pointed out the foot holes in the bottom of the seat back in front of him and the handles to grasp. "Hold on tight, Flint!"

"Do you really think you need to tell me that?"

"Sir Larkin Leader, Sir," Eldan called down to Hickory, "as soon as we secure the top of the Larkin stronghold, we will give you the signal. That's when you send in the group of Larkin to handle the vents. Then just follow the plan."

"I can see them coming!" Tobin shouted. "This wind is going to make it difficult for them to land, but we can't stop things now. We've got to go! Hang on!"

Tobin then called out, "Chatter, up!" and the huge squirrel sprang to his feet. With a cry of "chick, chick," Tobin sent the powerful animal racing through the brush toward the Larkin stronghold.

Flint had never experienced speed like that. The bushes, grass, and trees they passed were a blur. Their dash to the top of the Keep was so fast that Flint almost didn't have time to cry out . . . almost.

Chatter burst through the brush and into the clearing surrounding the Keep. He had covered most of the distance to the Larkin stronghold before any of the Renegades on the Watch Deck spotted him, and even then the Renegade guard thought nothing about it. Not until Chatter was inside of a bow shot from the Keep and was still racing towards them did the now wide-eyed guard stammer a warning. As the other guards turned to see what concerned their companion, they heard a loud, scratchy thump, and suddenly a huge, powerful grey squirrel landed in their midst. With cries of panic, many of the Renegade guards dropped their weapons and ran for the steps leading into the stronghold.

A couple of the enemy guards with long, sharp pikes stood their ground and prepared to attack Chatter's flanks. But seeing the danger, Tobin gave the command, and his furry companion suddenly spun rapidly to his left, effectively clearing the Watch Deck of all enemies and almost robbing Flint of the last meal he had eaten.

"Well, that was easy enough!" Jay called to the others when he saw that Chatter had left them as sole inhabitants of the Watch Deck.

"Quickly, everyone," Tobin yelled as he leaped off Chatter's back, "dismount! We've got to keep the Renegades pinned down in the chamber below!"

Each of the friends slid off Chatter, threw the coils of rope and packs onto the deck, unslung their bows, and ran to the opening. As Tobin and Savin reached the edge of the steps leading down into the lower chamber, an arrow flew out of the darkness and whizzed between them.

"It's too dark in there!" Savin yelled as he and Tobin threw themselves on the floor of the deck and signaled the others to stay back. "I can't see where they are!"

"Just keep them down there," Tobin yelled. "The Rangers are coming in!"

As Savin, with Jay's help, began to launch arrows into the shadows of the darkened room below them, a dull buzzing sound could be heard directly above the Watch Deck.

CHARGING THE KEEP

Looking up, they saw six Makerian whirly-bugs emerging out of the woods with their rapidly spinning rotors made of the winged seeds of the maple tree. They were trying to hover over the top of the Keep. Riding each whirly-bug were two Rangers, one on top and one below. When the Ranger in the top position saw that his whirler was positioned directly above the Keep, he pushed up on a rod that rubbed against the spinning maple seed blades. This slowed the rapidly rotating, fan-like propeller on top of the whirly-bug, which caused the machine to descend. The wind began to gust just at that moment and pushed the lightweight flying machines toward the woods to the east. One by one, the six whirlers descended toward the Watch Deck of the Keep, and each time the wind pushed them away from their intended destination.

"Oh, no!" shouted Jay as he and the others watched in frustration as the flying machines on which the Rangers rode were blown past the Larkin stronghold.

"This is bad, right?" Flint asked as they watched the Rangers land their whirly-bugs in the grass just at the edge of the woods to the east of the Keep.

"We won't have the help up here that we had hoped," Tobin answered reassuringly, "but we can still make it work."

"You don't want it to be too easy, Flint," Rush said, nudging his friend, "or anybody could do it."

"They're shooting arrows up at us from the Watch Chamber," Savin added from where he crouched near the stairs leading down to the chamber below, "but it's too dark to see them."

Quickly Tobin pulled out his light stick from where he had been wearing it around his neck, shook it, and tossed the carved resin vial down into the murky lower chamber. Immediately the dark room was illuminated with an iridescent green glow.

"There they are!" shouted Savin as he and Jay began launching arrows at the shadowy figures below.

With screams of alarm, the Renegades turned and escaped into the deeper regions of the Larkin stronghold.

"They ran down the tunnel into the Keep!" Savin reported from where he squatted beside the steps looking into the room below.

"Eldan!" Tobin shouted. "Keep the Renegades pinned down inside that tunnel so we can take care of the vents."

"You can count on me, oh best brother of mine!" Eldan exclaimed as he leaped down the steps into the lower room. As Eldan ran across the large room toward the doorway into the tunnel by which the Renegades had escaped, he pulled out his own light stick. Shaking the resin vial to brighten the light coming from it, Eldan tossed the light source down the dark tunnel. As more of the shadowy forms came into view, he launched an arrow in their direction. This caused the Renegades to hastily retreat further into the shadows.

"Rush," Tobin called, "where are the air vents located?"

"There's one on the north side," Rush answered. "Jay, you and Savin bring two of the coils of rope."

They all followed Rush as he ran to the north wall of the Watch Deck. Leaning far over the edge, Rush visually searched the wall on that side of the Keep. Eventually he found what he was looking for. Air was brought into the interior of the Larkin stronghold through three air vents cut into the sides of the great cedar stump. There were two other windows in the side of the Keep used as emergency air vents, but these were always kept closed unless needed. The vents, round and nearly one half the height of a standing Larkin, were located close to the bottom of the stump but were still five to six Larkin high above the ground. Wooden bars were pegged across the openings to keep unwanted creatures from crawling in.

Once Rush spotted the north vent, he stood above it and waved to the others to identify its location. As Savin,

347

Jay, and Flint raced to the indicated spot, Tobin ran to the south wall and signaled with his arms that the second part of the plan was beginning.

When Hickory and the others saw Tobin's signal, the order was given, and Hawthorn with three others ran quickly from their place of concealment in the brush to the north side of the Keep. They each held the edge of a flat piece of bark that they carried between them as they ran. Another warrior ran behind them carrying a backpack and two rolls of leather.

By the time Hawthorn and his companions reached the north wall, Rush and the others had uncoiled the two ropes and had dropped them over the side. The ropes fell on either side of the air vent and reached to the ground. As soon as they arrived at the spot, Hawthorn and his group began tying the ropes around each end of the bark slab. When this was done, Rush nodded to his friends, and they began taking up the slack in the ropes. Down below, the backpack and one of the leather rolls were tossed onto the flat piece of bark. Then Hawthorn quickly climbed on himself and grabbed both ropes.

"Are you ready, Thorn?" Rush called down to his friend.

"Ready!" Hawthorn called back up. "I'll tell you when I get to the level of the vent."

"All right, fellers," Rush said, addressing his friends, "let's pull together. We got to keep him level and steady."

Rush, Flint, Tobin, and Savin pulled on the ropes as Jay leaned out over the side of the wall. In a short time Jay heard Hawthorn call and wave his arms to indicate that he was now at the level of the vent.

"That's it!" Jay called. "He's there! Now hold it steady."

As the friends held the ropes, Hawthorn quickly opened the backpack and pulled out a stone-headed hammer and several very sharp, fire-hardened thorns.

Unrolling the leather so that it covered the vent, Hawthorn quickly pinned the leather in place by driving the thorns through the leather and into the bark of the cedar stump. As soon as Hawthorn had finished covering the vent, he was lowered to the ground, and all of the friends hurried over to the east wall where the second vent was located. The process of covering that air vent was repeated. When both vents were covered with leather, everyone ran to the south side of the Keep where the last of the three air vents was located.

At that same moment the friends standing on the Watch Deck heard Eldan call up from the chamber below them, "Better hurry, fellows! The Renegades are massing for an attack down here!"

"Hurry, Thorn!" Rush called down to Hawthorn and his group. "We're about outta time!"

As Hawthorn and the others were piling sticks and leaf litter onto the bark platform, they suddenly heard a chorus of war cries coming from nearby. A war party of Renegades charged through the front gates of the Keep and around to their left to attack Hawthorn's small group. Rush, seeing the danger, called down to his young friend, "Quick, Thorn, jump on! We'll pull you up to the vent!"

Hawthorn threw himself onto the flat piece of bark as the others in his group fled toward the brush to escape the attackers.

"Pull, fellers!" Rush yelled as they used all of their strength to lift Hawthorn high enough so Renegades could not reach him.

By the time the Renegade war party arrived under Hawthorn, Rush and the others had managed to get him almost five Larkin high. Several of the enemy warriors tried to throw their clubs at Hawthorn, but with the young Larkin lying flat on the bark platform, they caused no harm. When Hawthorn reached the level of the vent, he yelled up to his friends to stop pulling. Hawthorn began shoving tender and leaf litter through the bars of the air vent. When he had enough piled inside the vent tunnel, the young Larkin started placing larger sticks and pieces of wood on top of the tender. Suddenly he stopped, and with a look of panic, he began looking frantically around the bark platform and in the backpack.

"Hurry, Thorn! Hurry!" Rush called down.

"I can't start the fire!" Hawthorn screamed back up. "The others took the bundle of coals with them when they ran away!"

"Hold the ropes, fellers!" Rush yelled at his companions. "I got to get somethin'!"

Rush ran over to Chatter and found his own backpack where he had dropped it. He ripped open the top and dumped all of the contents onto the floor of the Watch Deck. Shoving everything else aside, he grabbed a dark brown pouch about the size of his fist and ran back to the wall. Leaning over, he yelled back down to Hawthorn, "Here's my fire startin' rock and a flint! You're gonna have to catch it!"

Suddenly an arrow flew by Rush's ear.

"Watch yourself, Rush!" Flint called as another arrow slammed into the edge of the wall near where Rush stood. "Some of the Renegades brought their bows with them!"

"Yeah," Rush returned as he ducked behind the wall to escape another feathered missile, "those rascals ain't as dumb as they look."

When another arrow flew past, Rush leaped to his feet and called to his friend below. "Here she comes!" Rush took careful aim and dropped the pouch just as another arrow sliced through the sleeve of his tunic.

Hawthorn wanted to sit up or get on his knees to catch the heavy pouch, but with the arrows smacking into the side of the Keep all around him, he didn't dare. Lying on his back with his arms extended up towards the oncoming pouch, the best that he was able to do was slow it down before the speeding sack smacked into his chest. The heavy pouch stuck him a bruising blow, but Hawthorn was able to hang on to it.

At that moment Rush heard Eldan's excited call from the room below them. "I can't hold 'em, fellows! There's too many!"

"Jay," Rush barked as he dropped down to take Jay's place holding the rope, "Help Floppy!" Jay leaped to his feet and charged down the steps leading to the chamber below.

The large room just below the Watch Deck was called the Watch Chamber. It contained the great hollow log used to send signals through the Keep, but mostly the Watch Chamber contained weapons to be used by those who were defending the Keep from the Watch Deck above. As Jay ran to Eldan's aid, he snached a bow and two quivers of arrows from pegs on the wall. Dropping one of the quivers beside Eldan, Jay joined his friend in launching arrows as fast as he could down the dimly lit passageway leading into the Keep.

By now Hawthorn had the heavy stone and the piece of flint out of the pouch. Holding the fire stone in one hand and the flint in the other, the young Larkin stuck his arms through the bars covering the vent. Stretching out his arms, Hawthorn was able to reach the pile of tinder and wood that he had constructed inside the air vent tunnel. By striking the flint against the heavy stone, a shower of sparks began to fall on the tinder. After repeating this several times, Hawthorn noticed a faint trail of smoke curling up through the near edge of the tinder. He pressed his face against the bars and tried to blow the smoking tinder, but he was too far away. In desperation he began to fan the glowing spark with his hands, and suddenly it burst into flame.

"Hurry, Son!" Hawthorn heard his father call from the top of the Keep. "We can't hold you much longer!"

The fire in the air vent was burning strongly now, and Hawthorn began shoving in all the rest of the leaf litter that had been piled onto the bark platform. Then, just to make sure, Hawthorn pulled off his hunting shirt and shoved this through the bars and laid it on top of the fire. "Okay! I'm done!" he called up to his father and friends.

"He's done," echoed Savin. "But what are we going to do? We can't drop him, or the Renegades will kill him."

"As weak as we all are from holding him," Flint answered, "we don't have the strength to pull him up."

"No," Tobin agreed, "but Chatter does. Can you fellows hold the ropes without me while I get him over here?" No one answered, but they set their teeth and gripped the ropes with all of their remaining strength.

Quickly Tobin ran to Chatter and, with very little effort, walked the huge squirrel over to where they were. Tobin then took the remaining ends of the ropes and drew these one at a time around protruding portions of the wooden saddle and cinched them tight. Next Tobin walked Chatter across the top of the Watch Deck toward the north wall. By doing this, they were able to lift the bark platform on which Hawthorn lay to the top of the Keep.

"Hey, Wretch," a voice called from the chamber below, "tell Chummy that he did it! There's lots of smoke coming up through this tunnel, and we can hear a whole bunch of coughing from below."

"Tell him yerself," Rush called back. "He's up here with us."

"Uh-oh!" Eldan exclaimed. "Something's happening down here. I think we need you—all of you!"

Grabbing their weapons, the tired friends quickly descended into the chamber below. The room was heavy with smoke as they worked their way across the room to join Eldan and Jay. "What's happenin', Floppy?" Rush asked anxiously when he arrived beside his two friends.

"With all of that smoke," Eldan began, "there's no way they can stay in the Keep for much longer. They're either going to have to run out the front door or come up here to get fresh air. By the sound of things coming from this tunnel, I'm guessing that a bunch of them are heading this way."

"And here they come!" yelled Jay, who was watching down the tunnel.

War cries, coughing, and lots of crashing and banging echoed up from the darkened tunnel as the desperate Renegades fought each other to get to fresh air.

"Let me in there, Floppy," Rush said, pushing his friend aside so that he could take his place next to the tunnel opening. Rush was holding a long lance that he had pulled down from some pegs on the wall.

"Here, Jay, hold onto this," Rush added as he passed the butt of the lance over to his friend on the other side of the opening. Rush and Jay held the shaft of the lance at about shin height across the opening of the tunnel. Just then Renegades blinded by the smoke came charging out of the tunnel opening and, tripping on the lance, fell face first onto the floor. As more of the choking enemy warriors charged into the room, they crashed on top of their fallen comrades.

The rest of the Larkin began pulling Renegades out of the pile and quickly tying them up with rope, slings, and leather straps stored on the pegs and the shelves around the room. Those Renegades that needed it received a stunning bonk on the head to make them more cooperative. In a quarter of an hour, there were eighteen trussed up Renegades lying in the fresh air on the Watch Deck of the Keep.

"Hey, everybody," Hawthorn called from where he stood by the southeast wall of the Watch Deck, "look at this!"

When the others joined him, they saw that Hickory had lined up most of the Larkin warriors on one side of the path leading away from the gate of the Keep, and Sir Comfrey, Ranger Troop Six, and the rest of the Larkin were lined up on the other side of the path, all with weapons ready. Between the two lines marched an army of coughing, watery-eyed Renegades with their hands in the air, desperate to leave the smoke-filled Larkin stronghold and breathe fresh air again.

"How about that, Eldan?" Hawthorn said, slapping his Makerin friend on the back. "Your plan worked!"

"Why, I'm downright offended, Chums," Eldan said in mock hurt. "My plans always work!"

"Not always," Tobin muttered.

"Now, Bubs," Eldan shot back, "I was gonna say 'except for that time by the creek,' but you didn't let me finish. I can't believe you keep bringing that up. You did eventually heal, you know. And besides, that time by the creek wasn't totally my fault."

CHAPTER TWENTY-EIGHT

CARRYING THE CROSS

While the fight for the Keep was going on, the ladies, children, and the few remaining guards of the Third Clan of Larkin were trying to make the best of their situation as they anxiously awaited news of the outcome of the battle with the Renegades. Between wood gathering, cooking, and cleaning, no one had any trouble finding something to occupy their time. This was true for the Makerians in the camp as well. What with treating Spruce, Mumbles, Stub, and herself, Carineda stayed very busy performing her healing duties.

At first it was just Rose, Juniper, and her mother who would occasionally visit with Carineda and Jillia, but later Spruce's wife Cassia came over to talk to the two Makerian strangers.

Once again Cassia expressed her gratitude for their work in saving her husband's life. "You are very kind to say that," Cari returned with a tired smile and a couple of coughs, "but truthfully, it is the Maker and His Son Jehesus Who you should thank, not us."

"Yes," agreed Jillia with a warm smile, "that's true. It was King Jehesus who wanted us to care for your husband, and it was the Maker who said yes to all of our prayers for his healing."

"I heard Rush mention that King's name when he said his prayer," Cassia began. "Who is He, and what does he have to do with any of this?"

"Oh, Lady Cassia," Cari said as she reached out and grasped Cassia's hand, "we would love to tell you about King Jehesus! It is the most wonderful story you will ever hear. But you need to know something. This is a story that the Shaman do not want you to hear, and hearing it may put you in some danger."

"Hmmm," Cassia said thoughtfully, "maybe I'd better talk to my husband first."

The rest of the day was spent in collecting dew from the leaves for drinking, gathering wood for the fires, preparing food, and anxiously waiting for news about the battle.

Several minor injuries were brought to the healers during the course of the afternoon. One was a burn on the hand of one of the Larkin ladies while she was tending the cooking fire. Cari applied aloe and goldenseal juices to the burned area to stop the pain and to prevent the burn from turning foul. The injured lady and her friends were amazed at how fast the pain stopped.

The worst of the other injuries was a child who had fallen carrying some sticks and had received a deep cut in her arm. Once again Carineda and Jillia exercised their gifts of compassion and healing. With more of the aralia juice, they numbed the wound, and while Jillia playfully entertained the little girl, Cari cleaned, treated, and sewed up the deep cut. After this there were many more friendly visits from the Larkin ladies, some of whom came bearing gifts of food or hot drinks.

It was late in the afternoon when one of the Larkin guards heard a greeting from the brush near the entrance to the shallow cave where the Third Clan had camped. After talking with them for a few moments, the guards, on hearing that the newcomers were Larkin, invited them to approach the camp. Slowly the strangers walked single file out of the woods with their hands in the air. As they drew closer, the Larkin guards from the Third Clan noticed that these six warriors carried make-shift weapons. Two carried long straight sticks that had been rubbed to a point on one end. The other four carried large pieces of wood that they were using as clubs.

"My name's Slate," the leader of the newly arrived group announced. "And we're on a special mission for the High Seven Shaman."

"What do you want with us?" the Third Clan guard asked.

"We've been sent to track down some escaped prisoners and some Renegade spies. I see one of 'em right there!" Slate snapped as he looked straight at the bruised face of Carineda.

Cari shuddered involuntarily as she saw the familiar Shaman guard. Carineda was knealing beside the bed on which Spruce lay, changing his bandage; Jillia stood beside her. Slate and his warriors pushed forcefully past the Larkin guards until they were standing next to the two Makerian ladies.

Slate grabbed the neck of Carineda's tunic and turned to the Larkin guards. "What's she doing here?" Slate demanded.

"She and some friends of hers came in yesterday," one of the guards answered.

"Who came with her?" Slate snapped angrily.

"I did," Jillia answered calmly.

"Seize her," Slate ordered, and Poke, who was close behind his leader, grabbed Jillia by both shoulders.

"Also those two wounded fellows over there," the Larkin guard offered nervously as he pointed to Mumbles and the bed on which Stub lay.

"Bind those two spies!" barked Slate. Two of the Shaman guards hurriedly pushed their way over to the two injured Rowdies and roughly began binding their hands behind them. Mumbles and Stub tried to resist, but they had nothing with which to fight and were forced to submit.

"Hey!" one of the Larkin guards called out, "Be careful with those guys. They're both hurt!"

"That's the least of their worries," Slate snapped back. "Mind yer own business if you don't want to go with them. Now where are the rest of these lowlifes? There had to be more of them."

"They left," the now angry Larkin guard returned with a hard stare.

"Left where?" Slate demanded.

"West," the guard returned, determined to provide as little help as possible to these rude and arrogant warriors.

"When are they comin' back?" Slate asked again.

"Don't know," was the short answer.

"You better hope that you're not holding out on me," Slate threatened.

"No," the guard returned coolly, "that's not what I'm hoping right now."

"Get 'em up!" Slate ordered. "We're leavin', . . but we'll be back." As he said this last statement, Slate turned loose of Carineda's tunic and grabbed a fistful of her hair, yanking her painfully to her feet.

"Aiiii! PLEASE DON'T DO THIS! PLEASE DON'T DO THIS! OH JEHESUS, HELP ME!"

On hearing Carineda's scream of pain and fear, Mumbles yelled, "D-D-DON'T HURT HER!" and lunged forward, bumping his shoulder hard into Slate and knocking him away from Cari. Slate sprang at Mumbles in a fury, jamming the club in his hands hard into Mumble's stomach. With a grunt of pain, the tall Rowdy doubled over, his hands still bound behind him.

"NO! DON'T!" Carineda screamed when she saw Slate aim a powerful swing of his club at Mumble's unprotected head, but it was too late. Mumbles crashed senseless to the ground.

"MUMBLES!!" roared Stub in a rage. "NOOOOO!"

Both Cari and Jillia yelled in grief stricken agony. Carineda threw herself on top of her fallen friend to try to protect him from further injury.

"You had no call to do that!" snapped the Larkin guard.

"We serve the High Seven," Slate spat, "and we do what we want! That guy had that comin'."

"I think you killed him!" Carineda exclaimed through her tears.

"If I did, then he got off easy compared to the rest of you. Now on your feet, sister. We're leavin.'" This time Slate grabbed Cari by the tunic instead of the hair. He only had her part way up when a clay pitcher smashed into the side of Slate's head, knocking him to the ground.

"You're leaving, all right," Rose said angrily as she reached over and grabbed another clay pot to throw, "but you're leaving alone!"

Slate sat up, rubbing his head. He glared at Rose as he started back to his feet. "Why you ol' hag, you can't stop me from taking them." Suddenly another clay pot came crashing into the side of Slate's head.

"She can with my help," Cassia said angrily.

"And mine," said both the lady with the burned hand and the mother of the girl with the cut at the same instant that they threw a pitcher and a large pot at the heads of the two Shaman guards who had grabbed Mumbles and Stub. Holding their aching heads, both guards stumbled forward to get away.

"Hold it right there!" Rose ordered the two Shaman guards as she shook her pot threateningly in front of them. "Pick that leader of yours up off the ground. He's going with you." By now over fifteen of the Larkin ladies had joined Rose, Cassia, and the other two, all with grim, determined looks and all holding pitchers, pots, or large bowls.

"You can't do this!" one of the two remaining Shaman guards snarled. They were standing closer to the cave entrance. At his words, all of the ladies turned as one to face them and drew back to throw their pottery. With a yell both guards turned and ran.

"Nod . . . giddaway . . . wi' 'dis," Slate slurred drunkenly as his two injured companions lifted him to his feet. He struggled to focus his eyes on Rose and said, "Ah'm comin' back!"

"Good!" Rose snapped, looking Slate squarely in the eyes. "I'll look forward to giving you THIS!" As she said the last word, Rose jammed her pot under his nose.

"Aiii! Don't hit me!" Slate screamed as he flailed his arms to protect his head.

As the three Shaman guards stumbled toward the entrance to the cave, Rose turned and saw Poke standing with his mouth open, still holding onto Jillia. Rose stepped up to him and lifted her pot. "Young Poke," she began, "your parents were two of the finest people I ever met. Your mother was one of my very best friends. When she died, it broke my heart. When we lost your father a few weeks ago, my heart broke again, and I felt a deep sorrow for you. But since then you have made some terrible decisions . . . decisions that neither your father nor your mother would be proud of. I do not feel sorry for you anymore. Now you turn that girl loose this instant, or I will give you what I gave that no-good leader of yours!"

With wide eyes Poke released his grip on Jillia's shoulders and turned to follow the retreating Shaman guards.

By now the straps holding Mumbles and Stub had been cut, and Mumbles had been rolled over onto his back.

"He took a breath!" shouted Stub as he knelt over his friend. "He's still alive!"

Carineda bent down and, lifting Mumble's eyelids, studied his eyes.

"How is he, Lady?" Stub asked anxiously.

After several moments she lifted her face to Stub. There were tears streaming down her cheeks. "It's bad, Stub!" she cried. "It's very bad!

"Someone get me some water and a cloth," Cari called to those around her. One of the ladies quickly filled her pot with water, pulled off her apron, and handed these to Jillia, who stooped down beside Carineda. With the wet apron, Cari began to wipe Mumble's face with the cool cloth. After several minutes she noticed that her injured friend was trying to move his lips. Leaning down with her ear close to his mouth, Cari could just make out the words, "Can't s-s-see."

"Try not to move," Cari said gently. "You've been badly hurt."

"You s-s-safe?"

"Yes, Mumbles, we're all safe, thanks to you," Cari answered as she fought back the sobs in her throat.

"Had t-t-to do s-somethin'," he managed to get out. "King wanted m-m-me . . . d-d-do something."

"You were wonderful, Mumbles," Cari responded. "King Jehesus must be very proud to have a follower like you."

"N-n-not m-m-me. It . . . King. I j-j-just c-c-carry cross."

"Hang on, Buddy! Hang on!" Stub cried as he reached over and grabbed his friend's hand, but it was too late. Even as Stub said the words, Mumbles stepped into the presence of his King.

Cari and Jillia hugged each other and began to cry very hard. Rose, with tears beginning to stream down her face, gently helped the two Makerian girls to their feet and led them away from their fallen friend. Four of the Larkin guards, with Stub's supervision, wrapped Mumble's body in a blanket and carried him to the back of the cave where the injured Stub sat down to keep a vigil over his friend.

It was nearly two hours later when Cassia and a group of the Larkin ladies approached Carineda and Jillia where they sat with Rose, Verbina, and Juniper. "We just wanted to say," Cassia began, addressing the two Makerians, "that we are all very sorry about your friend's death and how all of you were treated."

Cari managed a sad smile and said, "That's sweet of you ladies to say that, but we know that it wasn't your fault."

"We need to be thanking you for standing up for us," added Jillia.

"Oh, yes," agreed Carineda, "thank you all so very much!"

"Well," began Cassia again, "we've been doing some talking among ourselves, and we've decided that we want to hear more about this King that you and your friends serve. If He is the one Who has you do all of these wonderful things, then we want to hear more about Him."

"We would like very much to tell you about Jehesus," Cari answered.

"But there's just one thing," Cassia added. "When you tell us about this King of yours, you need to do it over by my husband's bed, 'cause he wants to hear about Him, too."

For the next two hours, Carineda and Jillia captivated their listeners with the Good News about King Jehesus. When asked how they found out about the Maker's Son, Cari and Jillia spent a few minutes explaining that all of their information came from their great ancestor Larkin the Great. In his travels Larkin discovered the wonderful news about King Jehesus. Larkin even learned to read the Maker's Book, in which the Maker reveals His plan to save all of those people in the world who will trust in the sacrifice of His Son Jehesus as the payment price for their crimes against the Maker and who will make Jehesus the ruling sovereign of their lives.

"I thought you said that the Maker offers to save people as a free gift?" Spruce asked from his bed.

"I did, Sir Spruce," Cari answered. "These gifts of forgiveness and favor from the Maker are free in the sense that you cannot earn them. How can anyone be good enough or do enough good deeds to be worthy of the terrible suffering and abuse that King Jehesus went through when he died for us? You can't earn that! That type of supreme sacrifice is given as a gift."

"Kind of like what your friend did for you," Cassia said, expressing her thoughts out loud.

"Yes, that's right," Cari returned sadly as she looked over at her dead friend and at Stub who was still sitting beside Mumble's body.

After several moments of silence, one of the other ladies spoke up. "Excuse me for asking," she began, "but I was standing beside you when your friend died. The last thing I heard him say was that he was carrying the cross. I know you said that the Maker's Son died on a cross, but what did your friend mean when he said that he was carrying it?"

"Mumbles was referring to a conversation that he and I had earlier in the day when I was changing his bandage. He said that since he had decided to follow King Jehesus, he wanted to know what Jehesus had to say to people like him. There is a story in the Maker's Book where Jehesus was talking with people who wanted to be His followers. Jehesus said to them, '*He who would come after me, let him deny himself, take up his cross daily, and follow me.*'

"When Jehesus said this," Cari continued, "He was on His way to die on the cross. Jehesus had given up His own will in order to do what the Maker, His Father in Heaven, wanted Him to do. If anyone is going to be a follower of King Jehesus, then He is saying that they must be willing to do the same thing. That's what Jehesus meant when He said that any follower of His must deny himself, take up his cross daily, and follow Him. So while the forgiveness King Jehesus offers is a gift from Him to us, becoming His follower requires that we offer ourselves back to Him.

"When Mumbles saw that Jillia and I were being hurt, he said he knew that King Jehesus wanted him to do something. So for Mumbles, carrying his cross to follow Jehesus meant that, even though he was tied up and had no weapon, he opposed those who were hurting us."

"Even though it cost him his life," Jillia added.

"That's right," agreed Carineda. "For Jillia and I and the others, carrying our cross for Jehesus meant that we came here to warn you of the danger of the Renegade ambush and to try to help your injured."

"Even though you might have been captured or killed," Cassia said thoughtfully.

"Jehesus wants followers, Cassia," Jillia returned, "but not halfhearted ones. Before anyone decides to become His follower, King Jehesus wants them to decide if they are willing to give Him their whole life. But it's really a great deal!"

"How's that?" Cassia asked

"Because if we are willing to give Jehesus everything we have, then He will give us everything He has."

It was almost sundown when a shout was heard by the guards at the front entrance of the shallow cave. When asked to identify himself, the one who gave the shout walked out of the brush. It was Hickory, followed by Flint, Savin, Hawthorn, and another Larkin named Cedar.

"What are you doing here?" the surprised guard called to his friends. "You fellas are supposed to be fighting for the Keep!"

"The battle to retake our home has been fought and won," Hickory shouted with a big smile, "and we didn't lose a single Larkin! The plan that our new friends came up with worked perfectly!"

THE GREAT GATHERING

By now an excited crowd was gathering at the entrance of the cave to welcome them back and to celebrate the good news.

"But how did you do all of that and get back here so fast?" the confused guard wanted to know.

At that question Hickory and those with him began to laugh. "Well," Hickory chuckled, "I'm gonna answer that question, but I thought I needed to prepare you first. Don't panic over what you're about to see." Having said that, Hickory turned and faced the brush out of which they had just walked and waved a signal.

On cue, out came Tobin, riding on the back of a very large, muscular grey squirrel. Because he didn't want to terrify the Larkin of the Third Clan, Tobin stopped Chatter before he got close to the cave entrance. Then he slid off the great squirrel's back and walked over to join the others.

"The Maker answered the prayer Rush offered for us!" Hickory proclaimed loudly. "Tobin here, Flint, Savin, Rush, Jay, and Tobin's brother did all of the fighting. With the help of Tobin's squirrel, they were able to capture and hold the Watch Deck on top of the Keep. Then Hawthorn risked his life to seal up two of the air vents and start a smokey fire in the third one. That did the trick! With the Keep full of smoke, the Rengades just gave up and marched out. We were anxious about all of you, so Tobin offered to ride a few of us back here quickly on his friend over there."

"So what's the plan now, Hickory?" another guard asked.

"While some of our warriors are securing and airing out the Keep, a large party of our warriors is already marching here to us. They will travel through the evening and should arrive sometime around the last watch of the night. With them to help guard us, we will travel back to the Keep tomorrow."

"But my husband is in no shape to walk that far!" Cassia called from Spruce's bed.

"He won't have to," Hickory said reassuringly. "Our friend Tobin has offered to let our severly injured ride back on his squirrel."

"Thank you, Sir Tobin," Carineda said to her Makerian friend, "but I'm not sure my injured ribs could handle bouncing on Chatter's back."

"There's no need to worry, young one," Tobin said with a smile. "I will walk him."

CHAPTER TWENTY-NINE

A PLACE TO CALL HOME

For all of the excitement leading up to it, the trip back to the Keep proved to be very uneventful. Either from shame for their failures, or more likely, from the large number of Larkin warriors and Makerian Rangers guarding the old path, the Renegades were not to be seen.

True to his word, Tobin kept Chatter at a slow walk all the way back to the Keep, providing a relatively comfortable trip for Carineda, Stub, and Spruce. After several hours of travel with the large squirrel, the Larkin grew so at ease with his presence that a few of the children asked if they could ride on him.

As the long day of travel finally came to an end, everyone was glad to at last arrive at the great cedar stump that the Third Clan called home. An enormous amount of work had been expended, airing out the Keep and cleaning away the layer of soot that covered everything. Even the Rowdies and Ranger Troop Six volunteered to help. The Keep's cooking fires were hot, and pots of soup were nearly done when the caravan arrived late that afternoon. Everyone was so appreciative of the Makerian's help that the clan leaders invited them all to stay for the meal.

Sir Comfrey graciously declined the invitation, sighting the long march ahead of them to get back to the High Place to report in. The Rowdies were also invited, but they wouldn't stay because they were all still heartbroken from the death of Mumbles.

Jay and Rush were standing outside of the gate of the Keep as the sun was beginning to set when Hawthorn walked out of the gate and up to his friends, "Hey, fellas."

"Well hey, Thorn," Rush said cheerfully. "How're ya doin'?"

"To be completely honest, I'm worried, Rush," Hawthorn began. "I'm proud of how my mother stood up to that brute from the High Shaman, but when they drug him off, he said that he was coming back. What if he does, and what if he comes after my mother?"

"You don't need to worry about him," Rush answered confidently. "I've had run-ins with his kind before. That guy's a coward. Oh, he's a tough guy when he's got his gang to back him up, but alone he's nothin'. Besides, ol' Slate has much bigger problems than gettin' even with any of us."

"What do you mean?" the young Larkin asked.

"He, he, he," Rush chuckled, "when he and his no-good sidekicks drag themselves back to the Steps, they've got a whole heap of explainin' to do to the High Seven Shaman. Not only did they not bring any captives back with them, but their heavy-handed brutality caused most everyone in the Third Clan to turn against 'em, which is probably the last thing that the Shaman wanted. If Slate winds up getting hisself banished, I figure he'll have gotten off easy."

"So what do you think the Shaman will do?" asked Hawthorn curiously.

"Wel-l-l," Rush drawled thoughtfully, "as slimy as the High Seven Shaman are, I expect you'll see a friendly delegation from them show up here in a week or so, sayin' that they never sent Slate and his goons and how sorry they are about the whole misunderstanding. They'll probably say that they have come back to help the clan and to make sure nobody speaking for them ever has a chance to do anything like that again—or something like that.

"What they will want is to take control of the clan again, but after all that's happened this week, I don't think our older warriors and clan elders are gonna let that happen. I figure the Shaman will have to be content with just being advisors, and even then they'll have to watch what they say and how they say it, since everyone is suspicious of them."

Hawthorn was thoughtful about all of this for a moment, and then he asked, "Do you really think the Shaman will put up with just being advisors?"

"Oh, they won't like it," Rush returned, "not one bit."

"Then why will they do it?"

"Because they've got to know what's happening in the Third Clan to control it, if possible, and to try to keep what's going on here from spreading to the other clans. If their spies get the right kind of information, then the Shaman might be able to turn the rest of the clans against us."

"Do you think the Shaman will get the other clans to fight us?" Hawthorn said, speaking his thoughts.

"They would if they could," Rush answered, "but you know how the clans do things. If the Shaman start tryin' to turn the other Larkin against us, then the clans will be honor bound to send delegations to talk to the Third Clan leaders before any kind of fighting could start. The Shaman wouldn't want that, because then more clans would learn about King Jehesus. But with so many people in the Third Clan interested in Jehesus, the other clans are going to eventually hear about Him anyway."

"So what do you think is going to happen?"

"First of all, I figure you've been to your last Great Gathering," Rush answered confidently. "The Shaman would be stupid to let that happen again. As far as the Third Clan is concerned, I figure it'll be tense around here for a spell with the Shaman nosing around. But unless they can figure out a way to brainwash all the other Larkin, the Shaman are eventually going to lose control of the clans. It may take a while, but eventually the truth will get to all of the Larkin clans. And when it does, that will be the end of the Shaman."

There followed a period of thoughtful silence. Finally Hawthorn remembered why he had come. "Have you fellas seen Eldan?"

"He's over there helping his brother tie the Ranger's whirly thing-a-mees on the back of his squirrel," Jay answered.

When Hawthorn called to his friend, Eldan turned and walked over to join them. "I've been looking all over for you, Eldan," Hawthorn began. "My mother's got two big bowls of hot soup for you and Tobin."

"That mother of yours is a real treasure, Chums . . . a real treasure! You tell her I said that. I know that the soup must be delicious, because I can smell it from here, but unfortunately my able-bodied brother and I won't be able to enjoy it. The Rowdies are leaving now to grieve over and bury their friend that was killed. Tobs and I thought we'd go with them and help them get through this. In a way, Tobs and I are kind of responsible for them, and we don't want them to fall back into their heathen ways, if you know what I mean."

"So you're leaving?" Hawthorn said with some disappointment.

"I'm afraid so, Chums," Eldan returned. "It's what the King would want us to do."

Hawthorn nodded his head in agreement.

"I saw the Rangers leave a little while ago," Rush observed. "Did Sir Comfrey take all of the Makerians with him?"

"All but Miss Cari," Eldan returned. "She was hurting from traveling all day. We talked about it and decided that she needed to rest. Chummy's mother and Miss Juniper are going to look after her until tomorrow."

"Why just 'til tomorrow?"

"Because tomorrow my big brother Tobs is going to fly back here on his bird Nightwing and ferry her back to Stillwaters. That should put the least amount of stress on her injuries. Flying with Tobs on his crow will also get her to our healers much faster."

"So Tobin is gonna ride his squirrel back to Stillwaters and then get his crow and fly back here?" Rush asked.

"Well, that's the brief version of the plan," said Eldan. "He's actually got a secondary mission. Being the fine, upstanding Bubsy that he is, he agreed to haul all of the whirly-bugs back to the High Place for the Rangers. So after we spend a little time consoling and encouraging the Rowdies, Bubsy will travel to the High Place to unload the whirlers and then head to Stillwaters to get the bird."

"You fellers shor' do stay busy," Rush observed. "It makes me tired just hearin' about it."

"All in a day's work, Wretch . . . all in a day's work."

"So then I guess this is good-bye again," Hawthorn said, sticking out his hand to Eldan.

"At least until next time," Eldan smiled back, giving Hawthorn's hand a firm grip. "I expect you'll be too busy answering all of your clan's questions about King Jehesus to miss me much."

"It is pretty exciting!" Hawthorn responded. "All that's happened in the last two days has really caused people to want to know more about the Lord. Cari is up there teaching a small crowd right now. We don't really know what's going to happen. My father thinks that sooner or later some of the Shaman will come back. If and when they do, we will face whatever comes from it. But until then we're going to teach as many people about the Lord Jehesus as we can."

"Well," said Eldan thoughtfully, "it didn't happen the way we planned it, but the results have been much better than anything we could have hoped for. But that's the way the King does stuff."

"Yep," Hawthorn agreed. "One of the verses the Makerians wrote down for me when they gave me copies of some of the Maker's Words was that He can do *"exceeding abundantly above all that we ask or think."*

"That's shore what happened this time," Rush agreed.

"I just thought of something, Eldan!" Hawthorn said excitedly. "You can't leave yet."

"And why not?" Eldan asked with a confused look on his face.

"Because you still haven't said good-bye to Juniper!" Hawthorn's said with a huge grin. "You are going to tell her good-bye, aren't you?"

Eldan just stood there with a stunned look on his face, trying to gather his thoughts. Finally he looked at Hawthorn and said, "You know, Chummy, sometimes in life there are things that are best left unsaid.

"Well," Eldan continued, looking around, "I see that Bubs is about ready to leave, so I'd better be going."

"Hey, Floppy," Rush spoke up, "do you think it'd be all right if'n me an' Jay tag along with you and yer brother?"

"You don't have to leave, Rush!" Hawthorn exclaimed. "I don't think anyone in the clan believes what the Shaman said about you."

"I know, Thorn," Rush said, putting his hand on his young friend's shoulder, "but the leaders of all the Larkin clans have branded us as traitors. If'n we was to stay here, then the Shaman might declare the whole clan in rebellion, and that just might be enough evidence to convince the rest of the clans to side with them. With the Shaman scheming to get their power back, they could use something like that to start the clan war they want. Nah, the best thang for me an' ol' Jay to do is to clear out."

"We all knew something like this might happen one day, Thorn," Jay added with an encouraging smile. "Besides, we'll be around."

"Well, shore we will!" Rush said enthusiastically. "Here, I'll leave you my caller, an' you can send us a message whenever you need us. I'll get Floppy to help me make another one, an' then we can message each other. You do remember the caller signals I taught you, don't you?"

"Yes, yes," Hawthorn returned with some frustration, "but are you sure about this?"

"Hawthorn, you saw what those brutes from the Shaman are like," Jay responded. "They killed Mumbles, and they would have killed all of the rest of us if they had gotten the chance! The Shaman have declared war on the Makerians and all of those connected with them. That means Rush and I are on the kill list, and if we stay here, all of you will be on it, too. If we go, then the Shaman have got nothing to use against you."

"We've already talked to your father about it," Rush said. "He don't like it any better'n you do, but he agreed with us that our leavin' would be the best."

"I hate to break this up, fellas," Eldan said, "but Tobs and the Rowdies are leaving now. If you two are coming with us, we need to get going."

Heartbroken, Hawthorn had to watch as his dear friends marched off into the fading light of the day. He stood there until they disappeared into the brush to the west of the Keep; then he turned and walked sadly back through the gate.

Tobin and Eldan kept everyone moving steadily due west for the next four hours. It was long past dark when the sad caravan came to a sandy clearing on which were located numerous patches of grass of varying sizes, all scattered around the clearing like so many grass islands. Tobin, using the green glow from his light stick, led his group past several of these clumps of grass until they came to a particularly large one.

At this point Eldan walked up to the wall of thick grass and carefully pushed through the tall blades until he disappeared from view. It was several minutes before they heard him coming back through. "It's all clear, Bubs," Eldan reported. "You can send them in."

"This is it, Pike," Tobin announced. "This is one of the hidden Makerian safe places I was telling you about. You can have the Rowdies carry Mumbles in here.

"Rush and Jay," Tobin continued, "I would greatly appreciate it if you two fellows would help Eldan and me unload Chatter."

After several minutes of work, the whirlers were unloaded from Chatter's back, and the squirrel's saddle was removed. Tobin took a moment to give his furry friend a greatly appreciated ear rubbing before he sent Chatter up a nearby tree.

Everyone was eating a quiet supper of bread and dried meat when Tobin climbed through the wall of grass to join his friends. Inside the grass wall was an open area with a sandy floor large enough to comfortably lodge twenty warriors. A rock wall went around the inside edge of the grass. There was a small cave built into the rock wall on one side, with a fire pit near the front of the cave.

"Eldan and I thought that this might be a good place to bury Mumbles," Tobin said to them all. "It's safe and peaceful, and only our friends know about it." The Rowdies took in this information with nods of agreement.

After their meal some pieces of bark were procured to use as shovels, and a deep grave was dug in the sandy soil. When the sad job of burying their friend was finished, Tobin and Eldan took turns telling the Rowdies what the Maker said in His Book about those followers of His who die.

"Now wait just a frizzelin' minute," Buzzard interrupted after listening to the Maker's Words. "We just finished burying ol' Mumbles right over there. I can still see the mound of dirt coverin' him. So how can you stand there and say that Mumbles is with King Jehesus right now?"

"We buried his body right over there," Eldan answered, "but not his spirit. The spirit is the part of you that makes you alive. Your spirit is the part that makes you YOU, if you follow me. When we die, our body stays behind, but our spirit is the part of us that goes to be with Christ Jehesus."

"How do you know that we go to Jehesus when we die?" Little Snide asked.

"Because in the Maker's Book, the great disciple named Paul, who the Maker used to write a large part of His Book, wrote a message to a group of believers living in a place called Philippi. In that letter Paul, talking about his own death, said that to depart—or die—and to be with Christ was far better to him than to keep on living. He also said that to keep on living was to serve Jehesus more, but to die was gain."

"So you're asayin' that when followers of King Jehesus get kilt, they leave their dead carcass behind an' go straight to be with Jehesus?"

"That's right, Buzzard," Tobin answered. "That's what the Maker's Book tells us."

"Well, I'll be a blue-nosed grubworm!" Buzzard spat in frustration. "I might have knowed that rascal Mumbles would pull somethin' like this. There he is up thar havin' hisself a grand ol' time with King Jehesus while we're all stuck down here!"

"Hurrumph!" Thug said in agreement.

"King Jehesus is anxious to have all of His followers with Him," Tobin explained. "Jehesus' best friend, a follower named John, wrote about it in the Maker's Book. On the night before He died, Jehesus prayed a long prayer for His followers. In that prayer King Jehesus asked the Maker that all of His followers would come to know Him, to be like Him, and to be with Him. Jehesus wants all of us to be with Him as much as he wanted Mumbles; it's just that Jehesus has some more work for us to do here."

"What does He want us to do?" Muckly asked with great interest.

"He wants us to be busy doing what He prayed for in His prayer," Tobin answered. "First, He wants us to know Him like a close friend . . . like you know Lil' Snide and like Buzzard knows Thug. Secondly, He wants us to be like Him. King Jehesus wants us to learn to trust Him enough to let Him live inside of us so that we say what He is saying and we do what He is doing and we think what He is thinking. King Jehesus wants people to look at you and see Him."

"Do you think that'th why Mumbleth did what he did?" Possum asked. "Cuz I don't think that I could do that."

"If you could ask Mumbles," Tobin returned, "he probably didn't think he could do that either."

"Why, that's just what I was a'tellin' Thug when we first heard about Mumbles givin' his life for the girl,"

Buzzard exclaimed. "'Thug', I says, 'I didn't know ol' Mumbles had it in him.'"

"More than likely, he didn't," answered Tobin. "That was something King Jehesus was doing. Mumbles, as a faithful follower of King Jehesus, let Jehesus do it through him."

"But what if King Jehethuth wanth you to do thumthing that you don't want to do?" Possum asked with concern.

"That's when you find out if He's really your King," Tobin answered. "If He's really your King, then you do it. If He's not your King, then you don't."

The next day when the first rays of the morning sun began to slice through the forest shadows, Tobin had their group already on the move. They traveled south until they came to a low rocky ridge in the woods. At this landmark Tobin turned and headed more to the southeast. Just before midday they arrived at a large clearing with a gigantic oak tree on the west side.

"I remember that tree," Jay said his thoughts out loud as they entered the clearing.

"Hey, that's right," Rush agreed. "That there's the big oak that yer High Place is in. We just came at it from a different direction this time."

"Eldan," Tobin called to his brother, "I'm going to leave all of them with you. Chatter and I are going straight up to deliver the whirlers, and then I need to leave for Stillwaters."

"How long will it take you to get to your home at Stillwaters?" Pike asked.

"If we hurry, Chatter and I can skirt the edge of the Meadow and be at Stillwaters in two hours. That should give me plenty of time to get Nightwing, fly back to the

Larkin Keep to pick up Carineda, and return to Stillwaters before sunset."

"What's it like to fly, Sir Tobin?" Little Snide asked in wide-eyed amazement.

"I'll tell you what, young one," Tobin answered with a smile. "I'll take you with me sometime, and you can find out for yourself."

Tobin then looked at the rest of their new friends. "This is the North High Place. It's one of our outposts. This is a safe place where you can rest and get some hot food. I would suggest that you fellows rest up here for a few days before you start for Stillwaters. Eldan, Jay, and Rush will stay with you until you are ready to leave; then Eldan will take you to our home across the Meadow."

"Us Rowdies want to say thank you, Tobin, for all that you and Red and the others have done for us," Pike said as Tobin prepared to leave. All of the others nodded their agreement.

"It has been our privilege, friends" the red-bearded Makerian smiled back. "But you know, it really wasn't us."

"Yeah, we know," Stub said, cutting Tobin off. "It was what King Jehesus wanted you to do." Tobin and Eldan both nodded their agreement as everyone laughed.

"You know thumthin'?" Possum said with a sly look. "That'th what I figured they wath gonna thay."

"We had best quit all of our dallyin'," Eldan announced. "I'll bet lunch is almost ready up there, and we got a long climb ahead of us. Do us a favor, Bubs. When you get to the block house, tell 'em that we're on our way up and to save us some food."

With a nod Tobin gave the order, and Chatter sprang up the trunk of the great oak tree and disappeared.

"Okay, fellows," Eldan announced, "follow me, and if you want something to eat when we get to the end of this climb, you'd better keep up."

When Eldan and his party finally managed to drag themselves into the doorway of the large wooden building in the top of the giant oak tree, they were all sweating and breathing hard. Eldan had pushed them all as hard as he could to try to get them there before the food was all gone. "Did we make it?" Eldan huffed as they burst into the large meeting room of the High Place. "Is there any food left?"

"No need to fret none," boomed a voice over by the cooking fire. "Your brother's been here and told us you was a'comin'. Little Bark saved you blokes a few baked tubers, and you can have what's left of the stew. There's also a basket of seed bread for you that we kept the Rangers away from."

"Oh, Barkus," Eldan exclaimed with obvious relief, "you are my hero!"

"Barkus?" questioned the dumbfounded Pike when he saw the large Makerian cook standing by the pot of stew waving a large spoon. "Is that really you, Barkus?"

"Great hairy caterpillers!" Buzzard shouted. "Why, it's ol' Barkus an' his son come back from the dead!"

"Barkus!" several of the other Rowdies shouted in disbelief as they ran to greet their old friend.

"Lookee here, lookee here!" Barkus roared when he recognized Pike and the others. "Just look at this herd of scum-suckin' mud puppies what Eldan done brung to us! HA, HA, HAAAA!" Barkus shouted a great roaring laugh, threw his spoon in the air, and hurried to embrace his old comrades.

Jay, who was observing all of this, leaned over and spoke to Possum, who was standing beside him, "Apparently they know each other."

"Tho it would theem," Possum answered.

After the excitement began to subside, Pike grabbed Barkus by the shoulder and asked the question they all wanted to know, "Barkus, how did you get here? All of us thought you and your family were dead!"

BARKUS GREETS THE ROWDIES

"Come on over here and get something to eat," Barkus said with a laugh. "I'll sit with you and tell you my story while your'a fillin' yer bellies.

"Once when I was out with a Renegade raidin' party," Barkus began when they had all seated themselves at one of the long tables with their food, "we got caught in a storm, and I wound up getting' washed away from the others. I would have drowned if some Makerians hadn't a fished me out of the stream. I had hit my head on a rock, and I was pretty cold when they finally saved me, so they took care of me for a few days until I was strong enough to go back to the Lair. But by that time, they had been so good to me that I didn't want to go back.

"I asked 'em if I went back and got my wife and my boy, if we could join up with them. They agreed and told me how to find them when I had my family.

"The next time a wood gatherin' detail went out from the Lair, I made sure my family was a part of it. Once we got where the others couldn't see us, we took off and found these good folks. HA, HA! I gots me a good life now. Believe it or not, I'm in charge of this place.

"So what brings you grubworms here? Did you get yerselves captured?"

"Well," Pike said thoughtfully, "the truth be told, with the help of Red here an' his brother . . ."

"An' the Chummy!" Muckly reminded.

"Oh, yeah," Pike continued, "and the Chummy, we got ourselves captured by King Jehesus."

"PRAISE THE MAKER AND BLESS MY BELLY!" Barkus shouted as he jumped to his feet. "That there's the best news you swamp eels could'a told me. Me an' the Missus and Little Bark, we're all followers of the King, too! Best decision we ever made! You fellers won't regret it."

"But we got us a problem, Barkus," Pike said with some concern. "We really appreciate what Red and his brother and the others have done for us. And we believe in King Jehesus—at least most of us do. Those of us who do are gonna follow the King just like the Makerians follow Him. But we aren't like Red and his people. They're all nice and proper and . . ."

"Clean," Buzzard added.

"Hurrumph!" agreed Thug.

"And, well, you know," Pike continued, "that ain't us. It's not so bad bein' around one or two of 'em at a time, but to go and live amongst a whole hive of 'em is just more niceness and cleanness than we can handle, if you know what I mean."

"He, he, he," Barkus chuckled. "I know exactly what you mean. I had the same concern when we joined the Makerians. That's why we're here rather than over at Stillwaters.

"Here's a thought," Barkus continued. "Why don't you bog weevles just stay here with us? There's always plenty of work to do, keepin' up with this outpost. With all the Renegade activity in this part of the woods, the Rangers could sure use an extra patrol once in a while."

"Hey, yeah!" Stub exclaimed. "Why don't we just stay here with Barkus?"

"Yeah!" the others agreed.

Suddenly there was a scream and a crash coming from one of the back rooms. "SOMEBODY GET THIS VARMENT OUTTA MY KITCHEN!"

Snap, snarl, snap, doink, doink!

At the noise Stub quickly looked down and discovered his open and now empty backpack. "Oh, no! Doink! Don't hurt him, lady!" Stub leaped to his feet and raced to the door of the kitchen.

Snarl, doink, doink.

"GET HIM OUTTA HERE!" Peony screamed at Stub, who ran in to grab his fugitive pet.

In a moment Stub reappeared, holding a very agitated young whiptail. Suddenly a large wooden spoon came flying out of the kitchen and bounced off Stub's head.

Doink, snarl!

"Ahh, ain't he cute," Stub said with a smile.

Snarl, snap, snap!

"Yeeow!"

"I think we've found ourselves a place," Pike said, addressing the other Rowdies. "It's startin' to feel like home."

The End

www.ingramcontent.com/pod-product-compliance
Lightning Source LLC
Chambersburg PA
CBHW070357260626
47161CB00001B/169